T0078012

THE CHANGING
MYSTERIES
OF PARKDALE COURT

MIKE ROBERTSON

authorHOUSE®

AuthorHouse™
1663 Liberty Drive
Bloomington, IN 47403
www.authorhouse.com
Phone: 833-262-8899

© *2021 Mike Robertson. All rights reserved.*

No part of this book may be reproduced, stored in a retrieval system, or transmitted by any means without the written permission of the author.

Published by AuthorHouse 11/19/2021

ISBN: 978-1-6655-4544-0 (sc)
ISBN: 978-1-6655-4545-7 (hc)
ISBN: 978-1-6655-4543-3 (e)

Library of Congress Control Number: 2021923755

Print information available on the last page.

Any people depicted in stock imagery provided by Getty Images are models, and such images are being used for illustrative purposes only.
Certain stock imagery © Getty Images.

This book is printed on acid-free paper.

Because of the dynamic nature of the Internet, any web addresses or links contained in this book may have changed since publication and may no longer be valid. The views expressed in this work are solely those of the author and do not necessarily reflect the views of the publisher, and the publisher hereby disclaims any responsibility for them.

CONTENTS

THE APARTMENT

I t was called Parkdale Court, a building that housed one and two bedroom apartments with hardwood floors, decorative fireplaces and bow style windows. It had been built in the Queen Anne Revival style and had been designed by an architect who had provided the building with part of its history by hurling himself to his death from the balcony of a third floor apartment of the building. It was just after he had finished playing a game of whist with three older women who lived in the same building. It had become a story that was told in the pages of the city's chief newspaper for a week or so back in the 1940s.

John Delaney had been given this information by a representative of the Ambassador Realty company when he inquired about any apartments for rent in the building. The representative, whose name was Robert Butterworth, told Delaney, as he told every potential tenant, that the building had been and remained popular with university professors, young professions and writers ever since it was built in 1936. Delaney was looking for a place after living several years with a woman named Sharon, the inconvenience of being married for three or four of those years depending on how you define marriage. The building was situated on Bank Street just south of the Queensway in Ottawa.

He first saw the place in 1975. It was one day in the spring when he saw a small sign in the lobby door of Parkdale Court. He was on his way to his job at a car rental on the corner of Patterson and Bank Streets. The apartment building was on the other side of Bank Street, a block south of his place of employment. He knew he needed a

1

place to live, his soon to be ex- wife having given him three months to find his own apartment. That was six months ago. He continued to live with her at her address even though she had been the only name on the lease for the last year. It was a penthouse apartment on Frank Street near the Rideau Canal. They were living separate lives although she often, if not always allowed him to share her bed, that aspect of their relationship never having gone cold. Nevertheless, in the last month or so, she had begun to increasingly mention her request, if not her demand for him to move, ironically sometimes after making love. Over the past week or so, he worried that she would bring it up during rather than after sex, a possibility that while unlikely, still seemed real enough to enter his mind occasionally. It seemed, therefore, somewhat serendipitous that he had noticed the sign in the lobby of the Parkdale Court when he did. He had mentioned it to his soon to be ex-wife before he left for work that day. He said that he intended to visit the building on his way home. He hoped that mentioning it would give him another month of rent free accommodation.

After the morning rush at the Economy Car Rental, when cars were returned and then rented out, there was little to do at work. There were only four people working at the place. There was the boss, a fastidious little man named Daniel Mayhew whose wife June actually ran the business. Delaney later become aware, further to a rumour that he heard the first week he moved in, that the apartment building across the street was actually owned by June's family. Mayhew spent most of his time in his office on the telephone with the door closed. Sometimes he would go into the garage to speak to the mechanic Jeff who seldom came into the office to speak to either the boss, John or a totally superfluous counter person named Debra, a woman in her early forties who dressed like someone twenty years younger. John suspected that she had had some sort of strange relationship with the man who hired her. She liked to flirt with any male customer who looked half decent, an inclination that included John who sometimes entertained her in the penthouse on Frank

Street when Sharon was at work or was out socializing with people who John never met and didn't know.

With his plan to visit Parkdale Court in mind, he left the car rental thirty minutes early that day in the spring, leaving Debra to handle any customers until closing, a duty she wasn't exactly comfortable with. It was his thought that he might stand a better chance of catching the apartment caretaker before dinner time. He was right. The manager or the caretaker or superintendent of the building, whatever he called himself, was an older, almost elderly man. He buzzed John in and answered the door to his apartment 106 on the first floor. Aside from ensuring that John knew his correct title for the day --- manager he called himself this day ---- he introduced himself as Kenneth Casey. He was a pale, thin, frail looking man who did not appear strong enough to change a light bulb. He told John that he and his wife, who was moving around unseen in the apartment as he spoke to John outside in the corridor, had been managing the building for more than thirty years.

John stood in the corridor as Mr. Casey informed him that there were three vacant or soon to be vacant apartments in the Parkdale Court, two one bedroom and one two bedroom units, the latter being available immediately. It was a relatively brief conversation during which Mr. Casey seemed to be unwilling to allow John into his apartment, leaning his head out the door, only a sliver of space between Casey's apartment and the corridor in which John stood. Casey then slid an application form through the space between the partially open door and the door jam itself, telling him to complete the form and return it to him or the office of the builder's current owner, Donaldson Property Management which was just a couple of blocks north on Catherine Street. Mr. Casey then bid him adieu and gently closed the door to his own apartment. The door creaked.

As he walked home, John realized that he had not asked to see the vacant apartment nor had manager/caretaker/superintendent Casey offered to show him. Nonetheless, he was prepared to rent the place if he had the opportunity, sight unseen, realizing that he may not be living on Frank Street much longer. As soon as he got home, he told

Sharon that he was likely moving out shortly, showing her the form that Casey gave him. It had taken him fifteen minutes to complete the form ---- basic stuff that one saw on every form of that nature. Sharon seemed pleased, an unusual reaction for her anytime she dealt with John, except of course during or after sex. She congratulated him and then handed him $20, the standard fee anytime she wanted him out of the house for the evening. This night she was hosting one of her dinner parties, hardly an appropriate soiree for her wayward husband. As for John, he planned to invest the $20 in pizza and beer at a tavern on Preston Street, as he often did. He assumed that his friend Greg would be at his usual table, by one of pillars in the middle of the room, sitting at one on those old fashion bar stools and talking to one of waiters or one of the other frequent patrons. So he expected to see him that evening. He left the apartment around seven. He expected to be home around eleven, by which time his wife's cocktail party would be over, the apartment would be empty, and his wife would be in bed. He would not be waking her up.

During a late lunch the next day, having convinced Debra to take the early lunch by quickly making a casual caress of her butt. John walked to the office the Donaldson Property Management Company on Catherine Street to submit his rental application. He gave it to a nervous looking young man who had been on the telephone and accepted it without comment. John then had enough time to stop by the Chinese joint on Bank Street near Patterson to read the newspaper over a lunch of chicken fried rice, two egg rolls, and a chocolate milk shake. He was back behind the counter with Debra for maybe ten minutes when he received a call. It was a woman who introduced herself as Mrs. Thompson who offered to allow him to inspect the apartment the following week, possibly by Monday. John then asked if she could contact Mr. Casey for him, explaining that Casey had not volunteered to show him the apartment he was applying to rent. Mrs. Thompson apologized and agreed, promising to speak to him that afternoon. He was also told by Mrs. Thompson that Kenneth Casey, who was known around the office as "lantern jaw", a reference to his most prominent physical feature, had been elevated to "manager" by acclamation after the previous manager died suddenly several years ago. There had been no obvious successor but for a burnt out janitor named Casey who lived in the building and had been with the current company and its antecedents for thirty years.

As long as the subject of Casey was being discussed, Mrs. Thompson advised John to avoid Mr. Casey as much as possible, claiming that he was difficult, if not strange. He didn't have neither the time nor the inclination to ask Mrs. Thompson to explain the comment. He could tell that she wanted to hang up. It didn't seem to matter anyway he thought. He would find out more about Mr. Casey once he moved into Parkdale Court. As promised, Mrs. Thompson called within the hour to inform him that Casey was prepared to show him the vacant two bedroom apartment late that afternoon if he could get over there by five o'clock. For the second day in succession, John left work early to visit Mr. Casey. He answered his buzz with a standard gruff greeting and allowed him in, the door to apartment 106 already open. Casey came out of his apartment walking slowly, hunched over, looking like he would soon be navigating behind a walker. He was carrying a skeleton key, a key that Casey said, with a curious pride, would open every apartment in the building. Casey was a couple of feet outside of his apartment when he and John ran into each other. John held out his hand but Casey looked at him dismissively and stepped back a bit. It was clear that Casey was not in the habit of shaking hands.

Casey then spoke in a low, rumbling voice, the almost guttural voice John had heard from him before. "I am supposed to show you the vacant apartment, right?"

"Right." answered John.

"You should have asked to see the place yesterday." said Casey, more an admonishment than some idle comment. "It's a big pain climbing up to the third floor, you know. My legs are really acting up today.", a predictable admission given his long time position in the building. John wondered for a moment whether Mrs. Casey, or who he presumed was Mrs. Casey, helped him with his duties, whatever they were. Maybe there was someone else helping Casey.

John tried to look understanding, thinking that he should be sympathetic with a cantankerous old man with a serious limp. He then had an inspiration. "Sorry to hear that. Look, why don't you just give me the key and I'll just go up there myself."

They both just stood there, looking at each other. Mr. Casey then put the key in his pocket, as if John was about to take the key from him. "No, I can't let you do that." He hesitated for a moment and just stared at John. "Mrs. Thompson would have my butt if I let you up there unsupervised." John smiled and offered a solution. "I won't tell. Honest. Fact is that I don't think Mrs. Thompson would care." Casey just showed him a creepy little smile and answered. "You don't know Mrs. Thompson."

John then put both hands up in submission, recalling that he had been ready to rent the place without first seeing it anyway. Standing there, an old woman walked by, John had to move a couple of feet to his left to allow her to pass. She was pushing a small cart. She stopped and spoke to Casey. "Kenneth, do you think you could send Mitchell up to move a dresser for me?" Casey quietly assured her that he would be sending Mitchell, whoever he was, up to her place sometime before lunch tomorrow. Before the old woman thanked him and continued down the corridor,she looked at John and then turned to Casey. "I hope this young man here intends to move in. We could use some younger tenants." Casey nodded with a vacant look look on his face, explaining that the old woman was named Florence Quinn and that had lived in the apartment for more than fifteen years. He then commented. "The woman is a little eccentric if you know I mean. I wouldn't worry about her." Casey went on to explain Mitchell's function in the apartment building. "He's a young guy who helps me out occasionally." John nodded and concluded, in view of Casey's apparent disabilities, that Mitchell was probably doing most of the duties. He wondered how much Mitchell was getting paid to help Casey out and whether Mrs. Thompson knew about him.

The two of them watched as the old woman pushed her cart down to the end of the hallway and opened the last apartment on the right. He and Casey faced each other again, John smiling and turning to leave. "Don't worry, Mr. Casey, like I said yesterday, I am ready to rent the place without seeing it. I will be back to see the place before I move into it. I'll call on you to see when Mitchell is available." He then turned toward the lobby door, again no handshake. Casey then slowly backed into is own apartment without saying a word. John knew he would be seeing Mr. Casey again. Frequently.

MOVING OUT AND MOVING IN

⸻◆⸻

As expected and as promised, Mrs. Thompson telephoned on the following Monday morning to inform him that he could move into the vacant apartment anytime, asking him to visit the office to sign the lease at his convenience. The lease was for a year and specified a monthly rent of $275. For reasons that John didn't understand, she repeated the monthly rent several times. It seemed unnecessary he thought but John then told Mrs.Thompson that he did not have a car, his use of his wife's Pontiac Astre foregone once he moved himself, thereby not needing a space in the small garage in the Parkdale Court. All he had to move was his clothes, four milk cartons of record albums, several pieces of furniture, that being a chair, a wreck of a couch, a single bed, a television set and sitting in storage on Frank Street, a trunk containing assorted junk and kitchen utensils, all of which John was unlikely to ever retrieve. Although it had not occurred to him until Mrs. Thompson telephoned him to remind him to come to the office to sign the lease, that he would have to obtain additional furniture, specifically a bedside table, another chair, a kitchen table, and maybe a coffee table. He assumed that he could transport whatever furniture he had inherited and whatever furniture he could purchase at the second hand place further down Bank Street in a small van he could arrange for at no charge from his place of employment. He also assumed that his friend Greg and maybe the latter's roommate Mike would help him move into Parkdale Court.

As promised, he visited Mrs. Thompson three hours later, again during his lunch hour. He signed the lease agreement and was given a key to his new apartment. It was numbered apartment 302. She again repeated that he could move in the place at any time, asking him, if not directing him to inform Mr. Casey of the day he planned to move in. She gave him a telephone number for Mr. Casey but advised him to contact him in person at the building. She said that calling on Casey personally was the preferable option, noting that Casey seldom answered the telephone during the day and Mrs. Casey was apparently in charge of answering the telephone. However, she was hard of hearing and would invariably hang up if it was somebody other than her sister calling. In any event, he could easily walk by the apartment building on his way home from work that day.

Having been suitably advised of the conditions of moving in, he took the lease document from Mrs. Thompson, folded it and put it in his pocket. By the time he returned to the car rental, he had decided that he would move a week from Friday. He would advise his boss Mr. Mayhew that he would be taking that Friday off, reserve a van for that day and inform Mr. Casey. He completed the rental paperwork by the end of the next day. It was fortunate that the larger of the two vans that the place had for rent was available.

As planned, he stopped by the building to inform Casey that he would be moving his belongings into the building in eight days. An interesting fact had emerged during his conversations with Mrs. Thompson. She had told him that apartment 302 had been vacant for almost two months, the previous occupant being an elderly man named Hector Dennison who had been living there alone for decades. He had a massive stroke, dropped dead and wasn't found for more than a week. In a subsequent conversation, Casey told him that Mitchell found Hector when he noticed that his mailbox was almost full and knocked on his door for five minutes before he ran downstairs to borrow Casey's skeleton key, who he had initially been unwilling to turn over. He then ran upstairs to open Hector's door. The man had fallen face down in the living room, a broken nose, and a small pool of blood on the floor. The television was still on, the news channel still mumbling, and a half full cup of tea still sitting on the coffee table. Mitchell had gone down to Casey's apartment and explained the situation. Casey was still standing by the door to his apartment, waiting for his key no doubt, looked at him with a dismissive look on his face, and quietly swore. "Are you sure the old man's dead?" Casey asked, with more than an annoyed look on his face. He then shook his head and looked like he was ready to anger. In response, Mitchell felt frightened. "Well, if he's dead up there, you better call the cops." said Casey, as if it was Mitchell's responsibility. Mitchell who, after hesitating at the door, brushed by Casey into the latter's apartment, an apartment which he had never entered, even though he had supposedly worked for Parkdale Court and Kenneth Casey for five years. "Where's your telephone?" asked Mitchell in a semi-panic. Casey looked at him, a puzzled look on his face and asked, befuddled. "My phone?" Mitchell continued to look around apartment 102, observing that practicably every single item in the living room of the two bedroom apartment, the only room to which he had access, seemed to be some sort of antique. It reminded Mitchell of a shop south of Lansdowne Park which sold old furniture and other items of vintage interest. He was confused.

His confusion slowly waffled away while he waited nervously with eyes darting all over Casey's apartment. Casey finally managed to point to a telephone on a small table by the couch. Mrs. Casey, who up until then had sat in apparently bemused silence, also pointed to the telephone and smiled, as she was somehow proud of herself for identifying the telephone. Mr. Casey did not move so Mitchell picked up the receiver, dialed 911 and informed whoever was on the line that he had just found a dead person in an apartment. He related and then repeated the address of Parkdale Court. There was a brief delay as Mitchell waited for instructions. Mitchell said he would meet the officers at the entrance to the building to take them up to apartment 302. He assured the person on the line that he did not touch the body. He then hung up the telephone and looked at Casey who just shrugged himself out of a momentary stupor and commented "Happy now?" He then stepped further into his apartment, telling Mitchell to go to the lobby where he could as he promised wait for the police.

Two officers, a bald middle aged man looking bored and a much younger man who looked a little scared, arrived in the front of the building in a squad car. As they got out of the car and started to ascend the steps to the building, an ambulance stopped behind the squad car with its lights still flashing, suggesting to Mitchell that they may have gotten the message wrong. The two police officers waited on the steps of the building as three paramedics, two men and a woman emerged from the ambulance, unloaded a gurney and began to carry it up the steps. Mitchell had had the presence of mind to place door stops in both the front and inner doors. He directed the officers to the stairs and twice repeated the directions to apartment 302. Kenneth Casey had completely retreated into his apartment, apparently disinterested, as he usually was in anything that required him to take any action, no matter how trivial or how important. Meanwhile, Mitchell continued to act as the doorman.

The older officer offered a predictably sardonic remark. "Third floor and no elevator, right?" His partner just shrugged and continued up the stairs. One of the three paramedics offered an exasperated groan while the other man and the woman struggled with the gurney. Mitchell offered a lame through familiar excuse. "I know, its an old building." The younger officer started up the stairs at a good pace followed by two paramedics, one of them pulling the gurney while the woman was half pushing and half carrying it up the stairs. The other paramedic followed the three of them up the stairs. Out of the curiosity he supposed, Mitchell followed the three men, the woman and the gurney. He then turned back to look towards the front door when he noticed that a small crowd had gathered outside the building. The older officer, the bald one seemingly guarding the entrance to the building, was standing there on the front steps smoking a cigarette.

Mitchell heard the gurney shuffling up to the third floor. He also heard a couple of doors opening and then closing. The younger officer had reached apartment 302 first. The door was closed but unlocked, Mitchell having left it that way after finding Hector Dennison. The younger officer waited by the door upstairs until the paramedics with the gurney arrived to enter the apartment. There was a strange silence on the third floor, the only sound coming from the television in Dennison's apartment. Almost by reflex, after entering the apartment, one of the paramedics, the woman stepped over the body and turned off the television, something that Mitchell had neglected to do. The paramedics then put on rubber gloves on their hands.

The paramedics had stood over the body for a time, considering the details of the scene, wondering why people from the coroner's officer had not been called, if not at least notified. The older paramedic made a derisive comment and shrugged. The other two paramedics, the younger man and the woman, then lifted the body of Hector Dennison, placed him as gently as they could on the gurney, and started to roll him out of the apartment. They then started to slowly carry Dennison and the gurney down the stairs. The younger police officer closed the door to apartment 302 and then hesitated for a moment, contemplating. He put his ear to the closed door and then stood there with a perplexed look on his face, as if he was still hearing the television inside the apartment. He opened the door and then closed it again, the silence returning. He then followed the paramedics down the stairs. By the time the gurney reached the lobby of the building, there were dozens of people outside, milling about, speculating among themselves about the events that had just occurred on the third floor. They knew that someone had died, an event that was obviously unusual for Bank Street. Even as the crowd outside the building continued to murmur among themselves, a certain reverent tranquility fell over the crowd as the gurney was lifted and then placed in the rear of the ambulance which then slowly drove away. The older police officer, who had been on what turned out to be crowd control since the police and the paramedics turned up, put our his last cigarette and joined his young colleague in the car. It too drove away. The crowd slowly dispersed. Hector Dennison was gone.

———————⇒•◦•⇐———————

As he had been told, the apartment had been empty for nearly two months when John first rented it, having declined to check the place out beforehand. The floors were hardwood, the ceilings high and the walls painted a dark brown colour, giving the place the look of a funeral parlour, an appropriate environment for the death of its last tenant. The apartment was designed consistent with the design of building itself. The master bedroom was in the front of the apartment, just to the left of the door and right behind coat rack, the living room and a small dining room to the right down a long corridor to the kitchen and to the left of that, a bathroom that reminded John of his grandmother's place in Toronto. Finally, there was the other, smaller bedroom in the rear of the place. In the middle, there was a narrow kitchen. Within a week of his death, there was little evidence of Hector Dennison's decade or so of living in apartment 302 at all, a thorough job of removing all his possessions was complete, the only exception a framed photograph left on the ledge above the decorative fireplace, a memorable feature of every apartment in the building. It was an old picture of a family, seven people and a small dog in the arms of a young boy. There were four, including the dog, sitting on a bench and three standing behind a bench in a park, a park which could have been the park adjoining Parkdale Court. It was a black and white family portrait maybe taken sometime during World War I: frozen faces, nearly out of focus expressions, people in their Sunday best, posing for a camera that might have weighed ten pounds. Maybe Hector Dennison was one of the children although John couldn't tell. He thought of giving the photograph to Casey but decided against it. He decided to keep it. It was such an interesting picture that he decided to leave it where it was.

It was eight days later. As arranged, he arrived at his place of employment to pick up the van. It was a Friday. He took possession of the van, at least for the next eight hours. It was a two year old van with an array of dents for which a good number of customers paid $500 each time a new dent appeared, the deductible for any insurance claim, which Mr. Mayhew always maintained was less than the cost of the actual damages. It was always the habit of the fastidious owner of the rental agency to charge the customer the deductible and then never get the van repaired. As for subsequent renters, Debra, John, the Saturday guy, a guy named Chris, and even boss himself, would carelessly indicate on the rental contract most but not all of the dents on the van. Customers would return the van and damage not indicated on the rental contract would be pointed out. Either the full deductible would be charged or a lesser amount, depending on the alleged severity of the damage and whether the amount was paid in cash. In any event, Mr. Maynew would simply pocket the cash.

As for John, he never signed any rental agreement nor did he pay anything for the van. He just picked up the key from Chris, picked up his friend Greg and Greg's roommate Mike at their place off Preston Street and drove over to Frank Street to pick up his furniture and belongings. Thankfully, he realized that he would be seeing his wife for possibly one last time, or so he thought. John was not surprised that Greg seemed unusually enthused about the idea of seeing her again. He thought that maybe his best friend would see her again after John did. The thought did not trouble John. He had long suspected that something was going on between the two of them.

They picked up John's possessions without much trouble, the elevators in the Frank Street apartment a comparative convenience. On the other hand, moving into the Parkdale Court apartment building was entirely different, no elevators making moving anything up those three stone stairs laborious, if not difficult to say the least. His records in the four hard milk plastic cartoons proved the most difficult to transport, each surprisingly heavy, holding maybe a couple hundred albums each. In addition, the three of them had to carry the milk cartoons up all three floors a little hung over, the consequence of a rough night spent in a tavern on Preston Street. They lost their grip on their fourth cartoon, spilling its contents on the landing between the second and third floors, watching in bemused horror as maybe two dozen albums settled in a dishevelled pile on the second floor landing. Greg and Mike were laughing as John ran down the stairs to reassemble the fourth cartoon. As he was placing the spilled albums into the milk cartoon, he thought he faintly heard a song from a Who album, one of the albums he was now picking up from the floor and returning to the cartoon. He thought the song was coming from apartment 204. As soon as he placed the Who album in the milk cartoon, the music stopped. He was able to pick up the cartoon by himself, less than six dozen albums in it, and walked it up to apartment 302 where Greg and Mike were sitting on the couch in the living room of John's new place. He didn't mention hearing the Who song to the other two. He began to think that he had imagined it.

Once he put down the milk cartoon, Mike took up a position on the floor while the other two remained on the couch. All three of them were smoking and staring at the four milk cartoons, discussing how long it would take them to assemble the stereo system. Greg then asked John to turn on the television set. He started to plug the set in when there was a knock on the door. John got up to answer the door. It was Mitchell. He introduced himself as Mr. Casey's assistant and shyly welcomed him to the building. He said he helped Mr. Casey take care of the building, careful to note that he only worked five days a week, Sundays and Mondays off. John introduced himself and also introduced Greg and Mike. John told him that there would be additional deliveries to the apartment over the next couple of weeks. Mitchell cautioned him about leaving the truck or the van in front of the building too long, particularly on the weekdays. While he said that while the city usually looked the other way when furniture was being moved into the Parkdale, their patience was not inexhaustible. Mitchell also said that the city was well aware of the fact that space in the Parkdale Court Building garage was limited, saying that the Parkdale was built "a long time ago when a lot of people didn't have cars".

John mentioned briefly hearing music coming from apartment

204 when he was moving in. Mitchell looked puzzled and told John that he never heard music coming from the tenant in apartment 204. John shrugged, thanked Mitchell for dropping by, closed the door and went back to his partially furnished living room. He still had to return the van. He was late but it didn't matter. That evening, he slept in a single bed for the first time since he lived on Cooper Street in a bachelor. As he was drifting into slumber, he was somewhat troubled by late night traffic noise coming from the street. After all, it was Bank Street and his apartment did face the street. He briefly thought about hearing that Who song again that day.

⟫·◉·⟪

His first couple of days living in the apartment were somewhat disjointed, the duty of assembling housekeeping a tiresome requirement, particularly for a recently separated man who had only lived on his own for several months six years ago. He found organizing the kitchen, its pots, its pans, and its other utensils plain annoying. In addition, while he had a refrigerator, a relative antique model left by the previous tenant, the deceased Mr. Dennison, he still needed a stove. He wondered why Mr. Dennison had not left his stove behind, his immediate thought being that Mr. Casey had managed to sell the stove but could not sell the refrigerator. In any event, he mentioned his need for a stove the next day at work in the car rental. Jeff the mechanic overhearing this suggested that he might consider purchasing a used stove from Ben's Used Appliances, a place out on Merivale Road. Maybe Ben's Used Appliances had bought Mr. Dennison's stove. Anyway, Jeff said that the store was open until seven o'clock five days a week. John decided that he would take another one of the vans, if one was available the next day and purchase a used stove. Another development on that first day back at work after moving into his new apartment involved Debra who convinced him, without too much effort, that they audition the single bed that he had just installed in the apartment just after work. There was a definite improvement in their amorous activities, the location and meaning of which about being discovered in John's previous place of residence was no longer applicable. From his third day in the new apartment until she left the employ of the car rental agency four months later, their romantic adventures were a little more relaxed, and if not, a little more adventurous.

That first Sunday, he didn't get out of the bed until late, maybe a few minutes after noon, the rigours of drinking on Preston Street usually a problem for John, particularly now that he wasn't subject to an informal curfew, one of his wife's presumed curfews now no longer relevant. However, he did have difficulties that first night of freedom. Aside from spending more than an hour trying to persuade Debra to ignore the traffic noises outside his bedroom window, they both had to ensure that whatever gymnastics they were pursuing did not result in either of them falling out of the single bed. He also had to prepare things before things got started with Debra. He had spent that afternoon arranging things around the apartment, pots, pans and dishes in the kitchen, ironing and placing his clothes in the small dresser he had inherited. He realized that he may have to start filling the refrigerator and kitchen cabinets with actual food, his original plan, as absurd as it turned out to be, was to take most of his meals in local restaurants and diners. But this Sunday, the day before Debra's first visit, only several convenience stores were open to sell him anything to put in his kitchen.

While he was placing a dozen or so kitchen utensils in the kitchen drawers, he came across another faded black and white photograph that looked like it had been taken sometime around World War I. It appeared to resemble the photograph that John had found on the ledge about the decorative fireplace that first day. There was a major difference between the two photographs, the copy he found in the kitchen showing five instead of four children but no dog. He brought the kitchen photograph into the living room where he compared it to the photograph he found above the fireplace. The photographs were amazingly similar. The kitchen photograph was taken by the Brown Studio of Ballantyne Street in Verdun, an English working class enclave of Montreal while John had noted that the Blair Studio of

Sparks Street in Ottawa had produced the other photograph, the one found above the fireplace. Aside from the number of children and the clarity of the kitchen photograph, the two photographs looked strangely similar. John decided he would keep both photographs in the top drawer of his dresser in his bedroom and contemplate their mystery at a later date. To John, they were always like relics of Mr. Dennison's history in apartment 302.

After cleaning up the apartment that first Sunday, he went out for dinner, the absence of a stove leaving the three television dinners he had purchased from the convenience store that was three blocks away just sitting in the refrigerator. Aside from the dinners, he had bought some milk, some bananas, which looked a little suspicious, not that he would know the difference, a couple of large bags of potato chips, six cans of coke, and his weekly cartoon of smokes, Player's Light the only brand in the place that was recommended as being fresh according to the kid behind the counter. The convenience store was called Abbey's although no one knew or had ever seen anyone named Abbey.

So without anything in the house for dinner that Sunday, John went out to his usual haunt, a local diner named Fido's where he usually had a discussion with the owner, a congenial guy named Joe, who always remarked that he always saw him for dinner on the weekends, weekdays reserved for lunch. John confirmed his regular presence, eliciting little, if any comment from Joe and interest from a waitress named Beverly who said she was single, as she often did. He had dinner, tried to avoid eye contact with Beverly, and was back in his new apartment by seven o'clock. He wanted to telephone his wife, as he had promised Friday evening, his purpose to arrange to pick up some his clothes that she said he had left in her place. Before he opened the door to the apartment, he realized that Bell Canada wasn't coming in to install a new telephone until Wednesday. She would be pissed, nothing new. At least the television was working.

He watched "Sixty Minutes" and an episode of "Columbo", during which he had three beers, which were as left out of a case of twenty four that Greg had brought over during yesterday's move. He watched "Colombo", an episode involving a murdered writer. As usual, Peter Falk was hounding the murderer into a confession.

The next morning, his first day reporting to work from his new address, he happily told Debra of the successful move. They were both standing behind the counter of the office when she whispered her plans to accompany John to his new place on her way home for some "more exercise" and then laughed. An erection started to stir. She noticed it. Neither Mr. Mayhew nor Jeff the mechanic mentioned anything about his move, even though he thought that he and Debra had discussed his plans in the office a number of times and therefore they should have been aware. In fact, Debra would sometimes remark that they could see his place from the car rental parking lot, remarking on the convenience of having his residence so close to his place of employment. With that comment, Debra made a provocative gesture, pulling up her skirt, which was already indecently short. She held the skirt up for a moment and smiled suggestively. She was wearing tiny violet panties. She said they were expensive.

For the rest of the day, they briefly discussed their planned amorous appointment for that afternoon, served several customers and his new apartment's furniture needs. Regarding the latter, John had to endure a couple of hours listening to Debra's suggestions for appropriate apartment decor, including the history of her and her husband's efforts to decorate the three houses in which they had lived since they had married in the mid-1960s. Debra recommended a number of potential interior designs, practically all of which evoked in him thoughts of magazines that were kept for patients in medical offices. Her taste, or apparent taste in apartment design, seemed to John to be a fantasy, unless her taste in fashion, at least the clothing she wore to the work, was contrary to the impression she created with the talk of interior design.

She wore clothes that did not appear on the racks at Holt Renew, her only extravagance the wearing of quality undergarments. It was an understandable combination of personal characteristics. She sometimes considered herself a middle aged woman with a middle aged body. She was almost ashamed of her body, an impression that she created when they first had sex. They had discussed it for a couple of weeks before actually doing anything about it. By the time they arranged a time when John' wife wasn't around, he felt like a sixteen year old who had tired of frequent self abuse. Despite their expectations, that first time, it took Debra fifteen minutes to remove her clothes, worried that her cellulite and a surgical scar would be inhibition enough to keep any potential adultery a fantasy. In fact, at the time, that first time, she suggested that she only remove her underwear until they were ready to complete the deed, no foreplay required it seemed. John eventually convinced her to remove her clothes, including the expensive underwear. It was the beginning of her taking her clothes off every time they made love. The more frequently they made love, the more promiscuous it seemed that Debra became.

They eventually worked out a routine, one day a week being the usual schedule but with the new apartment, they would take the opportunity to increase their frequency, now that John wasn't living with another woman with whom he could also have regular sex, despite his lack of interest in continuing any long time arrangement, that is, their marriage. In any event, the first time they decided to move the venue for their affairs to his new apartment, Debra was surprisingly enthusiastic about their encounter. Twenty minutes after they were together in bed, they were both naked and weary, smoking cigarettes, having exhausted their passion. After she got up from the bed and put on her expensive undergarments, she left the bedroom and went into the kitchen for a drink. She was gone for maybe ten minutes when she returned to John still laying in bed. She was holding a beer and two photographs that she said she had found in his bedroom dresser. John did not know how she found them.

John rose up out of the bed up on his elbows, like some sort of sexual Lazarus. "Where did you get these?" asked John. Debra then answered. "Like you told me the first time here, they were in the top drawer of your dresser." John then asked a second question. "What were you doing in the top drawer of my dresser?" Debra took a swallow of her beer and offered an explanation that didn't seem difficult to believe. "Curiosity, I just wanted to see what you had in your drawers." Debra started to laugh and then asked if the two photographs were pictures of his grandparents or something. She added that the two photographs were different but remarkably similar fto each other, noting the major differences being that one of photographs showed a dog while the other didn't and one pictured five children while the other portrayed only four. John simply explained his interest in them. "I know the two photographs are different. I can't really explain why I kept them. I just liked them. And, by the way, neither of them are photographs of my grandparents or any of my relatives." Satisfied with his own explanation, John dropped back onto the bed and asked if there was any beer left in the refrigerator. He also asked Debra to put the two photographs back into the top drawer of his dresser. She turned, replaced the two photographs and confirmed that there were three beers left in the fridge and started out of the room to bring John one of them. He watched her walk out of the room. As usual, her expensive underwear certainly looked good on her.

⎯⎯⎯⎯⎯◈⎯⎯⎯⎯⎯

Three weeks later, after work on a Tuesday, Debra was over at the apartment for their usual therapy session. They were enjoying post-coital cigarettes when Debra, who had been blowing smoke rings at the ceiling of John's bedroom, a working class Sistine's Chapel he called it one evening, whispered something about the framed portrait on the nightstand, a recently added piece of bedroom furniture. She saw that the photograph, a relatively pedestrian shot of a little league baseball team, of which John claimed to be a member, had replaced a family portrait. John admitted that he had decided he thought that it was necessary to replace the family portrait since he was not particularly thrilled by the picture in the first place. Debra just nodded and lit another cigarette. She said that not only did she not find the family portrait interesting but its replacement by the little league picture entirely understandable. Within ten minutes, Debra had left the apartment. It was almost seven o'clock.

Next day, his plan was to have a quick dinner, the stove finally having been delivered by Ben's Appliances, then to join the boys for pickup basketball and a few post game beers at a strip club called Luster's on Richmond Road. He figured that a couple of hours running up and down the gym and, after that, an hour or so of drinking beer and barely noticing the subdued gyrations of naked women in Luster's, would be enough to get his mind off his confusion. He got home around midnight. He was inebriated enough to have difficulty opening the inner door of his building. A young couple was leaving the building as John was coming in, stepping up the steps. They seemed as befuddled as he was, almost stumbling down the stairs as John went up. He arrived on the dimly lite third floor, his key in his left hand. He dropped the key and suddenly found himself with his elbows on the marble floor. He looked up to see the vague shape of what appeared to be an elderly aged lady in an evening dress standing at the end of the corridor. The shape appeared to be facing the window at the end of the floor, swaying as if slow jazz music was playing. As he pushed himself up into a sitting position, he simply stared at the form of the woman, mystified. He was mildly frightened. He first thought was that he may have been staring at a possible apparition, beers and a little coke supplied by one of his basketball buddies a possible explanation. Now he was standing, the corridor was silent, the only sound his breath echoing down the corridor. He stood and watched the lady for a couple of minutes until she stopped swaying, turned and went back into her apartment, which John assumed was apartment 308. John was now standing tranquilized, He took a couple of steps, took out his key, and finally opened his own apartment. The corridor grew silent again. It was fifteen minutes after midnight, his usual bedtime for a Wednesday. He was still thinking about the lady as he got ready for bed. He thought about her until he drifted off, ten minutes later. He concluded that the lady might have been Mrs. Quinn, who he had casually met while he was talking to Mr. Casey a week or so before he decided to move into the building.

━━━━━◆━━━━━

He arose at the usual time in the morning, a little after seven. On his way to the washroom, the lady in apartment 307, the lady swaying in the corridor around midnight the previous evening materialized in his head like a persistent memory. He wondered about the lady, that is if she actually existed. He wondered whether she swayed during the daytime as well. He thought of asking Mitchell, a more dependable source of information, more than Mr. Casey who was hopeless in John's estimation. He thought the incident interesting enough to bring it up with Debra. When he raised it, she laughed quietly, suggesting that John was maybe imagining the incident. John did not accept Debra's comment happily, giving her an expression that may have been on its way to a dirty look. But he stopped. She usually didn't respond well to dirty looks, she being a person who provided people with dirty looks rather than accepting them. In addition, given the circumstances, John thought it advisable to permit Debra to have her observation about John's imagination without comment.

He continued to think about the lady in apartment 307 throughout the morning. Occasionally the thought that he had imagined the scene floated through his head like one of those songs that arrived and then stayed around long enough to threaten insanity. By the time lunch time arrived, the notion of the nocturnal activities of the lady in apartment 308, imaginary or not, had permanently left his mind, to be replaced it seemed with his usual collection of salacious thoughts about Debra and, somehow not surprisingly, his soon to be ex-wife, the responsibility for the future of their relationship if there was one, almost entirely hers. Ironically, he had a date that evening with his wife, his expectation that he would show her his new apartment for ten minutes or so and then the both of them would head into the sack, the best thing they ever did well together.

Several months later, in a conversation with a friend of his wife during an encounter on Sparks Street, he was told that the only reason she allowed him to stay in the penthouse apartment on Frank Street as long as she did was their comparability in the bedroom, something he already suspected. When she arrived, she spent maybe five minutes checking out an apartment that reminded her, and presumably John as well, of the place they both lived on Cooper Street, and then spent the remainder of the evening having sex. John was unusually cheerful when he reported for work the next day. Even the boss Mayhew commented on the fact that he was cheerful, which was surprising since he seldom remarked on anything more personal than the number of customers due to rent cars on a specific date. Oddly enough though, he felt a little guilty when he greeted Debra that morning. He didn't quite know why he felt that way. He had the strange thought that here he was fooling around on the woman with whom he had been previously around with. He guessed that fooling around on your girlfriend with your wife was a twisted enough arrangement to prompt anyone to consider it curious. It sounded like a script for a half hour situation comedy.

John spent much of the remainder of the day wondering about the dalliance with his wife. He had left the situation open, no particular plan. Not that he discussed much about his soon to be ex-wife with anyone, including Debra or Greg or anyone else for that matter. When they were together, he and his wife sometimes discussed his ambition, or lack therefore, his car rental job being the last in a series of lousy jobs. In contrast, his wife, who had a good job in a government department, had been promoted twice in the last three years and thereof was fairly familiar with ambition. He had to admit, usually to himself in the middle of the night, that ever since he left university and maybe even before that, he didn't have much ambition, however you define it. Sure, he used to pursue the occasional artistic endeavour, like writing poetry or short stories,mainly in university. Strangely, they did not discuss any arrangements for the future, that is if there was a future, that is if their separation, now several weeks old, were to become permanent, which seemed to be a certainty. As she left his place, she just gave him a chaste kiss, smiled and left without a word. He was still in bed. It was eleven at night.

Two mornings later, he happened to glimpse, or thought he glimpsed, an older woman at the end of the corridor as he was leaving his own apartment. It may have been but it wasn't the lady from apartment 307, the lady who was swaying in the corridor a couple of evenings previously. She just looked like the woman. He knew he didn't know her. Fact was that, aside from Mr. Casey, Mitchell and Mrs. Quinn, John Delaney was not familiar with another soul in Parkdale Court. He had seen maybe five or six people the Saturday he moved. They were older, not close to elder but old enough to possibly regard John's arrival as an annoyance, the possibility of excess drinking, loud music, disjointed conversations, and other possible late night foolishness lingering in their minds. After all, it was a quiet building, as he was assured or maybe been warned by Mrs. Thompson of Donaldson Property Management when he signed the lease. He thought, however, despite his temporary misgivings, that his new neighbours had regarded him politely, without any mistrust. Not that he could blame anyone if they did. They had exchanged deferential nods, nothing more, nothing less.

Still, John had lived in the building for less for than two weeks but had not exchanged anything more than cursory nods with anyone other than Casey and Mitchell. The residents immediately adjacent to his apartment, his closest neighbours, were a late middle aged couple who John assumed had just moved into apartment 304, John thought that they were either recently retired or were downsizing from a much larger place, probably a house. There was little doubt that someone in John's situation would almost always entertain such a conclusion. In any event, they exchanged those standard nods although John wanted to engage them in something beyond the nods, particularly the woman who looked like someone he might have seen when he first moved in. Aside from himself, the middle aged couple, and the swaying lady in apartment 308, he thought there were five other residents on the third floor of Parkdale Court. He wondered who they were, a wonder that evaporated by the time he ordered breakfast at Fido's diner and was working though the sports section of the *Ottawa Citizen*. He was at work twenty minutes later, the identities of his neighbours a continuing puzzle.

It was ten in the morning, after the usual rush of rentals by business types, when Mrs. Quinn was dropped off in a taxi, She looked like she hardly ever drove a car, let alone rented one. She was dressed in an expensive navy midi dress with a silver belt, a completely inappropriate outfit for a morning visit to a car rental agency. Adding to the unsuitable impression that the woman made was what appeared to be a cosmetics look better suited to a circus clown, lipstick smeared across her mouth like a traffic signal. Debra, who had been filing her fingernails with the lassitude of a bored stripper, was at the counter when the woman walked in. She greeted the lady and, after a brief internal, looked over her left shoulder with a pronounced eye roll and a smirk. The woman stepped closer to the counter and John, who was standing behind Debra, could detect the scent of an expensive perfume. John heard her ask for the most luxurious automobile available. Debra chuckled, as if the woman was making a humorous suggestion. John, who had moved closer to her before she had a chance to answer, whispered that the agency had only one luxurious automobile available and it was rented out for the day.

"I'm sorry, madame, we have only one luxury car, or what anyone would regard as a luxury car, and it's out on rental today." Debra had stepped back from the counter and made a curious gesture as she walked back into the office, leaving John to continue to deal with the woman who wanted to rent a luxury automobile. The woman, who John had quickly identified as Mrs. Quinn did not think Mrs. Quinn knew who he was, stood at the counter for a moment with a quizzical expression on her face, apparently incredulous. She then turned and pointed out through the side window of the office to a Mercedes that was parked in the far corner of the lot. "How about that one, sir, isn't that a luxury car?" the woman asked with a certain enthusiasm. John leaned over the counter and replied in a low, soft voice. "I can't rent you that car ---- it's the manager's." The woman stared at John and then commented with a certain seriousness. "That doesn't matter. I don't want to drive the car, I only want to sit in it for a few minutes. Couldn't you just let me sit in that car?" She asked casually, as if she were asking for the time of day." He thought that she was going to call him darling or some other similar affectation. He started to think that she may be some sort of actress. He already knew that she was a dancer, or thought she was. The thought, however, was fleeting.

Nonetheless, it was not surprising that John looked at the woman as if she had just removed her expensive navy midi dress with the silver belt. He understandably stumbled, speaking almost in a high register. "You just want to sit in the car!" Debra had heard John's dumbfounded, flabbergasted declaration. She spread her hands out toward the ceiling in exasperation and then crept back into the office. Neither Debra nor John thought that Mr. Mayhew, who was sitting behind his desk in the office with some paperwork, had heard the exchange. The woman, seeing John's discomfort, which was pretty well obvious by then, immediately modified her request, which may have been her objective anyway. "I only want to sit in the car for a few minutes, only a few minutes, that's all." She then leaned across the counter again and touched John's right hand. "Only a few minutes, darling, only a few minutes, in that car over there." And then she took her hand away and turned her back to him. She started to walk out. It reminded him of something, something very familiar. He wondered if she would dance or sway. John then nodded and took the key to the Mercedes from the hook directly behind him. He was certain that Mr. Mayhew would not notice. John then followed her out of the door into the parking lot, holding the key to that luxury car.

As he followed her into the parking lot, he noticed again that there was something reminiscent of her, something he had seen before. He had passed her before she got to the car. He opened the passenger side to the car, held open the door and invited her into the car. She got in, sat down, daintily swinging her legs into the car, and gestured for him to join her, patting the front seat behind the wheel. John gently closed the passenger door and went around to the driver's side of the car. He opened the door and got in. As soon as he slid behind the wheel, she reached into her purse and handed him a camera. He once again looked at her with another puzzled look. "I want you to take my picture." she said, a beguiling smile on her face. "And I want you to try to include part of the apartment building in the background, the top floor if you can." She then looked straight at John. "Take the picture now." she commanded. He did, a corner of the Parkdale Court in the upper right corner. Delineating the request, the woman said that she lived on the third floor of the Parkdale Court. John already knew that.

Debra had been watching the two of them out in the parking lot. Not surprisingly, Debra asked about the strange transaction that John had just managed to complete. Debra had this strange smile on her face, as if she had some sort of clue as to explain the elderly woman's curious behaviour. All John would say was that she obviously had some sort of fixation for luxury cars and left it at that. Debra shook her head, shrugged her shoulders and provided John with one of her decadent snickers, just to suggest to him that she suspected that the elderly woman was certifiable. With that, Debra waved her hand and said that John had maybe come across a woman with a strange personality trait and little more. John responded with a dumb look on his face and started to ruminate about the woman, a process that was to consume him for the next week or so. He had come to at least one conclusion. It was likely, or so he thought, that Mrs. Quinn had some sort of consuming attraction to the building. He also concluded she had a strange interest in expensive automobiles, an interest strong enough to compel her to ask John to take a photograph of her sitting in one. Again, he knew he would be obsessing about the woman for a while.

The incident was still very much on his mind by the time he got home that day. He sat on the couch, had several beers and then drifted into a contemplation of the woman, the car and the resulting photograph, which he would probably never see unless its subject chose to share it with him once it was developed. He thought of a picture of his mother taken at a masquerade party that his parents had hosted in their basement maybe fifteen years ago. She was dressed in an outfit that she later told he and his brother was worn in the flapper era, the so-called Roaring 20s. John wished that he had the picture itself, which he figured was now in some forgotten photograph album in their retirement place somewhere in Florida. He was momentarily convinced that his mother, the picture of which he had just recollected, looked like the woman who had appeared in one of the pictures that he had recently found in his apartment.

He also had awoken to the conclusion that the woman in one of the photographs wasn't really his mother but a woman who resembled his mother. He was still wondering whether it was a case of mistaken pictorial identity, that apparition was the answer to his confusion about the other two pictures he had originally found in apartment 302. He felt like he had been magically transported into something out of a *Twilight Zone* episode.

One week later, another Monday evening, having almost forgotten about the photograph of his mother's now imaginary lookalike, he was coming home after having dinner at the Chinese restaurant down the block when he saw Mrs. Quinn, of whom he had recently taken a picture in a luxury automobile. She was staring out out the window at the end of the corridor of the third floor, gently swaying to unheard music. Just like a couple of weeks ago, her back was to him. He stood at his door, thinking of approaching her. He took one step toward her and then stopped. She then turned to her left, walked toward the door to the last apartment on the right of the corridor and opened the door to the apartment. She suddenly turned to him and gave him a theatrical wave. She then closed the door. The sound of the closing echoed down the hall like it was a confessional in a silent church. Again, he thought of walking down the corridor and knocking on the lady's apartment. But he didn't. It was just another peculiar circumstance. At the moment, as he closed his own apartment's door, he thought, for a split second, that Parkdale Court should have been called something else. The Hall of Mirrors seeming to be an appropriate name.

That night, he had a dream, an unusual occurrence for John but more likely given to the unexpected incidents that had befallen since he moved into the place a month ago. The dream, again strangely, was inspired it seemed by the apartment itself. It was haunted he thought. In the dream, it was the old photograph that was bedevilling him. He was holding a black and white terrier. He was standing between the lady that had had her photograph taken in Mr. Mayhew's automobile parked across the street from the Parkdale Court and his replica mother Edna. The two women seemed to be looking at each other. The photograph seemed to be moving somehow, forward and backward. Every time the photograph moved though, the two women seemed to change position, from left to right and then back again. They were facing stationary, facing front, then facing the other way. The dream was mercifully short. It had awakened him.

He had tried to remember the dream the next morning. He had spent some time sitting on the side of the bed trying to recall the entire dream. Sometimes, when it came to dreams, he remembered them, sometimes he didn't. In this case, however, he managed to recall the dream. In the bedroom, he stared into the mirror and then wondered about seeing the lady in the corridor the previous evening. As usual, he couldn't really explain it. That and the dream were mysteries. He rehearsed the same questions to himself practically every time he had a dream, which he thought were connected to the strange events. It was his normal practice. For a moment, he almost hypnotized himself while gazing at himself in the mirror. In fact, he almost fainted. For a fleeting moment, he had been thinking, as he had on several previous occasions, that each one of the bizarre events that he had experienced were illusions that he had imagined as dreams. As usual, that thought did not last long. He finally got out of bed, went to the kitchen for a cup of coffee, and thought about getting ready for work. That usually did not take very long. After all, his place of employment was right across the street. It was a Tuesday.

Nothing happened over the next few days. By the Friday of that week, he had pretty well abandoned his obsession with his so-called "strange events". During his customary Thursday evening out on Preston Street, his buddy Greg spent much of the evening debating the qualities of his two last girlfriends, both of whom were still around to demonstrate their attributes to Greg. Oddly enough, they were both named Cathy, a curiosity that did not seem to stand out to either of them, since neither of them knew about the other. According to Greg, who had often characterized both of them as being difficult to deal with, calling both of them "crazy" at times, out of their presence of course. One of them, a twice married woman who claimed to have been intimate with guitarists from every amateur band in the city, believed in things like angels, seances, and barely watchable art house movies. All these general interests suggested to John that maybe this Cathy was not exactly all there, a judgment that he sometimes shared with Greg. In response, Greg would just shrug, saying that she was very attractive, liked vigorous sex, was popular with his buddies, liked to drink and probably wasn't dangerous. He also said that for these reasons, he was willing for the most part to overlook the deficiencies of their relationship.

The other girlfriend was also quite attractive, younger but less unorthodox. In fact, since Greg started his liaison with the younger Cathy, John would fantasize about her, regardless of any relationship he had with his soon-to-be ex-wife and his workplace mistress Debra. But Greg said she was demanding, and he seemed was more interested in the other Cathy. In another event, when talking about either of them, Greg would shake his head, call both Cathys "crazy" and order another beer.

John would just listen, pretending to sympathize with Greg although he could never understand his friend's continuing relationships with either Cathy, a fact that prevented John from seriously pursuing either one of them romantically. John did however have a brief fling with the crazier of the two Cathys, a fling that lasted two hours at a downtown nightclub. Sure, she was a little more deranged than the other, a character flaw she demonstrated on that date by handing John her underwear after the second drink. By the fourth drink, however, that particular Cathy had deserted their table after getting into a disagreement with John over the relative merits of the band that was playing at the club. At some point in their discussion, she said she was going to the ladies' room and disappeared. He never told his friend Greg about their so-called date. Regardless, he did, however, feel a little guilty. Even if Greg knew, John doubted that he would have cared. John later thought, once he had started having the strange sightings on the third floor of the Parkdale Court, that maybe the first "Crazy Cathy" could have provided him with an explanation. Perhaps she would have said that the place was haunted, ghost identification likely being one of her natural aptitudes or so she believed.

It was a Thursday, like any other Thursday, John, after listening to a recitation of Greg's travails for a couple of hours, considered raising his own anxieties with the incidents on the third floor floor of his apartment building. His intentions were disrupted, however, when they were joined by two of their former colleagues from their old jobs at the Royal Canadian Mint, which was where Greg and John first met, preparing materials and chemicals for eventual pouring of cooper slabs for the pressing of pennies. John forgot one of their names, the other being named Ed, a teammate of both John and Greg on the Mint hockey team. They stood and then sat at their table for a few minutes before they left. By then, both John and Greg had decided to leave as well. John therefore never got the opportunity to bring up his paranoia regarding those third floor sightings.

Two days later, a Saturday during which he was working, it being his turn, he and Debra alternated Saturdays, he spent most of that day staring over the counter out the front window into the parking lot. There was little business aside from renting out the cube and cargo vans for moving furniture and the like. Around four o'clock that afternoon, which was usually the deadline for returning the daytime rentals, the evening rentals got the remainder of the weekend, the instruction was to leave the van on the lot by midnight Sunday, as monitored by parking lot cameras. On this Saturday, the cube van was rented for the day while two vans were leased through the evening. John also rented six cars, went to the Chinese restaurant for lunch, talked to his soon-to-be ex-wife on the telephone about the whereabouts of the winter tires for her car, and watched people waiting for the city bus on the northern corner of the parking lot. It was two in the afternoon when he saw an older man who looked very familiar standing across the street. He was standing on the steps of the Parkdale Court.

While he looked recognizable, he also looked peculiar. He was wearing an old fashioned three piece striped suit accessorized with a polka dot pocket square, a gold chain and watch fob combination, and what looked like, if one could have have imagined, white spats. He was leaning on a cane. People were walking by looking agog, like he was some sort of street performer. All he needed was a monocle and he would have resembled the theatrical "Mr. Peanut". John starred at him until he started to see double. He did look more than familiar though. He knew it but could not put his finger on it and it wasn't just based on the man's likeness to "Mr. Peanut". Although the image was a trifle faded, he may have looked like the man in the photograph that he had originally found in the kitchen drawer. With with the cane, however, the Mr. Peanut masquerade seemed believable. He was the father. He was the only common figure in each of the three photographs. Maybe. He was still staring when "Mr. Peanut" brought his cane to his side, and started into the lobby of the Parkdale Court, opening the front door and disappeared. Since he had used a key, John concluded that the man lived in the building. He thought of walking across the street and following "Mr. Peanut" into the apartment building in which they both lived.

⊶•⊷

He was laid off by the rental agency two months later. It was July. He remembered the day. Mr. Mayhew came out from behind his desk in the back office to the front counter to personally cashier him, weakly telling him that "We can hardly keep the lights on the way business has been going the last month or so." Jeff the mechanic told John that Mayhew invariably laid off office staff after six months or so as to avoid giving them raises, a habit that Jeff suggested allowed the family to purchase a new luxury automobile every two years. Another theory, again propagated by Jeff the mechanic, habitually dumping office staff on a regular basis because he liked to demonstrate to his wife that he was decisive, firing someone supposedly indicative of that quality. Jeff said, "I'll bet they'll be somebody new standing at this counter within a couple of weeks." Funny thing, his prediction turned out to be accurate. From his living room window a month later, he saw a young man with a beard standing behind the counter talking to Mr. Mayhew. By that time, John was working over at Tunney's Pasture on Scott Street for the Department of Health and Welfare as a casual short term clerk. Within two weeks after leaving the employ of Mr. Mayhew, he had been hired. He thought getting a job so fast was a miracle. Debra, who he saw one more time after he had been let go, agreed that it had been a miracle. As for Debra, at her husband's suggestion, she said that she was taking the rest of the year off.

It was the end of August. As he did most mornings, John was standing at the bus stop on the corner of Bank and Patterson Streets. It was seven thirty in the morning. He had given Jeff the mechanic a salute, as he normally did anytime he saw him. As the bus going north approached, he saw the man and the lady from one of the photographic apparitions step out into the street from the front door of Parkdale Court. It looked liked the father and the mother from one of the photographs. It was the first time since the middle of May that he had seen anyone that had appeared in any of the photographs. He had almost but not quite forgotten them. Some nights but not many, he could not get to sleep. Then the photographs would come back to him like a bad memory, illusions still but not forgettable.

He thought of not boarding the bus, his surveillance now more important than getting to work on time. But he had one foot on the bottom step of the bus door and four or five passengers behind him in line. He also checked his watch, a little worried about the time, being late to a casual clerical job unlikely to inspire much hope for full time employment. So he got on the bus, paid the fare, found a spot standing on the street side of the bus, continuing to study the man and the woman on the steps of the Parkdale Court while the bus started up and headed downtown. He continued to gaze at the man and the woman, following them down the aisle out of the back window of the bus until the Parkdale Court was out of sight. He then took a seat on the bus, bewildered by another example of the ever shifting photograph. He almost missed his transfer, so spellbound he was by his latest observation. By the time he arrived on the fifteen floor of the Jeanne Mance Building, he had decided that he would investigate these apparitions, not just ruminate about them. He wanted to get to the bottom of the matter.

Fortunately or not, his position at the Department of Health and Welfare provided him with enough spare time to contemplate plans to scrutinize these presumably imaginary but still strange occurrences. There were now six episodes he thought, all of which were connected to a single photograph that he had found in the kitchen drawer of his recently leased apartment, a photograph that was then found sitting on his phony fireplace and then transferred into the top drawer of his nightstand, a photograph that, at last examination, seemed to include a picture of his own mother. His first move, therefore, was to carefully check the photograph, to specifically determine who was actually in the photograph, including his duplicate mother and the man who appeared to be the father of the family and who had appeared in front of the building twice in the last few months, most recently that morning. He arrived at that decision after lunch with a woman named Patricia with whom he had occasional sex, including the previous day in the stairwell between the fourteenth and fifteenth floors. He had suggested one of the staff rooms on either floor but both happened to be occupied when they were prompted by their passions.

On this Thursday, although Patricia made the offer, claiming that the staff rooms on the two floors weren't occupied, John declined. When she looked disappointed, he told her that his stomach was a little queasy, a condition he blamed on the cafeteria food. Instead of regretting a failed opportunity for intimacy with Patricia, he spent most of the afternoon deliberating about the possible identification of the man and the woman who he had seen that morning in front of his apartment building. Around quitting time, he came to the conclusion that if he could somehow convince building manager Casey, or perhaps his assistant Mitchell, to talk to him about the building's occupants, most specifically the occupants of the third floor. At least that gave him a plan. He thought about calling on Casey or maybe the more amendable Mitchell. He wanted to ascertain the identity of the third floor tenants.

He temporarily lost interest in further investigation of the photograph. So it was not a surprise that John never got around to calling on either Kenneth Casey or his assistant Mitchell on either the following day, the weekend or even the next week. He did, however, see Mr. Casey that Saturday hauling groceries into the building, holding the door for him and his wife. He never mentioned his interest in seeking the names of certain Parkdale Court tenants. He had been waiting to meet Patricia who was coming over for a quick romp in the hay before heading out for dinner and then the remainder of the evening at a club in Hull, where they would dance until they were exhausted. They would then take a cab to either of their apartments although Patricia always preferred John's place. His place was larger and closer to the club they frequented in Hull. In any event, with his Saturday recreation with Patricia taking all his time, he never had the opportunity to ask either Mr. or Mrs. Casey anything. And Mitchell wasn't around on the weekend.

※━◇━※

Three weeks later, during which time his relationship with Patricia started to bloom, she persuaded him to invite a number of people from Health and Welfare and anyone else they could think of to a party at his place. She had convinced him that he had a great place for a party, with a fairly large living room and a small dining room. While John hadn't attended many parties, let alone hosted a party since before he was married, he grudgingly agreed. He and Patricia then celebrated the plan by having sex on the dining room floor, grappling with each other until John hit his head on the radiator.

They had selected a Saturday night three weeks hence for the party. Patricia had complied a list of invitees of some forty people, most of whom worked at Health and Welfare. John added another dozen or so, including Greg, Dan, Mike and a couple of their softball teammates and their dates. On a related matter, he told Patricia that he had slipped invitations under the doors of every other apartment on the third floor of his building. Patricia initially thought that it was an idiotic idea, using the term repeatedly when he first informed her. But she changed her opinion after he explained his reasoning for those invitations. According to John, invitations might pacify the floor neighbours who might otherwise be tempted to complain about noise that would likely to be emanating from the apartment. For the some reason, based on having seen the dancing lady once at the end of the floor, who may or may not have been imaginary, he was convinced that every other occupant on the third floor was past or close to retirement age and therefore would be likely to object to loud noises on a Saturday night. Anyway, Patricia eventually thought it was worth a shot. In any event, neither thought that any of them would actually show up.

Over the next three weeks, Patricia advertised the party to practically everyone she came across, most if not all of them having already been invited. Not surprisingly, they had not invited any of their managers, thinking that if they asked any manager, a woman named Georgina was quite popular around the office, it would be difficult not to invite any other manager. Regardless, it looked like the party would be well attended, a prospect that somehow worried Patricia who started bothering John about things like drinks and appetizers. Predictably, John was not concerned. There was also the matter of entertainment, music and whatnot. For reasons that Patricia never could understand and asked John to forget about, John and Greg went ahead and produced a series of presentations that he thought would amuse the party. They were basically satirical takes on advertisements and recent movies. They also intended to hold a quiz, with a series of prizes. Patricia argued that party goers really didn't need entertainment. John said that he and Greg said that it wouldn't hurt.

———◦———

It was an impressive crowd by any account. By nine o'clock on the night of the party, there were at least four dozen people already spilling over the living room into the dining room. As more people arrived, most carrying wine, beer and liquor, the crowd started to move from the living room and dining room into the corridor, the kitchen and even the small bedroom. There was a heavy cloud of smoke in the place, a blue haze requiring the opening of all the windows. There was an alarming level of noise by ten o'clock, music and the din of overlapping conversations dominating the room. It was a slightly concerned John who, aside from serving drinks, playing the music, and earlier in the evening, playing supposedly amusing videos, was occasionally checking the hall for potentially complaining neighbours. He continued his monitoring until eleven o'clock or so without any appearance by anyone. None of the third floor neighbours had appeared. By the time John and Greg unleashed the quiz on the crowd, most of them were more interested in remaining upright than answering some dumb questions from the hosts of the party. It was no surprise when John didn't bother finishing the quiz. There was a lot of razing, people hollering ridiculous answers to equally dumb questions about movies, music, television shows and, just for the hell of it, current events. The music was turned up every time either John or Greg tried a question. Still, overall though, the party was a roaring success. There had to be fifty or sixty people in the apartment, including at least two dozen people who John did not recognize. Several people appeared to have been accompanied by their parents, three older women and two older men, both of whom were armed with cameras.

There were people laying on the floors of the living room rather than on the overcrowded couches and folding chairs elsewhere in the apartment. There were people sitting cross-legged on the floor, couples in the bedroom trying to rearrange their clothing, one couple making out under the clear glass coffee table in the living room and two guys in the kitchen arguing about, at least according to people coming out of the kitchen shaking their heads, Marxism or something like that. Aside from having to compel a few people to leave the party involuntarily, the gathering broke up without any problem around two in the morning. Only John and Patricia were left to wake up in the apartment late Sunday morning. Greg and his date Valerie, his most recent replacement for either of the Cathys, had wanted to stay the night, claiming that they were too plastered to go home, an excuse that could have been used by practically half the people who attended the party. Greg and Valerie were declined lodging at the Parkdale Court for the night and then sent home by cab.

On the following Monday, however, there were numerous stories of incidents that may or may not have occurred that Saturday night circulating on the fifteen floor of the Health and Welfare building. Patricia thought that the stories were somewhat amusing while on the other hand, John spent much of that day commenting on whether this or that event had actually happened. Fact was that the reports about the party, no matter how incredulous, were held in high regard. Many attendees expressed their hopes to be invited to the next party. As Patricia was to say with a certain mirth that the party was definitely a success, no matter how stoned the guests were. People were still talking about the party weeks later, after which time recent promotions, affairs and similar news came to dominate the office rumour mill.

John did not tell Patricia of the photograph he found underneath his door the morning after the party. It looked like the original fireplace photograph although, on closer inspection, it had looked entirely different. In this case, instead of the mother and the father in the photograph, it was Patricia and John casually standing staring into the camera. They were holding a small picture of the four children and the white terrier as they appeared in the original photograph. Although he did not check with Patricia, he was certain that there was a couple of guests taking photographs at the party. That might have provided some sort of explanation, as mysterious as it seemed. Besides, neither John nor Patricia knew every guest. Like each time he saw the photograph change after that first time, the source of the modification was a mystery. Along with the three other haunted family photographs, including most particularly the original, which he had started to believe may not have been the original at all, he secured it in his nightstand. He stood and lingered, staring at the wall above the chest of drawers for several moments, almost hypnotizing himself into paralysis, until he woke out of his stupor.

He had heard Patricia clattering around in the kitchen, offering up the occasional expletive as she started to clean up after the party. But John thought that the place was not as messy as it should have been. Actually, after an evening of hosting a horde of more than sixty guests roaming around with drinks in their hands, the apartment was remarkably tidy, that is it was not as messy as one would have expected. Patricia had instructed John to start cleaning up in the living room. He quickly broke himself out of his vacant stare. Patricia was always right. John was lazy and messy. Still, he started to pick up the beer bottles and placing them in boxes, muttering and more accurately grumbling under his breath.

As he often did when performing unpleasant tasks, pretty well any domestic chore would qualify, he started to daydream. Not quite daydreaming. He started to drift into fantasy. He was reviewing his options for investigating the photographs, including most particularly re- interviewing Kenneth Casey or his assistant Mitchell. He had not spoken to either of them about the other third floor occupants but it still was a possibility. He also considered contacting Mrs. Thompson of the Donaldson Property Management about the tenants on the third floor. While she would most certainly know who was living in one of the Donaldson buildings, she might be reluctant to share that information, confidentiality being a possible explanation. The other alternative was to research the newspapers, which was probably an unlikely source of information unless you counted obituaries, the most recent of which being the notice about the previous occupant of apartment 302, Hector Dennison. He also remembered the story he had heard from Mrs. Thompson about Parkdale Court even before he had thought looking for an apartment to rent. Back in the 1940s, the architect of the Parkdale Court had committed suicide by hurling himself off a balcony from the very building he had designed. According to Mrs. Thompson, that event had precipitated a couple of days of newspaper stories. Maybe there were other stories about the building, John thought that maybe the mutating photographs were indicative of an eccentric history.

In the living room, there were two folding chairs left from the party. One of them was marred by a wobbly chair leg under which someone had placed a folded piece of paper. He picked up the chair. It was a page out of a newspaper that had been stabilizing the chair. It was almost a piece of parchment, the front page of the *Ottawa Journal* newspaper for April 5, 1949. There were three articles on the front page. In the upper right front panel was the most significantly sized of the three articles. "Ottawa Architect Kills Himself". It identified the architect as George Fenwick who, as John had been told when he was looking for a place to live, had jumped from the window of an apartment in a building he designed, i.e. Parkdale Court. The front page article only provided three paragraphs before advising readers to turn to page six. He was immediately surprised, pondering the circumstances of the architect's suicide in the building in which he now lived an obvious fascination. It did not take him long to decide to research the newspaper archives to find the entire article. Given his recent obsession about events in his apartment, he was compelled to expand his research to include any article that mentioned Parkdale Court.

———⟫•◦•⟪———

After asking around at work for a day or two, he was informed that access to newspaper archives, including the *Ottawa Journal*, was available from the main branch of the Ottawa City Library. After ensuring that the library was open, he made plans to research its newspaper archives on Saturday. He told Patricia about his weekend plan, which more or less necessitated admitting to her that he was initiating or maybe re-initiating his investigation into the origins of the photographs, an admission that, was momentarily disturbing to Patricia, but did not result in any further discussion. Although he had originally decided not to let Patricia know that he was continuing to explore the mystery of the photographs, the fragment of the *Ottawa Journal* found under the folding chair in the living room was the rationale for his decision to change his mind. So he finally showed the partial newspaper article to Patricia and then explained his intention to locate the rest of the article, suggesting that maybe it could provide him with a clue as to the origins of the photographs. He admitted that it was a long shot but he said that there had to be a reason for the placement of the newspaper fragment under the chair, something that John thought was doubtless intentional.

Patricia had looked at him with a puzzled look on her face. "You mean, you think that someone who was at the party brought part of a newspaper and then placed it under a chair so that somebody, like you presumably, would find it. Who would do that and why would they do it?" John looked equally puzzled. "I don't know but I can't get it out of my head." he answered. Patricia looked at him and shrugged at him in an endearing sort of way. "I guess I can let you have your hobby, if that is what it is." assured Patricia. She then continued. "Well, as much as I think you're wasting your time, it's your time. So go ahead. But please," she said with a gentle look on her face, "don't start obsessing, like I think you could." John would accept her advice but would be visiting the library on Saturday anyway.

For the remainder of the week, John tried not to think about the newspaper fragment. Thinking that it might distract John, Patricia assisted with that effort by insisting on sex in the stairwell on Wednesday, sex in a manger's abandoned office on Thursday and, just to ensure that John's mind was not fixated on a visit to the library the next day, they performed spectacularly in a women's washroom cubicle after work on the Friday. Aside from any ulterior motive, the sex was also unusual for another reason. It was predictable that, since Patricia moved into apartment 302, the pursuit of sex between the two of them in the environs of Health and Welfare would decline. It didn't. By Friday evening, the couple was exhausted and most of their office colleagues had been provided with considerable material for gossip.

The next morning, as planned, John arrived at the main branch of the Ottawa Public Library at ten o'clock. A woman named Lynn Monette, a name plate on the front desk identifying her, greeted him. He explained his purpose in visiting the library. She smiled and responded. "We don't have that many requests for newspaper archives. They're in a separate room. I'll take you there." She closed the book that was spread out in front of her and beckoned him to follow her. To the right behind the collection of newspapers on those wooden sticks were two microfilm readers behind which there were file cabinets in which Ms. Monette said were the microfilm rolls, indexed by newspaper and year. Ms. Monette said that the archives went back to the 19th century and included a dozen Canadian newspapers, including the *Ottawa Journal*. Regarding the latter, she told John that the microfilm records on the *Ottawa Journal* dated back to 1885, the year in which the newspaper was established. She then motioned John to follow her to the file cabinet where she pointed out a drawer identified as the *Ottawa Journal* for the years 1941-1960. She then pointed to the two microfilm readers on the table.

She stepped aside and opened the microfilm roll for the years 1946 – 1950. He picked it out of the drawer and the file folder for the year 1949. April 5 of that year was a Tuesday. He found the article on the front page for that day. It continued on page six. He noticed at the bottom of the front page was a large advertisement for the Caplan Department Store on Rideau Street. He read the entire article.

OTTAWA ARCHITECT
KILLS HIMSELF

———◆———

George Fenwick, an Ottawa architect known for designing buildings in the downtown area, killed himself yesterday by jumping from the open window of the top floor of Parkdale Court, a twenty one unit apartment building he designed in 1935. According to building landlord Lawrence Wallace, Mr. Fenwick, who was unmarried and was living alone, was a well spoken and courtly gentleman who was the perfect tenant. "He always paid his rent on time, never disturbed his neighbours, and maintained one of the most tastefully decorated apartments in the building." said Mr. Wallace.

According to several of the tenants who had gathered in front of the apartment on Bank Street where the body was found, Mr. Fenwick seemed to be distressed recently, nervous about something or other. According to other tenants, who spoke to this reporter, Mr. Fenwick was not close to anyone in the building, having few friends, if any friends in Parkdale Court. Police have indicated, however, that the circumstances of Mr. Fenwick's death appear to be obvious and therefore did not warrant any further investigation. Officially, Mr. Fenwick's death would likely be ruled a suicide.

According to city records, Mr. Fenwick had either designed or had a hand in designing over a dozen downtown

apartments and was commonly regarded as one of the most prominent architects in the city. Mr. Fenwick was 52 years old and had lived in apartment 302 of Parkdale Court since the building opened in 1936.

Sitting there in the library, John quickly recognized that the last sentence in the story might be a clue. More than 35 years ago, it was evident that the man who had designed the building had moved into the same apartment that John and Patricia now lived. It was not entirely difficult to believe, however, that the apartment in which they now lived was "one of the most tastefully decorated apartments in the building", though its architectural benefits may have faded over the years. Aside from wondering about the monthly rent on the apartment in 1949, he also pondered how many tenants had lived in apartment 302 in the intervening years, aside of course from Hector Dennison, Patricia and himself.

He started to speculate about the nature of the circumstances that led to Mr. Fenwick becoming "distressed" and then eventually leaping out of the window out of his apartment. Maybe it was the apartment itself. That was his first thought. Sitting there, he started to think that maybe the apartment was haunted or possessed or cursed or something. He also realized that, aside maybe for an obituary for Hector Dennison, he could continue to sit in the library and look through the microfilm of every *Ottawa Journal* edition for the next 25 years and not find another reference to Parkdale Court. Still sitting there, he was now determined to speak to Kenneth Casey. He figured, at least based on his aged appearance, that Mr. Casey had been a custodian of the Parkdale Court long enough to have some knowledge of the building's history.

It was the next day when he decided to call on Casey in apartment 106. It was one in the afternoon, having remembered that he had seen he and his wife going to the United Church three buildings down from Parkdale Court. He thought that they probably attended every Sunday. He had tried to convince Patricia to accompany him to see him, thinking that her presence might encourage him to talk, a quality that he didn't usually exhibit, at least during the few conversations he had pursued with him. He stood before apartment 106 for maybe two minutes before he responded to John's knocking on his door. He was still dressed in a black suit with a white shirt with a frayed collar and an undone maroon cravat, presumably his outfit for church. John had never seen Casey in anything other than a grey work uniform. It was obvious that he had not changed his clothes since he and Mrs. Casey had returned from church. It was also obvious that they had just finished lunch.

"Hello, Mr. Casey, I'm John Delaney from apartment 302." Casey looked at him with an annoyed look on his face but still acknowledged him. "Yeah, I know. We met. You know that I know everyone in the building. You're up in apartment 302, moved in about four months ago, right?", a comment that seemed and no doubt was intended to be sarcastic. He then continued, his tone predictably irritated. "I assume you have a complaint." John should have been but was not prepared for his reaction. "No, I have no complaints, none at all." Casey snickered and pointed out his own complaints. "As a matter of fact, I have received some gripes about you, mainly about the music you play." John expected that. He muttered an apology and looked down at his feet. He noticed a ring of keys hanging from a hook by the door. He stared at then for a moment and looked back."I'm sorry but nobody let me know the music was bothering them."

Casey shrugged his shoulders. "They should have let you know, they should have." Casey then stepped back and motioned John into the apartment. Mrs. Casey, who sat on the couch holding a cup of tea, looked up and gave him a funny little smile. As instructed, John sat on a faded petite point chair. He was momentarily worried that the chair would collapse. Casey took a seat on the couch besides his wife, who he introduced as Gladys, and asked. "Then why are you here, Mr. Delaney? Some sort of trouble with the apartment?" John shook his head and leaned forward, the back feet of his chair coming off the floor. "Well, I thought I would pick your brain, so to speak, about the history of the apartment, specifically the tenants who have lived on the third floor. I'm guessing that you have been working in the building for a long time." He looked at Casey who actually seemed to him to be listening intently, which seemed to be surprising. "Gladys and I have been taking care of this place for more than thirty years." He delayed for a moment and added. "For your information, we replaced a guy named Prentice who I think may have been the second or third custodian here in Parkdale Court." Gladys looked up at John and offered him cup of tea. He accepted.

As Gladys got up from the couch and headed for the kitchen, Casey asked John what he wanted. "Well, to be honest, Mr. Casey. I'd like to know what you know about the tenants on the third floor." He tilted his head a bit and asked. "Why would you like to know that?" John should have been ready for the question but all he could come up with sounded like a rather feeble explanation. He had concocted it the previous evening, just before he went to sleep. He thought about his concern about the photographs he found in his apartment but decided against it. He thought that no one would believe him. "Well, I'm taking a course at Carleton University." He looked positively mystified, as if John was speaking a foreign language. "A course? What kind of university course are you taking?" John had invented a course with which he was relatively certain that George would not be familiar and therefore would not dispute. "It's a Canadian history course. The students have been asked to submit papers on local history. I decided to write a paper on Parkdale Court, starting with the architect Mr. Fenwick's death on the third floor of the building and anyone living on the third floor who might known anything about the history of the floor." Casey looked a little dumbfounded. John added some further information in which he thought he might have an interest. He was wrong but he went ahead with a comment anyway. "I'm auditing an evening course, just taking the course for interest." Kenneth's bewilderment remained. "Okay, you say you have an interest in writing something for a course that you are just taking for the helluva it. You don't have to write anything for this course, right?" John nodded. Casey then laughed. "Okay but I still don't get it. And what the hell does that have to do with the tenants on the third floor." It appeared that the entire story wasn't making much sense to him.

Again, John wasn't too confident about his prepared answer to a question he had expected but it was only the one he had. "Well, I just want to talk to anyone who has lived on the third floor or maybe anyone in the rest of the building who might be acquainted with the building's history." Kenneth then made another obvious inquiry. "Why the third floor?" John also had a reply to that question. "There are a lot of tenants in the building. So I just decided to concentrate on the third floor. Besides, I live on the third floor." He was focusing on the third floor of Parkdale Court for an answer to the mystery of the photographs and not for a paper on the history of the building.

The three of them sat silent in the living room for a few minutes. Mrs. Casey offered the two of them another cup of tea. John smiled and accepted a second time. Her husband declined. "So you want information on tenants on the third floor. What exactly do you want to know about or from tenants on the third floor?" John took a gulp of tea and repeated his request in a little more detail. "Actually, I'd be happy if I could just get their names and maybe a little bit of info about each of them." Casey again snickered a bit, folded his hands and leaned back on the couch. "Right, so you thought you'd ask me and you thought I'd tell you." John tried a smile and then replied. "I hope so." Again, he waited for a response. He looked like he was preparing for his afternoon nap. "So you hope so.', he allowed.

Casey then stood up, took his wife's tea cup from her lap, circled the couch and walked toward the kitchen. "I guess I could do that." he said from the kitchen. John sat up straight and waited for Casey to return from the kitchen. He came back from the kitchen and sat down again. He put his hands together and looked at John. "Aside from you, there are six other tenants on the third floor. Do you know any of them? Have you spoken to any of them?" he asked. John just shook his head, not mentioning the lady he imagined he saw dancing at the end of the corridor one evening. "No, I haven't spoken to any of my neighbours. But I've seen most of them since I moved in, you know in the hall. They all look like they are retired." Casey, who had sat back down on the couch, looked a little surprised. "You know you may right, at least as far as I know." He paused and then asked a question. "What makes you think that" John had an answer for that. "Well, I have never seen anyone on the third floor going to work in the morning or coming home from work in the evening." Again, he didn't mention the dancing lady. He didn't mention the discarded photograph either.

Gladys pointed to the roll top desk sitting by the door where she said there was a small note pad and a pen in the top drawer. John assumed that he was about to receive a recitation of a list of the third floor tenants. For the first time during his visit to the Casey apartment, Kenneth actually spoke to his wife. "Thanks, Mother. I think John here is gonna need that pad and that pen." he said, in an unexpectedly pleasant tone. He then took a couple of steps toward the desk, opened its top drawer, and removed a pad, a pen, and a tan file. He George opened the file and a sheet of paper. "Well, I have the current list of tenants right here. Get your pen ready." Kenneth then started to read off the names and John wrote down their names, their current status, and the duration of their residence at Parkdale Court. With each name, they would add short commentaries which John did not record. According to the Caseys, most of them had lived in the building for years, if not decades. It took Kenneth ten minutes to completely read the list. Once finished, Gladys announced that it was time for her nap. John had been in apartment 106 more than half an hour. He thanked his hosts for their time and hospitality. He had the list. The possible next step was to interview his neighbours. Maybe.

<hr />

John was casually watching a baseball game on television with Patricia as he shared the third floor tenant list with her. He went over the situation with her. The other clue or clues suggesting that something eerie was transpiring on the third floor where on two occasions he saw the man who he thought was the father in each of the family photographs that he had found in the apartment. They were sitting on the living room couch as they both studied the list. There were seven tenants listed on two pages, four on one, three on the other. John read the names aloud. According to Casey, as John suspected, the occupants were all retired but he and Patricia, there being two men, two woman, and three couples. The occupants were:

Apartment 301 – Allan Goudreau, tenant for 13 years, wife passed away 6 years ago

Apartment 303 – William Anderson, tenant for 9 years, unmarried

Apartment 304 – Alice Stewart, tenant for 13 years, husband passed away 8 years ago

Apartment 305 – Beverly Miller, tenant for 15 years, husband passed away 4 years ago

Apartment 306– Desmond & Mary Gibson, tenants for 8 years

Apartment 307 – Harry & Florence Quinn, tenants for 21 years

Patricia leaned back on the couch, looked up at the ceiling, and asked with a shrug, "You now know who lives with you on the third floor. Now what?" John responded with a shrug of his own. "I don't know." He starred at the two small sheets of paper and just continued to sit there, contemplating his next move. He joined Patricia in leaning back on the couch. He felt like taking a nap. But then Patricia rose up from the couch, removed her shirt, and straddled John. "How about doing something to get your mind off the tenant list?" John smiled and started to remove his t-shirt. His concentration on the list disappeared quickly. Later that evening, after their amorous struggles on the couch and dinner at a local Italian restaurant, John had an inspiration.

He had concluded that he would consult with the two couples who lived on the third floor, the couples in apartments 306 and 307, to determine whether one of them had been standing in front of the apartment that day he had boarded the bus. He thought, though unlikely, that one of the two couples might provide him with some sort of explanation for the photographs. Maybe one of the couples were magicians or wizards, a suggestion that Patricia made when John had told her his plan. He wasn't happy about her idea. She thought that John was being ridiculous. It had been a strange inspiration.

After dinner on Monday, he called on the two couples who lived in apartments on the third floor. He was hopeful, as he told Patricia and himself, that one of the couples would give him a hint of the circumstances that might have led to or caused the delusions he thought he was having about the photographs. He hoped he might recognize one of the couples. Patricia had called John's plan a dubious ambition. His visits to both couples had proved futile. Both could not understand the reason for John's calling on them, his explanation not making any sense to them. He would introduce himself, which he thought on reflection ironic since they lived doors from each other. They would just stand at the door and gawk, obviously unable to understand John's purpose in showing up at their doors. John began to think that he may be forgetting his purpose of his visits as well. Finally, and almost reluctantly, he turned to apartment 307 and the tenants who lived there longer, the Quinns, Harry and Florence. He knocked on their door and the two of them appeared. While he knew that he would recognize Mrs. Quinn, he expected that she would not recognize him, his experiences with her dancing and her interest in being photographed in a luxury car not giving her any hint. There they were, Mr. and Mrs. Quinn, alias Mr. Peanut and his wife, the couple he saw from the bus. They answered the door. Harry smiled. Then, he and Florence, who looked to be dressed in formal evening outfits, greeted John by executing a nice swing move. It was obvious that the two of them were proficient in their dance moves, particularly for people their age. He also remembered her as having accompanied her husband that day when he saw the two of them in front of the building as he was boarding a city bus. Mr. Quinn, who was wearing his Mr. Peanut tuxedo, had greeted him warmly. Mrs. Quinn had stopped executing any sort of dance move and was standing behind her husband with a coquettish smile on her face. She was wearing an abundance of theatrical makeup.

"So nice of you to drop by, Mr. Delaney, I have been expecting you." said Mr. Quinn. John had not expected the reaction. He just stood there stunned, trying to figure out how Harry Quinn knew his name. Maybe he had simply read it on the mailbox. He extended his hand. John shook it. Florence Quinn gave John an expansive wave. John waved back. Harry then invited him into apartment 307. John paused for a moment, walked into the apartment and sat in a chair after Harry had patted its seat. "What can I do for you?" John suddenly had no real answer, or at least no answer that would make any sense. What did he expect Quinn to say? "I think I know what you're looking for, Mr. Delaney. You have been mystified by certain events around the building, are you not?" asked Mr. Quinn with a mischievous smile on his face. With that question, Quinn pulled a flower bouquet out of his left sleeve and bowed with a theatrical flair. Mrs. Quinn laughed and clapped. He then showed John, now apparently his audience, a deck of playing cards and then went through several simple card tricks. Mrs. Quinn was now standing beside him, watching her husband mystify their guest. John just sat there casually dumbfounded, eyes wide and a strange blank look on his face. John pondered. Is Mr. Quinn attempting to impress him with card tricks and a juvenile magic trick involving a flower bouquet? What exactly was Mrs. Quinn trying to do?

Harry Quinn recognized that his guest was perplexed. He was clearly baffled. He decided then to clarify things for him. He produced a copy of the picture that John had found in his kitchen several months ago. In addition, there was a photocopy of the Tuesday, April 5, 1949 edition of the *Ottawa Journal*. John looked like he was about to faint. After several moments of uncomfortable silence, John managed to ask Quinn about the original photograph he found in his apartment, the father, the mother, the three boys, the little girl and the white terrier. Harry then replied with a certain dramatic flair. "Well, Mr. Delaney, I have been a magician for almost fifty years. I deal with illusion and trickery. And as you can see, I have tricked you with the photograph. And as I said before, I have been expecting you." John's uncomfortable silence started to diminish even though he had no specific idea as to what he could say and what specifically the Quinns had in mind with their impromptu show.

YEARS BEFORE THE
PARKDALE COURT

I t was a couple of years before the beginning of the World War I when George Fenwick first visited his father's office in the Parliament Buildings. Back then, he was a student in Ashbury College, a private school that his father had also attended, when he convinced his father, who was an assistant to the Under-Secretary of Foreign Affairs, to host a group of his classmates on an architectural tour of Ottawa. His home room teacher at the time, a man named Haley, had been impressed by a composition that George had written on the building of the Royal Canadian Mint. The essay focused also entirely on the design and construction of the building by its chief architect, Norman Ewart. It was evident that George had an abiding interest in architecture in general, often decorating the walls of his bedroom with drawings of structures around the city, both buildings and private homes. George's father was also interested in architecture and was pleased with his son's ambition to attend the architectural school at McGill University in Montreal.

Toward that objective, George had managed to convince his father to accompany him to Montreal to visit the school on two occasions before formally applying to it. It was during the second call on the architecture school that he met Professor Simon Fokke, the sole member of the architectural faculty in 1917, the other three professors having gone overseas to serve in World War I with twelve of the fourteen students who had attended the year before. Professor

Fokke was glad to meet with George. If George was accepted by the school, a likely result since it appeared that only three students had plans to apply to the school for the coming year, the good Professor being happy to have anyone to teach, a year without an available teaching position a real possibility.

During their audience with Professor Fokke on that visit to McGill, which was understandably brief since the elder Fenwick did most of the talking, explaining to Fokke that his age had disqualified him from military service. He suggested that he would probably turn out to be useless as a soldier anyway. That led the two of them to conduct a long discussion of the progress of the war and its absurdity, which George thought was a little strange since his father was, after all, a fairly senior official of the Canadian government, a participant in the war. George was more interested in a brief conversation they conducted about the university's fees, Fokke telling his father that the university had decided to reduce, if not waive them, hoping to keep as many students as they could, the war attracting more volunteers than they had anticipated. Fokke said some of the departments, including architecture, were concerned that they would be eliminated. The university administration had come to the conclusion that reducing tuition, perhaps even to zero, might keep students engaged in their education rather than boarding a ship headed for Europe. George's father was pleased it appeared. So was George who was not, unlike many of his high school classmates, enthusiastic about going to war.

Fokke asked George a curious question as both he and his father were leaving the Professor's office. He asked George if he was interested in magic. George did not know how to respond. So he didn't. He did not see Professor Fokke again until school started five months later. He didn't have an answer then either although he found out later that he was to grow interested, if not obsessed with magic.

George Fenwick graduated with a Bachelor of Science in Architecture in 1922. As much as he enjoyed living in Montreal, a small flat on MacTavish Street his residence for the three years he spent attending McGill University, he chose to return to Ottawa with his degree. Aside from being instructed in general architectural theory and engineering practice, George had also learned about magic from Professor Fokken, who had implied an interest in the art the first time he met, when he and his father met with the professor five months before his admission to the university. In fact, in their second year together at McGill, the Professor started to reserve Friday afternoons to teach George and another student named Stephen Gilbert the fundamentals of magic. Stephen, however, did not appear to be that interested in magic and stopped attending the Professor's Friday afternoon sessions after only a few weeks, leaving George the only pupil of Professor Fokken's magic sessions. Actually, the Professor and George were pleased to see Stephen Gilbert leave Friday afternoons. His constant questioning of even the most elemental magic tricks was so annoying at times that Professor Fokken and George would simultaneously complain about headaches. It was a relief when he left. More importantly, George also found that his ability to grasp the magic tricks about which the Professor was educating him was a lot stronger than it was when Stephen Gilbert was still around. In addition, he wasn't getting headaches on Friday afternoons.

Professor Fokke had started with simple cards tricks. George remembered feeling some residual shame about the one time he had been ordered by his fifth grade teacher, a Mr. Clark, to learn and then perform a card trick before the entire class. After he was unable to adequately perform his trick, he sat in the corner of the classroom and melodramatically cried until another boy was unable to successfully perform his chosen trick, at which point he replaced George. His trick at that time in grade school was a simple and well used ploy called "The Power of Four". It involved shuffling cards, cutting the deck, and remembering the fourth card in the divided deck. Ten years later, Professor Fokke had George practice the same trick for a week before he was satisfied with George's performance. They then moved on to a more complicated trick. It was called "Pick a Card, Any Card", a scheme that Professor Fokken supposedly used he said before countless audiences. They spent more than two Friday afternoons practising that trick before Professor Fokke persuaded one of the university secretaries to sit as a live audience for George as he attempted to successfully perform the "Pick a Card, Any Card" trick. It took George four runs before he was able to get it right. Professor Fokke asked George to successfully perform it before two other university employees before moving on to the next contrivance, a comparatively simple trick called "Make a Prediction".

By the time George had mastered that trick, the Professor was convinced that his disciple was skilled enough to allow him to accompany him to a brothel located near the Crystal Palace, a popular cabaret on Saint Laurent Boulevard. Introduced to the brothel by a colleague who was still serving overseas, Professor Fokke had been invited a year ago to entertain the brothel staff with magic tricks, a skill about which the good professor often boasted. The colleague thought that the women might appreciate the occasional diversion while they were waiting for clients. Although Professor Fokken declined to enjoy the attentions of one, if not several of the ladies by way of payment for his efforts, he offered to perform for nothing, the opportunity to demonstrate his skills at magic enough to attract him to putting on a show for the ladies. He was tempted to enjoy the charms of at least one of the bordello ladies, a woman named Gertrude who reminded Professor Fokken of his wife Madeleine who had died a couple of years before. It was guilt that motivated the good Professor to resist the ladies' offers.

So it was that every Saturday night, he would stage a short stage show at the brothel on Saint Laurent Boulevard, combining a few simple card tricks and a variety of conventional magic tricks, from Chinese linking rings to the rabbit in the hat along with a few jokes. George was understandably excited with the opportunity to join Professor Fekken on a Saturday night in the brothel beside the Crystal Palace on Saint Laurent Boulevard. The Professor, who cautioned George against developing an interest, if not a passion for any of the ladies, introduced George to several of them who happened to be available as well as to the married couple who ran the place, Moise and Beulah Snyder. Despite his infatuation with one of the prostitutes, a term that he was told to avoid using, George, although admittedly a second if not a third rate magician compared to the professor, continued to entertain the girls with his efforts. He had become quite popular with not only the ladies but with the Snyders as well. In fact, the Snyders sometimes invited George, along of course with Professor Fokken and a colleague of the latter in the classics department named Dr. Cairns to dinner at their place at least once a month. George was fascinated by the stories that the Snyders and the two professors would tell about the origins of their families in the places like Austria-Hungary, the Republic of Poland, and Russia before the revolution. George become so enamoured with the stories that were told by the Snyders and the two professors on the occasional Saturday night that he started to regret not adding a history course to his program of study. Although he wasn't able to formally study history at McGill, he did manage to take European history on as a serious past time.

<hr />

George Fenwick continued to be interested in magic after he graduated from McGill University in 1922. He moved back to Ottawa two weeks after graduation, moving back into his old bedroom in the family home in a fashionable area of Ottawa called New Edinburgh. He told his father that he was giving himself a couple of months to secure a position with a local architectural firm and find his own apartment. Not surprisingly, while his father seemed more resigned than happy to see his son back from Montreal, his mother Edna was elated to have her son back in the house after four years of only living at home during the summers. She was normally not a particularly emotional person, seldom if ever demonstrating anything close to sentimentality. But with his return to the family home, Edna could not stop herself from hugging her son George every chance she got. George was somewhat embarrassed by Edna's increasingly maternal affections although he did enjoy clean linen and laundry every day, his favourite meals, and her almost mawkishness, something that came to annoy her husband. She told George's father that she missed her son terribly, having initially pleaded with her husband to discourage George from enrolling in McGill University. Despite his wife's entreaties, the elder Fenwick was determined to see his son pursue his interest in architecture by attending McGill, there being no university courses in architecture at the University of Ottawa.

George's father had grown accustomed to having the house to Edna and himself. He had never wanted children, he and Edna were late in life when George was born. Edna was not expected to have children at her age. Anyone who knew the couple, including her doctor, thought the birth was a miracle. While his mother was ecstatic, his father was disappointed, if not despondent with the miracle, sometimes pretending that he did not have a son. He had hired a governess to look after young George. Edna, who did not see the need at all, thought that her husband simply did not like children, even his own, and wanted to ensure that he would spend as little time as possible with his son, thinking that his disapproval was shared by his wife. By the time he was four years old, however, George's mother had managed to convince his father that their son no longer needed a governess and she could look after him without assistance. Further, she dissuaded her husband from sending George to a boarding school in Montreal. He was to stay at home until he graduated high school and entered McGill University in Montreal. His mother was pleased and his father reconciled with the situation. Besides, his position on Parliament Hill demanded long hours and as a result, he didn't have to communicate with his son very often.

George applied for employment at several firms in the Ottawa area before settling on the JH Roberts Co, an all purpose architectural firm headquartered on Rideau Street. He was hired as an associate, which sounded like he was a lawyer. He was initially hired as a draftsman as opposed to an architect, preparing drawings for specific parts of a project, most particularly the plumbing of municipal projects, mainly if not always new buildings or the renovation of existing houses. He started drawing standard toilets, which prompted a number of humorous, if not sarcastic comments directed at him by his new colleagues, of which there were two in his department, specifically two architects concerned with lavatory facilities. From the first day he reported for work, George realized that he was the most junior member of the firm, even lower than the young clerk that worked for the two architects who gave George his instructions as to which kind of toilets to draw. On the other hand, he was told by the man who was responsible for giving him his $35.00 in weekly wages that he was making more than the young clerk. He explained that the disparity between their respectively salaries was based on the fact that George had a university degree while the clerk, whose name was Keith, joined the firm after graduating from grade seven.

He was paid weekly with cash in a brown envelope, cash with a small piece of paper advising the recipients of the taxes submitted to the government. For some reason, George had been under the impression that he would be paid by cheque, as was his father and most people who were regarded as professionals. At his previous jobs, it was always cash: delivering groceries for a couple of summers in high school and then, during his university years, his summer jobs working at a lumber yard on the Montreal Road in Ottawa, mowing lawns for the City of Ottawa, busing tables at a fish restaurant in the Glebe section of Ottawa, and then, after his third year in university, cleaning offices in the Arts Building at McGill. The most he ever earned during those years was 30 cents an hour before that last year in university, the minimum wage being established the year before. That first year at JH Roberts, he was getting paid more than three times what he was earning that last year before he managed to acquire that full time job. His father, once he was informed, told him that he was proud of him, his profession and even his salary.

⇒▷◦◁⇐

Like most architectural firms in the city, JH Roberts designed buildings for residential as well as commercial properties. At first, George spent most, if not all of his time at the firm submitting drawings for the design and placement of toilets in the houses and more accurately the mansions that the firm was currently building. Most of the houses were large structures in which most of them featured at least two bathrooms, one large lavatory on the main floor and a much smaller powder room on the second floor, usually off the master bedroom. There were usually standard designs although every now and then, there was a request which would require special designs and therefore necessitate special drawings. At first, the requirements for special lavatory drawings prompted a certain reluctance in George. He confided in one of his friends, a guy whom he had known since both of them had attended elementary school at the Mutchmore Public School on Fifth Avenue, that he was not looking forward to his next several years spending his time drawing designs for toilets. He and George had rekindled their friendship after he graduated from McGill and returned to Ottawa. His friend, whose name was Barry, felt lucky to have found a position as a clerk in the Department of Supply. He also had attended Ashbury High School although he did not graduate from there, his father, who was a police officer, having decided to return him to public high school, specifically Glebe Collegiate, after he failed grade ten at Ashbury. The two friends had predictably grown apart over the six years during which they had attended different schools and then lived in different neighbourhoods.

When Barry first heard that George had returned to town where he was hired by one of the largest architectural firms in the city, he had been reluctant to re-establish contact with him despite his mother's advice, who had always liked George and had encouraged them to become friends again. He was hesitant. He had not seen George for more than six years, their relationship having been abandoned once he went to different schools and then Montreal to attend university. But when Barry's mother had run into George's mother at a rummage sale at a church in the Glebe that summer, the two of them had agreed that Barry and George should renew their friendship. When she returned home, she encouraged Barry to contact George. He did. They got together after work one day at the oldest tavern in Ottawa, the Chateau Lafayette on York Street. Barry noticed that George looked a lot older than the last time he had seen him. He had grown a moustache.

They had a couple of quarts each during which they exchanged news on their lives over the past several years. Barry had little to report except his job at the Department of Supply, his marriage to a woman named Lorraine, who he said he met a month after he started at the Department, and their two children. It was no surprise then that Barry was more interested in hearing about George's academic career at McGill University, Professor Fokken, his interest in magic, and his position as a junior associate at JH Roberts than his own pedestrian account. It was simply no surprise. His experiences with the women at the brothel on Saint Laurent Boulevard, which were predictably platonic despite the temptations that a bordello could offer, his academic achievements as well as his surprising interest in magic, were all events that fascinated Barry, particularly compared to the daily grind that he, Lorraine, and their two children faced most of the time. For his part, George's interest in Barry's life was limited to the latter's domestic situation, an accomplishment, while generally mundane and experienced by most people, was something that George had pursued in his daydreams for years. The simple act of having a wife and family seemed something that George wanted to attain. He had realized that such a state was and could remain an elusive objective for him. Fact was that George Fenwick had never even had a girlfriend, let alone a wife. Additionally, he did not know a woman who could possibly be a candidate. He blamed it on the schools he had attended, all of which were segregated by gender.

As he listened to Barry's story about his life, he thought about seeking his counsel, not on his career choice, drawing toilets having been a major disappointment, but on his love life, which was more than a disappointment. It was pretty well desolate. But he decided to complain about his job instead. "As I told you, I'm sick and tired of drawing toilets. The two architects who give me my orders, you know, give me my instructions, seem to snicker, if not laugh every time they hand me a blueprint, point out where the bathroom is and tell me to draw a toilet. Even the clerk we got working for us giggles every time one of the two architects hands me a piece of paper, any piece of paper it seems."

Barry almost giggled himself but managed to control himself long enough to commiserate with and then acquaint George with his own humiliation. "I can understand, I can sympathize. Do you think I'm having a good time at my job? All I do all the time is file purchase orders, contracts and stuff like that. You think you're the bored? You think people I work for don't laugh at me? You think you're the only one that thinks he has a lousy job?" observed Barry. "And at least your job can lead somewhere, somewhere higher in the firm. I mean, isn't that the way careers in your kind of profession go. You start with a job like drawing toilets and a couple of years later, you're designing a building downtown."

George appeared to be contemplating Barry's observation for a moment or so, a thoughtful look on his face. He then asked Barry a question about his position as a clerk in the Department of Supply. Barry explained. "You're kidding, aren't you? I mean, clerks are promoted, at least within that classification but usually nothing higher. The best I can hope for is maybe a couple of bumps upward to the top of the clerical group. But there isn't any guarantee, not like your company which I think hires people like you to promote them. I mean, weren't you hired as a junior associate? It kind of suggests that you will become a senior associate at some point in the future. Right?"

George nodded. "Yeah, it's probable. We all expect it, That's why anybody who gets a position with an architectural firm starts at the bottom and knows that sooner or later, he'll be moving up in the firm. But still, I didn't expect to be drawing toilets when I started with the firm. I mean, it's really quite boring. Sometimes, maybe even all the time actually, I can hardly stand it. The whole thing is quite depressing."

Barry interrupted with an obvious question. "Have you spoken to anyone who you work for? You know, simply asking them for another responsibility. You could ask for a transfer to another section of the firm. Or, if you feel that strongly about it, you can always apply for another job, a position at another firm. There might be something in another firm that would be more to your liking. Do you ever think about another position in your company or some other company?" Barry waited for an answer as George looked like he was considering a reply. Barry anticipated a reply, something predictable.

George looked serious and answered in the affirmative, as Barry thought he would. "Sure, I thought of talking to Mr. Denman ----he's the company manager --- but first I wanted to speak to one or both of the guys I worked with." George paused for a moment, chewing his nails, waiting it seemed for inspiration to provide him with an answer. It wasn't predictable. "But after thinking about it for a while, I decided not to. I was worried that the guys would laugh at me and that Mr. Denman would laugh at me as well. So I didn't speak to anyone in the company. I know it was kind of cowardly. No, it was definitely cowardly. I just couldn't speak to anyone in the company."

Barry then gave his friend George a sympathetic shrug of his shoulders and asked for a second time if he was thinking about seeking employment somewhere else. George then pointed out that JH Roberts was the largest firms in the city and that if he wanted to stay working in Ottawa, he didn't know where he'd look. "I mean, there is no company in the city that is larger than JH and I don't think any of them have an opening, at least not until the next spring, when a new batch of architects, maybe a dozen in Ontario and Quebec enter the employment market and already employed architects leave the market by either retiring or, sorry to say, passing away."

The discussion of George's job situation ended with the two old friends concluding that he had little choice but to continue drawing toilets for JH Roberts until, Barry assured him, he was promoted. Besides, Barry had grown weary of listening to George's troubles, the third quart of beer having been planned but not yet been ordered. Predictably, it was Barry who changed the subject, selecting the subject of what George did with his spare time, possibilities such as sports and politics, issues in which Barry had quickly discovered that

George had little interest. It was during a return to their discussion of George's possible hobbies that Barry resurrected his questioning of George's interest in magic which he had said he had developed during his time at McGill. George said that when he returned to Ottawa, he continued his interest in magic, having resumed his practising of a variety of magic tricks, hoping he said he could return at some point to performing magic in public, the evenings spent entertaining the women of the bordello with Professor Fokken a fond memory.

Barry then asked George if he was a customer of Fred's Magic Shop, a small store on Laurier Avenue that specialized in selling potential magician and illusionist products that would assist them in demonstrating or practising their craft. Barry said that Fred's Magic Shop might advertise magic shows. The shop might even provide customers with the name of entertainment agents and other sources that might provide potential magicians with opportunities to ply their craft. George said that he was familiar with Fred's Magic Shop, often frequenting the place to such an extent that he had become friendly with Fred himself, who, despite his creepy appearance, was surprisingly friendly. He was more than willing to help aspiring magicians with their hobbies, if not their possible careers. When asked by Barry if he ever considered performing magic rather than than just practising it, George said that he was was taking lessons from Fred and other magicians who also gave guidance regarding a career in performing magic. To that end, he also told Barry that he was a dues paying member of Fred's club of amateur magicians in which magicians from Montreal and Ottawa would appear to not only perform at the store but also provide club members with lessons and advice as how to stage magic shows.

George said that he had attended four meetings since he joined the club when he first returned to Ottawa. He reported that the largest audience at any of the four meetings was maybe a hundred people. That surprised Barry who said that he didn't think that many people actually were interested in magic. George pointed out that maybe only ten out of the hundred people who attended the shows were curious about magic, the others only entertained by magic.

According to George, Fred was planning to host a magic show in several weeks, performances to be provided by members of Fred's club. George said that he, as well as several other members of the club, would be entertaining. He said he was always nervous but so were his fellow club members. Barry assured him that he would likely put on on a good show. He also said that he would be happy to attend his performance, whenever it took place. He was also happy to hear about George's interest in magic, most practically because he at least had something to divert his attention away from his disappointments at work. Not only that but Barry was more entertained by George's story about his fascination with magic than continuing to hear about his dissatisfaction with drawing toilets for JH Roberts.

George was comforted somehow by his meeting with his old friend, particularly Barry's encouragement of his interest in magic. To his lesser degree, he was also consoled by his friend's implied assurance that he would not be sketching toilets forever, his move up the company organization inevitable, at least according to Barry. George returned to work the next day with an enthusiasm that he had not had since his first week at JH Roberts. His current job involved three toilets that were to be installed in a mansion that was to be constructed on the corner of Gilmour and Metcalfe Streets downtown. Placing three toilets in any house, no matter how large, was an unheard innovation in the 1920s, which provided George with a certain passion that he had not felt since he drew his first toilet when he joined the firm less than a year ago. So he approached the job with a renewed vigour. His senior colleagues, who were busily designing the bathrooms in which the toilets were to be installed, noticed that George was surprisingly eager, so much so that they frequently commented on his changed disposition, which had previously bordered on the solemn and maybe ever occasionally morose but now had somehow transformed himself into a character that was almost congenial, if not cheerful.

A couple of weeks after his transformation into "an okay guy", an opinion shared by his two colleagues in the lavatory department, George was invited into a club of young architects, a group that got together every month or so to discuss buildings and houses that were being planned around the city, which firms were bidding for them, and the kind of architectural styles that were being contemplated for the landscape and the general surroundings, the streets, the other buildings in the neighbourhood. At first, George was intimidated by the range of opinions that were being expressed at the meetings. He was fortunate that he had kept some of his university textbooks, references to assist him in contributing to the discussion by the group. He studied the textbooks closely enough to eventually join in the discussion of proposals and suggestions that the group was pursuing.

His preference for the Edwardian style of house building put him in a fairly good stead with his fellow architects. In addition, George's talent for magic, an ability that he was able to admit after maybe a couple of meetings, impressed his colleagues in the architect group. On the other hand, however, a few simple card tricks were enough to entertain the architects who found themselves more interested in being distracted by George's illusions than they being bored by discussions about Frank Lloyd Wright, the rise of Art Deco and Neo-Gothic and other consequential matters relevant to their careers. After three months or so, George also added comedy to his presentations, borrowing gags and witticisms from Vaudevillians like Charlie Chaplin, Stan Laurel, Oliver Hardy, and Buster Keaton, and adding some of his own jokes, usually about things like hockey, misquotes, and to specifically play to the room and his own ego, the architecture of outhouses. He soon found himself becoming fairly popular in the company and in fact was attracting more than just young architects to the meetings at which he was performing.

Consequently, George soon found himself growing optimistic about his career prospects in JH Roberts.

To assist in his optimism, within less than three months, the company won a contract to construct a swimming pool complex at a place to be called Plant Bath on the corner of Somerset and Preston Streets. It was scheduled for completion in 1924. The winning of the contract for the design and construction of the Plant Bath, the first municipal swimming pool of its size in Eastern Ontario, elevated a man named Warren Lorentz to the position of the Chief Executive Officer of JH Roberts, replacing the longtime company boss Ross Drury. His appointment merited news stories in both the *Ottawa Citizen* and the *Ottawa Journal*, not to mention the *Construction Quarterly*, a journal that was published by Temico Inc., the largest construction company in Ontario. There were four local architectural firms which were large enough to advertise in the *Construction Quarterly*. In addition, Warren Lorentz was lionized to such an extent that he was encouraged to replace Napoleon Champagne as mayor, who stepped down from the post after only eighteen months in office. Predictably, there was a controversy related to the awarding of the contract, rumours of influence peddling which explained Mayor Champagne's rather short stint as mayor. The local newspapers were particularly interested in playing up the possibility of bribery, hoping reporters were able to obtain the ingredients that rivalled the municipal scandals of Montreal, the unrivalled champion of Canadian municipal corruption.

Regardless of the supposedly tainted circumstances leading to the contract, it was exciting news to the employees of JH Roberts. The expectations of George's department, George and his colleagues, Elmer Gibson and Allen Wilkerson, were understandably high, thoughts of promotion frequent when the three colleagues were assigned the design of not only the men's and women's washrooms but the men's and women's locker rooms as well. The designs of the washrooms and locker rooms required the addition of a fourth architect, an older man named Levesque who had worked at JH Roberts since the company was established more than a couple of decades ago and before then, a company called Reid and Rollins, one of the earliest builders of schools in Ottawa. Given his experience with designing and building schools, he was asked by company management to supervise the completion of both the washrooms and the locker rooms. Mr. Levesque, whose first name was August, assigned the locker rooms to Gibson and Wilkerson while George predictably received the task of designing not only toilets but the washrooms as well. While George was somewhat disappointed with working on the washrooms, his friend Barry, with whom he was now in regular contact, suggested that it could be his big break. Both the washrooms and the locker rooms would require a complicated architectural plan, much more sophisticated than the plans for the usual commissions that bore the JH Roberts imprimatur.

George remembered the day that he, Gibson, and Wilkerson were asked to report to the main board room on the sixth floor of the Freeman Building on Rideau Street. They were formally introduced to their new boss, August Levesque as well as to two rudimentary blueprints of the bathrooms and locker rooms of the Plant Bath. The men's washroom was particularly challenging, the first plan for a public lavatory that any of the three architects had ever worked on. It contained a half a dozen toilet stalls, a standing circular hand washer, and, for the first time for the firm, a series of bowl urinals against one wall. Normally, at least in his experience, public urination was accomplished by emptying one's bladder into a mental or ceramic trough, like a latrine in a prison. On the other hand, urinals were a relatively new plumbing device, a gadget that provided owners with the convenience of standing up rather than having to sit down to urinate.

<hr />

It was over a year before George was to finalize his efforts on the Plant Bath toilets, three complete drawings of toilets of three different styles, one circular, one square, and one triangular, all with different coloured seats, including one that was not black, not brown but a strange dark red colour, almost a maroon, a choice that went to Mr. Levesque who actually thought of bringing it up to CEO Lorentz before agreeing to it. George Fenwick's repeated representations led to a successful conclusion, Mr. Levesque's rumoured doubts notwithstanding. On the other hand, his colleagues had seen their reputations fade somewhat when they failed to impress management with their design of the Plant Bath urinals, which had been loosely based on those installed in the Kresge Building in New York City ten years previously. This kind of architectural plagiarism, however, was not unknown in the profession but not particularly prized by JH Roberts.

It was almost a month after a celebratory dinner following the opening of the Plant Bath that JH Roberts landed another municipal pool project, the Champagne Bath on King Edward Street downtown. It was not a surprising triumph, considering that the firm, with the Plant Bath project, had become the city's principal, if not its only builder of municipal pools. By the time the responsibilities were assigned, George was given dominion of both the washrooms and the locker rooms. His former colleagues were no longer benefiting from the company's successes, Elmer Gibson having left JH Roberts for a small construction company called Williams Structures while Allan Wilkerson moved up from the lavatory department to take over from Mr. Denman who had retired. Their replacements, a young guy named Mark Nolan and an older man named Brian Baxter who liked to address anyone younger than him "kiddo", an inappropriate nickname seeing as how George was no longer a junior to cither of his new colleagues or to anyone else in the firm. Fact was that George was now a supervisor, a promotion that was announced at the dinner celebrating the completion of the Plant Bath project. Weary of working on washrooms, George decided soon after being given responsibility for both the washrooms and locker rooms of the Champagne Bath that he would assign the new men, Mark Nolan and Brian Baxter to the washroom design and take on the locker rooms plan for himself. Although he had no experience with designing locker rooms, the only experience in the firm having either migrated to a new company or had been promoted out of architectural operations, he looked forward to the challenge, the idea of further advancement another consideration.

To prepare for the locker room project, George thought he would examine similar facilities in local schools for ideas. When he heard of George's intention, his new boss and former associate Wilkerson told him that he did not need to survey existing locker rooms for ideas for new locker rooms, pointing out that the construction of a locker room was hardly complicated enough to require the study of a duplicate. He thought of the locker room at Ashbury College. As he recalled it, it was a generally dreary looking place, only used when the students were compelled to prepare for a session in the gymnasium, an hour of boring exercise every two weeks to fulfill an obligation that Ashbury undertook with the parents of students. So George visited the man who had held the office of vice-principal when he attended Ashbury, a man named Dr. Allan Adkins who by then held the office of principal, to ask whether he could tour the locker room. While Dr. Adkins seemed interested in inquiring about George's career in architecture, about which he seemed to want to know a great deal, George's interest was in inspecting the school's locker room. However, when George mentioned that he wanted to inspect the school's locker for ideas on a locker room he was designing for a new project, Principal Adkins immediately got up from behind his desk and said that he would be more than happy to escort him down to the locker room.

Still, Principal Adkins remarked. "Why are you interested in inspecting our locker room? First of all, our locker rooms are pretty ordinary. There doesn't seem much of a challenge. I mean, a guy from a firm like yours should be able to design them with their eyes shut. It makes no sense, at least to me." George nodded his head. "I know, I know. It seems kind of unnecessary. In fact, it is unnecessary but you have to understand, as surprising as it sounds, neither me or anyone else in the firm have any experience with building locker rooms. So I just want to get an idea, by looking at the room itself, the lockers, the benches, that sort of thing. I mean, it's just better than looking at pictures or drawings." Adkins gestured by waving George out of his office, down the hall to the right, down three sets of stairs at the end of the hall, past the washroom, and then into the locker room. There were lockers on all four sides of the room, all in military green. There were two groups of benches facing each other in the middle of the room, and stairs at the end of the other end of the room. Above the lockers, of which there were probably fifty, were small frosted windows. Most of the light in the room was provided by six lamps hanging from the ceiling. They looked like they might be swinging.

George started to walk down the lockers on right side of the room, looking in every second or third locker. As expected, all the lockers seemed pretty well identically sized although he had neglected to bring any sort of measuring device, so his estimation may not have been entirely accurate. George examined the height and depth of each locker, including each shelve in each locker, and each door. In several of the lockers he opened, not that he opened each locker, he found gym clothes hanging; knickers, boxer shorts, singlets, all in white, vestments either forgotten or abandoned by participants who may have grown weary of the gym routines. George made mention of his observation regarding the deserted clothes in the occasional locker. The Principal said that, as disappointed as he was with any student who excused himself from physical education, a letter from a parent enough for dispensation, some of the students, as few as they were, could not endure the rigours of jumping jacks, climbing ropes, pull ups and push ups, and were therefore forgiven from participation in gym.

GEORGE FENWICK IS PROMOTED

———◆———

It was several years later. George Fenwick had been appointed vice-president of JH Roberts. Under the leadership of a man named Powers, a Toronto architectural engineer who had become the CEO of JH Roberts after the previous CEO Warren Lorentz died from a heart attack suffered during a dinner party. Under Mr. Powers, the firm had started to specialize in designing apartment buildings. Its first apartment job involved the addition of a fourth floor to an apartment located across from Dundonald Park on Somerset Street near Lyon Street. It was more a matter of engineering than architecture, basically copying the blueprints that had been liberated from the files of another Ottawa architectural firm, Bailey and Cole. Paramount Ltd., the owners of the apartment building, which was built prior to the turn of the century for lower income tenants, had decided to raise income from the building by increasing rents through refurbishing it, specifically by adding a fourth floor to it. They approached JL Roberts who agreed to the plan. George was given responsibility for the reconstruction. Unfortunately, George was also given the responsibility for dealing with city hall which seriously opposed the eviction of the tenants who had to leave the building while the building was remodelled and a fourth floor added. It was a consideration that was part of the deal.

A city counsellor named Thompson was particularly troublesome, having threatened legal action on a number of occasions but without any eventual consequence. it was rumoured, if not confirmed by a *Ottawa Journal* reporter who reported that money had changed hands and any contemplation of legal action forgotten, at least temporarily. George, whose experience with company manoeuvring usually involved ensuring that submitted architectural plans were authorized, was suddenly thrust into a situation about which he did not have possible expertise. To mitigate the issue of evictions from the apartment on Somerset Street, George proposed finding apartments for each tenant who was suddenly homeless, that is if they were willing to move into the apartments selected for them. Actually, the plan to relocate the tenants was suggested by George's friend, Barry who reacted to his friend's plight with the proposal. In any event, the idea went all the way up to the new CEO Jeffrey Powers who was impressed with the plan and approved it.

Three days later, JH Roberts hosted a meeting with the tenants who were slated to be relocated. It was a surprisingly relaxed meeting during which the plan was accepted by almost all the tenants attending the meeting, the only contrarian a middle age woman who said that she and her family could not see themselves living in the apartment that had been selected for her family and herself. She said that it did not allow dogs and therefore was unacceptable. A man attending the meeting with George, the apartment janitor, a man named Jean, interrupted the discussion by telling the complaining woman that he would try to find her family another apartment, one that allowed dogs, as difficult as that could be. George was somewhat concerned by the offer, realizing that the woman, whose name was Madeleine Benoit, her family and their terrier, would likely be on the front pages of the *Ottawa Journal* and the *Ottawa Citizen*, within days. In addition, there was a crescendo of applause from the tenants, maybe of whom knew the Benoit family and their terrier. After George replaced Jean in front of the crowd, he formerly offered the Benoit family an apartment that would welcome dogs. Madeleine Benoit saluted the room and, in a loud voice, thanked both George and Jean. The applause erupted again.

As soon as all the tenants left their apartments, there were thirty apartments empty of residents, JH Roberts began its reconstruction work. The plan was to add one floor to the building and to reduce the number of apartments on each floor from ten to eight. The total number of apartments would therefore increase to thirty two, only two additional units although the plan was to increase the income from the building, now named the Squire's Court, to almost triple its current level, the rent on the smallest apartment four times what it was previously. Accordingly, the possibility of any of the previous tenants, some of whom were almost indigent, renting any of the redecorated apartments was absolute zero. That had been the essence of the controversy that motivated city councillor Thompson to press the issue with the newspapers. Interestingly enough, Mr. Thompson had appeared at the tenant meeting organized by JH Roberts and hosted by George Fenwick but left when Jean the janitor said that the company promised to find similar apartments for the tenants slated to be evicted. Thompson dropped the matter when it became obvious that the soon to be ex- tenants were no longer alarmed by the possibility that they would soon be homeless, a likelihood that was no longer likely.

The rebuilding of the apartment began with the demolition of the original structure. Within a couple of months, the building was down to its foundation, everything else gone. The place looked like a Roman ruin, a scene that attracted bystanders who passed by on Somerset Street. Many of them stood before the construction scene, crowds gathering to watch the Dorchester Construction Company working, sometimes the city trolley cars stopping long enough to allow their passengers to get on and off the trolley and to witness the workers erect the Squire's Court, a new apartment being built was a matter of considerable interest. It was a news story of considerable interest. Within a week, the workers on the site grew tired of bystanders staring at them as they worked and shouting questions at them. After a continual stream of complaints from the construction workers, who grew tired of them, the Dorchester people decided to install a fence around the front of the construction site. Behind the site, there was another fence and a line of tall trees in the backyards of houses on Cooper Street.

⸻ ◦ ⸻

It was almost six months before construction of Squire's Court was complete and the apartments were available for rent. There were a large number of potential tenants that called on the temporary office of Paramount Ltd. The design of the refurbished apartment was unique, at least as compared to most apartments in Ottawa. The finished building was composed of four floors, comprised of two separate buildings between which was a cathedral entrance and lobby over which there was a large stained glass window. There was an elevator on each side of the building, another unusual feature for an Ottawa apartment building, most of them being without any elevators, marble stairs being the normal mode of transport between floors in the city apartments. Because of the notoriety of the apartment building due to the political turmoil generated by city councillor Thompson and the newspapers, George and JH Roberts Ltd had established a temporary office for Paramount in the lobby of the building to accept applications for apartment leases. The popularity of Squire's Court was such that the *Ottawa Journal*, which followed the original controversy surrounding the building before it was demolished, actually published a couple of articles about the newly rebuilt apartment building. One of its most attractive features, a veritable advertisement, was the installation of a garage which provided parking for twelve cars as opposed to the original building which furnished spaces for only six cars. The number of garage spaces in the original building did prompt complaints from tenants that had automobiles, Model T's the most popular model by far. On the other hand, most people didn't have automobiles in those days.

The attributes of the new building implied, to almost anyone who was aware of them, suggested that the new building would be fully rented within a limited period of time. Fact was that the building was fully rented or leased within weeks. New tenants started to move in, actions that the *Ottawa Journal* reported as well. Paramount Ltd.'s plan to generate more income out of the property had worked surprisingly well. Everyone involved, the owners, the architects and the construction company were all satisfied with the outcome. One could also add the former tenants to the list of the satisfied.

Once the building was fully leased, George and his three associates on the project, along with a number of other employees of JH Roberts, were fated at the celebratory reception, a standard company practice when management deemed a job complete and well done. During the function, after a few drinks, George confided to one of the company's secretaries, a woman named Grace, that he had been approached by the matriarch of the Benoit family, who had been moved from the original Somerset Street apartment a couple of months ago to a large apartment in the Sandy Hill area near the University of Ottawa, an apartment that accepted dogs. As a final part of their agreement to voluntarily leave the Somerset Street apartment, Madeleine Benoit asked George to leave a small photograph of the family in their old/new apartment, as a sort of homage to the family's fifteen years there. For a reason that eluded him at the time, George agreed to attach the photograph in the approximate location of the Benoit apartment in the original building. Its number was 106. He did not ask Mrs. Benoit for the number of the current family apartment in Sandy Hill. That was about as far as he went. He did not tell Grace that he attached the photograph, a fuzzy focus picture of the Benoit family, two adults, three children and a black terrier in place. Grace looked at George with a puzzled look on her face, as if she did not really believe George's account. George did not tell Grace that he had secretly hid the photograph by attaching it to the rear of the closet by the front door of an apartment on the first floor of the new place. In view of the size of the Benoit photograph,

George knew that unless any new tenants used a magnifying glass, the photograph would remain a secret.

⫸•◦•⫷

George Fenwick's next assignment with JH Roberts was to assume responsibility for the design and construction of a three floor apartment building on Bank Street a couple of blocks south of Highway 17. The apartment was to be built on a lot that had previously been home to Saint Louis, an Anglican church that ran out of parishioners and was demolished after the church was eventually sold to a company called Maitland Properties. The firm contracted JL Roberts to build an apartment that provided twenty one bachelor, one and two bedroom units. Unlike the previous job by JL Roberts, the Maitland Properties assignment did not involve refurbishing an already existing structure but to build an entirely new structure, complete with basement and foundation, construction with which JL Roberts had little experience, its history generally limited to houses. As a reward for his efforts to complete the Squire's Court, it was predictable when CEO Powers gave George the assignment of building the apartment for Maitland Properties. In planning the project, George provided management of JL Roberts with a project proposal that included the employing the same construction company, Dorchester Construction Ltd., which built Squire's Court and hiring an additional architect. While Mr. Powers did express a reservation regarding the addition of another architect, a doubt that George managed to deflect by complimenting him about the recent redecoration of his office, a desk. Asked about it, Mr. Powers said that it was bought from a local furniture maker and friend named Hennessy who, interestingly enough, recently moved into a house designed by JH Roberts. By the time Powers finished his explanation of his desk, he had forgotten about his problems with hiring another architect. Neither of them mentioned the matter again.

It was a little more two weeks after Dorchester Construction started to lay the foundation for the new apartment when there was an incident. When a steam shovel was in the process of evacuating the foundation, a man carrying bags of cement tripped in front of the shovel as it was picking up a load of dirt. The shovel fell on the man, whose name was Gauthier, who died within minutes. There was considerable press coverage of the mishap, it appeared above the folds on the front pages of both the *Ottawa Citizen* and the *Ottawa Journal*, not to mention the French language paper *Le Devoir*. There was considerable public interest in the accident, a characterization that was often disputed by observers who called the event a 'tragedy'. In fact, the project was delayed for two weeks as several local politicians, including a federal Member of Parliament named Chevrier, threatened to have the Bank Street project shut down a lot longer than a couple of weeks while Dorchester Construction was investigated for negligence. In the meantime, there was Mr. Gauthier's funeral, a service that attracted a considerable gathering of mourners. At the same time, regardless of the public complaints, the political pressure eventually dissipated and the project resumed.

From the architectural perspective of the project, rather than produce his own drawings, George oversaw the designs of the bachelor, one bedroom and two bedroom units that were produced by the four architects now working for him. For reasons that the four architects did not understand, George insisted on placing a painting in all twenty one apartments of the Bank Street building, claiming that it would make the rooms more attractive to potential tenants. Hector Gallagher, who was managing the project for Maitland Properties, could not understand George's interest in placing paintings in all the apartments either but raised no objections to his decorative suggestions. George had hired the Vincent Gallery on Queen Street to select the paintings which would be placed in the apartments, suggesting that portraits, particularly portraits of families, be the preferred type of painting to be displayed. The Vincent Gallery did not have enough portraits to satisfy George's request for that type of painting. As a result, the Vincent Gallery had to purchase portraits from several other galleries, including one in Montreal. In any event, as curious as George's decorating requests had been, JH Roberts management, specifically Mr. Powers himself, was more concerned with the cost of purchasing paintings, even though the Vincent Gallery did give the firm a volume discount on them, even though the gallery itself was somewhat resistant, claiming that it didn't offer bargains to art enthusiasts, no matter how prosperous. One enterprising gallery employee, a salesman named Jackson, managed to convince gallery manager Lamoureux that placing paintings in each apartment of the new building could function as an advertisement, particularly after enterprising salesman Jackson recommended that a small card be placed below each painting identifying it as being sold by the Vincent Gallery. However, the recommendation remained a recommendation.

It took the Dorchester Construction another two months to complete the foundation and begin to work on the upper structure of the apartment building, the frame, the shell, the columns, the walls, and finally the roof. As a consequence of the accident that claimed the life of Mr. Gauthier when a steam shovel accidentally fell on him, both the construction company and the JH Roberts put up a large sign on the street in front of the construction site recording the number of accidents on the site, one of the first such signs standing anywhere in the city. The fence around the partially completed structure stayed in place as did some of the crowds that had been spectating as the building had been going up during an earlier stage in construction. In fact, the city, led by city counsellor Thompson, thought that the posting of the safety record of a construction site was a good idea and pressed for the counsel to impose it as a municipal regulation. While the city was unable to establish an appropriate bylaw, Dorchester Construction had generated enough favourable publicity to ensure that the sign stayed in place. Over the next six weeks, two other construction projects around the city reported accidents, one involving a man falling down a partially built second floor stairs while the other had a carpenter badly cutting his hand in a job enlarging a grocery store. Strangely, both accidents did not merit much in the way of publicity, not being mentioned anywhere in the newspapers.

In the meantime, while Dorchester Construction started building the individual apartments without any other memorable incident, the only exemptions being several protests attempting to attract members to a recently established construction union. Interest in leasing apartments in the building was significant, the number of potential tenants growing as the opening of the building, which had been named "Parkdale Court" by Maitland Properties, was announced for the end of September, then October, then November. The announcement appeared in the newspapers and on the sign placed in front of the building. Like the renovated "Squire's Court", the rents on the apartments were a little on the expensive side but still attractive enough to attract a large number of potential tenants. Maitland Properties was compelled to hire part time help to handle the rental applications, the full time staff unable to manage the paperwork that for the most part was comprised of the leases and payments applicable to the properties owned by the company. In addition, Maitland Properties had to purchase another office cabinet to file relevant documentation, the number of applications so significant that at times, the office looked like it had just been robbed. In that event, Hector Gallagher of Maitland moved the opening of the building back another month, from November to December.

The closer the building came to completion, the closer George Fenwick came to finalizing his selection of paintings to be placed in the apartments. The manager of Vincent Gallery Lamoureux had collected fifty paintings for George's consideration for the twenty one paintings George ultimately wanted hung in "Parkdale Court". With the apartments ready to be prepared for furnishing, less than two weeks before the building was to open, Lamoureux and salesman Jackson met George at the gallery for the latter's artistic selections. Without making any comment, George picked ten of the first twenty six paintings he saw, mainly landscapes of mountains and forests, until he stopped examining the paintings and asked if the rest of the selected paintings had any images of families, specifically a father, a mother, two boys and a black terrier. Both Lamoureux and Jackson expressed a certain surprise, looking at each other as if George had suddenly asked about paintings of nudes. Lamoureux asked for a reason for George's insistence, a request that to them seemed curious. George just shrugged and then responded by saying that he simply liked pictures of families. Both Lamoureux and Jackson stood mute for a moment. Mr. Lamoureux then said that the Vincent Galley would have to canvas galleries to search for paintings with such specifications.

It was three days later when Jackson contacted George inviting him down to the gallery to examine eight paintings which showed families with the exact characteristics as stipulated by George. Fortunately, George was able to select a number of paintings which showed various families. Only two of them were representations of families with parents, two sons, and a dog while the other six paintings showed families with parents and children ranging from three to five children, boys and girls but without any dogs. As disappointed as George was with some of the selected paintings, he accepted them and made arrangements for the Vincent Galley to deliver them to the apartment building by the end of the week. Those people lucky enough to be chosen as tenants were slated to start moving into "Parkdale Court" within two to three weeks. Strangely, George insisted on deciding which specific paintings were placed in which specific apartments, a decision that most of the people in JH Roberts, Dorchester Construction and finally Maitland Properties, who were familiar with the situation, started to wonder about George, at least as far as his interest in decorating apartments was concerned. No one in the three organizations involved in completion of "Parkdale Court" were previously aware of any strange predilections that George may have held for apartment paintings. No one knew, however, that George had hidden a photograph of the Benoit family in apartment 106 of the recent renovated "Squire's Court". That choice, however, had nothing to do decorating the apartment. It was a memorial to a family that no longer lived in the building.

GEORGE FENWICK IN
THE PARKDALE

———————◆———————

Parkdale Court officially opened in 1936. For reasons that should have seemed obvious, having designed the apartment building himself, George Fenwick was one of the first tenants to move into the building. He moved into apartment 302, a two bedroom place on the third floor of the building overlooking Bank Street. In fact, George was the second to rent an apartment in Parkdale Court. Previously, he had been renting a small two bedroom house on Lisgar Street, an A frame house that had been built sometime in the last century. It was the second place in which George had ever lived since he moved back to Ottawa from Montreal after completing his degree in architectural science from McGill University. He had lived with his parents for several months after he returned to Ottawa. He admitted, at least to himself, that he admired the house, its elegantly haunted look suggestive of a picturesque romantic novel. Occasionally, people would linger in front of George's house to invest a few minutes considering its mystifying beauty. George was often approached by people interested in purchasing the house and he would refer them to a local lawyer named Kelley. In addition, there were countless amateur photographers using Kodak Box cameras standing in front of the house to take pictures. Sometimes, there were also fledgling artists who would stop, lean against one of the elm trees across Lisgar Street and work on a drawing of the house. So there was nothing surprising about George's veneration for the house.

In the six months prior to the official opening of the Parkdale Court, Hector Gallagher of Maitland Properties advised personnel of each one of the companies involved in the construction of the apartment building as well as the widow and children of Pierre Gauthier who was crushed by a steam shovel during the construction of the apartment building that they would have the opportunity to rent one of the units at a preferential rate. George and a vice president of Dorchester named Bassell took apparent advantage of the employee discount, though the rent was fairly costly compared to most apartments in the region. Despite George's longstanding sentimentality for the house on Lisgar Street, he decided that it was a point of pride that he move into one of the apartments which he had designed. He chose a two bedroom apartment in the front of the building, in the south east corner, the first tenant to sign a lease with Maitland Properties. His current landlord, a younger man who was left the house after his father died, was surprised when George informed him that he intended to move. Having first rented the house on Lisgar Street from the man's father and having lived there for more than eleven years, the landlord, as represented by the lawyer Kelley, was understandably disappointed with the loss of a long time resident.

When George moved into Parkdale Court, he was the second renter in the building, the apartment's newly hired janitor, Ronald Miller, his wife Helen and their son Patrick having moved into a smaller two bedroom apartment on the first floor a week previously. George chose apartment 302 on the third floor toward the front of the building, principally for the view, a field of vision that was aided by the three windows, one in the front bedroom, one in the living room and another in the small dining room, a wall separating the latter two rooms. There were only two similar two apartments in the building, the other one on the second floor and the janitor's two bedroom apartment, both having fewer windows and no dining room. There were six other tenants who moved into the third floor of the building over the next two weeks. Only one of them had children, an understandable circumstance in a building in which a one bedroom apartment would set renters back more than one hundred and twenty dollars a month when the average monthly salary for people in Ottawa was less than fifty dollars. Predictably then, the other six denizens of the third floor appeared to be prosperous, no apartments available to working class citizens having been rented in the building.

Over several months, George slowly became acquainted with his neighbours on the third floor as well as with Mr. Miller with whom he had become familiar because they both had been or were employed by one of the companies that were responsible for the construction and subsequent management of the building. Both of the Birches were professors of the University of Ottawa, Tom Birch taught physics while Ellen Birch was chairman of the classics department, an interesting academic combination. Next to the Birches lived a man named Greg Hughes, a Member of Parliament who represented a riding north of Toronto where his wife and his three children lived while he was in Ottawa. Of the four other tenants on the third floor, George had gotten friendly with Michael Mulvihill, a semi-successful bachelor lawyer who sometimes performed magic shows under the stage name "Magic Mike", a theatrical sideline that George discovered when he found one of Mulvihill's handbills. As he later admitted, he had placed handbills in each one of the mail boxes in the lobby of Parkdale Court. George's passion for magic, which had waned as his architectural career grew, slowly returned. So he was reminded of an almost forgotten diversion, if not infatuation, George decided therefore to attend the "Magic Mike" show. It was scheduled to be held in the gymnasium at the Glebe High School in two weeks. The cost of a ticket was $.75. So, aside from his practice, he was a working magician, at least on occasional weekends and evenings. George was a sudden admirer.

George ran into him several days later on the streetcar travelling south down Bank Street at the end of their respective days. During their conversation, they exchanged information on how the two of them made a living. George was informed that he worked in the law office of Fagan and Segal on Queen Street while Mulvihill was informed that George was an architect, listing a couple of buildings that he had designed. Like a lot of lawyers, he said that he did a fair amount of work for the government although he was not particular about the category of government work in which he specialized. George guessed that he may have had something to do with the tax code. But George was more, much more interested in his pursuit of magic than an explanation of tax law. He asked him about his act, confirming that he intended to attend his magic show in any event. He laughed, explaining that this act was fairly standard. He said that most of his audience didn't really care about his act, as long as there was an act, saying that the simplest trick, for example like the Chinese linking rings, or easy to learn card tricks were usually enough to entertain the kind of audience he was attracting. By the time the streetcar reached the stop just past Parkdale Court, George had agreed to meet with him for a drink at the Gilmour House after work the next day.

George was happy with streetcar trip down Bank Street with Mulvihill. As soon as the two of them arrived in the lobby of the Parkdale Court, they both checked their mailboxes. Mrs. Miller happened to be on the first floor near the stairs with a mop and a bucket, cleaning up some sort of mess. As both he and George passed her to climb the stairs, Mrs. Miller looked up long enough to inform the latter that she had received his handbill about his magic show, mentioning that she and her son Patrick were looking forward to the show. Mulvihill smiled and started up the stairs with George. They both complained about the stairs, Mulvihill remarking that they must be perilous to anyone over sixty years old. George agreed, mentioning that he often saw Marge Delorme, an older woman who lived in apartment 306 with her husband, an ever older man, struggling up the stairs with groceries. As both he and Mulvihill opened the doors to their apartments, the latter said that he was going out to dinner with an associate and bid him good evening. As George was closing the door to his apartment, Mrs. Wheeler, who lived in apartment 307 at the end of the corridor, was completing her climb up the stairs with her ten year old son, whose name was

Victor he thought, and several packages. George waited for a moment to provide Mrs. Wheeler and her son with a curt nod and then disappeared into his place. He listened to the two of them struggling down the hall through his door. George noted that Mike had closed the door to his apartment without acknowledging the Wheelers. He wondered whether Mrs. Wheeler, or her husband Frank, were aware of his part time hobby. George thought that they might consider taking their son to the "Magic Mike" show.

BEER AND PICTURES
ON THE WALL

The next evening, George met Mike at the Gilmour House, generally a blue collar place in which the two of them, a lawyer and an architect, should have felt out of place. While George tried, in so far as he could, to dress down to the surroundings, Mike arrived dressed like the attorney he was, explaining that he didn't have time to go home to change clothes, although he did volunteer that he had previously frequented the Gilmour House in his pinstripes. After greeting Mike, George predictably asked, "Don't you feel a little out of place? I mean, I do and I'm not dressed to go to court." Mulvihill responded with a gentle laugh, asserting that no one in the place actually cared about what the patrons actually wore. In addition, he did volunteer again that he had frequented the Gilmour House in his pinstripes. In any event, however, the discussion did not last long.

Both George and Mike further introduced themselves to each other by discussing their respective occupations. He seemed particularly interested in the buildings that George designed or had had a hand in designing. He showed an unusual amount of enthusiasm when George told him that he had been significantly responsible for the design and construction of Parkdale Court, his new drinking buddy adding with an embarrassed smirk that he was the second tenant to be granted an apartment in the building. Mike said that he had arranged for his apartment several weeks later, having been told by Hector Gallagher of Maitland Properties that he was among the first tenants to be provided with an apartment in the building. They did not discuss their respective monthly rental rates, both sensing that George, as the architect of the building, might have been a beneficiary of a favourable rate. However, George in particular did not want his new friend to be informed that he had paid more for his apartment. This could have been a potentially sensitive issue between the two of them since George was paying less for his two bedroom apartment than Mike was paying for his one bedroom apartment.

Of course, they discussed the neighbours on the third floor. George admitted that he was regrettably indifferent with the idea of meeting the neighbours although he said that he had briefly met nearly all of them anyway, his next door neighbours the Birchs, the Wheeler family, the Delormes, the Member of Parliament Hughes, and now Mike Mulvihill. That only left the Hudsons, a middle aged couple that seemed extremely enigmatic, usually slipping by their neighbours with their heads down, not responding to anybody's greeting. Mike told George that he thought that the Hudsons owned a small tailor's shop downtown although he wasn't certain. However, he said that building custodian Miller believed that both Mr. and Mrs. Hudson worked in the main Ottawa library downtown on Metcalfe Street. But he wasn't sure although he did think that, regardless of their positions, the Hudsons were a strange couple.

After about an hour of drinking beer at the Gilmour, George working on maybe his third or forth draft while Mulvihill was in the process of ordering his third quart of Molson Export, Mulvihill asked George about a painting that was hanging in his new apartment when he moved in. He then asked George if a painting was also hanging in his apartment when he moved in and whether he, as architect of the building, had had anything to with what he referred to as a curious decorative touch. He had an assertive look on his face, the edge of a grin appearing. He was certain that he knew the answer to his inquiry. George explained that he was responsible for the paintings in each apartment, a plan that was inspired by his father's interest in accessorizing the rooms in the family home in the same way. He added that his father changed the placement of the paintings, which were placed in the house' s four bedrooms, its living room, its dining room, its kitchen, its lavatory and even its vestibule, every three months or so.

When Mike observed that his father's hobby, which was how he described the practice, was strange to say the least, George agreed without any commentary. He leaned over toward George and asked whether anyone, particularly his mother, ever offered any sort of assessment of George's behaviour regarding the paintings. George responded by acknowledging that his mother questioned his father every time he decided to change the paintings, her main complaint being that he was continually and foolishly buying new paintings to hang in the house. His mother suggested that with the walls of nine rooms to adorn, he could simply rotate the paintings among the rooms. His parents compromised when his father said he would replace only one of the paintings every time he rotated the paintings among the nine rooms. In addition, Mike asked about the dominate motifs of the paintings. George said that there were mainly portraits of individuals, either alone or with other people, including most particularly families. George also mentioned that a good number of the paintings included a likeness of a dog, usually a terrier. George did not have an explanation although he did mention that while his father may have liked dogs, his mother disliked them and would not allow them in the house. However, she did permit them to be in the paintings that father like to hang in the house."

When prompted by another question, George said that he had no idea as to reason for his father's interest, if not obsession with paintings on the wall of the family home. "No, I've thought about my father and his peculiar habit. Fact is that I spent a fair amount of time wondering about him and his paintings. I never came to any particular conclusion. Aside from the paintings, my father was a pretty odd man to begin with. He worked a lot, late hours, weekends, that kind of thing. He was a senior man in the government. It seemed that he was always working." He then asked about her mother. "Wasn't your mother a little puzzled about her husband's habit?" George leaned back in his chair, spread his hands out and answered. "As I told you, I'm sure she was but I never heard them discuss the paintings or anything else for that matter." Mulvihill nodded and then pointed out that they must have discussed the matter of the dogs. "I seldom heard them talking about dogs, much less arguing about having them around. I just knew that my mother didn't like them. So I guess she didn't care about any dogs in the paintings." George then shook his head. So did Mike. It was a mystery to the both of them.

<hr />

The two of them then returned to an exchange about the other tenants on the third floor of the Parkdale Court as they started walking down Bank Street. It was around eleven o'clock. Both George and Mulvihill had finished their beers and had settled up with a waiter named Sam. As they walked the eight blocks home to the apartment building, Mikeulvihill brought up a fellow tenant on the third floor, the Member of Parliament Henry Hughes who may have known George's father, at least by reputation although Mike was not certain. Again, there was another shrug of the shoulders from George, who said that he doubted that Mr. Hughes knew who the elder Fenwick was, not only because George's father was not that well known but also because Mr. Hughes, MP was not that active on matters that would be relevant to George's father, specifically matters relevant to the Justice Department. Mulvihill remarked that he had only spoken with Hughes once and for only a couple of minutes, probably about the weather or some other equally banal issue. By the time the two of them reached their respective apartments, they had nothing else to discuss. They heard a door to one of the other apartments on the third floor briefly open and then close. They then both said good night to each other.

George had difficulty drifting off to sleep that night. He spent most of the night staring at the painting that he had removed from the wall in his apartment. Actually, the painting looked more like a grainy photograph than a painting, an artfully black and white rendering of a family, a father, a mother, four children, three boys and a girl, and a black terrier. It looked like the family was relaxing after or perhaps during a picnic, a hazy representation of a river and a bridge showing in the background. George carefully inspected the painting, which was one foot wide and maybe six inches high in an antique frame. He must have invested twenty minutes gazing at the figures in its frame, almost waiting for inspiration that never materialized. Like his new friend and current neighbour Mike, he wondered about the origins of his father's apparent obsession with paintings, including the painting he was holding in his hands. He thought about his father's family, members whom George never met, both his grandparents having died before George was born, and his one uncle and his two aunts having been relocated elsewhere in Canada, also before George was born. Accordingly, the consequence of a lack of family history led George to consider trying to get in touch with someone connected to his father's family. He decided to explore the history of his father's family. Talking to his father or maybe his mother was probably the best, if not the only way of researching his father's fascination with paintings.

He would start his mother. He doubted that his father, normally a taciturn individual, would be amendable to any discussion of his personal history.

———◦———

George got an opportunity two weeks later when he was in the neighbourhood of the family home to scout the location of his next job for JH Roberts, a planned four floor office building for the Department of Industry. The current site for the construction of the new building was currently occupied by two large houses which the client, the Government had purchased, intending to knock them down and replace them with a new office building. George visited the site with a surveyor and a representative of the McGill Construction Company, which the Department of Public Works chose to construct the new building. After the three of them concluded their business, George visited the family home in New

Edinburgh, as he had arranged with his mother the previous week. During their telephone conversation, he had briefly spoke to his father, who told him that he had recently attended a dinner at which Prime Minister MacKenzie King had put in an appearance. It was curious. George's father boasting about highlights of his senior government position, a position from which George wondered why his father had not retired at his age.

His mother, unexpectedly, was willing to discuss the origins of her husband's apparently aberrant infatuation with the paintings or pictures on the walls of houses. After all, his mother Edna was a surprisingly cheerful woman in view of the fact that she had been married to a fairly sombre individual for almost fifty years. She did, however, ask about the purpose of her son's inquiry. He explained his interest. She didn't seem surprised. She addressed him as she always did. As expected, she offered him a cup of tea before they started their conversation.

"Georgie", she asked, "why do want to know about your father's family, his background?" Her voice was shaky, as it normally was, no suggestion that she was in any way surprised by George's interest in his father's history. In fact, Edna had often wondered about her son's lack of interest in his family's initial genealogy, particularly his father's. She had told her son about her own background, how she was born in a small English town near London called Hackney, met Richard Fenwick during World War I at a country dance and was married to George's father within a month. The story was that the newly married Mrs. Fenwick, whose maiden name was Richards, was sixteen years years old while Richard Fenwick was in his early thirties although that was, at least according to his mother, just a guess. "I know it is somewhat confusing, even to me."

There was a delay while George's mother presumably thought about her husband's history. After thinking about it for a moment, Edna offered some evidence of her husband's biography, at least what she knew about it. "I remember finding a couple of letters from somebody your father said was his brother who lived in Calgary. When I found them, I asked your father about him." George moved forward in his chair, a maroon armchair, in an attempt to hear everything his mother was saying. His mother shrugged her tiny shoulders and continued with her historical commentary. "Your father was very reticent anyway, so anytime I asked him about his family he wouldn't talk about it. He told me that his brother, whose name was Douglas, had moved to Calgary after a friend of his from Scotland – Logan was his name I recall – had accompanied his family to somewhere in the province of Alberta after his father joined the Hudson's Bay Company. He had applied for a position with the company during liberty from the British navy in the port of Montreal." George was becoming more interested in his mother's commentary. It reminded George of listening to a history text, like an Ashbury teacher named Austin who used to read stories about various historical episodes from index cards, standing in front of the class wearing an academic gown and smoking endless Sweet Caporal cigarettes.

George urged his mother to continue with her explanation of how her husband, his father, ended up in Ottawa working for the Government. "I know I shouldn't be telling you this but your father, after getting those two letters from his brother, decided to move to Canada. Your father told me that Douglas had invited him to move from Scotland and stay with him in Calgary. He even offered to lend him some money to get to Calgary, to take a ship from Glasgow to Montreal and then a train from Montreal to Calgary. Logan also told your father that he could get him a job at the Hudson's Bay Company. Then..." his mother then lowered her voice, leaned closer and started to whisper, "your father told me that his brother said that he couldn't bring his family with him, at least not until he got settled." George's fascination with the story of his father's background intensified while his mother continued with her story.

"Anyway, your father decided, like I think his brother may have decided and suggested, that he would just leave. Your father admitted that he just got on the ship by himself without his wife, whose name he has never told me, or his family, two boys and two girls, whose names and ages he never told me either." Edna delayed for a moment, George noticed that his mother had started fiddling with a tissue that she had removed from the right sleeve of her sweater. She was nervous, he thought her veins would soon burst. At that point, George tried to reassure his mother by telling her than he had heard or maybe read of similar situations, i.e. fathers who permanently left families for a better future in Canada. It seemed to subdue his mother somewhat. So she continued the biography of her husband. "When your father first told me his story, which was years after we were married, I really didn't believe it." With a certain quiet delicacy, George then asked his mother how she could have agreed to marry his father, who was maybe twenty years older than she was. His mother looked up at George pensively, as if she was afraid of answering her son's question. She then looked down as she gripped her fidgeting fingers together. George thought she was about to faint. She then replied. "Things were terrible at home. There was a war on, we were all very poor; all of us, my mother, my four sisters, my brother and my grandmother. But my father, when he wasn't beating my mother or any of us, was down at the pub spending money that we needed to survive."

His mother then stopped talking and had started to silently weep. Her head was down, almost in her hands. She was leaning forward and back. George sat, staring soundlessly. He was waiting for her to continue. "That evening, when I met your father, my friend Mitzi and I were invited to this dance by a teacher at the Hackney school. I danced with him all evening. I remember dancing to that old song about the home fires burning. Your father seemed so nice." She looked up at her son. A small smile had emerged on her face."I can't tell you how wonderful your father seemed, at least compared to the ways things were at home. I didn't go home that evening. I remember staying at Mitzi's house for a couple of weeks after that dance. My mother understood but I felt bad because my father, that terrible man, only made things worse for the family." Again, the two of them sat in silence. George then asked his mother when she and his father got married. "Less than a month later. We had a short honeymoon at a Blackpool guesthouse. I then stayed with my aunt

Thelma until Richard got out of the service --- he was a cook in the army or so he said." George then got a puzzled look on his face and exclaimed. "So that's how he got a job running a small meat processing firm, first in Calgary and then in Toronto where we lived when I first came with your father to Canada. From there, he joined the government department of agriculture and then he ended up with a senior job in Ottawa." His mother paused and looked up at George with a knowing look at her face. "But you may know that already. Maybe he told you that already."

His mother then offered George a second cup of tea. For some reason, she asked her son to forgive her for not having offered him that second cup of tea, an omission that she repeatedly expressed regret and about which she apologized. George took a sip and answered his mother. "Yes, he told me how he ended up with that senior government position although I never knew that he started as a cook in the army." His mother nodded. "He had enlisted in the British army but was not enthusiastic about finding himself in the trenches. He did have experience working as a slinger, a cook in a pub in Hackney. George laughed a bit and remarked "I guess being a cook was better than being in the trenches." His mother agreed.

The two of them had been sitting for a moment when George finally got around to asking his mother for a possible explanation of his father's apparent fascination with paintings. His mother looked at her son with a perplexed look on her face. "Yes, he likes to hang paintings all over the house, always did. He never really explained it, at least not directly. He just told me that he liked paintings, liked to move them from one room to another. He said that the paintings reminded him of a museum he used to visit in London, one that showed a lot of portraits. He took me there once. Your father went from room to room staring at the portraits, especially ones of families. He seemed captivated, absorbed ---- he never said anything about it, never explained it." With that, Edna offered George an inconclusive smile. It was obvious that she had nothing more to add to the story of Richard Fenwick.

A SEARCH FOR PAINTINGS
AND PICTURES

—◇—

As intriguing as his mother's account of his father's previously unknown history was to George, it was not as informative as he had hoped. His new friend and neighbour Mike Mulvihill pointed out that he could hardly have expected an explanation of his father's behaviour. After all, he said, his father's apparent fascination with certain types of paintings could hardly be explained by his past. Fact was George's interest in his father's previous endeavours began to move away from an investigation into the man's obsession with paintings to pondering the possible reasons for his father's abandonment of one family in Scotland to the beginning of another in Canada. He quietly suggested that it might have happened more often than one would have thought, laws and regulations in most countries hardly stringent enough to prevent people like George's father simply deserting his wife and family in one country and then moving to another without any permission whatsoever. Mike offered conjecture that was already on his friend George's mind. "Just imagine. Your father gets a letter from his brother in Canada. Presumably he tells him that things are great and suggests that he consider emigrating." George then was asked about his father's family in Scotland. "My mother told me that my father had a wife and four children in Scotland. He probably couldn't afford to bring his wife and family with him to Canada. I don't know what my uncle would have told him, if the matter came up." Mike then put forward another idea. "Maybe your uncle might have suggested that he could send for the family once he got settled in Calgary."

The two of them looked at each other, doubt all over their faces. George settled the question. "I got the impression from my mother that my father would not have sent for his wife and family in Scotland once he got settled here. It seemed that my father, like a lot of immigrants I suppose, wanted a clean start in a new country. In addition, he could avoid all the burdens that he would have to bear if he had to bring his wife and his family over to Canada. I know it's pretty low behaviour but I'll bet a lot of people looking to emigrant might have pulled something like that." The two of them shook their heads and then went back to staring at each other. George then made another observation. "I wonder whatever happened to his wife and his family in Scotland after my father left for Canada." Then a puzzled look appeared on George's face. "I have another thought. I wonder whether his first wife thinks about how her husband is doing in Canada, if she knows where her husband went. I mean, for all she knew, her husband just deserted the family one day, left home without a word, and disappeared." George paused for a short moment and then continued with a question regarding his sudden theory. "What was his wife to do, particularly in rural Scotland, call the local constabulary, that is if there was a constabulary? Anyway, even if there was, why would any local peace officer bother with somebody's missing husband, particularly in rural Scotland, particularly if he went to another country? I'll bet there were a lot of Scottish husbands missing in those days."

Mike nodded in acknowledgement and then shrugged. He then offered George another opinion. "The story about your father's first wife is all very interesting and all but I don't think it gives you any hint as to why your father is obsessed with paintings or photographs. You have to admit it though, it's a good story." George agreed and then asked Mulvihill if he had any suggestions regarding his father's strange habits. They again sat in silence as they presumably contemplated possible ways of further investigating Richard's weird photographic practices. After a few minutes, the two of them changed the subject and began to discuss a couple future projects that JH Roberts was pursuing, Mike recommended that George might consider researching paintings and photographs that could have prompted his father to focus on certain types of scenes. Mike went on to recommend that he consult either the Ottawa Public Library on Queen Street or the library at the University of Ottawa. He added that if those two institutions were not sufficiently helpful in finding any paintings or photographs that could provide George with clues as to his father's hobby, he suggested that he might consider visiting the Museum Art Association of Montreal, one of the largest, if not the largest art museum in the country. He admitted that it was a long shot. For his part, the mention of the Montreal museum prompted pause in George. He told Mulvihill that he was somewhat embarrassed that he had never even heard of the Museum Art Association of Montreal, a cultural oversight in view of his years of attending the School of Architecture in McGill University.

After his evening of discussing his father's occasional painting/photography psychosis with Mike, he spent several nights struggling with sleep, ruminating about the possibility of exploring the two libraries in Ottawa and the museum in Montreal for hints of his father's compulsion for hanging paintings or tacking photographs on the walls of the houses that he lived in. After a couple of partially sleepless nights, George decided that he would start his research into art at the Ottawa public library as soon as he could. He thought of informing Mike but decided against it, waiting until he had already visited at least the library at the University of Ottawa, most likely the smaller of the two libraries. He visited the university library on his lunch hour a couple of days later. He was informed that the library was open five days a week during normal banking hours. meaning that the place closed at three o'clock in the afternoon. He was also told that if he wasn't a student at the university, he would have to apply for a special library card, easily obtained because of his attendance at McGill University. George quietly complained to the librarian, a predictably older woman, that he would have to take a day off from work. He also asked for a special library card, which was issued immediately.

When George arrived at the University of Ottawa library, the place was close to empty. He went straight to the counter where a younger women, likely a student, looked up and waited for George who asked for the section where the art books were housed. The volunteer librarian asked him whether he was looking for anything specific. George explained that he was looking for a certain type of painting or photograph although he did not intend to explain the purpose of his search, that is a certain type of painting that could have fuelled his father's obsession. She nodded, pointed to the rear of the library and went back to whatever she was doing when George walked in. He thanked her and walked back toward the reference section of the library. He didn't even have to show his special library card.

⟫⟩-◦-⟨⟪

The reference section of the library yielded little in the way of anything useful. Aside from the photographs of famous people, George was still looking for portraits of families. But he did not came across any photographs of families that included anybody who could have been a younger version of his father. In fact, most of the families seemed older, likely too old to include someone who looked like a younger Richard Fenwick. Still, his search did result in a couple of pictures that attracted George's interest. They captured two families, four individuals in one picture and six in the other, looking down from two windows. It was a poignant picture. George stared at the two pictures for several minutes. He then looked up at the clock on the wall above the four shelves of reference books and realized it was approaching four in the afternoon. Closing time was due. George noticed that the librarian was clearing the counter. She checked the clock as well. By the time George left the library, he decided that he would show the picture he had removed from a reference book in the library to his mother, seeking to explore her perspective as to whether that image of the young father in the photograph of the family on a picnic blanket looked like a younger version of her husband and his father. He thought he would then decide whether he would visit the Ottawa Public Library or the Museum Art Association in Montreal or both.

His mother was delighted, as he could have expected, with her son's second visit in a week. He called her to invite himself over to discuss the results of his visit to the library at the University of Ottawa. She asked him to lunch. He reluctantly agreed although he pretended to respond enthusiastically to his mother's proposition, the reason for his hesitation his mother's culinary shortcomings, lunches of lentil or hot water soup with barely buttered stale bread and deserts of stewed prunes or mouldy oranges high on the lunch menu. Still, his mother brewed a tasteful pot of tea and was usually an entertaining conversationalist, at least compared to his father, who was dour and almost entirely taciturn. In addition, during family meals, George's father would read newspapers or government memoranda, make the occasional note on envelopes which he kept in one of his suit jackets, attire that he always wore everywhere but in bed. And on the other hand, there were the cookies, marvellous confections that his mother always seemed able to serve to anyone who dropped by.

Initially, his mother had chastised George for tearing the photograph out of the reference book, more concerned it seemed with violating library rules than potentially identifying the man in the photograph that was removed. George expressed some guilt but also offered an explanation --- in other words, an excuse. "I just saw the picture. The man looked like my father might have looked if he was thirty years younger. I mean, I just couldn't help it. I had looked at a whole bunch of pictures and this one sort of popped up." He then looked down on the picture, looked up at his mother and handed her the picture. With a shaky hand, she accepted the photograph, nodded and looked down to examine it. She adjusted her glasses and then bent down so her nose was practically touching the photograph. She was farsighted. She started to softly whistle, then looked up at George, and commented. "Yes, I can see why you stole this picture, which you shouldn't have." She held up the picture and then brought the picture down to her lap. "You know I don't see very well but the man in the picture could have been your father, maybe thirty years ago or so, with more hair and no moustache." She then tittered in an old lady way.

They both sipped their teas and continued with their chat. His mother then asked a question that, surprisingly enough, had not occurred to George. "Why do you want to know if the man in your picture here is your father?" His mother was now holding the photograph up. George shrugged and answered. "I don't really know. I just thought I could find a clue to his interest in certain types of pictures." His mother looked up with a startled look on his face. "I know more than you do that your father has an interest in pictures, paintings or photographs. Always did I think, probably before we even married. That's why the house still has a picture in every room. Aside from your curiosity, I don't really know what good that would do." George shrugged again. "Mother, as I told you already, I don't really know."

Both George and his mother discontinued their consideration of his father's interest, if not obsession, to have their lunch of cucumber, egg and watercress sandwiches. As they ate their lunch, George asked his mother about his father's habits, his occasionally curious behaviour, and his authoritarian approach to parenting. As expected, George was particularly interested in more detail about his father's history in Scotland. His mother opened their discussion of her husband's history, in so far as she knew about it, by observing."Your father wasn't very parental if you know what I mean. I don't know how he felt about the children he said he may have had in Scotland but I always had the impression --- you'll forgive me dear ---- that he may not have been too happy about your arrival." George was somehow not surprised. After all, he apparently had left four children in Scotland without explanation, at least without any explanation that was available to anyone, including his mother. She tried to comfort her son. "I don't think that your father treated you badly in any way. He just wasn't particularly affectionate, with you, with me, with pretty well anybody. People from his work, at least the ones I've met, have told me that while he was is generally well mannered, he is not particularly friendly. While he is good at his job, he is generally stern. He gets along with his colleagues but I can't say that any of them like him."

They ate their lunch in silence for a few moments while George considered his mother's comments. He immediately wondered about what may have attracted his mother to his father. He was reluctant, if not entirely unwilling to ask her mother that question. Still, she must have had a premonition or something. "I know what you're thinking, dear, don't be embarrassed. You're wondering why I married your father." George still had a blank look on his face, still stunned in silence. "When I first met your father at that dance outside London during the war, he seemed so nice, at least compared to what I was used to." George nodded, recalling his mother's story about the misery of her family life. "When he asked me to marry him, it had to be within a couple of weeks of meeting him. I have to admit, I couldn't wait to get married. As I told you, we got married within a month. Then, you came along, shortly after we got to Canada."

They both relaxed. His mother offered George some cinnamon cake and encouraged him to have another cup of tea.

<hr />

While he had learned a good deal about his father's past, George was no closer to explaining his father's preoccupation with wall art, whether paintings or photographs. He lay in bed that night for hours again ruminating, if not trying to remember the plan he had contrived when he decided that he should investigate his father's fascination. It came as no revelation then when he decided that he would again consult with his relatively new inspiration, his neighbour Mike Mulvihill. As far as the possibility of visiting two other libraries for more pictures, he concluded that he would first speak with Mike. After all, he could not shake the frequent boredom he endured during that his last two hours of looking through the art books in the library at the University of Ottawa. Consulting the two other libraries he had selected was an alternative that he had anticipated but not yet decided. He would wait until he spoke to his friend Mike.

MORE NEIGHBOURLY ADVICE

H e caught Mikel leaving his apartment on the following Tuesday morning. He waited for him before the two of them headed down the stairs. George greeted him cheerfully, asking him if he had performed as "Magic Mike" over the past week or so, their previous meeting at the Gilmour House almost two weeks ago. Mike answered with equal cheer, telling George that he presented his magic show to groups of kids at the Sandy Hill Community Centre and Saint Gabriel's church over the past two Saturday afternoons. He answered happily, saying that kids were always enthusiastic about his shows, his only reservation being that he had agreed to perform for free. Mike explained that he had hoped that a free concert might generate publicity, particularly from two city newspapers and at least one radio station, featuring radio personality Andy "Loud Mouth" Kelly, who attended the concerts. By the time the two of them reached the street, they agreed to meet at the Gilmore House, George brought up his recent activities in his quest for an answer to his father's fascination with placing paintings and photographs on walls. Arrangements were made for Thursday.

Mike knocked on George's door around seven o'clock on the next Thursday evening for their appointment at the Gilmore House. Unlike the previous time they went together to the Gilmore, Mike was more casually attired than he was that last time they met. In fact, he was actually wearing blue jeans, surprising since he was sporting a three piece pinstripe suit the last time they met there. They decided to walk down Bank Street to the Gilmore. During their walk, they initially discussed, at Mike's suggestion, his recent dealings with the Department of Agriculture, entertaining George with stories of the department's bureaucrats, many of whom he claimed were "a bit looney", a characterization that George assigned to the department's personnel policy, which he claimed was based more on the recommendations of local Members of Parliament than it was based of the qualifications of the individuals applying for positions. When pressed for specifics of those recommendations, Mike reported perennially vulgar language and profound dislike for anything to do with government, a curious combination to say the least. George did not bother letting Mike know that he recognized the irony of the situation. He imagined that he already he knew it. George contributed to the exchange by telling Mike that his father sometimes amused his mother by relating stories about Ministers and bureaucrats from other departments, including some from the Department of Agriculture. He pointed out, however, that according to his father, people representing agriculture, whether it was the government department or the industry itself, were almost constantly aggressive, if not outright rude. On the other hand, his father also said that agriculture people were not alone in offending the government. As they got to the Gilmour, standing in the entrance, Mike remarked, "I thought you told me that your father seldom talked to you about his position in the government." George laughed a bit and told him that he overheard most, if all of his father's comments about his meetings with people from other government departments from conversations his father and his mother occasionally conducted in the living room. George also added, as a humorous, if not valuable aside he thought, that his father always wore his office attire until he went to bed. This time, Mike laughed.

The two of them were seated by one of the concrete pillars in the Gilmour within two minutes, at which point they were immediately approached by one of the older waiters, a man named Lou, not Sam who had served them the last time they frequented the place. Both Lou and Sam managed to meet every one of the usual qualifications for a waiter at an established tavern: middle aged, corpulent, grumpy, and amateur city historians. Mike ordered a quarter of Molson's Export while George asked for three drafts, just as they had during their previous visit to the Gilmour. George then asked Mike about his father. When George asked, Mike looked a little uncomfortable, like he didn't really want to talk about his father. "Why? I kind of thought you might want to talk about anything you might have found out about your father since the last time we were in this place." George shrugged and answered somewhat tentatively. "Well, maybe I'm just noisy." They both laughed. Lou arrived with the beers, made change and then departed without a word. They then both took a couple of gulps from their beers and Mike put down his glass and assured George. "Look George, I'm willing to continue to talk about your father. You don't need to convince me by asking about my father, if that's what you're trying to do." They both nodded and went back to their beers.

Mike spoke first. "So what you have found out about the old man? Did you go through any books at those libraries you said you intended to visit? I know you thought it was a long shot but what the hell." George slightly nodded and began to explain his afternoon spent at the library at the University of Ottawa. "I came across several pictures that included men that looked like a younger version of my father. In fact, I took a picture out of one book ---- you know, ripped it right out of the book, ---- and showed it to my mother who thought that he could have been a younger version of my father." Mike looked at George with a bemused look on his face. "And so?" George responded by giving him a perplexed shrug. "And so.... nothing." George was telling his friend the truth. He had spent hours laying in bed, staring at the ceiling, waiting for slumber while he searched his thoughts for any future plans. He could not come up with anything except for searching the other two libraries he had previously identified. "I don't think you have any other choice except to continue investigating books in those libraries, for whatever good that will do you." George confirmed his friend's observation. "I know.... I know." They sat in silence for a time.

Soon,after ordering another quart, Mike asked another obvious question. "As I say, what good does finding someone that might have looked like your father twenty years ago provide you? Suppose someone, your mother I guess or maybe your uncle, maybe the one that convinced him to leave Scotland, positively identifies him in any picture, what could it prove about any personality quirk he may have? To be specific, even if you discover that your father had such an idiosyncrasy, as strange as that is, what could it mean, why would he continue to pursue it?" It didn't take George long to realize that Mike was probably right to ask the question. No matter what evidence George would uncover, it would be difficult to assign any particular justification for George's father belief or behaviour or whatever it was. George silently drank the remaining draft sitting in front of him and signalled to Lou for three more drafts. Mike ordered another quart of Molson's Export when Lou arrived with the drafts for George. Lou didn't look happy, giving Mike a dirty look. He also thought he heard Lou mutter a vulgar complaint under his breath. Neither of them knew why.

After several minutes of silent quaffing, George asked Mike if his own father, who drove a truck for Rush Metals Company, one of the oldest such companies in the city, ever had any habits or demonstrated any behaviour that he might have thought was a bit strange. Mike first looked at him as if the question was entirely inappropriate. He then answered, "Not really but on the other hand, I hardly knew the man. He hardly paid any attention to us kids ---- there were four of us. Luckily, we were all good kids, never made any trouble, so we never really had to deal with his bad side, that is if he had a bad side. My mother basically ran the house. He never made any trouble at home. He just went to work, sometimes to the curling club, where I guessed he may have drank a lot, and liked to play cards on Preston Street with the guys from work. He liked playing pinochle or euchre I recall." George just sat there listening to tales from the Mulvihill household, surprised by how ordinary the Mulvihill household actually was. But he continued to pursue with him his original question. "You mean that your father never did anything peculiar, never once?" Mike leaned in, lowered his voice, almost whispering, and told George that his father wrote poetry, examples of which he kept hidden in the basement of their house on Dorchester Avenue. Mike said he only knew about his father's verse when he was looking for an old pair of skates.

There were about two dozen poems in the coffee can he had used to conceal them. Before he had returned the poems to the coffee can, he read several of them, namely "Punching Out For Good", "Cutting Steel", "Work Time", "Canteen Euchre", and his personal favourite of the poems he read "Anguish At Quitting Time". They were surprisingly eloquent works given the subject matter, surprising because his father Hector Mulvihill left school in grade six and seldom, if ever demonstrated any sort of literary acumen. "I was stunned, more than stunned. To discover that my father who I thought might have problems reading the comic page composed poetry, any kind of poetry, was astounding. I just couldn't believe it." George had to admit that he was stunned as well, to hear Mike tell him that a manual labourer with a six grade education wrote poetry. "Did you bring your discovery to the attention of your father? Did your mother know that your father was writing poetry? Did anyone know?" asked George. Mike shook his head a couple of times and replied. "I thought that it would embarrass him. I mean, the fact that he kept his poems in a coffee can in the basement of our house tells you something, doesn't it? It was obvious, isn't it? Maybe he just didn't want anyone to know." He shook his head again.

Then Mulvihill added to his explanation by asking George a similar question. "Why don't you ask your father about his pictures on the walls, why he seems so interested? I'll bet you have the same reason I have for not approaching my father about his poems." Mike smiled. He wasn't waiting for an answer. He already knew it.

ANOTHER LIBRARY, MORE PICTURES

W hile he didn't think it was a particularly good idea, he still felt compelled to visit the next library on the list, having been reluctantly convinced by Mike to continue to pursue his original plan. So he arranged for another day off the next week, this time to spend at the Ottawa Public Library which he understood held more books than the University of Ottawa. He choose the next Wednesday. The library was located on the corner of Queen and Metcalfe Streets in a building that George knew was designed in the Neo-Gothic style more than fifty years ago. It was a large building with three floors and a large statute of Colonel By, the founder of Ottawa's antecedent Bytown, in the middle of library's first floor. He arrived there at nine in the morning, when the library opened. There were more than a dozen people waiting outside for the place to open, including seven elderly women, three university students, a middle aged man who may have been a university professor and George. An older man in a rumpled corduroy jacket opened the front door. He greeted all but one of the elderly ladies, all of whom were carrying shopping bags. It was obvious that the older man was acquainted with the ladies. He also seem to know the university professor but not the three students. He certainly wasn't acquainted with George either. George was the last to enter the library. The man with the rumpled jacket then returned to a desk he was occupying by the front counter.

George immediately recognized that the reference section was similar to the reference division of the University of Ottawa library. In the back was a middle aged lady in a navy blue tweed dress transferring large reference books from a cart to the shelves. She was having difficulty handling some of the books, lifting them from the cart. By the time George arrived in the reference section, the lady in the navy blue tweed dress had turned around, clenching a large book with both hands to her chest with the startled expression on her face. She was barely able to hold onto the book, which George noticed featured a picture of a church, a medieval church to be specific, most likely an European cathedral. It was obvious that the lady with the book expected George to ask her for information. She turned around and placed the book she was holding on a shelve, turned back and, in a quietly nervous voice, offered to help him.

George approached the lady and asked if she could direct him to books that featured pictures, specifically paintings or photographs, of families in late nineteenth century. The lady stepped around the cart and motioned George to sit down at one of the tables, as she did. In a quiet voice, the lady made an observation. "That seems like a curious inquiry." She paused for a moment and then asked. "Are you an artist?" George, who was now sitting across from the lady, was understandably surprised with the question. "An artist? Why do you ask?" She looked a little perplexed and expounded on her original question. "Well, I have had a few patrons, people who are painters who have asked for books for reference material, either paintings or photographs, on which they could base their own paintings. In other words, they were looking for something to copy, to get ideas. I know it is something that you don't see every day but it makes a certain amount of sense when you think about it." George sat across from her and thought about her comments. He had never heard of any aspiring artists consulting libraries for ideas but he had to admit to himself that it was a pretty good idea. After all, what better way to practice a certain style of painting or discover a certain subject matter, when accorded with many examples.

The lady in the tweed continued by asking George for more detail as to his interests in family pictures. At first, George was confused.

She gave George several examples of what she meant. "Sometimes, artists will provide particular detail as to what they are interested in, like you are in pictures of families. Some have told me that they wanted pictures of certain types of landscapes, places, people, certain types of faces, even things, like furniture for example ---- one man, an older man, wanted paintings or photographs of a Victorian dresser or roll top desk, another wanted pictures of something as absurdly specific as a nineteenth century gravy ladle. As I say, people wanted all sorts of things." George was surprised by the lady's comments, wondering why he had not requested the same information in the library at the University of Ottawa. In view of the information provided by the lady, George decided that she could provide useful advice about he was looking for, despite the fact that he was not quite sure of that. He said to the lady that he was looking for young men who might have looked like his father. As an aside, he also mentioned that his father spent his early years in Scotland. It was a detail that prompted the lady to suggest a specific reference book.

He thanked the library lady, carried the book, entitled "The Faces of Scotland", to the one of the tables, sat down and began to flip through the pages of the book. There were several sections, each including faces from specific Scottish cities: Aberdeen, Dundee, Edinburgh, Glasgow, Perth and Stirling. Each section featured faces who lived in the respective cities listed, all presented in natural locales. George opened the book and found dozens of faces and their families living in Aberdeen, one of the seven towns and cities, meaning that there were over seventy people on their own and with families pictured on those pages. He started to look through the Aberdeen Section, noting that there were several faces that had been painted and the remainder photographed. There were pictures of at least ten families.

Looking though the pictures, George was entertained. He saw that most of the men in the pictures were predictably wearing kilts, sporrans, different types of paid jackets, and different types of caps and hats, none of which George had ever seen his father wear. On the other hand, the women were wearing billowing dresses, long skirts, various types of scarfs and sashes, and tightly curled hair. Half the pictures were of families ---- fathers, mothers, children, and older people, presumably grandparents, aunts or uncles. He also noted that some of the men were playing bag pipes and many were sporting beards and/or moustaches. As for the central objective of his investigation, there were several men who could have been identified as his father in his younger days but there was not a positive identification. One looked to be much slimmer than his father was although George could not be sure since he estimated that more than two or three decades tended to add more than a few pounds, a likely judgment given that the older Richard Fenwick lived a much more affluent life than the supposedly younger Richard Fenwick in the picture. After examining the picture with his magnifying glass for a second time, he concluded that he was mistaken. The other two men who he could have identified as his father were apparently taller and in addition, were not accompanied by families. He had compared the pictures to a recent photograph of his father, which his mother had given him during his last visit to the family home. Unfortunately, his mother did not have any pictures of his father in his younger years. He also had two other pictures on him, photographs of himself when he was in his late teens and then one which was taken several weeks ago. There was maybe twenty years between the faces in the two pictures. While not identical, there was enough of a resemblance to use for the purpose of juxtaposing pictures in the reference book and his father, if he needed to.

After quickly flipping through the comparatively few pictures of people in Dundeen, where he did not locate anyone who even remotely looked like his father several decades back, he started investigating the maybe two hundred pages of pictures that constituted the Edinburgh Section. The library lady walked by the table that George was using, stopped for a moment and asked if he had found anything. George replied in a pleasant tone, "No, not yet but some of these pictures are quite nice". She smiled in a kindly manner, "I would imagine that they would." she replied, "I briefly looked through "The Faces of Mexico" when we first got the book. I found the pictures in the book very interesting, fascinating faces. You know, people in Mexico have different ancestral backgrounds, mainly the indigenous population, who were here before people from Europe arrived and people who are descended from those people who had arrived from Europe. The faces in the pictures in that book are fascinating." George smiled and nodded. "Thank you, maybe I'll look at that book if I get a chance." She left and headed toward the front counter. George turned back to the Edinburgh Section of the "The Faces of Scotland".

In the hundred or so pages, George came across at least a dozen pictures that could have been a younger Richard Fenwick although of course he could not be even remotely certain. One of them was a painting of the younger man with a family of a wife and two children, the four of them sitting on a bench in front of a cobbler's shop in Edinburgh, the only colour picture in the batch. Ten of the other eleven pictures were black and white photographs of families, husbands, wives, with families with one to eight kids, in ages ranging from infants to maybe ten years old. There were no children in the remaining photograph, an unusual portrait of a single man for the Edinburgh Section. In that regard, George had come across maybe twenty photographs and two paintings in which there were no children, most, if not all of them were young couples although three of the wives looked to be expecting. Comparing the eleven other pictures in which men could have been lookalikes, doppelgangers of his father, to the picture George had brought to the library. He was not convinced that any of the pictures, as intriguing as some of them may have seemed to him, could be definitely identified as a depiction of his father maybe thirty years gone. He had to admit to himself that he was getting tired of the entire enterprise, no matter how many pictures he had inspected. Besides, he was already getting tired and a little despondent.

As he was entering the library that morning, he had noticed that there was a diner right across Queen Street. It was called Big Al's. Around noon, he thought of the place. It was time to have lunch.

Although he was reluctant to return to the library after lunch, he practically forced himself to return to his investigation. He returned to the chair he had previously occupied at the table in the reference book section. The book "Faces of Scotland" was still open on the last pages of the chapter devoted to the people of Edinburgh. For some unknown reason, he came across a picture of two men, presumably inhabitants of Glasgow, sitting across each other at a small circular table in an unnamed pub. Not looking at each other, they were staring straight ahead, presumably posing for the photograph. He interrupted his gaze for a moment and wondered about the name of the pub in the picture. None was shown. George hesitated for a moment. He thought, based on his reading of the book so far, that there were perhaps more than a hundred of public houses in Glasgow. He wished he had not returned the magnifying glass he had borrowed from the counter lady at the Ottawa library. He seriously pondered the two men in the picture, bringing his eyes to a squint. They actually did look like each other, probably brothers George thought, but they both also looked like his father, a discovery that should have startled him but didn't for some reason. He sat there, contemplating his next move, if there was to be a next move, waiting for another burst of inspiration that would provide him with some sort of direction.

He wanted to remove this picture from the book, to show it to Mike rather than his mother this time, not to confirm some sort of identification of a face in a picture but to seek advice as to the future of his investigation. Once again --- it seemed many times now --- he began to seriously doubt his pursuit of his father's apparent and sometimes consuming passion. He had scanned countless pages of paintings and photographs to hopefully discover the secret, if there was a secret, beneath his father's ardour. There had not been nor was there any hint of a solution to his predicament regarding his father. No matter how often he tried, it just could not leave his mind. Why was he doing this? What did he expect to accomplish? Even though he had tried fairly strenuously to forget about what he was obsessing, realizing that he was developing or had developed an obsession of his own about his father's obsession, admittedly a strange intellectual quandary that could be considered almost academically. He was stumped, as he often was, about the project, enthusiasm for which was again evaporating.

He then returned to gazing at the two Glasgow men and suddenly became conscious of an accidental solution to his problem. The two men in the picture were obviously friends, this seemed obvious at least to him. He thought, like the kind of notion that came to him in the middle of the night when he was struggling for sleep, that they could confide in each other, telling each other things like they might not tell anyone else, not their wife, not their mother, not anyone else in their family. This was one idea that had not previously occurred to him, perhaps if he could find a good friend of his father to ask, that is if he had a good friend to begin with. Rather than consulting with his mother, whom he had bothered for information about his father's obsession at least twice in the last month or so without any success, he would interview a friend. In view of his sudden realization that there may be another course of action in his quickly vanishing pursuit of his father's fixation, he knew what his next move would be.

So he decided, rather than pointlessly pursuing clues to his father's curious habit among a multitude of countless paintings and photographs, he would look for a friend of his father and seek from that friend any intimate information he may have had on his father. With that, he closed the "Faces Of Scotland" reference book. For good he concluded.

A FRIEND OF RICHARD FENWICK

F or the third time in a little more than a month, he planned to visit his mother. Once again, she was more than happy to see him. In fact, she was almost unrestrained with her elation, squealing like an old lady with excitement. Like his previous visits, George ensured that he could take the weekday off and that his father would not be at home, which was almost instinctive in his case. They agreed to meet for lunch on a Friday in a week from his decision to abandon his survey of pictures in library books. He had concluded that his investigations of paintings and photographs in the two libraries were hopeless efforts that would result in nothing of any consequence. For the first time in months, George felt that he was finally on the right track and would not be wasting his time. Maybe his mother knew something she didn't know she knew.

When George called on his mother for lunch, her ebullience having not subsided, she greeted him with a sincere hug and informed him that she had prepared for lunch Scotch quail eggs with whipped strawberries for desert. She stepped into their living room and asked George to follow her with the tea service from the kitchen. It was obvious to George that his mother was making every effort to ensure their lunch was even more festive than it was the last lunch they had together. George immediately thought that his father must be in one of his moods. It was always hard on his mother who was in the habit to reacting to his father's moods by providing a nice meal, little more than a bribe but an approach that seemed to work not only on his father but on George as well. Whatever the purpose, George always appreciated the meal.

His mother wanted to know the purpose of his visit. "Well, I want to ask you about dad's personal life, you know what he does when he isn't working or he isn't here at home, reading all those newspapers." replied George. In that context, Richard Fenwick usually read, in addition to the two Ottawa newspapers, the Financial Post, the Montreal Gazette, the Montreal Star, the Toronto Globe and Mail, and the Toronto Star. At times, his mother would ask about the cost of subscribing to seven daily newspapers. His father would usually react by simply saying that he needed to know what his Minister's constituents were thinking. Anytime they discussed the matter, his mother would allow a vacant expression to appear on her face and the conversation would come to an end. When he was living at home, George would occasionally wonder about his father's apparently excessive reading habits as well, only to conclude that his father must have an important job. Unlike his mother, George never asked his father anything about the newspapers. Fact was that George usually lost interest fairly quickly.

"Does Dad have any friends, you know like personal friends, men that he might have confided in?" asked George. He left out the further explanation that he was looking for someone who knew more about his father's daily life than she did. He thought that his mother would be embarrassed if her son somehow suggested that her husband had a life in which she did not participate. His mother answered somewhat tentatively, "Well, as you know, your father is a secretive man, always has been. If he has a friend who I don't know about, I'll wager his secretary would know. You know, he has had the same secretary for at least two decades. Every time he moved to another department, to another ministry, she moved with him. If anyone would know if he had any friends who I don't know about, she would." He nodded and smiled. She paused for a moment and continued. "Her name is Carruthers, Miss Carruthers. Her and I talk all the time, by telephone of course, so we are fairly friendly. I can talk to her about your father's friends, that is if he has any, if you're too shy to call her yourself." She then giggled, giggled as she usually did, like an old lady. George continued to smile. They made an arrangement.

<hr />

His name was Nelson, Michael Nelson. His mother told him that he worked in his old department, the Department of Agriculture where he had worked for almost twenty years, ever since George's father had hired him. According to Mrs. Carruthers, who his mother said was more than happy to disclose the details of his personal life with her, Michael and Richard had been close friends for almost the entire duration of their government careers, from Agriculture ultimately to the Under Secretary of State via the Department of Finance. His mother had passed along Mrs. Carruthers' observation that as a result of their working relationship in three government departments for almost twenty years, they had become close personal friends. She had told his mother that his father's friend Michael would know things about his father that his wife would not know. His mother told George that she agreed with Mrs. Carruthers that Michael probably knew a lot of more things about her husband than she did. Regardless, it was now George's plan to contact Michael as surreptitiously as possible in order to probe him for clues about his predilection for paintings, photographs and pictures. His investigations in libraries were over without any result whatever. He was no closer to knowing anything.

He found his telephone number by contacting the office of the Under Secretary of State and asking for Michael Nelson. He said that he knew Mr. Nelson worked for the Under Secretary of State somewhere but had lost his number, that is if he ever had it in the first place. The woman on the other end of the telephone was about as helpful as expected, sounding understandably annoyed but did provide George with the number, presumably with a certain degree of reluctance. George then sat by the telephone and planned his call to Michael. He was admittedly nervous, considering a plan to persuade Mr. Nelson to disclose confidential personal information about his father, particularly whether he had any unusual interests or predilections, habits that he thought might explain his obsession with pictures, however they were exemplified. A sudden inspiration descended on him like some sort of cloudburst in the middle of the night. He would tell Mr. Nelson that he was putting together a commemorative album for his parents' wedding anniversary. Initially, he thought that he would inform Mr. Nelson that he was planning a party for their anniversary but realized before he said anything that he would expect an invitation. So he decided to ensure that the deception was foolproof. That was why he went with the commemorative album story. He thought he was being particularly clever.

Michael Nelson came on the line, the expected officious tone not evident. In fact, he sounded almost friendly. "Hello, Mr. Fenwick, Michael Nelson here.", George not getting an opportunity to introduce himself, although he immediately realized that it was unnecessary. As affable as he initially sounded, he went straight to the point. "What can I do for you? I hope I can help you." George thought he would continue with Mr. Nelson's evident candour. "Well, Mr. Nelson, if you'll excuse me, and I hope you don't mind, I'm calling to ask you a big favour." Nelson answered almost immediately. "A favour, a big favour? I'm always doing favours. In fact, I like to do favours." George explained the purpose of his call. "I understand that you have been fairly close to my father for a long time and you may be able to help me." George was worried that he might have been too direct but it was out there anyway. So he continued. "I should tell you that I am planning to put together something for my parents' wedding anniversary, their fourthieth." Nelson sounded puzzled. "Something, what do you mean, something?" George replied as astutely as he could. "I thought that I would ask you, that is if you are agreeable, if you are aware of any habits, practices, or routines that are generally unknown to most people, including his wife and his son ---- you know, something that may be a secret to most people." There was a silence on the other end of the line as Michael presumably considered his reaction. George assumed that he was probably a little, if not more than a little puzzled by the request. In fact, George would not be surprised if Michael would decline his peculiar request to share one of his father's secrets, that is if he had any.

After delaying the conversation for a moment, Michael resumed their conversation. He apologized and in a voice that sounded like it was on the verge of trembling, told George something about his father that was predictable. It was something that he expected. "You may not believe it but your father is an artist, someone who has always painted. In fact, he has a small bachelor apartment, has had it for years. He uses it as a studio ----- that's where he paints." Before George got the opportunity to reply, Michael asked. "Does your mother know about your father's painting?" George answered simply, "No, I don't think so. She would have told me at some point if he did." Michael didn't wonder why George didn't know, which was obvious, although he did remark. "I'm sure that you know that your father is a very secretive man, at least as long as I have known him. Why he chose to hide his interest in art from both your mother and yourself is beyond me. I just could never figure it out." Neither could George now that he knew.

George did not have any thoughts, at least momentarily. After Michael finally hung up, his parting words were surprisingly hopeful. "I hope what I just told improves your parents' commemorative album and makes your parents' celebration of their anniversary happier." With that salutation, Michael quietly hung up. After they completed their telephone conversation, George had little on his mind except his doubt about the next step in what he thought was his increasingly pointless investigation of his father's obsession. He already knew the source of his obsession. It was obviously the pursuit of his art. He wondered about the fate of his paintings after he completed them. He did not know how many paintings he had completed but he was more interested in their ultimate fate. Did he stow them somewhere in the basement, a location about which he knew little, having avoided venturing into cellar as if he expected ghosts, rats or frightening reptiles. Did he give them or sell them to people? And then it came to him. It was such a conspicuous conclusion that he felt like a complete idiot, an appellation that his father used to apply to George often enough as he would actually remember the specific occasions. He realized, or seriously guessed, that his father hung the paintings he completed in every room in the house. Based on his infrequent observations of his parents' house, some rooms went unseen for months, he began to assume that his father would rotate the paintings among the rooms and then, once each painting had been displayed in every room, his father would donate the paintings to local galleries, which could try to sell them but more likely give them to libraries, hospitals, community centres, theatres, hotels or even the building in which he worked, including in particular the large conference room adjacent to the office of United Secretary of State where he was able to hang eight paintings. No one seemed to notice any time he changed them, which he managed to do every four months or so.

It seemed like months since he had started his investigation into his father's obsession with what he now knew was painting. Now that he understood one of his father's major attributes, he was now worried that it would become one of his.

HIS FATHER'S PAINTINGS

Although he had developed serious doubts about continuing the investigation of his father's obsession about painting, now that he had managed to connect it to his pursuit of art, he still wanted to determine what his purpose in painting actually was. Enjoyment, relaxation, some unknown artistic inspiration. In any event, the subject of his paintings was or could be the final clue to the mystery that continued to endure. Perhaps he could actually ask his father about his collection, inspect the paintings in his parents' house, which of course would require another lunch with his mother which, while pleasant enough, might encourage his mother to consider their lunches a habitual event, if not a responsibility. He thought that unnecessary. Having rejected from the start of his quest the possibility of simply asking his father, he decided that he could somehow discover where his farther took his paintings after he had either grown tired of the ones that were hanging on the walls of his home or he had produced new paintings which he wanted to place on those walls. Michael Nelson had told him that his father would bring the paintings he wished to discard to one of the city's art galleries where they would be sold to individuals or to institutions, e.g. hotels, hospitals, libraries etc that had walls using paintings not as art but as decoration. He would then visit the galleries to look for examples of his father's work.

There were four art galleries in the city, two of which were prominent enough to attract his father's most significant patronage. The Temple Galley was the city's largest, presumably the gallery with the most paintings and other objet d'arts. It was located on Sussex Drive. He would visit the gallery sometime during the weekday, possibly next week, ask to see the selection of the paintings by Richard Fenwick and ascertain whether there was anything in any of the paintings that could explain anything about his father. The other large gallery in the city was called Desloges, which sounded more arty than the other three galleries, including of course Temple and the two others, the Boivin and Garneau Galleries, both small places that specialized in certain genres of art, including in particular abstract paintings in the case of Boivin and sculpture in the case of Garneau. He telephoned the two smaller galleries to ask if they had any paintings by Richard Fenwick. Only Pierre Boivin, who introduced himself on the telephone as an impresario, said that they accepted paintings by Fenwick fairly often, pointing out that the gallery currently had three Fenwick products for sale. On the other hand, the director of Garneau Gallery pointed out, with slight pique, that his gallery was only interested in sculpture and therefore did not offer any paintings for sale.

George planned to stop by the Boivin Gallery after leaving work the following Monday, having been assured that it was open until six o'clock. He had decided that he would scrutinize each Fenwick painting available in the gallery looking for clues. Interestingly, he had never told anyone at JH Roberts of his continuing research into his father's painting. In fact, other than perhaps his mother, who may have understood her husband's artistic ambition, at least on her good days, and certainly his neighbour and friend Mike, with whom he discussed his father, no one knew. While that thought lingered in his mind, as it frequently did, he seldom pondered the absurdity of continuing to pursue his quest of discovering his father's hidden fascination. He figured that if he spent enough time staring at his father's paintings, perhaps he would understand whatever meaning his father intended with each painting, that is if he considered his paintings to have meanings at all. Most, if not all of the paintings that his father had hung in the house, at least the ones he recalled, envisaged a group of people, presumably a family but not always.

There was invariably a man, maybe a father, maybe an uncle, sometimes just a bystander. Most of the time, there was also at least one woman and some children although only the man was a constant. There were not any cityscapes, not any landscapes, not any wildlife, not any buildings, not anything even suggestive of the abstract, no niches other than paintings with people in them. But aside from that general analysis, George's impression was that he liked such paintings and stayed with that format regardless of any temptation his father may have had to paint in any other style.

With that in mind, George stopped by the Boivin Gallery on York Street in the so-called Byward Market, a few blocks north of the main street, Rideau Street. It was a small gallery, a store no larger than a restaurant that seated maybe thirty people. Mr. Boivin was a short rather portly man who advanced to the front of the gallery in a rather brisk pace. He greeted George with a wide grin, pumped his hand enthusiastically, and asked him about the kind of paintings in which he had an interest. George responded by mentioning that he telephoned the gallery several days ago to inquire about paintings by an artist named Richard Fenwick. "Sure, I remember your call. I told you we have three paintings by Mr. Fenwick, Would you like to take a look at them?" With that invitation, he swept his arm toward the rear wall.

There were six paintings surrounded by frames hanging on that wall, three of which were authored by his father. He felt a trifle strange looking at his father's work hanging in an actual art gallery. It made his father's paintings seem to be legitimate art, just like the ones he had been scrutinizing in the reference books in the two libraries he had recently visited. Each of the three of his father's paintings portrayed several people, including most particularly a middle aged man who looked a lot like his father. One of them showed the man sitting on a veranda at what George presumed to be a summer cottage. On the lawn below him was a group of children dressed in swimming attire playing with a beach ball. The middle aged man, who was apparently reading a newspaper, was dressed in a three piece suit. The other two paintings portrayed another solitary middle age man, waving, one looking straight forward and the other looking to his left. There was no one else in either picture. In both cases, the solitary man had a curious smile on his face, as if he was unsure of the purpose of his wave. He looked like he was either greeting someone or bidding farewell to someone. There was some sort of message in both pictures.

George wondered why his father would paint nearly identical scenes. It just seemed odd. He turned to Mr. Boivin and asked him about the two paintings. "What do you think those two paintings mean? I mean, why would any artist paint nearly identical scenes?" Mr. Boivin smiled and approached the paintings, smiled and looked back at George. "To be honest, I just don't know. Artists are always difficult to understand." He paused for a moment, a confused look on his face. He shrugged and then made a comment. "You should have a better idea than I do as to what was on his mind when he was painting those two pictures. After all, I thought you knew him." George then admitted that Richard Fenwick was his father. Understandably, Boivin expressed a certain surprise. "He's your father? He didn't share his work with you? You haven't seen that work before? The way you looked at them, it was obvious that you haven't see them before." George then continued with a narrative about how, for whatever reason, his father kept his painting secret from his family but shared it with a lot of other people, people he worked with, people he knew, people who ran art galleries, any person it seemed but his mother and his son. He also told Boivin that his father had been painting in a rented bachelor apartment for years, using it as an art studio. George admitted that while he did not know the origin of his father's artistic vocation, he was convinced that his father's calling as a painter was legitimate.

"Speaking as an art gallery owner," said Boivin, "I have to admit, regardless of why or how your father paints, he seems to know what he's doing." George smiled and returned Boivin's handshake which he had offered as he gazed at his father's paintings. "By the way, did you ever sell any of my father's paintings?" Boivin suddenly looked serious, like he was trying to remember, like he was contemplating something. George almost expected Mr. Boivin to excuse himself so he could start looking through his receipts to find any pertaining to his father's paintings. After several moments, Boivin finally became aware of the sales he made on behalf of Richard Fenwick. "Well, I think we have been representing your father for at least two years. Over that time, I think we might have sold maybe a dozen or so of his paintings. I recall that a few might have gone for at least $100." George nodded and asked how often his father brought paintings in for the Boivin Gallery for sale. "Well, he brought a painting every three months or so. As long as we had space in the gallery, we would hang his paintings on our walls. I think the three we have now is pretty well normal." George nodded and continued to wonder about whom the two solitary middle men in the paintings were waving. As for the man in the three piece suit and the kids in bathing suits, George had no idea. However, like the other paintings, George thought that there was a message in there somewhere.

<hr />

A week later, on another Monday, this time at noon, George visited the Desloges Gallery on Queen Street near Lyon. It was a larger gallery than the Boivin Gallery, maybe double its size. There were maybe more than fifty paintings hanging on bricks walls on the first floor and maybe two dozen paintings along with several sculptures on a second floor that began with stairs more than halfway down the length of the gallery. As far as the width of the gallery was concerned, it was sometimes difficult for three people to pass each other without twisting sideways. In fact, clientele sometimes gently collided with each other. A young man sitting at a small desk greeted George, rising to shake his hand and ask whether he had any preferences. George shook his hand, smiled and asked if the gallery had any Richard Fenwick paintings on display. The young man, who had introduced himself as Philip Nadeau, assured him that there were a number of Fenwick paintings hanging on the walls on the second floor. With that, he gestured toward the rear of the gallery and pointed to the stairs up to the second floor. "I know that we may have maybe eight of his paintings. And I think we've sold a couple of his paintings as well, at least over the past six months or so." George smiled, nodded and started to head toward the stairs. While he expected the Desloges Gallery to report that it was holding that a number of his father's paintings, he was disappointed that this gallery, which was obviously larger than the Boivin Gallery, had sold fewer paintings than the Boivin Gallery, bearing in mind that neither gallery had sold very many of his father's paintings.

As advised by Mr. Nadeau, there were eight Fenwick paintings hanging on the north wall, four above each other. He was alone, strange he thought because it was the noon hour and he expected at least one other art aficionado, maybe on the first floor. He stood maybe a foot from the paintings, then started to inspect them, noticing that his father's surname was ascribed in small, nearly indescribable letters in the lower right corner of each painting. For the first time he could recall, his father had autographed a painting. The picture was a portrait of a man, again a man who looked amazingly enough like his father, just like the three men in the paintings he had observed at the Boivin Gallery. He was sitting behind a large desk, apparently reading a document of some sort, head down, arms spread out to the edges of the desk, apparently concentrating. The next painting, which was to the right, had another of his father's dead ringer still sitting behind the desk, his arms still out to the edge of the desk, but his head facing forward, a blank expression on his face. The third painting had his father's lookalike still facing forward but smiling this time. The sequence continued with the fourth painting showing the desk now empty, its occupant gone, its destination unknown. All four paintings were autographed, although each signature was located in a different corner of the picture. All four paintings were identically sized and held in identical back frames. As surprised as George was with the four paintings themselves, he could hardly believe that Mr. Nadeau did not provide him with any hint of their idiosyncratic natures. He wanted to ask Nadeau whether the paintings were to be sold as a set.

He then looked down at the other four paintings. They each showed entirely different scenes although the man in all four paintings, although dressed differently, still looked like his father. Aside from ruminating about his father's obvious penchant for secretly painting, he also thought about the eccentricities in the paintings themselves, most particularly the placing of someone who looked an awful lot like himself in every scene he painted. To confirm his perplexity, which had been caused not only by the four newly identical paintings on the top row of his father's paintings but also by the bottom four paintings, which depicted four heads all facing away from the artist. Each head showed less hair but was otherwise identical. He was not, however, familiar with the back of his father's head and therefore was in no position to compare to the top row of paintings. He did realize, of course, that he may have been jumping to conclusions, as strange as they were. What was his father trying to suggest with his paintings? What did they mean? Did they mean anything?

The Temple Gallery, the city's largest art gallery, was located on Sussex Drive across Clarence Street from the Notre-Dame Cathedral. It was a three floor building that was fronted by two full length windows on the first floor and several small windows on the two other floors. The building itself was constructed in the 1850s and was supposedly intended as a seminary for Catholic priests and a rectory for the priests attending to the Cathedral. According to Jordan Morris, the gallery host, the building was sold when Saint Paul's University was enlarged to accommodate seminarians. The building was then purchased by a man named Maurice Provost, who owned a number of buildings in the Byward Market, lived in the Rockcliffe Park, was well known in Ottawa social circles and collected artwork. So in 1910, when he purchased the building from the Archdiocese Parish, he turned it into an art gallery, the first in the city. He named the Temple Gallery further to a suggestion from Archbishop Purcell of the Notre-Dame Cathedral. At first, Mr. Provost filled it with some of the items from his own art collection but over the next decade or so, he was able to fill all three floors of the building with a variety of objet d'arts, everything from paintings and sculptures to Russian icons and glass figurines.

On entering the Temple Gallery, George asked his host Morris if he had any paintings by Richard Fenwick. It was as if Morris had anticipated George's request. He immediately responded by mentioning, in a casual way, that they had more than a few Fenwick paintings, which were being shown on the first and second floors. George was understandably astounded, having already thought that the eight paintings by his father that were on display in the Desloges Gallery was significant. It meant he guessed that there were a lot of his father's paintings currently on sale in the city's galleries. The realization suggested to George that his father's painting was more than was just a hobby. He also wondered how his father managed to paint so prolifically while holding a senior position with the Under-Secretary of State. When did he have the time he thought to spend so much time in his artist's loft? While he remembered that his father did seem to spend a fair amount of time at work, he just didn't think that he would have enough the time to produce the number of paintings he appeared to have produced. Of course, he did not know how long he had been painting to produce such a significant inventory. In addition, George had no idea how many other paintings he had sitting in the closet of his artist's loft, not available for sale in three of the four galleries in the city. He also wondered whether his father's paintings were available for sale in Montreal which could have had ten galleries, including he understood the largest gallery in the country.

As George considered the enormity of his father's evident success, looking at the multitude of paintings on the walls of the first floor of the gallery, he wondered how many of them were authored by his father, he turned back to Jordan Morris and asked him to direct him to the Richard Fenwick section, that is if there was such a section. Morris said that the Fenwick paintings were grouped into two segments, one on the first floor and the other on the second. He also volunteered that although a good number of his his father's paintings were somewhat unorthodox, they sold fairly well, particularly for a local artist. He also commented that his father had been bringing in his paintings for several years.

George thanked Mr. Morris and started up the stairs to the second floor, his plan to appreciate the paintings on the second floor before the first floor paintings, which he thought would be superior somehow. He then paused for a moment and turned back to Morris to ask a question that had been mystifying him since he first saw his father's paintings at the two galleries he had already visited. Did either Mr. Boivin or Mr. Nadeau think that any of the men whose faces appeared in any of the paintings that were on display at either of their two galleries looked look like the artist that created them? He wanted to suggest that his father was actually painting his own face into his paintings, a Van Gogh approach as bizarre as that seemed. But he didn't ask, leaving the idea that his father was in his own paintings a possible figment of his imagination. By the time he arrived on the second floor, the thought had faded for the most part. He went to the north wall toward the front of the store, where Morris told him a segment of his father's paintings were on display.

The second floor segment of the Richard Fenwick paintings was a series of paintings of what George was pretty sure were certain streets of the city of Ottawa, a fellow patron who was also looking at his father's paintings had casually made the same whispered observation to him. On the streets, which were varied, from Montreal Road in the Eastview district to the comparatively desolate area around Lansdowne Park, where pedestrians, all four of them included a man whose face looked like the face of his father. The other patron was a older man who was holding a valise in his right hand and staring as George was at the row of the Fenwick paintings of Ottawa city streets. Both he and George stood there for more than five minutes, transfixed. The other art enthusiast leaned closer and whispered to George, "Each one of these paintings picture a lot of people, men, women and children, but are individual, a man in different clothes in each painting, sometimes with a hat, sometimes without, each one seemingly with a different expression on his face, looks like they could be the same man." George felt a little anxious for a moment and agreed with the man. George had mumbled his agreement and watched his fellow Temple Gallery patron walk toward the stairs and the first floor. For a brief moment, George wondered whether the other would be art connoisseur shared his own suspicion that his father had an apparent strange and unusual artistic preoccupation. Of course, George did not mention that he knew that the artist, the name Fenwick having been scribbled in the right bottom corner, was his father.

George stood for a few minutes, pondering whether he was becoming haunted by the continuing spectre of his father's face, before he headed down to the first floor where he hoped for a little variety in subject but pessimistically expected more Ottawa street scenes. He passed Morris on his way to the rear of the first floor where the Fenwick paintings were hung. He nodded. Morris smiled. There were at least twenty visitors on the first floor, most of them crowded around a painting by AY Jackson of the recently founded Group of Seven, obviously a celebrated artist. It was a World War I landscape entitled "House of Ypres". Mr. Jackson was a Canadian painter who had become quite acclaimed and therefore was able to sell paintings at most art galleries in the country. The Jackson painting was for sale by the Temple Gallery, explaining the crowd around the painting. Its price was unknown although judging by the $90 posted price of his father's paintings, at least the ones on the second floor, suggesting that the price for the "House of Yves" was much higher. In any event, George stood by the edge of the crowd for a moment and then went on to the other Richard Fenwick segment on display in the Temple Gallery.

He came across the Fenwick paintings. Unlike the street scenes of his paintings on display on the second floor, the four paintings on the first floor resembled the similar style he had exhibited in the Desloges Gallery. The paintings presented nearly identical renderings of the family home in New Edinburgh. It displayed four portraits of the front of the family home, each with four windows, two on the first floor and two on the second. Each painting showed the house with each of the four windows displayed differently. One of the windows was empty while the other three windows showed what appeared to be his father's face, his unsmiling and stern countenance in the centre of the window on the west side of the top floor of the house; the face of his smiling mother, appearing for the first in any of the paintings, in the window just below the window in which his father's face appeared; and then, in the bottom window, both the father and mother apparently waving to someone or something on the street in front of the house. George stood transfixed for a moment as he recollected or imagined a memory in which sometimes his father and most times his mother would wave farewell to him as he left for school most days.

He had wondered whether his father had been inspired to paint those houses by actual or imagined events. So muddled was George's consideration of the house paintings in particular that he decided, as he stood on the first floor of the Temple Gallery, to purchase the fourth painting in which portraits of his father and mother were shown waving from the window on the ground floor. It cost him $80, a sum that George thought a trifle exorbitant but his obsession about his father's evident obsession was such that he dismissed any reluctance he may have made. He would investigate his father's painting further. He didn't know on what basis he would do so. In any event, it might be the last time.

THE DELANEYS GET MAIL

---◆---

They decided to move after the birth of their son Tyler in April. While they were generally happy with apartment 302 in Parkdale Court, even with the imminent arrival of their first child, an unexpected event that Patricia announced one night after she suggested that she move in with him. Surprisingly, at least to Patricia, John was pleased with the news, hardly concerned at all with the possibility that he was about to take on a responsibility that he spent his adult years so far evading. In fact, within minutes, he was asking Patricia for her opinion on whether they should get married before the baby arrived, in at least six months according to her. Patricia reacted to John's query, as unexpected as it was, by leaning across the kitchen table and suggesting that they might want to wait until the baby is born. John then asked whether she had told her mother.

Patricia answered enthusiastically. "Oh, she was very happy with the news. The idea of being a grandmother got her so excited that she could barely talk for a couple of minutes. Then she started making plans. She even offered to help us with the down payment on a house, even though I had told her that we had no plans to get married, at least not until after the baby is born, then said we may talk about it. After that, she said she had to start calling the relatives although she admitted that some of them disapprove of having a child out of wedlock." She then rolled here eyes. John remarked, "Yeah, but all of them wear nothing but black dresses that fall to the floor." Patricia gave John a look and then quietly noted, "Don't forget, most of them are elderly and old fashioned as hell." She then tried to introduce a balance to the conversation after John suggested that it might make family gatherings a little uncomfortable. "They will probably forget about it after they see the baby. I remember how my mother told me that my grandmother, her mother, wanted to throw my aunt out of the family after she had a baby girl before she married my uncle. But as soon as she saw the baby, she completely changed her attitude." Neither Patricia nor John brought up his parents, both of whom hadn't spoken to their son for over a year, the consequence of the two of them having spotted the expecting parents leaving Parkdale Court at eight in the morning.

They then started to discuss the possibility of moving to a place that didn't involve carrying a baby, a baby carriage and groceries up three flights of marble stairs. They also began to discuss purchasing a car, the second requirement necessitated by the arrival of a newborn. On the latter, John reminded Patricia of the size of the underground garage in Parkdale Court, pointing out for maybe the hundredth time it seemed that since the apartment was built in 1936, there were only ten parking places available for tenants, meaning of course that if they were to purchase a car, they would have to find someplace to park the car. Patricia said that there always seemed to be places to park on Powell Avenue, that is if you were able to arrive before nine in the evening. John was unhappy with the prospect, proposing that he could speak to superintendent Casey about whether any parking spaces would become available in the spring or the summer, the baby expected sometime in mid-to-late April. They both decided to postpone making any moves until the arrival of their firstborn become a little more imminent. Besides, Patricia would have to convince her mother to lend them enough money to first buy a car and then arrange to move to a larger place. Presumably she said the birth would doubtless motivate her mother to help them out.

As far as John's parents were concerned, they could forget about receiving anything from them. John said that maybe the arrival of the baby would prompt his father, who was less opposed to their status than his mother, who had been ready to disown him, to contribute to their situation. If Patricia's mother gave them any money, John said that his father, whose name was Norman, would likely give them something, provided that his wife, John's mother Marjorie, never found out. Patricia hesitated, hopefully theorizing that his mother would have not keep up her acrimony regarding their liaison forever. She said that her best friend, Cynthia, had a mother who didn't speak to her for over five years because her husband spoke to her harshly at a Thanksgiving dinner. Neither of them could ever explain her mother's anger. Nonetheless, Cynthia's mother eventually abandoned her animosity because, at least according to her brother who was still in the good books with his mother, the mother was so impressed with Cynthia and her husband's new house that she completely changed her attitude. Neither Cynthia nor her husband could ever explain it.

⟢─◦─⟣

It was a maybe a month after Patricia told John about the impending birth that he received the photograph in the mailbox. It was the size of a small index card, small enough to be slipped through a grill of the mailbox without requiring a key. It was black and white photograph of the street shot from Parkdale Court toward Bank Street south. It was curious, almost magical. John had not found a photograph anywhere in the apartment for months, let alone one delivered via the lobby mailbox. In fact, John could not remember finding any photograph since Patricia moved in with him although she was acquainted with the couple of photographs that he had found and then showed her when she had started to stay the night At the time, she had counselled him to be cautious around the apartment, tentatively suggesting that perhaps the door to his apartment was easily opened. Similarly, John thought of some of his neighbours who might have been responsible for this macabre prank. He immediately conjured up a reflection of the Quinn couple. They were somewhat eccentric, more like whimsical than anything else. Harry impersonated Mr. Peanut and Florence liked to dance in the corridor of the third floor, not to mention of the living room of apartment 307. On the other hand, perhaps the photograph in the mailbox, especially the subject matter of the photograph, was hardly symptomatic of something ominous.

Although he thought about it frequently, he would not share the most recent picture receipt, as unsettling as it was, with Patricia. He was worried that she would allow her previous paranoia, if that's what it was, to escalate, a situation that would be uncomfortable. He recalled his aunt, his father's sister Helen, scaring the hell of the nephews and nieces with her stories about ghosts that she said she was convinced were inhabiting the attic of their house. Her husband, who was hardly fascinated with the concept of sceptres inhabiting any room in the house, avoided the subject anytime his wife brought it up. His reaction, if he was compelled to have one, was to usually commiserate with Helen, pretending to listening to her and her apparent lunacy. Over time, with an almost continual decline in her references to the possibility of the house being inhabited by ghosts, the issue eventually disappeared. So John decided that he would keep the mailbox photograph to himself. He pondered the possibility of receiving further photographs, worrying that Patricia would find any future photographs since it was now apparent that they were being left not in the apartment but dropped into the apartment's mailbox in the lobby. He thought about arranging to have their mail delivered to a box in the post office but he would have to explain the change to Patricia, which he could not do. Consequently, he decided that he would adjust his work schedule to allow him to arrive home earlier than Patricia, whose hours at the pharmacy had her arriving home at around five thirty. On the other hand, John usually got home around five o'clock although he decided that he would leave work twenty minutes earlier to ensure that Patricia would not be in a position to pick up the mail before he did.

It had to be over three months before the apartment received another photograph. Before the second photograph arrived, it occurred to John that it was unlikely that the photograph was delivered by the postman ---- after all, there was no address, no stamp, nothing to indicate that the photograph was actually mailed. It was obvious that whoever sent the photograph walked into the lobby of the Parkdale Court and slipped it into the mailbox for apartment 302. It was another black and white photograph of the street shot from Parkdale Court. However, this picture showed a shot from the Parkdale Court headed toward north rather than south, towards downtown, the opposite direction from the previous picture. In addition, despite the fact that the photograph showed the Bank Street in an opposite direction, it also showed a man on the east side of the street also facing downtown. John scrutinized the photograph, musing on the intention of showing the man. Did it mean anything? Was there a point? He thought about it for a couple of minutes but could not fathom anything that made any sense.

Later that evening, after Patricia had gone to bed, he compared the two photographs with a magnifying glass on the kitchen table. Aside from the man facing different directions, there were at least three differences that he noticed. In the earlier photograph, on the other side of the street from the man, on the west side, there were four dark coloured cars --- it was a black and white picture ---- while in the second paragraph, there were four light coloured cars. The second discrepancy was the appearance in the first photograph of the number three on the bus stop on the heading north on the corner of Bank and Pretoria Streets. In the second photograph, there was no number on the bus stop. While there were bicycles in both photographs, the first picture had the bicycles heading south while the second picture had the bicycle heading north. Again, like the two other comparisons, John had no idea as to the meaning of the differences between the two photographs. Having ruminated about those differences until maybe midnight, he went to bed without having come to any conclusions. Unlike the pictures that he had previously found in his apartment, the similarity of the pictures that he had found in the apartment mailbox with the actual scenes they had photographed to exhibit was simply too strange to forget. Although he was disappointed that he could not figure out what was going on with the two photographs, another major concern was to ensure that Patricia never came across the two photographs.

He kept the two photographs in the bottom drawer of his dresser underneath his unpublished manuscripts, stories that he had written and collected since he was in college which, for the most part a pointless exercise in drugs, rock music and a collection of English literature courses, and the other two family pictures that he had found in the apartment before Patricia moved in, buried and forgotten. He recalled telling Patricia about the photographs when she first found them but he was now certain that she had forgotten all about them. However, he was equally certain that she wouldn't forget about the two recent photographs or at least not forget about them in any hurry. So he hid them. While he placing the photographs under the manuscripts --- there were dozens it appeared ---- he started to leaf through them. At the bottom of the pile, he found several stories that he wrote in his last year of college, some of which were intended as entertainment for a group of girls with whom he was occasionally had intentions. He specifically remembered that one of the stories, coincidentally entitled *Mistaking Penny*, was unfinished, prompting him to consider completing it. Consequently, he pulled it out of the pile, deciding that he would first have to read the story before figuring out how to finish it. He then decided that he would select a few stories from the collection in the bottom drawer, including a lengthy narrative that was, more often than not like a diary or a journal than a short story or even a novel.

He recalled that back then, maybe once a week or so, he would produce a recent narrative, much of which was based almost entirely on the group's activities. John had been remarkably content with the enthusiasm that his friends showed pretty well every time he shared his narratives with them. They realized that John often embellished his stories, allowing them to drift into fiction, not always but frequently enough to add a certain panache to his readings. There was another characteristic of the literary presentations that was a dilemma for John. Fact was that his audience for his narrations was limited to a group of ladies. Some of his male friends and even some of his male acquaintances were aware of John's literary pursuits. They did not approve of his writing, most of them thinking that he wrote simply to attract women which may have been true, jealousy a possibility.

In any event, John had kept the stories for reasons that he could not quite explain and now he had come across them again. Now that he had rediscovered them, the memories returned.

He sat there. He counted eleven stories, three or four of which were unfinished. Unlike his journal/diary stories, most of the recently detected stories were entirely fictional, genres like straight drama, crime, fable, fantasy, romance, satire, science fiction, and even comedy which John entitled *Entertainments*. The discovery of the previous stories, not to mention his dairy entries, prompted John to seriously consider resuming his writing career which he had been pondering for a while. The thought usually came to him during twilight time, just before he fell asleep, but now, with a number of stories for source material, he could reinvigorate his literary career without much difficulty. As far as his future projects were concerned, he started to realized that he could use his experiences as a series of memoirs, short stories that could cover all sorts of youthful activities, from elementary school misbehaviour through high school to university hi-jinks.It was almost three o'clock on Wednesday morning when he realized that he had been reviewing his previous literary attempts for almost four hours. He collected the stories, shuffled them into a half of dozen file folders and placed them in the bottom drawer of the dresser, underneath dozens of pairs of socks. John then took the pictures and placed them in his battered briefcase, which had been standing in the closet by the front door of the apartment. He hadn't forgotten his worry about Patricia discovering the photographs. While the bottom drawer still seemed an appropriate place to hide, he was still concerned.

⟶⟩⟨⟵

The next day at work, he had had a difficult time staying awake, having not slept much the previous night, he told Patricia about the previously written manuscripts he had found in his dresser. She was momentarily pleased, recalling how enthusiastic John used to be about writing, at least according to the conversations they used to have when they first met. It was then when they used to discuss their ambitions, she at one time having dreamt of being a doctor while he claimed to have wanted to be a writer. When they first started seeing each other, John would occasionally share with Patricia a short story, a poem, even a play, all of which was intended to impress her. When Patricia moved in with John, he told Patricia that he had no intention of allowing his ambition of writing to disrupt their daily routine. He tried to complete a page of prose a day, some of which was written during his workday, his clerical position offering him so little challenge that John could have worked the job asleep. Since a fair amount of his writing was actually achieved at home, Patricia could not help but take notice of his efforts. Accordingly, she would sometimes encourage John to consider submitting his literary efforts to publishers.

John was initially intimidated by the process of submitting his work to publishers. The process was laborious. He had to type the stories on a creaky old Underwood that his mother had purchased from the classified ads for his first year at university, a year which he had failed spectacularly, and then photocopy the pages, usually on the machine in the office. The latter took a fair amount of time, particularly since he had to do his photocopying surreptitiously, at the machine that stood between his section's two secretaries. John was worried that one or maybe both of them would bring his unauthorized photocopying to the attention of somebody in authority. He was worried that being caught would terminate his photocopying and maybe his job. He was forced to pursue his secretarial efforts when the ladies went to lunch or left for the day. He had gone to the department's library in order to research book publishers. He didn't know which publisher or publishers to chose, an important consideration since he planned to limit the submission of his manuscript to three publishers.

When he showed the list to Patricia, who had not been consulted about his plans to submit anything to anyone, she suggested that he submit his work to a literary agent, who would be in a better, a much better position to assess the viability of his literary efforts than simply submitting his work to random publishers in New York, which evidently was by far the most prominent centre for book publishing in North America. It made sense to John who asked Patricia to help him with a recommendation. She replied by asking John to bring her a a list of literary agents and she would make a recommendation. She said that her guidance would be to select agents whose offices were located somewhere in New York or even Toronto. The next day, Patricia was handed two lists, one showing six New York agents and the other with three Toronto agents. Patricia sat in the living room with the two lists spread out on the coffee table and made her selections: representing New York, McGovern Agency of Fifth Avenue and Hickman Inc of Broadway Avenue and representing Toronto, Beverley Agency of Bloor Street. She advised John to compose a compelling query letter in order to introduce his collection, having decided to include eight short stories to all three agents: two straight forward dramas, two fantasy satires, a semi-fairly tale, a science fiction story, a mystery story and a thriller. John was prepared to follow her instructions to the letter, even offering to have Patricia edit his work, a task that Patricia previously regarded as beyond her capability ------ after all, he was the writer. They both agreed that the query letters and his submissions would be mailed within the month. That evening, they had spectacular sex, even better that normal. John imagined the best for his efforts. He was expecting some sort of success. He seemed to have no doubt. Patricia didn't say anything.

Having chosen the stories, the literary agents and the method of submission, John actually managed to construct a schedule, that he seriously hoped he would follow faithfully. When he presented the schedule to Patricia, she feigned being impressed, familiar with his behaviour long enough to predict his ability to follow up on his pledges, including every resolution he had made since she had met him three years ago. She had initially intended to encourage John to continue to write, acknowledging that the organization of his submissions to the three literary agents was a fair amount of effort. But she limited her comments to asking him every couple of days about the progress of his submissions. Within three weeks of sending out his submissions, which took more than a month to assemble and mail, he received a letter from a Mr. Rice of the Beverley Agency in Toronto, informing him that the firm was not accepting any new submissions for publication at this time and was not anticipating any new submission for publication for at least six months, adding however that his stories would be kept on file and possibly considered for review. He told Patricia who consoled him by noting that to be honest, she had not expected the Beverley Agency to respond to him. In other words, she said that he should be hopeful.

By the time John received the first response to his three submissions, Patricia was five months pregnant. They had decided that they would not consider moving to a larger place, preferably one which featured at least a front lawn and maybe a back yard, until the baby was born. She was having difficulty in sorting out her maternal benefits. Her employer, Johnson Pharmacy, did not have an obligation to provide her with any maternal benefits, her only available assistance being unemployment insurance, a government benefit with which John but not Patricia had had some experience. Over the past several years, two or three years during which he drifted from lousy job to lousy job, he had managed to qualify for UIC several times, until he lost his benefits for not being able to prove that he was looking for gainful employment. A week later, he was hired to clean offices, a position that he held for less than a month, after which he started at the bottom of the heath department, a temporary clerical job that required him to distribute mail to several of the floors of the Jeanne Mance Building. From there, he was able to climb up the bureaucratic ladder to his current position as a CR-3, the qualification being a high school education and a semi-affable disposition.

In any event, Patricia was happy to benefit from John's advice. She was told by an official down at the UIC, which she had visited on Carling Avenue, that she would be receiving benefits equal to 40 percent of her regular pay for a period of three months. She therefore would be receiving $80 a week, an eventuality that concerned John who began to actually consider getting a second job. When he raised the possibility with Patricia, she pointed out that although she would have help with the baby from her mother and she would have three months of unemployment benefits, they would still need some financial help. As usual, the discussion almost developed into an argument, which invariably resulted in John either surrendering or spending a night on the sofa in the living room. Having escaped domestic detention, he was laying in bed that night wondering about their future when he remembered a conversation he overheard in the cafeteria three days ago. The tax department, the main office down at Bronson and Baseline, was hiring for tax time, specifically from March to May. He discovered that clerks were being hired for the evening shift, from six to eleven o'clock, five weekday evenings, at four dollars an hour, processing tax returns. The job sounded relatively easy, the catch being that an inability to maintain a certain quota, which continually increased, would led to immediate dismissal.

After informing Patricia, who expressed a certain sympathy but agreed wholeheartedly with his decision to apply, provided he was prepared to leave the job once the baby arrived, John went down to the tax office, which he understood was open to seven o'clock in the evening to take applications for part time work. There was a lineup going out to Bronson north, college kids mostly, more girls than guys, with the occasional jobless and even miscreant around John's age or older mixed in. For one unfathomable reason, aside from taking note of the college girls in the lineup, he wondered about whether there were others of John's situation looking for a part time work, that is, other people with jobs looking to supplement their income. A week after he submitted his application, he received a telephone call at work from a woman who introduced herself as a clerical supervisor named Cynthia. She told him to report to the tax office at quarter to six the following Monday. It was the second week of March.

The following Tuesday, he was ushered into a room the size of a small gymnasium where he sat between an older, moody looking guy with a Van Dyke beard and an attractive college girl named Carole about whom he developed an immediate infatuation. Within a week, he was conducting a remarkably caste affair with Carole, who seemed to John to be not only too beautiful for the office but was probably too smart for the office as well. Although he seemed to speak to her practically every day, their relationship never went beyond a platonic origin. They never discussed it although he suspected that Carole's affection for him was never to the same degree as his for her. He thought about her constantly but it never came to anything. It was a fantasy in reality he thought. Amazingly enough, his thoughts about Carole never had any effect on his relationship with Patricia. Over time, after he left the tax department job, his thoughts about Carole never had much of an effect on himself either.

It was late April. John had been working the two jobs for more than two months. The baby was due within weeks when John reluctantly resigned from his part time position at the tax department. It was time he told Patricia who was both pleased and relieved at the same time. Patricia had a week until she was to go on her maternity leave and was having difficulty doing her job, even though her colleagues were doing everything they could to help her with her duties. Fact was that she was doing little more than sitting behind the pharmacist counter in a comfortable chair. It was a miracle of irony. Her last day was a day prior to John's departure from his job at the tax department.

⋙➤-◦-⊰⋘

It was the Monday after her last day at the pharmacy and his last evening working in the tax department. He was standing in the lobby of Parkdale Court a little after five in the afternoon, his earliest arrival home in more than two months. He opened the mailbox and removed a Bell Canada envelope, doubtless the telephone bill, an advertisement from a local sporting goods store, and a black and white photograph. It was the third of the photographs that had been found in the mailbox over the past several months. The background scene was identical to the backdrops of those two photographs: looking several blocks north up Bank Street from Parkdale Court. In the foreground were two different forms, a woman pushing a baby carriage north on the west side of the street, at the corner of Bank and Pretoria, and a woman shown from the rear on the east side of the street, also heading north, also at the corner of Bank and Pretoria. The woman pushing the carriage looked to be at least as tall as John and with dark coloured hair while the woman on the other side of the street looked to be shorter, also with dark coloured hair. He was tempted to share the photograph with Patricia but, like the previous two photographs that were left in the mailbox in the lobby of Parkdale Court, it was to be concealed in the bottom drawer of his nightstand. It would be difficult to identify either woman since both were photographed from the rear.

That Tuesday, after dinner and a couple of hours of television, Patricia wet to bed, John returned to the spare room and the dresser where the hidden photographs were kept. With the magnifying glass, he scanned the photograph as if he were studying a chess board. It must have been maybe fifteen minutes before his frustration evaporated his intention to solve the mystery of the latest photograph to be left in their mailbox. He pushed the drawer closed. He left the spare room, went to the refrigerator for a beer, and sat down in the living room after turning on the television. He started to watch a hockey game. He wasn't paying attention to the game itself, speculation, if not fantasizing about the two woman in the most recent photographic puzzle, now his main objective. It took him most of the third period to come to a conclusion that seemed surreal. Still, he took them out of the drawer to examine the picture for a thousandth time, wanting to be sure that he hadn't imagined them. The two women in the most recent picture could be Patricia and Carole, John now thought. It was the photographer's most recent ploy, if that's what it could be. A ploy, a stratagem, a trick he thought, a thesaurus of similar descriptions went thought his mind. Maybe he was being misled, misled all along. By himself.

———◆———

Tyler was born the next afternoon. Although it had become quite the trend for expectant fathers, John did not accompany Patricia to the delivery room while she was giving birth. Both new parents agreed. Patricia did not want John, or anyone else for that matter, to witness her in the most unbecoming pose possible. As for John, he did not understand the interest that new fathers had in in watching new mothers struggle in the most unappealing way to give birth. Although he might deny it, he secretly preferred the traditional practice of having new fathers nervously pretending to relax in the waiting room, cigars in their pockets, occasionally pacing, discussing their expectations with total strangers, and anxiously waiting for a report from a nurse or an obstetrician. He had taken the day off when Patricia entered the hospital, his colleagues at the work seemingly as expectant as John was. As for the Patricia's co-workers, three of them dropped by the waiting room of the maternity department of the Civic Hospital although they did not stay to see Tyler Richard, who was registered in City Hall as Tyler Richard Monette, Patricia's family name. Tyler Richard Monette would have his name changed within months, Patricia's opinion that Delaney was a more pleasant family name and a more appropriate name once they were married.

Patricia's mother was overjoyed, spending much of her time --- she was retired --- helping the new parents, not only with the daily chores related to the baby but financially as much as she could. About possibly moving to a new place, while John thought that a family needed a lawn and a backyard, much of his childhood having been spent in a suburban bungalow, Patricia was not particularly enthusiastic, their dreadful economic situation her main rationale. She counselled caution, repeatedly pointing out that even if her mother was willing to contribute anything, it was unlikely that they could afford a decent place with a lawn and a backyard. Fact was that the less expensive and available houses were understandably located in less attractive neighbourhoods, at least according to Patricia. Further, again according to Patricia, moving to any such neighbourhood would make the purchase of a car necessary. That would place a further financial burden on the new parents. Patricia then raised the possibility, however unlikely, of John contacting his parents. He said that he couldn't imagine it. They then both reluctantly agreed that they would have to forego both moving and purchasing a car. They further agreed that would have to wait until at least the fall when Tyler was six months old.

———————⟶⊱⊙⊰⟵———————

Patricia went to back to work when her unemployment benefits ran out. Although they had a few more bucks coming in, they also had a few more bucks going out: baby clothes and bedding, a portable crib that the new parents took delight in wheeling around the apartment, a second hand carriage in which Tyler travelled around the neighbourhood, the main difficulty being carrying the carriage up and down the stairs to and from the third floor in Parkdale Court, and the babysitter, a middle age woman who lived on Powell Avenue and looked after Tyler and several others during the day. For the occasional evening out, they retained an old lady who looked like the Wicked Witch of the West from the *Wizard of Oz*. Even with a little help from Patricia's mother, they were always short of funds. They spoke frequently of restoring John's relationship with his parents. Aside from the thought that a reconciliation with his parents would be a good thing for the the family, now that they actually had one, the promise of John's parents helping them out financially seemed far fetched. John promised Patricia that he would think about it, his primary objective to break the news that his parents were now grandparents. He was already considering contacting his father at his place of business, Eaton's Department Store in the Bayshore Shopping Centre where he was the manager. John had long told Patricia that his father was much more compromising than his mother when it came to moral or religious issues, like having a child out of wedlock.

Despite John's parents' misgivings, several of their neighbours were more than generous, leaving cards, little gifts for the baby, and cookies either in their mailbox or on the stoop of their apartment. Notes were attached to some of them, people with whom they barely or not acquainted, people on the first or second second floors although, strangely enough, no one from the third floor. Although they did not have expected it, apartment manager Casey and his wife did not acknowledge the apartment's newest tenant either. Enclosed in a plain, parchment envelope, slipped under the door was a faded black and white photograph of an infant boy dressed in a vintage baptismal outfit. The boy was sitting on a bench in a park that looked a lot like the park that had been pictured in the framed photograph that had been left on the ledge above the decorative fireplace in the empty apartment when John moved into it. It could easily have been the same vintage. Neither the photo nor the envelope were signed. For a moment, John thought that it should have been signed by the previous resident of apartment 302, the late Hector Dennison. He mentioned his imaginary musing to Patricia who shrugged, thinking that John's rumination was indicative of his curious fantasy about the two pictures that she knew he had found in the apartment and shared with her. That didn't include the newspaper fragment that was found under the leg of a chair in the apartment after a party in their place. John finally concluded that it had been left by a third floor neighbour.

After going through the cards and the gifts, again assuming that most of the benefactors were tenants in Parkdale Court, neither he nor Patricia were familiar with most of them. They were surprised, if not fascinated with the evident generosity of their barely known neighbours. In addition, like they had with the photographs that John had found when he moved into the apartment, they were momentarily perplexed although they eventually theorized that perhaps the photograph of the unidentified little boy in the park was donated by the same party that may have had something to do with the newspaper fragment regarding the suicide of George Fenwick and the other two photographs.

Contemplation of the photographs, however, was a relatively minor part of their days. Both John and Patricia awoke around six on work mornings, usually after Tyler was up for the third or fourth time after being "put down" sometime after dinner time. First, Tyler was fed and then dressed, John and Patricia dressed themselves for work, both ate a quick breakfast, and then watched a little morning news on the television. About fifteen minutes before seven, Patricia walked south down Bank Street to Glebe Avenue, took the bus west to Carling Avenue, and then another bus down Carling Avenue to the Carlingwood Mall where she worked in the pharmacy there. Fifteen minutes later, now around seven, John placed Tyler in the carriage, started down the stairs to the the front door of the apartment building, and started south for one block to take Tyler to babysitter Ethel Baker's small house on Powell Avenue. Mrs. Baker was a rather pudgy woman in her late fifties with short silver hair and a selection of house dresses that John's mother used to call "dusters", fashion statements that were usually reserved to women who cleaned houses. She also looked after two other children, four and two year old boys named Ronald and Stephen respectively, who were accompanied by their mother, Grace Little, a young woman who, like John, worked somewhere in the government. The two Little boys usually arrived about fifteen minutes after John and Tyler arrived. Mrs. Baker liked pointless conversation, meaning that John occasionally had difficulty extracting himself so he could catch the number six bus heading north on Bank Street. He would arrive downtown to Bank and Wellington, take another bus along Queen and Scott Streets, and then either another bus ride or a long walk to the Jeanne Mance Building to the area called Tunney's Pasture. John worked on the fifteenth floor where Patricia used to work as well.

The end of the day was just as hectic. Patricia was responsible for picking Tyler up from Mrs. Baker's house at little after five, which was the latter's deadline, and that was generally fairly loose. Mrs. Little's boys were usually gone by then and Mrs. Baker was almost always looking forward to her favourite television show, *The Price Is Right*. If Patricia was late picking Tyler up, Mrs. Baker invariably got annoyed and the two of them would be worried that their arrangement, which John and Patricia felt quite fortunate to have, would possibly be under threat. As good as she was with young children, particularly Tyler, she also had a quick temper, which seemed a peculiar personality trait for a woman who looked after children. Patricia remembered Mrs. Baker informing her, when she agreed to take care Tyler during the day, that she didn't allow people to take advantage of her, admitting that the parents of one of her previous charges left owing her three weeks of fees. Anyway, Patricia or John, if Patricia knew she was going to be late and had to enlist John to leave work early, took care to arrive to pick up Tyler on time.

It only took them two months before Patricia suggested that buying an automobile was pretty well necessary for them, for John in particular who continually complained to Patricia about how much time the both of them were spending on bus rides to and from work every day. So the following Saturday, after spending Friday evening in a local restaurant discussing the purchase of a car, they took a couple buses to visit several car dealerships on Richmond Road. There were at least three dealerships within a block or so of the corner of Richmond Road and Woodroffe Avenue that they saw advertised in the *Ottawa Citizen*. They also seemed to have a large selection of used cards, all three advertisements showing lists of used cars for sale. The first dealership was called *Richmond Road Chevrolet* and aside from new Chevrolets, they had a large lot full of a variety of used cars, prominently General Motors models, principally Chevrolets but also Pontiacs and Oldsmobiles for sale. .

Standing in the *Richmond Road Chevrolet* lot, John and Patricia were immediately approached by a man who introduced himself as Desmond Nasseh, a relatively stout man in his late thirties who seemed to be unable to restrain himself from constantly talking. His sales pitch, which seemed to consist mainly of explaining his history of buying cars, concluded by recommending that they consider one of the many compacts they had on the lot, mentioning that two cars, a 1974 Chevy Nova and a 1972 Pontiac Astre, just came in and were particularly attractive buys. For a minute or so, John and Patricia looked at each other a little dumbfounded and said that they would have to do a little browsing. Mr. Nasseh retreated, put his hands up in supplication and told them that he would be in the office if they needed any help. For the next fifteen minutes or so, the two of them wandered around the lot looking at cars. Fortunately, the price, which they had heard was always negotiable, was affixed on each car's windshield. Both of them were completely confused, their preference for any car based entirely on its appearance, they realized that they were wasting their time. So they left the lot and walked further down Richmond Road to the next dealership, *Ottawa Ford*.

They were there for several minutes, unbothered by either of the three salesmen that were sitting at their desks in the showroom. It seemed strange since the two of them were casually inspecting the used cars that were parked by the front windows and should have been seen by one if not all of the salesmen inside the building. John and Patricia were therefore free to roam about the lot on their own. John was inexplicably attracted to a 1975 AMC Pacer, an absurdly designed compact automobile that only lasted five years before the management at American Motors decided that they could no longer expose the Pacer to the ridicule it was attracting. Patricia was waved over by John to show her the grey Pacer that was priced at $2,500, as indicated in a large sign on the windshield, suggesting in a surprisingly excited voice that he wanted purchase the car. "I know it looks weird but I think it is a great car and at a pretty good price, at least for us." Patricia looked at John as if he needed medication and observed. "You have to be kidding. I mean, this vehicle looks like it was built to be driven on the moon. I'd be embarrassed to drive this thing. You have to admit, it looks like like a fishbowl." John looked like he was expecting her comments."Look I know but I've read some pretty good things about the car and I think we should buy it."

Patricia, who had been looking at a used Mazda, a black sporty number that was $500 more than the Pacer, immediately disagreed with John's choice and began to push for the Mazda. John walked over to the Mazda and pointed out that the car had a manual transmission, which neither of them knew how to operate. Patricia responded by pointing out that John's friend Gord's car had a manual transmission and he had been operating a manual transmission since he started driving, at seventeen and could instruct them both. John replied, "Hey, it took you a couple of months to learn to drive an automatic. How long do you think will it take for you to get comfortable with a standard? You know, learning a standard transmission may be a lot harder than you think. I know, I could never get the hang of it." He looked at Patricia, waiting for an answer. Instead, he got a question. "So you think we should just buy the Pacer, right?" John nodded and added some comforting words. "Look, we can buy it right now. We can walk in there right now and one of those guys on those desks will sell us that Pacer, arrange the financing, get a license on it and we can drive it off the lot next week." Patricia tilted her head to the right, offered John a slight smile and exhaled. "Okay, okay I give up. I agree that we should get the car, no matter how dumb it looks."

They then hugged and headed inside the office of the *Ottawa Ford*. They presented themselves to the woman behind a bank of telephones at the front counter. John simply announced that he and Patricia wanted to buy a specific car in the lot, pointing to the grey Pacer. The woman immediately picked up a telephone receiver, pressed a button and a telephone rang on the floor behind her. She spoke into the receiver, "Mr. Lapointe, we have some customers out here looking for someone to talk to." Lapointe answered as promptly as he could. Before the telephone woman hung up, Mr. Lapointe, a smallish man wearing a rumpled black suit with a couple of unidentifiable stains on the trousers, arrived at the counter. He cheerfully introduced himself, "Hello, I'm Andre Lapointe. I understand you two are interested in a car, in fact that car." With that observation, Mr. Lapointe pointed to the Pacer in the parking lot. John nodded, "Yeah, we've have definitely decided on that one. We're ready to buy today. We have no trade-in and not much of a down payment, if you need one." Lapointe immediately replied, having anticipated John's admission. "Hey, we can have that vehicle prepared for you by the middle of next week, ready to be driven off the lot." John and Patricia both nodded enthusiastically. He then invited them to accompany him to his desk toward the rear of the building where they began to fill in the forms they would need to complete the sale. The three of them completed the forms within twenty minutes or so. They all smiled, shook hands and John and Patricia headed out to the street to catch a bus going east.

The next Thursday, five days after they first visited *Ottawa Ford*, they picked up the car. As usual, Patricia seated herself on the passenger side, despite the fact that John offered to let her drive, an ironic move that he submitted with a devilish smile. After all, she didn't want the Pacer in the first place. Two days earlier, John had received his fourth mailbox photograph. It was the familiar picture of Bank Street, this time looking south. But, unlike the other three Bank Street pictures, there were neither women, parked cars, nor bicycles in the photograph he had just received. The street was almost empty. The fourth photograph pictured showed two vehicles travelling in opposite directions on the Queensway, which was above the Bank and Catherine Street intersection. Going east was a black Mazda while going west was a grey Pacer. There were no other cars in the picture. John slid the picture in his jacket pocket, prepared to hide it in the bottom drawer of his dresser. This was no way he was showing it to Patricia.

THEY DRIVE THE PACER

W hile Patricia would have preferred to driving the Mazda that was available at *Ottawa Ford*, that is if John could operate a standard transmission, they were both still pleased to have access to the Pacer that they purchased there. John was particularly delighted with the new arrangement. He was now able to drop off Tyler at Mrs. Baker's on Powell Avenue and then drive straight to Tunney's pasture. It reduced his morning travel time to work by maybe thirty minutes, depending on traffic and the day of the week. Although it took him a week or so, he was able to secure an outside parking space behind the Jeanne Mance Building. As for Patricia, her inconvenience was not reduced in any way, still having to pick up Tyler at the end of the day after taking the bus from the pharmacy at the Carlingwood Shopping Centre. As they both expected, he arrived home a few minutes before her, the drive from Tunney's Pasture cutting his afternoon commute by more than twenty minutes. Consequently and understandably, Patricia eventually persuaded John to add picking up Tyler at Mrs. Baker's house to his daily list of duties. He still was able to arrive home before she did.

Aside from adjusting his daily schedule and ensuring that he managed to secure a parking spot at work, he applied for a parking space in the basement of the apartment building, a difficult prospect given the size of the building parking lot, which was designed and constructed in 1936 when most potential tenants did not own automobiles, and the current number of applicants for one of them. John was advised by one of his colleagues at work, an older man named Mark Gore, that he should consider offering the apartment's manager some sort of incentive to be awarded a next vacant parking spot. Since John did not have any experience in offering anyone a bribe, he decided that the most obvious approach would be straight forward. So that evening, he went down to apartment 106, knocked on the door and greeted Mr. Casey. It was around seven thirty in the evening. "Mr. Casey, my wife and I just bought a car. You know, we have a baby boy and we needed one. So we would like a parking spot in the building." Casey looked at him with a curious, almost vacant look on his face. "We thought that maybe you would be aware of any open parking spot. We would be very appreciative, more than appreciative in fact if you could find us one." Casey took a couple steps forward into the hall, gradually closed the door to his apartment and started to whisper. "Mr. Delaney, I'm not sure what you are saying but the building has been keeping a spot open for a special tenant for some time. That person might be you." With that assurance, Casey held his hand out as if he was asking for something. At first, John knew that he was asking for something but he just didn't know that it was. He felt that he had entered a confessional.

John didn't have anything clever to say, so he just decided to play it straight. "So what can I offer you? I really need a parking spot. I know I can try to find a spot on the street, like Powell Avenue for example, but you can never be sure, especially at night." Casey nodded and offered a helpful hint. "You know, you can try to get a permit for parking on the street from the city. I think that some of our tenants have permits for Powell, some for Renfrew, some for Clemou, some for the streets across Bank Street, like Patterson. As you may know, we have almost two dozen tenants and I think they all have cars. In fact, I think some of them may have two cars. And there are only fifteen spaces for the building." John acknowledged the building's history. "I know, that's the way it was built. Not too many people had cars then and, well, there is not any way the building could be enlarged to provide for additional parking spaces." He knew that he had to acquire that available spot to which Casey had referred.

Casey then returned to the original though apparently confidential subject of their conversation, the price of the available parking spot. John responded with a straight forward approach. "I assume there is a price for this available parking place. I have no experience with this kind of arrangement ---- you know, providing money under the table.", embarrassed but subdued laughter followed. He expected Casey to be surprised in some way, maybe even shocked. He wasn't. Casey looked at him without expression. "Look, Mr. Delaney, in so much as you may not know this, I have sold the occasional parking spot in the past. In fact, it has always been up to me to decide on the parking and I've been in this job for almost twenty years. And yes, I have my own parking space." John looked at Casey with a glazed look on his face. After a few moments, he seemed to come to his senses. He then made Casey an offer. "I know that it costs $50 a month to rent a parking space in this building. I'll pay you personally the same amount every month for that special parking spot. I don't know if any other tenant pays you anything extra for their parking places. And if they do, I'll match whatever it is they're paying." Casey laughed with a sinister edge. "Good guess but you're a little high. They pay me only $40 a month extra. You can pay me $45 a month if you want but you don't have to." With that assurance, he held up his right hand and asked him to stand by the door. "Just wait. I'll get you an application." John raised his hand and told Casey that he had already filed a number of applications. Casey disappeared into the apartment and returned with a form. "You'll need to fill in a new application."

Three days after placing an envelope with the completed application and two cheques for $45 each, one cheque for Donaldson Property Management and another for Mr. Kenneth Casey in the mailbox for apartment 106, John and Patrica received their Parkdale Court parking sticker and an unnecessarily detailed printed map of the garage. John and Patricia had been parking on either Powell or

Patterson Streets since they took ownership of the car, having been issued only one parking ticket in the interim. It was only four days after they took possession of the Pacer when they first attempted to park in space number 307, which they thought strange since that apartment number was associated with Harry and Florence Quinn who did not seem to have a car. So why were they paying for a parking spot they did not use? That was a question for another day, an answer elusive as the question may have seemed obvious.

Initially, neither John nor Patricia were able to park their Pacer in their parking space without difficulty, sometimes taking more than ten minutes to maneuver it. First of all, the entrance ramp to the garage was quite steep and drivers had to be careful not to lose control while either entering or exiting. In addition, neither of them were particularly proficient at parking their car. Fortunately, not only for the two of them but for the other fourteen spaces available to tenants, John and Patricia were usually alone in the garage when either of them were attempting to park. Consequently, their attempts to navigate the Pacer into the space between a late model blue Buick and a moderately used rust coloured Plymouth Fury were usually exercises in mild futility. It was a miracle that there was not any damage to the two other cars although both John and Patricia occasionally dented both the Pacer's front and rear bumpers by striking one of the cement pillars that stood near their parking space in the garage. Usually on Sunday mornings, in a silent garage, when traffic in the parking garage was relatively light, if non-existent, both John and Patricia would regularly take turns navigating the garage entrance and then practising their turns in and out of their parking spot. They both admittedly felt like they were reliving their driver's examinations with the Ontario Motor Vehicle Office, John having failed the first time he tried, due mainly to his nerves he later determined. Eventually, they both passed their driver's tests and with several years of occasional practice --- John in his first wife's car and

Patricia in her father's station wagon --- became proficient enough to actually drive their own car.

———————◆◇◆———————

Predictably, there were incidents in the first few months of driving the Pacer that gave both of them pause in their decision to purchase the car in the first place. On Saturdays, the two of them would visit the store for groceries with Tyler who they would carry in a canary yellow baby stroller on wheels. They had managed to acquire both the carrier and the baby seat for the car in a used clothing store down near the Bank Street bridge. Tyler was happily ensconced in his backseat baby seat as they were parking the Pacer on Gilmour Street, a couple of blocks down from the IGA on corner of Bank and Somerset. John had opened the hatchback to the Pacer, having already secured the two front doors, when he dropped his car key in the car's trunk and then compounded that error by closing the hatchback with Tyler still in the backseat. Both John and Patricia immediately became excited, John swearing and banging the rear of the car while Patricia started to stop pedestrians on the street to ask them for help. Understandably, nobody could help. One man, an older man with a cane and a vague resemblance to someone or something, suggested that one of them walk over to Budget Car Rental on Kent and Somerset for help. He said that there was a pretty good possibility that Budget would have a mechanic on hand who could open a locked car door. As it turned out, he was right, a young man, who looked a lot like Jeff the mechanic in the car rental, did the job with a coat hanger. John gave the young man a ten dollar gratuity. For some reason, Tyler hadn't noticed a thing. He had been taking a nap.

John, who had never overcome his deficiencies when it came to driving a car, had the misfortune one evening of striking a Cadillac on Scott Street near Parkdale Street while hurrying to pick up Tyler at Mrs. Baker's house. He spent at least fifteen minutes pleading with the driver of the Cadillac to allow him to continue on his way to pick up Tyler, taking full responsibility for the accident to avoid calling the police and promising to pay full restitution if he could contact her after picking up Tyler. He explained to Mrs. Lebleau, a well dressed older woman, that his babysitter would not be happy if he was tardy in picking up Tyler and could severe their arrangement, which both he and Patricia much appreciated. He had asked for a pen and gave Mrs. Lebleau his name, his address and his telephone number. She seemed happy enough, got in the car and slowly drove off. John was relieved and also drove off, his frayed nerves settled enough for him to take the wheel and hopefully arrive by Mrs. Baker's deadline which, by the way, John and Patricia never missed. He spent the drive to Mrs. Baker's house ruminating about how he and Patricia were going to cover the cost of the repairs to Mrs. Lebleau's Cadillac, not to mention any repairs to the Pacer. Fortunately, repairs to both cars seemed minor, presumably well under $1,000. Still, any amount would cause them anxiety.

Because the damage to the Pacer was relatively minor and therefore easily overlooked, John chose not to tell Patricia about the accident. To cover the cost of the repairs to Mrs. Lebleau's Cadillac, John thought that he would need maybe $700 to $800, maybe more. He asked Mrs. Lebleau, who fortunately enough for John was a widow, to take the car to whichever garage she usually used. He decided that he would apply for a small loan with the Bank of Montreal branch at Laurier and O'Connor Streets. He had been banking there for almost five years, ever since he had moved to Ottawa from Montreal where he had maintained an account with the Bank of Montreal since he was in elementary school. So he decided to schedule an appointment with a loan officer at the branch and ask for $1,000, which seemed to be a reasonable amount given their circumstances. He did not tell Patricia about his intention to approach the bank to cover the repairs to Mrs. Lebleau's Cadillac. He did not want to tell her about the accident. There was already enough stress on Patricia he thought with her mother having recently told her that she had been diagnosed with bladder cancer. John thought that the news about her mother, along with her taking care of Tyler, was enough to plunge Patricia into a depression, which she once told him was a condition she occasionally faced in her teenage years.

———◦———

By the time John was able to schedule an appointment with a loan officer named Patrick Kessel, Mrs. Lebleau had telephoned him at work regarding the status of the repairs to her car. She told John that the repairs were estimated to be around $600, a sum that approximated John's own guess. It made John fell a little better about his application for a loan, now that he had a veritable reason for requesting the loan in the first place. That day, however, he came across another reason, however hypothetical, if not fantastic, that would further justify his applying for a loan. In fact, he began to think that he should significantly increase the amount of the loan for which he was applying.

In his mailbox, along with a couple of bills, a request for a charitable donation, was another photograph, this time of a garage on Gladstone that he recognized from his time working for the Economy Car Rental. It was called Richard's Garage, a relatively small operation that repaired cars for people in the neighbourhood. Business between the garage and the car rental was unorthodox, if not shady to say the least. It was conventional practice among car rental companies to ensure that applicants agree to pay a certain minimum deductible in the event of damage. It was usually $250 for a car and $500 for a van. In the case of Economy Car Rental, if there was any minimum damage, Daniel Mayhew, John's boss, would escort the renter over to Richard's Garage who would immediately provide the renter and Mayhew with an inflated repair estimate, invariably above the deductible level. The unfortunate renting customer would then pay the deductible, hopefully in cash. The damaged car would never be repaired and Maynew would pocket the deductible.

In the photograph, in the parking lot of Richard's Garage, was the wreck of a grey Pacer. John could not positively identify the car, its missing license plates, a missing trunk lid, all four wheels missing, its roof partially collapsed, and its windows smashed hardly indicative. In addition, there was a baby seat clearly recognizable in the backseat of the derelict, reminiscent of his son sitting in that very seat. Unlike the other photographs hidden in the bottom drawer of his bedroom drawer, it was a colour picture, not black and white. As he slowly pushed Tyler's stroller up the stairs of the three floors, he contemplated the significance, if there was any, of the colour photograph. By the time the two of them, father and son, arrived on the third floor of Parkdale Court, John thought for one forgettable moment and for one incomprehensible reason that he should get rid of the Pacer before it was too late. By the time John and Tyler entered the apartment, he had abandoned his plan, how fanciful it was, to leave the Pacer at *Richard's Garage* and purchase a replacement. He had taken the most recent picture as a sign rather than a question. The other pictures gave observers a choice. He didn't think the current picture gave anyone looking at it any sort of omen, maybe of things to come. Again, the possible insinuations of the most recent picture was another reason to keep it from Patricia who could be concerned, if not anxiety ridden if she started to understand the possible implications of the picture. Again, it was the question of troubling Patricia with more anxiety. When he thought about it, which was infrequent but lasted for about couple of weeks after he found the photograph, he was disturbed as well although not to the same extent he originally figured.

⟶✦⟵

John met with loan officer Patrick Kessel of the Bank of Montreal on the corner of Laurier and O'Connor on the next Tuesday. He turned out to be a middle age man who greeted him cheerfully. He was dressed in a brown suit that looked to be at least ten years old and was also at least two and three sizes too small, the belt to his trousers hanging well below his stomach. He invited John to take a seat at his desk, one of the three desks that were situated behind large windows on the southern side of the bank. For some reason that John couldn't comprehend, he then proceeded to introduce John to the interior details of the bank. He pointed to the other side of the three desks where he said that he and two colleagues served customers on a variety of banking services. He then said that more pedestrian banking activities were handled by the five tellers working to the left. There were also two standing tablets where customers completed their deposit and withdrawal slips before lining up before the tellers. Finally, across from the bank's entrance Kessel noted was the manager's office and his secretary's desk. John tried not to look annoyed. John was tempted to tell Mr. Kessel that he was familiar with the geography of the place. But he didn't. It was his impression that the man was just being sociable.

As he started to review his loan application, a one page form that covered the usual financial information, John was looking at people in the lineups at the three tellers whose wickets were opened. It was a few minutes after ten. He recognized that in the middle line was a long time Parkdale Court tenant named Beverly Miller. Aside from the her, in the line to her immediate right, was another Parkdale Court long time tenant named Alice Stewart. They were both widows and both had been residents of the third floor for more than a decade. They were chatting animatedly, presumably dealing in the usual gossip that elderly widows would normally exchange. They were both clutching their bank books in one hand and their withdrawal slips in the other while their purses were hanging off their arms. While Mr. Kessel went over the details of the loan, which he had authorized within several minutes of completing his review of John's loan application, John watched the ladies as they likely continued their conversations, this time with the two respective tellers who were now serving them. John barely read the loan document as he signed it. Gore said that the $1,000 would be deposited in his account by the end of the day. He watched the ladies leave the bank. He wondered whether the ladies had taken notice of him. John walked home, down Bank Street, stopping by *Anthony's Used Records* on his way, where he picked up an album by

T–Rex for $2.99. He also thought that maybe the $1,000 he had just been loaned by the Bank of Montreal was probably too little. He should have asked for double that. He was thinking about buying another car.

PHOTOGRAPHS CONCEALED

Initially, John did not think it wise to divulge the photographs that he had discovered in the mailbox. He had decided to keep the receipt of those photographs from anyone, including most particularly his partner Patricia. Considering Patricia's current judgment regarding the two photographs and the newspaper fragment he found in the apartment, he thought that discussion of any additional photographs would likely be even more distressing to her. That did not imply that he had dismissed any notion of the meaning of the photographs. He had, however, come to a conclusion that would have been, at least to John, difficult to determine. As enlightened as John thought he had been or was being, the nature of the conclusion he could have reached about the mailbox photographs seemed a little too curious to be believable.

From his viewpoint, each picture that John had found in his mailbox seemed to involve some aspect of the lives of John and Patricia, as if whoever had left it there was somehow clairvoyant. Each of the photographs portrayed scenes that were located around Parkdale Court and evoked, in some general way, circumstances and/or decisions that were reflecting events that were being faced by John or Patricia or both of them. The first two photographs showed Bank Street scenes, one facing the north toward downtown while the other faced south toward the Bank Street bridge. Both pictures included four cars on either side of the street, the cars on the east side of the street light in colour and the cars on the west side of the street dark in colour, any other definition of colour unavailable in black and white. There was a bus stop on the east side of the street, number five downtown with two people, an older woman carrying a shopping bag and a teenage girl who was reading a magazine. There was no bus stop on the other side of the street. In addition, both photographs portrayed two boys on bicycles, one light coloured travelling east while the other was dark coloured and was travelling west.

Although John did not have the frightening imagination that Patricia might have had in the circumstances that the hidden photographs depicted, he did come to an obvious conclusion. To John and likely Patricia if she were acquainted with them, the photographs were acting like a weird Ouija board. Every single picture was somehow related to their daily life and the choices either of them had made, specifically, the location of their residence, the choices that he had made with respect to the woman with whom John would eventually live, the automobile they would eventually purchase, and the possibility that that automobile would presumably get into a traffic accident that would seriously damage it. Those photographs, as well as the dream that John had with respect to the possible future of his son Tyler, continued to disturb John, principally in connection to the origin of the photographs. As for the dream, John eventually came to the conclusion that it was totally unrelated to the photographs and was probably the only sensible occurrence in the entire sequence of mystifying events.

⟢⟶⊙⟵⟣

It was more than a year later when they thought about moving from Parkdale Court. During that year, John and Patricia experienced a number of events that disturbed, if not occasionally distressed the two of them. While the mailbox to apartment 302 did not receive any more photographs during that period, John would occasionally recollect the previously received photographs, most particularly and perhaps not surprisingly given their eventual circumstances, the picture that portrayed *Richard's Garage* and the damaged grey Pacer. His recall was precipitated by several repairs to their Pacer undertaken by a local garage that had a propensity, if not the talent to consistently overcharge naive customers like John and Patricia It was of course their own doing, their own folly. It was entirely evident that the two of them had no notion whatever of the cost of fairly common automotive repairs.

Their first transaction with the garage, which was called the *Booth Street Auto Repair* and was recommended to John by his old colleague, the mechanic Jeff from his previous place of employment at the car rental agency, involved either a faulty alternator or a dead battery. Unfortunately, they were charged an exorbitant amount, a fee that was, as they later determined, more than twice what they should have paid. Several months later, they were convinced by a mechanic named Jack, while the Pacer was in for regular servicing, that the brakes needed repairs. Although neither John nor Patricia had noticed anything untoward about the brakes, they were in no position to disagree with Jack's diagnosis. Knowing nothing about cars, they agreed to allow Jack and the *Booth Street Auto Repair* to replace the brakes. This time, when added to the cost of the normal servicing of changing the oil and whatnot, John and Patricia ended up paying more than $500. It was during their eventual purchase of a two year old Pontiac station wagon from *Bronson Automotive* that a salesman named Campbell told them that brakes had never been replaced or fixed. John was contemplating the photograph of the damaged Pacer one last time when the mailbox received a final picture of *Richard's Garage*, albeit without the damaged Pacer in its frame.

LEAVING PARKDALE COURT

Tyler was a little more than six months old when his parents decided it was time to introduce him to his paternal grandparents. John had been secretly meeting with his father Edward at his job as an assistant manager in the Eaton's department store in the Bayshore Shopping Centre ever since he was made aware of Patricia's pregnancy more than a year ago. He was relatively reluctant, even nervous to approach his father at first. His father was initially startled, so much so that he could barely speak when his son John first approached him. In fact, he introduced him as James to a colleague who just happened to be passing by the two of them in the sporting goods department. James was John's brother. Eventually, at that first meeting, John was able to explain to his father that both he and his wife Betty, John's mother, should know that they were soon to become grandparents for the third time, his brother James and his wife having had two children, a boy and a girl several years past. His father accepted the explanation and in fact thanked him for it. Edward suggested that they retire to the store's coffee shop. They spent twenty minutes in the coffee shop, during which time John outlined their history, when and where they met, their decision to have a baby, which was not a decision at all, and any other detail John thought would be relevant or of interest to a grandfather.

Neither of them mentioned his mother Betty and the alienation between the two of them which had gone on for years. The precipitating incident was commonplace, ordinary, almost comic. It was eight o'clock on a Saturday morning. Patricia was observed by his parents leaving John's apartment, about to board a taxicab. His parents had decided to drop by his apartment on the way to their cottage up north. They did that fairly regularly. John's mother, a fervently religious woman who strongly disapproved of practically anything that could be considered sexually immoral, screamed something indecipherable from across Bank Street, where his father had parked the car. John stood silently while Patricia looked at John with a blank look on her face. She then giggled a bit, kissed him on the cheek and then got into the taxi.

John felt obligated to mention his initial rendezvous with his father to Patricia who had encouraged him to start meeting with his father in the first place, a practice that he began to undertake every month or so. They also discussed when he should introduce her to his father, when he should re-introduce himself to Betty, his mother, and when he should introduce Patricia to his mother. They mutually agreed that they would wait until the baby was born before they would present themselves to John's parents. John would meet his father every month on a Thursday evening at the store, Edward having to work a couple of evenings every second week. He would faithfully report the tenor of his conversations to Patricia who would usually shrug with indifference, his reports predictably dull although occasionally his father would mention that Betty was aware of the impending birth, was privately looking forward to the birth of a grandchild, regardless of what the circumstances under which the baby had been conceived.

They had been meeting surreptitiously for several months when the issue of the couple's finances had come up for discussion. Edward had asked about them in the context of their plans to purchase a newer car, the problems they had had with the Pacer indicative of their need. Aside from the fact that his father was somewhat disappointed that John had not consulted with him about the problems they had been having with the Pacer --- Edward Delaney considered himself fairly knowledgeable about automotive matters --- he was also dismayed that John had not approached him about some financial assistance. In reply, John admitted that he and Patricia would have to take out a third loan to pay for another car, with money left on the Pacer and a loan that the Bank had advanced him to pay for car repairs although he did not mention that the repairs were made to someone's else car.

"You should have come to me. I know you have had and still have problems with your mother but don't worry about them. Your mother doesn't have to know." his father stated, and then confided in him with a wink of the eye. "You're serious!" exclaimed John. Apparently, he was. Before they completed their discussion that evening, John had a cheque from his father for $2,000 in his pocket.

—◆—

They took possession of a two year old Pontiac station wagon the next week for $6,500, an arrangement brokered by a young salesman named Kevin Campbell. They immediately had a more significant problem parking the new car, it being appreciably larger than the Pacer. As a result, they were forced to find parking on the neighbourhood streets, a tiresome task that sometimes required more than thirty minutes or so. It was after such delays occurred on successive days that the couple decided to begin their search for a new place to live in earnest. They both now found that the parking problem, not to mention walking up the stairs to the third floor with groceries and a baby, to be too difficult to sustain. So within weeks of trying to park the new car within a reasonable distance of their apartment, they found a semi-detached three bedroom house with its own driveway in Ottawa South to rent. They were scheduled to move within a month. John was relieved with not only the new practical living conditions but also his presumption that he would no longer be troubled with the anxiety that the occasional mysterious photograph would be left in their apartment mailbox.

The next day after signing a lease to rent the semi-detached on Brighton Avenue in Ottawa South for $500 a month, they invested an evening in a dinner at an Italian restaurant on Preston Street, the Wicked Witch of the West, Mrs. Monfils, having been engaged to look after Tyler for the evening. Earlier that day, John, Patricia and Tyler drove to the Bayshore Shopping Centre to meet with John's father, the purpose of which was to plan a meeting involving the three of them with both of John's parents. They agreed on a visit to his parents' house for the next Sunday afternoon. Only Edward himself laughed at his own attempted witticism when he said that he would have to figure out how to inform Betty of the meeting. John and Patricia did not know it at the time but Edward had already decided not to tell her at all, a surprise seeming a better alternative than listening to his wife refusing to consider having her son, his girlfriend and their illegitimate son over for a visit. John's father said that, regardless of his wife's doubts, they were not to worry. Both of them would meet the "little family" as he put it. So Patricia bought a new outfit for Tyler, a matching shirt and short set, navy blue in colour. Patricia wore a one of the few dresses that she owned, a light lilac colour, while John decided to wear a mute checked suit jacket over his usual work outfit of light sports shirt and dark trousers.

A couple of days prior to the meeting with John's parents, something happened that gave rise to concern that he could not share with Patricia who understandably was already nervous in any event. On the Friday before their planned journey to the home of John's parents, he found another photograph in the mailbox. John thought that it would likely be among the last, if not the last mystifying photograph he would ever receive at Parkdale Court. It was a picture of a fairly new, palatial suburban home with two oak trees, a carefully manicured rolling lawn, the only sign of specific identification a number on an unnamed street ---109. Aside from the street number of the address, there was nothing identifiable in the photograph, John never having seen the house into which his parents had moved after arriving from a Montreal suburb more than two years ago. Like he had previously, he pondered the photograph like it was a conundrum. The superficial meaning seemed obvious but John still was puzzled, as he usually was with the mailbox photographs.

It remained elusive, like a dream that can be remembered at one moment but never recalled at another.

⟫＞-⊙-⟪＜

A week later, John was informed by his father of the address of his parents' place: 109 Linden Park Avenue in the Alta Visa area of the city. John was generally acquainted with that area of the city and had little difficulty in locating his parents' new home. They called on them at the agreed time on that Sunday afternoon. The three of them walked up to his parents' house and rang the doorbell. His mother, dressed in her customary house dress accentuated with compression stockings, greeted them at the door with a loud shriek as if she had just seen a ghost. She then burst into tears, proclaiming that Tyler, who seemed to be hiding in Patricia's arms while his grandmother was calling out, looked like John had at similar age, which was a trifle exaggerated since her son John did not arrive in the Delaney home until he was adopted more than eighteen months after his birth. His father stood behind Betty, smiling, introducing himself and his wife while her lamentations grew silent. Finally, she was quiet long enough to offer them slices of cake a selection of biscuits and cups of tea, neither of which seemed to have been prepared beforehand, suggesting to both John and Patricia that John's father had not advised her of their visit before they actually knocked on the front door. John later remarked to Patricia that his father had not been kidding when he said that he had no plans to tell her before they actually arrived.

The five of them sat in a well decorated living room, so well appointed that Patricia later said that it looked like the lobby of a fairly expensive hotel. John responded to her comment by later pointing out that the family living room in Montreal sometimes looked more like the front window of a discount store than the lobby of a hotel. In any event, the adults in the room spent the afternoon eating tomato soup cake, sipping tea, and listening to John's parents complain about housing prices in Ottawa, pointing out that they were nearly double than of those in Montreal. John's mother, Betty, repeatedly said that her husband had planned to retire after a couple of years of working at the new Eaton store in Ottawa, a plan that had gone awry when they were forced to take on an unexpected mortgage for the house in Alta Vista. Both John and Patricia feigned sympathy. They agreed that the situation facing John's parents was disappointing but tried to ameliorate things somewhat by announcing that they had just rented a three bedroom semi-detached house in Ottawa South and planned to move in within three weeks. While John's father congratulated them on the move and asked if he could help with the arrangements, John's mother sat there with a strangely stunned look on her face, like she didn't know how to reasonably react. Instead, she offered John and Patricia more tea. John replied to his father's offer of assistance with the move by politely declining it, explaining that he had already hired a moving company for the day. He was concerned that his mother would be mildly irate if his father helped him move.

<hr />

It was two years later, during which time they would visit each other's parents fairly regularly, when they decided to marry. After formalizing their relationship on a Tuesday afternoon at the City Hall with a municipal judge named Robillard, they hosted a wedding reception on the top floor of the Holiday Inn on Queen Street the following Saturday. More than fifty people attended the party, including both John's parents and Patricia's mother, the latter three of whom welcomed their marriage. John, Patricia and Tyler, who was almost three years old by then, had been living in the rented three bedroom semi-detached house in Ottawa South for two years and were considering buying a home, having had their eye on a small cottage in the west end of the city when two events conspired to accelerate their plans.

First, Patricia discovered that she was expecting their second child, a development that obliged the two of them to postpone any plans they had about buying a home, their finances hardly sufficient to buy a home and have another child almost insurmountable obstacles.

As delighted as they were with news of the impending birth, they were reluctant, if not unable to pursue the purchase of a house given their difficult financial situation. They both thought that they could appeal to John's parents for help but Patricia in particular didn't like the idea, particularly since her mother-in-law was occasionally critical about her raising of Tyler.

Secondly, and probably more importantly, Patricia happened to find an index sized photograph in the mailbox at 64 Brighton Avenue. It had been raining and the photograph was a little warped. It was not protected by an envelope. Patricia had been holding Tyler by the hand. As soon as she opened the door, she let him go, clutching the photograph with both hands. She knelt, holding the photograph as if it was a rosary. She had not sought an answer to any such photograph since John found those two antiquated pictures of families in apartment 302 of Parkdale Court more than three years ago. And even then, after years of occasional exploration, there was still no explanation, only pointless paranoia and aimless wonder.

Patricia was certain that John had pretty well forgotten the photographs but she had not. She had developed a number of opinions about the two photographs and although she didn't share all of them with John, she had abandoned pursuing even the ones she had shared after John began to ignore them when she raised them. She began to contend that the two families captured in the two photographs were in fact ghosts of residents who previously lived in the apartment in which they had lived. Patricia proposed researching the residents of apartment 302 of Parkdale Court to determine whether they resembled any of the people in the photographs. Based on the newspaper fragment that been left under a chair after one of their parties, both of them knew that the initial occupant was George Fenwick, the architect who designed the building and jumped out of the window of apartment 302 thirty years ago. Since that day in 1949, neither John nor Patricia knew how many people resided in that apartment. Much to Patricia's disappointment, two years or so went by but neither of them acted on her anxiety about ghosts. Even Patricia had eventually surrendered her anxiety about the ghost photograph, never mentioning it to John or anyone else for that matter, including her friends at work, many of whom were interested with Patricia's fascination with ghosts, particularly the ghosts of previous residents in apartment 302.

The details of the photograph placed in the mailbox at 64 Brighton Avenue were unmistakable and shocking. In the foreground of the picture was a For Sale sign placed on the lawn by a local real estate company. Behind the sign was a depiction of a young couple stepping down the stairs, leaving the house. There was a man in the door, presumably a real estate salesman, waving and making one last pitch to the couple. It was apparent that the couple, both of whom appeared to have just been married, was looking to buy their first house, presumably the semi-detached in the photograph being considered. The house looked to have been recently constructed, perhaps in the early 1950s.

Patricia had gotten to her feet and was sitting on the sofa of the living room staring at the photograph, with Tyler sitting on the floor before her playing with several toy cars that had been left underneath the sofa. She had the notion, however disturbing it seemed, that the couple resembled younger versions of her parents. It was a perception that so rattled Patricia that she wished that somebody was sitting on the sofa with her, somebody to talk with. She was thinking for a moment of her parents, a memory of which was drifting through her mind like a dream, a dream of their history, like they were ghosts that appeared and then faded almost as quickly as they had emerged. She found herself concentrating more on her father than her mother, he having passed away years ago. Amazingly enough --- it was almost thirty years ago ---- she could remember every detail of his father's younger face. She sat there contemplating the likely meaning of the photograph, aside of course from the obvious. The more significant mystery, however, at least in Patricia's mind, involved the origin of the photograph. She wondered, as both John and Patricia did with the two photographs John had found in their apartment in Parkdale Court, who left the picture in their mailbox at 64 Brighton Avenue and what was the purpose of placing it there.

As soon as John arrived home, Patricia showed him the photograph. Not surprisingly, aside from the interruptions caused by Tyler playing with his food during dinner, he and Patricia went on to discuss the matter until it was time for their son's bath more than an hour later. Most of their discussion was taken up with John attempting to placate Patricia who was spending some of her time crying. Even Tyler, when he wasn't making a mess, was occasionally soothing his mother as well in his own way. John was as sympathetic as he could be in the circumstance, concerned that he would allow himself to accidentally divulge the photographs that he had hidden in the bottom drawer of his dresser. He thought that if she was to learn of the existence of the secret photographs, her condition would hardly improve, particularly if her husband were to share with Patricia his evaluation of the meaning of the photographs.

Later in the evening, as the two of them sat silently on the living room sofa, John reading the evening newspaper while Patricia continued to battle her anxiety with almost constant trembling, so much so that John suggested that he take her to the emergency room at the Ottawa General Hospital. Patricia's experiences with afflictions related to her nerves were minimal. She was a little apprehensive as she was having Tyler although practically everyone she knew felt the same way when they were having their first born. Consequently, she was reluctant, if not opposed to going to the emergency room. John then had a thought flash across his mind. He asked her if she wanted a drink, an invitation that John seldom offered to wife and she seldom accepted if offered. However, as John tried to explain to Patricia, a couple of drinks might her calm down, regardless of who or what the source and/or purpose of the photograph actually was. Besides, again as John attempted to explain, they both would be in a far more favourable position to consider the actual meaning of the photograph if they were both suitably lubricated.

As John put Tyler to bed, who was misbehaving as he usually did, Patricia decided to finally respond to John's offer of a drink. By the time John had concluded his fatherly duty of convincing Tyler to finally put his head down on his Superman pillow, Patricia had her first drink and had calmed down enough to rationally discuss the curious photograph that arrived in the mailbox box at 64 Brighton Avenue. In fact, after exchanging similar comments on the mysterious nature of the photograph and concluding that a couple of drinks had soothed her enough to overlook or maybe even forget her susceptibility to ghosts and ghosts stories, John decided to reveal the existence of eight photographs he had been hiding in the bottom drawer of his bedroom dresser. As John had hoped, Patricia did not react as she might have previously behaved, unperturbed, as calm as if she had just been informed that he planned to rearrange the furniture in their bedroom. She looked at John, a small trifle of tears having collected in the corners of both eyes but otherwise she appeared to be serene. John admitted to having brooded about the photographs for months, describing each one of them in some detail and providing his analysis of each one of them. He sounded as if he was reciting screenplays out of an old *Twilight Zone* to Patricia, attempting not only to inform Patricia about the photographs but to somehow entertain her as well.

Patricia wasn't entertained although she did pay serious attention not only to John's reports but to his interpretation of their meaning, which in all but the most recent photograph seemed fairly obvious. He gently pointed out that he could not figure out the significance of a picture left in the mailbox at the 64 Brighton Avenue. In addition to his confusion about the photograph itself, he found it equally puzzling that while all but the most recent photograph were left either in their apartment or in the mailbox at Parkdale Court. The most recent one was left in another mailbox and almost six months after the previous snapshot was received. Patricia agreed with her husband that the fact that the photograph was left in their mailbox on Brighton Avenue as opposed to the mailbox in Parkdale Court was the major mystery in the situation. She then made a surprising recommendation, particularly in view of her previous apprehension about the photograph. Patricia, her tears dry and her expression relaxed, finally suggested that they consider seeking professional assistance to investigate the circumstances of the most recently received photograph, that is after questioning John about any inquiries he may have made about any of the photographs he found in the apartment or their mailbox for apartment 302.

"Did you ever question anyone in the building or anywhere else about any of the photographs? I mean, we talked about it for months. As I think I may have told you, I discussed it with my friend Angela and maybe a couple of girls at work. Anyway, I remember that you reported to me a number of times that you tried to find out about the photographs." She looked at John with a seriously inquisitive look on her face. She was obviously expecting a response from him.

"At first, I thought that the photographs of the two families that I found in the apartment may have been related somehow to a previous resident --- that old guy Hector Dennison who was found dead in the apartment. There was no way though that I could find out much about him. I mean, he had no family, no friends, he lived alone in the apartment for decades. I spoke to some of his former neighbours, all of whom are still living there. One of them, Alice Stewart, who has been in apartment 304 for years ---- you remember, she lived next door to us --- told me that she wouldn't be surprised if the Quinns, who've lived in apartment 307 for more than twenty years, might be behind the photographs. She told me that they were known as pranksters, that building superintendent Casey and probably every other previous superintendent that the place ever had, was frequently hearing about those two playing tricks on people. The way Alice Stewart told it, practically every tenant in the building who knows them were entertained by stories about their stunts. No one complained she said."

John paused for a moment and then continued his narrative with a further detail that would support the characterization of the Quinns as pranksters. "Remember, when I was looking for clues to those photographs I found in our apartment, I spoke to the Quinns. As I told you at the time, both of them seemed to me to be a little eccentric. I mean, I've seen Harry Quinn dressed like Mr. Peanut for god sake, not only in his apartment but even standing in the street outside the apartment. As for Mrs. Quinn, I've saw her dancing in the third floor corridor. She also asked me to take a photograph of her sitting in the boss's car when I was working at the car rental across the street." Patricia looked at John with a bemused looked on her face and commented. "And how is that weird?" John smiled and offered her an explanation. "Well, Mrs. Quinn insisted on having her picture taken in a luxury car and the boss's car was the only luxury car on the lot. In addition, she wanted to have it taken with the third floor of Parkdale Court in the picture. Now, that's weird." Patricia lowered her head and slowly nodded.

Patricia then raised her head, her fascination in John's report obvious, and then commented. "Okay, so maybe the Quinns have a habit of pulling the occasional prank. And maybe, just maybe they decided to hide those two photographs in our apartment, whether we lived there or poor Mr. Dennison did before he passed away. Look, you and I can convince ourselves that Quinns hid those photographs in the apartment but why would they do it, what would be the point?" John shrugged his shoulders and brought his hands up in doubt and confusion. "Maybe they just like to play tricks on people, like dressing up as Mr. Peanut for example, you know to entertain or mystify them, to joke with them but maybe there is another explanation, another reason for them to stash those photographs in some other apartment. I can't imagine what that reason could be but there might be another reason. Who knows, maybe those two are sorcerers or something." She then tittered a bit, looked at John and added another shrug to the exchange. She then asked John for another drink, an unusual request from Patricia who seldom had more than one. She was asking for her third drink of the evening.

"Sorcerers!" exclaimed John, with a wide smile appearing on his face. "That's pretty funny. I wouldn't be surprised. I mean this is a couple who to me seem to be a little unconventional but I don't think they're sorcerers." John then turned his smile into a laugh. Patricia responded with her own smile and another shrug. The two of them then sat in silence for a few minutes, looking at each other with befuddled expressions. Then Patricia reflected on the conversation they were having or had just had. "Maybe we should forget the whole thing. I mean, the Quinns may be responsible for the photographs, except of course for the one we received here but we probably will never know why." Then the two of them stayed quiet for another few minutes. Patricia, who was in the process of finishing her third drink of the evening, a Rusty Nail, then came up with a proposal, an idea that was original coming from her.

John was understandably surprised when Patricia again suggested that they engage a professional, most likely a private investigator although she admitted that she wasn't sure about how they would go about finding one but she did have a suggestion. "Some of the guys you play baseball with may have some idea. Aren't a couple of them with the police?" Another pause and a possibility. "Wouldn't they know some private investigators? Maybe they would have some suggestions." John looked quietly startled, not having thought of the idea that they could hire anybody to satisfy their curiosity, if not their own fascination. He agreed with Patricia's proposition. At first, the idea seemed fanciful. After all, their acquaintance with private investigators, with private dicks, PIs, gumshoes, whatever was limited to contrivances of fiction, that is books, movies, television, populated by famous sleuths like Sherlock Holmes, Mike Hammer, Sam Spade, Jim Rockford, Joe Mannix, even the Hardy Boys. But Patricia's suggestion did not seem as absurd as John had initially thought since neither of them had any other feasible plan.

AFTER ALL THIS TIME, PRANKS RECALLED

------◇------

It was years later. Fortunately, maybe amazingly, Harry Quinn, out of school for more than a decade and clerking for a bank, ran into Hector Dennison, also long out of school and working for a middle of the road men's clothing store. Harry was leaving the bank branch on Somerset Street when he came upon Hector walking by, apparently on his way to his apartment on the corner of Metcalfe and Somerset. They recognized each other almost immediately, which wasn't surprising since both of them were only in their mid-twenties and their appearances had not changed much. They spent the first few minutes together after almost ten years laughing instead of reminiscing, both thinking they were hopelessly fortuitous. They then, standing together in front of the bank, Harry's place of employment, began their respective reports on the histories that each of them had experienced since they last saw each other, that being when they were both just out of high school. Not surprisingly, neither of them was attached, either legally or any other way. Both reported on their jobs without much enthusiasm and admitted that neither of them had anything noteworthy to relate, again lapsing into laughter. Finally, they admitted to each other that neither of them had any plans for the evening and therefore were able to make immediate arrangements for dinner and drinks. It took them two minutes to agree on the Prescott Tavern on Prescott Street. And then it took them another two minutes to board a city bus down Somerset Street.

By the time they arrived at the Prescott, it was almost as if those years previously had never happened. Of course, it did not take them long to start exchanging information on their former high school classmates, in so far as they could recall any. Neither of them knew the reason for such remembrances but it was expected. As soon as they sat down and ordered their first beer, Harry mentioned Mike Fleury, a former classmate who had died in a streetcar accident a couple of weeks after graduation, the only alumni they had who had been mentioned in the newspaper in the last ten years or so. Hector also remembered Mike Fleury even though neither he nor Harry really knew him, he being in another class, his reputation based solely on the historical fact that a streetcar had run over him a few weeks after his high school graduation. Although it was never mentioned by the press, most of his classmates, including Harry and Hector, believed the story that he was on his way to pick up his rumoured girlfriend when the accident occurred. However, both Harry and Hector expressed more, much more curiosity about the supposed girlfriend, her reputation built on her beauty, which most people thought was spectacular. They both wondered what became of her, her fate more interesting to them than memories of the long dead Mike Fleury.

After they had exhausted their recollections of Mike Fleury and his rumoured paramour, they started swapping recollections of the classmates they could actually remember. The list of remembered classmates was relatively short, both of them wishing that one of them still had a school yearbook. By the time Harry and Hector had finished their abbreviated histories, relating a specific episode relevant to each individual in so far as they could, they had shared a large pizza, consumed several draft beers each, and a little information about their current situations, which they agreed was relatively scant. The evening was coming to a close, at least for the two of them, it being around nine. During a lull in the conversation, during which time they both finished their fourth draft beer and ordered another two draft beers each, Harry asked Hector if he still horsed around with magic tricks, a hobby that they both had pursued when they were still in high school. Hector shook his head reluctantly, as if he had regretted both his answer and the fact that he was compelled into making it. "I think some of my magic stuff is still sitting in the basement of my parents' place. I haven't touched any of that stuff since I moved out." Harry agreed with Hector. "Same here." he said.

After they were both served their two drafts, they sat in silent contemplation for a few moments. Harry then emitted a quiet laugh and then asked, "Do you remember that prank we tried at Parkdale Court when we were still in school?" Hector looked up from behind his most recent draft. "You mean, the thing with the pictures of paintings?" Harry nodded vigorously and smiled. "Yeah, I remember. Never had any effect, did it? Fact was that it was pretty well the only prank we ever managed, other than those dumb things we used to use to do in class." Hector responded by mentioning some of practical jokes they liked to pull, like putting glue on classmates' seats, leaving dog feces in peoples' desks or scribbling in other kids' textbooks. Harry interrupted his friend's nostalgic reminiscences by laughing and then reminding Hector, "Yeah, but everybody did that stuff. We wanted something bigger. Trouble was we didn't quite make it bigger. Still, it was kind of fun wasn't it." Then, the consequence of more than five drafts finally having an effect, Harry made a suggestion. "Look, why don't we try something bigger. I mean, I don't know about you but I've got plenty of time and ---- I just think that maybe it wouldn't be a bad idea to see if we could come up with another prank, a better prank. I mean, we've a lot of time to think about it." Harry then finished off his sixth draft and followed with a comment that was more like a question, that is after ordering another draft. "Interested?"

At first, convinced that Harry's proposal may have had something to be with the six draft beers he had already consumed, inebriation he thought always a cause of surprising suggestions, he pretended that he wasn't really listening to him. Harry repeated his query, expanding it a little. "Are you're interested in pulling a prank?"

Hector's attention improved. He looked like he was thinking about Harry's proposal, as unexpected as it may have been. "Well, what exactly do you have in mind? What are you thinking?" he asked, supposing that maybe Harry was only kidding. After all, Harry had already started on his seventh draft. Hector, who was thinking about risking embarrassment from the waiter by ordering a coffee, having finished only four drafts while Harry was working on his seventh, asked again, "You actually want to pull a prank like we did when we were in damn high school." Harry took another gulp of his beer and smiled casually. "Well, if we can think of something that might actually work, you know work as a prank, then maybe we should try it ----- try it, just for the helluva of it. Just like we did back then, but better."

So they remained at a table in the Prescott while they contemplated the possibility of contriving another prank, this time ensuring they hoped that it would have the intended objective, once they determined what the objective was or could be. After the failure of their previous prank, their previous, if not only consequential prank, they seldom conceived of any other prank. Further, fact was that neither of them were acquainted with anyone who could perform a worthwhile prank. Again, they looked at each other without commenting for a few minutes, Harry finished his last draft and Hector stared at the wall clock over by the washrooms. Their waiter, a younger guy named Matt, informed them that last call was early that night. Harry and Hector left several minutes later. On the cab ride home, they agreed to meet again in a week to exchange ideas on a possible prank.

———————⇒⊱•◉•⊰⇐———————

As agreed, the two of them met at the Glebe House on Bank Street within a week. Not surprisingly, neither of them had anything of significance to report. Harry asked why he wasn't married yet, or at least he hadn't had any plans to get married yet. Hector laughed and asked Harry the same things They both had neither taken any action nor made any plans. After they ordered dinner, it was a Friday and it was the fish and chip special, and ordered three drafts each, Harry asked if Hector had come up with a prank worthy of their efforts. Before answering, the drafts arrived. Hector swallowed half his first draft. He then meekly replied that he had come up with a proposal that he thought might work as a prank but that it might be kind of difficult to explain and therefore even more difficult to execute. Harry nodded and then smiled. "That's very good, Hector, congratulations. Now, what exactly is your proposed plan?" Harry looked confused while he waited for Hector's response. Hector looked puzzled as well, appearing to search for an answer by staring at the empty glass that had contained his first draft. He then took a swallow of his second draft and looked at Harry with a slightly apprehensive expression.

After another delay, during which time Harry and Hector both said that they recognized a couple of patrons also having dinner and drinks in the Glebe House, Hector ordered another two drafts and finally started to explain his proposed prank. "We could pick a guy, probably a guy with whom one of us is familiar and send him naughty photographs." It was a complete surprise, not foreseeable in any way. Two plates of fish and chips arrived without comment from either of them. Hector started in on his plate while Harry just stared, still perplexed with his dinner companion's proposition. "I have to admit that I never really expected anything like sending somebody dirty pictures. What made you think of that? I mean, I've never ever seen any dirty pictures. Anyway, how would you arrange something like that?" Hector looked up from his fish and chips and began to explain. "There's a guy at work named Roger. He works in the mail room. He's an older guy who apparently has been to jail ----- or so some of us think. Anyway, he occasionally shows us dirty pictures, you know obscene pictures of naked women, of people having sex, real smut he says." With that, Hector pushed a small black and white picture of a couple screwing which Harry immediately and quickly hid under the corner of his plate of fish and chips. Harry slowly slid the picture out from under the plate, leaned down and carefully inspected it. The couple, who looked to be at least in their thirties, were completely naked and were enjoying each other on an old sofa. The picture was understandably out of focus and seemingly taken from an odd angle. Harry then looked up and asked about the origin of the picture snapshot. "Well, Roger has a lot of friends and a lot of them know guys who take these sort of pictures." answered Hector. A shocked look spread across Harry's face and he naturally expressed his surprise. He asked. "You mean pictures like that are taken here? Taken here? I can't believe it." Hector replied as calmly as he could in the circumstances. "At first, I couldn't believe it either. But Roger kept on showing us new pictures, every week he would show up at work with a new picture. Sometimes, in fact quite a few times actually, you could recognize people in the pictures ---- fact was, fact is that we worked with some of them."

After a temporary interval during which both of them drank the draft beers and picked at their fish and chips, Harry finally asked Hector who and how he thought they should prank. Hector looked at him quietly, had another swallow of beer and then identified a co-worker named Proulx, a relentlessly miserable man who was universally disliked by everybody who knew him. "He's a bald headed jerk who's the boss of the file room. He treats everybody down there like crap. If anyone deserves to be a target of a prank, it's that guy. Anyway, we should start sending him dirty pictures. Think about it, the man has wife and four kids. Once she finds out, and she would I'll bet, his life will be ruined. She'll take the kids and leave him or something. The people at work will somehow find out and he'll be ruined there too. Not only that but I heard that he's a deacon in his church, an Anglican parish over in Sandy Hill. " They both ordered another couple of draft beers and Hector awaited Harry's comments, that is if he had any. For his part, Harry pointed out that maybe Hector's proposed scheme wasn't really a prank, more like a punishment for being a bad guy. "That's not really a prank, it seems more like a mean trick or something. You're sure you want to do something like that or even try to do something like that."

Harry looked at Hector with a funny little smile on his face. He then related his own proposal to Hector. "Actually, you'll probably recognize the idea, at least kind of recognize it. It will remind you of the failed stunt we pulled in Parkdale Court, the pictures of the paintings we slipped either in the mailboxes or under the doors of the tenants of Parkdale Court. Now, I thought that if we concentrate our trickery on one individual rather than more than one, we might be successful in creating some sort of reaction, particularly if our target is susceptible, you know influenced by the unexpected." While Hector thought it was a good idea, at least better than his idea, which he thought was worth pursuing anyway, he did raise an interesting point. "You know maybe we did come across somebody who was somehow influenced by one of those pictures but we didn't know it, which wouldn't be surprising since we wouldn't speak to anyone personally about their reactions, that is if they had any." Harry agreed with Hector, adding "Yeah, remember that the only report we have was based on me eavesdropping on my father talking with a few neighbours." Harry delayed for a moment and then continued with his supposition. "Besides, remember that the only neighbour who had any real reaction to any pictures of the paintings, some man from the first floor named Murphy, thought that the picture was some sort of prelude to a robbery or some sort of scam. But I don't think anyone ever thought that Murphy did anything about the picture. Maybe he ended up concluding that it was just a prank, just like his neighbours." Hector lightly laughed and offered a final remark. "I guess we'll just have to do better?"

Not having come to any conclusion that night at the Glebe House, they agreed to continue their consideration of a possible prank, again at a table in the Glebe House, which they both had previously agreed was the most convenient venue for their meetings. They also agreed that Fridays after work were the best time for their discussions. So they agreed to meet the next Friday for dinner and drinks. In addition, in discussing the arrangement, neither of them having detected a drop in the enthusiasm for the project.

Over the next several days, before their meeting, Harry had decided that Hector's proposal of sending naughty pictures to a specific individual was probably preferable to his idea, which was not nearly as well formulated as his idea and was admittedly vague and almost pointless, at least at the current time. Both of them had already ordered four drafts each, which seemed more convenient than ordering two drafts twice, and dinner, a hamburger for Harry and a steak sandwich for Hector. After ordering, Harry told Hector that his idea of harassing Mr. Proulx with pornographic pictures was probably the most practical means of ensuring an effective prank. Harry asked if Hector had any further thoughts about the proposal, particularly the details of the proposition. "Well, I thought of a better scheme than mailing a few dirty pictures to Proulx's home. We could start with his home and then start mailing them to him at work. Sooner or later, it is quite possible that everybody at home and at work will know that somebody is mailing him porn, suggesting that he was complicit somehow, like he was inviting the missives. And if that's doesn't wreck his reputation, we could maybe start sending pictures to the church." In a hesitant voice, Harry interrupted Hector and offered some advice. "Maybe that's going a little too far, don't you think?" Hector lowered his voice, looked Harry straight in the face, and agreed with him. "Yeah, maybe you're right." Hector then continued to clarify his scheme. He proposed that he purchase however many dirty pictures he could from Roger and inaugurate their plan as soon as they could. Harry agreed but asked his partner for a commitment that he inspect all pictures before they were sent to Mr. Proulx, his reasoning that the pictures not be "too dirty." Hector did not ask for any definition of what Harry meant by "too dirty".

After his deliberation with Hector, Harry did not volunteer his prank proposal, explaining his hesitation, "I haven't completed my plan yet. I still am thinking about it. Let's go ahead with your idea" Hector was immediately agreeable, not even mildly disappointed in Harry's delay. He was understandably enthusiastic, informing Harry that he should be in a position to start mailing naughty missives out to Proulx without several days, if not sooner, telling him that he had a couple pictures that he could send to Proulx almost immediately. To punctuate, if not prove his promise, he removed a couple of pictures from his suit jacket and slide them across the table to Harry just as their dinners arrived. There were two of them, both of them surprisingly chaste, one portraying a naked young woman facing away from the camera and the other showing an older couple, also naked, in an embrace. "Those are not very dirty, are they? So it is likely that Proulx won't know what to think and either throw them away or hide them somewhere. Do you actually think that they will frighten Proulx somehow?" Hector shook his head slowly. "I intend them to be just a taste, just to put the idea in his head that someone intends to play some sort of a trick on him." Harry still looked at Hector quizzically. But still he was wondering whether Hector's planned prank could have any effect on Proulx. Hector sensed some doubt on Harry's face and sought to assure him. "Well, we'll find out if it works on him once we start sending out the letters." Harry nodded in a solemn sort of way. Both of them had finished their dinners although Hector had consumed only two of his four drafts while Harry had finished all four of his, listening having given him more time to drink.

The two of them then dropped the subject of their proposed pranks to spend the rest of the evening finishing their beer and discussing a couple of historical pranks that Hector had found during his research last week at the Ottawa library. He reported that in 1912, an amateur archaeologist named Charles Dawson claimed to have discovered fossilized evidence of a missing link between humans and apes in a gravel pit in the town of Piltdown in England. The evidence later turned out to be a human cranium connected to a jaw of an orangutan. It took scientists over forty years to expose the so-called "Piltdown Man" as a fraud, a hoax, a prank. Harry nodded in acknowledgement and asked why he didn't start their discussion with the "Lock Ness Monster", noting that ever since sightings become fairly commonplace fifteen years ago or so, it would be natural to mention it. Hector immediately took exception. "I didn't mention the "Lock Ness Monster" because it's a myth, not a prank." Harry nodded and agreed with Hector's distinction. Harry then asked, "Did you find any others?" Hector smiled and resumed his recitation. "Well, there's the story of the Olympic marathon in 1904 when some guy named Fred Something or Other started the race, ran for a few miles, hitchhiked for ten miles or so, rejoined the race and then finished the race as the winner. Once he was found out, he called it a prank. And, then, there was something called the "Cardiff Giant", a fossilized ten foot man which turned out to be a sculpted statute that was exhibited for a fee by a man named Hull somewhere in New York state." Harry again interrupted Hector, suggesting that things like the "Cardiff Giant", or false histories of people like Davy Crockett or Shakespeare weren't pranks, hoaxes or frauds or myths, specifically mentioning the "Loch Ness Monster". After sitting for moments in front of his last draft, Hector agreed and waited for Harry to educate him further.

Harry returned Hector's now vacant gaze and then returned to his original purpose in raising pranks with which he may have been personally acquainted. "You must have a favourite. There must be at least one prank that you can remember. I know I can." Hector's stare quickly transformed, taking on a thoughtful look. He was pondering, almost a statute sitting there. The expression on his face suddenly changed, as if he had just awakened from slumber. A slight smile spread across his face, like someone somewhere was whispering a joke in his ear. It was clear. Hector had an inspiration, it had come to him like a recovered childhood memory. "Mat Night before Halloween. Don't you remember Mat Night? Now there was a prank! Do you remember?" Not surprisingly, Harry looked at Hector a little dumbfounded, not quite of course but close enough to create doubt. Hector shrugged his shoulders and tried to remind Harry. "You never heard of "Mat Night?" I don't believe you. Everybody knows "Mat Night. It's the night before Halloween. You collect dog shit, place it in a paper bag, put it before the front door of somebody's house, light the bag on fire, ring the front doorbell, and then run like hell." Now Harry recalled the remainder of the prank. "I remember now. People answer the doorbell, see a fire on their doorstep, and try to put out the burning bag by stomping on it with their feet." With a quick laugh, Hector finished the story. "And then they are stepping in shit."

Although he had already anticipated the punch line, Harry still had to let loose with almost a belly laugh, a reaction that prompted patrons at several adjoining tables to take notice. Fortunately, Harry had come to his senses. "Now that you tell me the story, I do remember "Mat Night". I never was involved but guys I knew sure were. I think some of them were arrested and spent some time in jail. Anyway, if you're thinking of pulling a "Mat Night" stunt, you should remember that it is traditionally a Halloween thing." Hector replied by suggesting otherwise. "Does it have to be the night before Halloween?" Harry answered, "I don't know. Besides, a stunt like that, well, you can't pull it more than once, once a year I mean. So if you thinking of using it against Proulx or anyone else for that matter, you'll have to remember that you can't trick it more than once. In any event, it's probably not worth thinking about it." Hector answered, "I wasn't thinking about it." He paused and asked, "Do you have any experience with pranks, you know, like in the past?" Harry mentioned a couple of practical jokes in which he was involved, peripherally he carefully noted, the sole responsibility he said belonging to older guys, some of whom were not even students of any high school. One of them, the less harmful of the two, required secretly gluing funny messages on people's clothes to see how long it would require the target, to become aware of the joke. "There was this one kid in high school, a guy named Ron Rydeau, who was a frequent target. His classmates would attach all sorts of things to his clothes, his desk, his books, his locker, hopefully to see how long it would take him to notice." Hector then asked about Ron Rydeau's reactions to the tricks that were played on him. "Well, Rydeau was surprisingly good natured about the whole thing. We used to think that he thought the tricks made him part of the crowd or something, you know, one of the boys. Of course, he was wrong but what the hell."

Harry then provided Hector with another example, telling him that in his second to last year of high school, he and several of his classmates, for no reason other than pointless trickery, unscrewed the wheels of every bicycle in the schoolyard. Consequently, when school was left out, always half past three in the afternoon, students went to the bicycle stands, unlocked their bicycles, and the wheels fell off the forks of every single bicycle. "There was chaos, especially since we left all of the screws that we removed in a bucket which we then hid in the school library. The guys with bikes either carried their bikes and their wheels home or left them in the stands. We left a note telling everyone that the screws were left under the door to the principal's office." There was a short pause and then Harry continued. "No one ever found out who did it even though the principal and most of the teachers in the school spent weeks trying to find out who did. They went after the usual guys ---- you know, guys who got in trouble a lot ---- but we got away with it. And after a while, I guess people forgot about it." Hector then asked if Harry was aware of any other pranks. "Not really, my buddy Nelson and I used to move guys' books from one desk to another. We did that for months in grade ten and then gave it up. I mean, guys would get mad and all but after a while, nobody seemed to care." Hector managed a shrug. Harry returned it.

⎯⎯⎯⎯⎯⟫⬦⟪⎯⎯⎯⎯⎯

After sending their first set of pictures to Mr. Proux, Hector was able to obtain a dozen of licentious photographs from Roger. He showed them to Harry who noted that each one was successively more explicit, if not more adventurous than the previous photograph. They ranged from simple nudes to the most graphic portrayals of sex acts that neither of them had ever seen. In fact, a number of the photographs showed acts that seemed impossible to the two of them. Since he was the original recipient of the photographs, Hector thought that he was the one that should select the next two photographs to be mailed to Patrick Proulx. Harry was shocked, starring at the first two pictures for what seemed to be at least a minute, embarrassed because he was unfamiliar with the activities in both pictures. Hector commented, "You have to admit, they're extreme but it may be the only way to get some sort of reaction out of Proulx." It prompted Harry to ask Hector what sort of reaction he expected or wanted. "I don't know, I honestly don't know. Just something I guess. I've thought of, in fact I've have gotten friendly with him. I found out that Proulx plays Euchre most days at lunch in the company cafeteria. So I managed to get an entree to the game through a guy named Pete Thompson who works for Proulx in the file room. I'll play for a couple of weeks and then may start telling the boys, including Proulx that I've been receiving dirty pictures. That might prompt Proulx to admit that he has also been receiving dirty pictures too and you know, get a reaction."

───────────◆◦◄───────────

Three weeks later, Hector telephoned Harry to confirm what had become their weekly meeting at the Glebe House. He told Harry that he had news about Proulx. Harry responded by informing Hector that he had planned to outline his own prank plan at the next meeting. He was sure that his plan, which he had finally finalized, at least in his own mind, would be acceptable to Hector. It was more complicated than Hector's plan and a successful result less likely, less predictable. In any event, Harry was ready to provide Hector with the details. However, he would have to wait to listen to Hector's news, whatever it was.

When Harry walked into the Glebe House the next Friday night, Hector was sitting at what had become their usual table with three draft beers sitting in front of him. A broad smile emerged on his face as Harry took his seat beside him, raised his hand in the direction of the waiter, and held up two fingers. Hector put down the menu that he had been consulting and greeted Harry enthusiastically. Harry started their conversation casually and then asked, equally casually. "What are you ordering?" Harry asked, pointing at the menu. "Haven't decided." replied Hector. The two of them sat there in silence as Harry's two beers arrived. Then, Harry asked the pivotal question. "So what's new with Mr. Proulx and his situation? To be honest, I would be surprised if there were any developments. After all, it has only been less than than a few weeks and even though he's probably received some photographs and knows you have received dirty photographs as well, he still may not have much to say."

"Well, you'd be surprised. Proulx and I ended up playing on the same Euchre team and we sort of became friends. After a couple of weeks, I told the group --- four of us, two guys who work for Proulx in the file room, Proulx and myself, that I have received dirty pictures in the mail, which prompted Proulx, who hadn't told anyone, that he too had received dirty pictures." Harry nodded his head and complimented Hector on a clever move. "So Proulx and you have something in common. You may be able to get a story out of him, particularly once he receives more pictures. I guess you can just keep talking about the pictures and hope that he'll tell you something about the effect that the pictures may have on him." Hector nodded again.

By the time they ordered and finished their dinners, both having had pizza, and were closing in their fifth or sixth draft, their consideration of the possible effect of their prank on Patrick Proulx became the main, if not the only topic of discussion. They both agreed that a prank was more than just a trick, more than just a practical joke, more than just a hoax. There was a certain touch of magic in a prank. Hector reacted to Harry's philosophizing by almost giggling. "Where did you get that stuff? Sounds like something Mr. Drolet might have said." he said, referring to a teacher under whom the two of them had suffered more than ten years ago. Drolet was famous, if not infamous for making bizarre comments that were often difficult to comprehend. Drolet was a teacher with two academic doctorates, which could not explain the reason a man of his qualifications was teaching high school. He was given to providing his colleagues, if not his students with observations that seldom made any sense to anyone, regardless of their qualifications.

Regardless of its definition, the two pranksters agreed that whatever trickery they were able to pull off on Proulx, it had to have some unfortunate effect on him. They also agreed that the effect, whatever it was, had to be obvious. Neither of them could, however, provide the other with an example of an effect that would be acceptable. Hector suggested that he could be somehow be reprimanded by his superiors on the job while Harry wondered whether there was a possibility that minister at his church or, even worse he thought, his wife would discover the photographs. On that point, both discussed the question of whether Proulx would keep the photographs, particularly the more entertaining ones theorized Harry.

The evening ended with both of them more than slightly drunk. Both of them were satisfied that with Hector now playing euchre with Proulx, they would have access to his reactions, if any, to the receipt of dirty photographs. At the moment, they realized that they had little to do but wait for news of the effect of their dirty pictures. In the meantime, at their next weekly meeting at the Glebe House, they began discussing plans for Harry's proposed prank. Harry started by providing Hector with a brief history of the apartment building in which his parents lived and where he had lived until five years ago. He told him that the man, an architect named George Fenwick, had designed the apartment building and had taken up residence on the third floor, four doors down from where his parents still lived. One of Fenwick's requirements for the building was the regular placement of paintings in the twenty one apartments of Parkdale Court on Bank Street. That would be the inspiration for the mechanics of Harry's proposed prank.

A LAST PRANK AT PARKDALE COURT

The Plan

After at least three weeks of regular meetings at the Glebe House, they had no news on Proulx despite Hector's regular euchre games with him, and the receipt of their dirty pictures. Harry asked Hector if he had any pictures left. He embarrassingly shrugged a bit and held up two fingers. Harry advised, "You may have to ask for more pictures." Before Hector had a chance to answer, their usual waiter Matt had arrived at the table to take their order. They both asked for four drafts each. Harry then ordered a club sandwich while Hector settled for fish and chips, a normal dinner for him at the Glebe House. Matt walked away while Hector responded to Harry's suggestion for additional pictures. "I don't think we'll need any more pictures. Proulx told the euchre guys that his wife, who he likes to refer to as a battleaxe, found some pornographic pictures he had been hiding in his dresser. So she ordered him to sleep on living room couch. She's also threatened to tell his mother, who Proulx said was worse than his wife, as well as the minister of their church." Hector then looked at Harry straight in the face and concluded that the pictures had an effect and were still having an effect. "Proulx told me that he's even worried about his job. I think we've accomplished what we set out to do. I don't think we'll have to send him any more photographs."

As they began to relax, Matt arrived with the beers. Harry and Hector toasted each other, declaring their prank on Proulx a complete success. As the two of them started to drink their beers, Hector questioned the efficacy of continuing to proceed with Harry's proposed prank, now that they have managed to successfully prank Proulx. Hector summarized his thinking. "I think you owe me one. After all, my plan worked. We have to see if yours. On the other hand, we may not need to stage another prank. I mean, we've successfully tricked Proulx and that is probably enough, don't you think?" Hector then leaned back in his chair while Harry leaned forward in his. Hector was obviously expecting a reply from Harry. "I don't know. Anyway, I would like to try my plan, to see if it works." At that point, Matt arrived with their meals.

As they began to eat their dinners, a usual silence descended on the two of them. After several minutes of quiet, the two of them listening to conversations swirling around them, Harry asked Hector if he wanted to hear about his plan, after which he could decide whether they should implement it or not. "After all, it may work as well as your plan has." Hector nodded, smiled and asked Harry to outline his plan for him. Between eating and drinking, Harry began his presentation. "As I told you, this man George Fenwick was the architect of the building and he had implemented a pattern of placing paintings in each apartment." Hector's gaze at Harry seemed to intensify. " Yes, my parents live in that building. Anyway, my father told me that George's father was obsessed with paintings, having purchased many of the paintings with which he then accessorized every room of the family home, usually rotating them every three months or so. It was also rumoured that he painted some of the paintings himself. In any event, George's mother accepted her husband's strange habit without question, often complimenting on his most recent addition, most of which were portraits of families, sometimes with dogs, always with several children."

Hector was still sitting in rapt attention over his fish and chips listening to Harry who continued with his commentary on George and his history. He was of course fascinated with the story of George and wondered where Harry was going with it. "George's fixation with paintings makes him an interesting target for a prank. You see, I'll place small pictures of certain paintings in his mailbox in Parkdale Court occasionally and see what happens, if he realizes that he has been pranked. My parents still live in the place and so I will have no trouble in knowing what effect, if any the paintings have had on George Fenwick." Hector asked, "Certain paintings? What paintings?" Harry started to finish the rest of his club sandwich and continued to further explain his prank plan for George. "Well, I have chosen several paintings that I intend to use in my plan. I have an idea that he might be interested, if not absorbed by them." Harry delayed for a moment, finished his second draft and carried on with the outline of his plan. "Well, it took me some time, the past month or so, but I had to engage an artist, a guy I knew from when I worked in the tax department, to paint portraits of George in various postures. I gave the guy some photos I had surreptitiously taken with my father's folding Kodak camera over the past month or so, in various postures, both inside and outside the apartment. Before you ask, Fenwick lives in the apartment that is the same size and layout as my parent's place which, as you know, is also on the same floor in Parkdale."

Hector had finished his fish and chips and was now settling into his third beer. He had a surprised look on his face, as if he was waiting for a further explanation, which was understandable. "Let me get this straight. You're going to place different paintings in his mailbox which will hopefully have some sort of effect on George." Hector had an obvious skeptical tone in his voice, as if no matter what Harry said, Hector was not prepared to believe him. "I know it sounds a little strange but I think it's possible that the paintings, which by the way I plan to leave in his mailbox in a certain order, will result in George acknowledging the prank. It may take a few paintings ---- Paul has already completed three paintings and he owes me two more. I'm sure that after receipt of three paintings or so, George will then quickly realize he has been seriously pranked. And unlike your plan with Proulx, I don't think they will harm the victim."

THE FIRST PAINTING

———————◆———————

The first painting found in his mailbox was a rather pedestrian portrait that rendered George Fenwick standing in front of the door to apartment 302. It arrived on a Tuesday afternoon in November of 1948. It was around six in the evening when the fifty two year old vice president of the architectural firm of JH Roberts stepped into the lobby of the Parkdale Court apartment building, opened his mailbox and found a large rectangular envelope. It was correctly addressed although he immediately noticed that there was no return address on the envelope. He was bewildered with the receipt of the envelope, not only because there was no return address on it but because he did not normally receive large envelopes of any kind, such communications usually sent to his office downtown. He carried the envelope as he climbed the stairs to the third floor, opened the door to his apartment, and laid it on the bedside table in his bedroom, which was to his right a few feet inside the apartment. Predictably, he stared at the envelope as if he were afraid to open it, he was worried, about what he thought may be inside.

He contemplated for several moments the possibility of the envelope containing something intriguing, mysterious, maybe even dangerous. He then picked it up and carefully started to open it. Inside there was a thick rectangular piece of paper the size and texture of a greeting card in it. There was a painting of a man facing the door to his apartment, apartment 302. The man was balding and wearing a black pinstriped suit. In his left hand, he was holding a black fedora with a small grey band in which there was a small red decoration, which looked like a feather. To George, the figure in the painting appeared to be a representation of himself, the suit, the hat, and the balding back of his head all looked right, as if he had stood in the corridor for a portrait by an artist sitting behind him. In that regard, the artist, who somehow managed to create the painting without meeting the subject, let alone having the subject sit for him, did not sign his work. George held the painting in his right hand, inspected it again with a detective's concentration and then placed it on the table in the dining room. He walked into the kitchen, opened the refrigerator, took out a Labatt Fifty, returned to the dining room table, and sat down on a chair looking out one of the windows in the front of the building facing Bank Street. He intended to continue as calmly as he could with an interpretation of the painting that he had just received.

At first, it was a joke he thought, a practical joke, not very humorous, in fact not humorous at all, but serviceable enough he supposed for whatever purpose the artist or the person that may have commissioned the painting had in mind when he placed it in his mailbox. It was possible, quite possible, at least to Fenwick, that there was a motive, a well thought out motive behind the painting, something out of his past. He could not imagine what it could be but he was willing to try. As he sat there pondering his history, he thought that maybe it was one of his colleagues, earlier at school, presumably McGill University in Montreal, one of his fellow patrons at the Fred's Magic Shop in the days when he attended magic shows, or at JH Roberts, the local architectural firm for which he had worked for more than thirty five years, or one of the contractors or other business associates, like art gallery owners where George Fenwick purchased one of the many paintings he used to decorate the twenty one apartments at Parkdale Court. Sitting there at the dining room table, George Fenwick began to formulate a theory, however unexpected it seemed. Someone from his past history, someone who was familiar with his own and his father's inexplicable obsession with placing paintings on the walls of homes and apartments, behaviour that the two of them eventually abandoned without really knowing why. Someone was sending him a message.

As absurd as it may seem, at least initially, the more Fenwick thought about it, the more it seemed to make sense. If he was right about the origins of the painting in the envelope, that left him with a consideration of the reason for it. Why he thought would anyone, and he had few candidates who could fill that role, send him a message, if a message is what it was, about a compulsion from which both he and his father suffered a long time ago. And if true, what message could that be? As he sat there behind another Labatt Fifty, having gone to the refrigerator without actually remembering that he did it, he concluded that probably the most likely explanation for the painting was an attempt by some unknown sender, motivation unknown, to remind him of his obsession with paintings. Perhaps it was his father deciding to play a joke on him, something he didn't often like to do. In fact, he could remember only one or two occasions on which he played a joke on anyone more.

The more he thought about it, however, and now he was on his third Labatt Fifty of thinking about it, the more he become convinced, despite evidence to the contrary, that his elderly father, Richard Fenwick, was behind the painting mailed to him. He concluded that he, regardless of the detail of the prank, did not need a rationale to pull any kind of stunt on his own son, nor anyone else. He thought of contacting his father, to let him know that he aware of his foolishness, if that what it was. That was his next move.

THE SECOND PAINTING

T he next day, after an evening of contemplating a painting received in his mailbox and concluding that his father may have played a prank on him, George Fenwick planned to telephone his father to inform him that he was aware of his deception. George was not normally enthused with the prospect of talking to his father. He could not specifically explain his reluctance to communicate with his father although he clearly remembered that their apparent antagonism started when the two of them disagreed several years ago over something he could not recall. In any event, he thought that a brief conversation over his father's apparent prank might let him know that he was aware of his practical joke but also possibly resolve their differences, whatever they may be. He planned to telephone his father in the morning, before lunch and before his nap in the afternoon, so he could limit their conversation, which George thought was likely to be worthwhile.

His mother Edna answered the telephone with a predictably enthusiastic greeting. Unlike her husband, his mother would express pride in her son's accomplishments every chance she got, which wasn't that often. Accordingly, it was no surprise then that his mother was more than happy to engage George in a discussion of his most recent accomplishments, whether real or not. Even the slightest triumph, a compliment from a superior for example, would prompt an avalanche of flattery from his mother. As pleased as he was with his mother's praise, he was also embarrassed, especially if he intended to speak to his father, who seemed to be more interested in George's faults than any of his successes. After fifteen minutes talking with his mother, he managed to get his father on the line.

"Long time, son. How are you?" his father greeting him in his usual business like demeanour. George was long familiar with his father's approach to almost every conversation. He almost always engaged anyone he spoke to as if he was in his office. Even in his childhood, his father generally treated George as if he was working in his office. Fortunately, that approach did not extend to his mother and his interest in magic and occasionally playing tricks on people. In any event, George answered as he always did. "I'm fine and my conversation with my mother was good." His father did not immediately reply. He only cleared his throat before he curtly replied, going straight to business. "Good. And what can I do for you?" George paused for a moment and then went to the point. "I got your envelope and the painting inside it. It took me a while but I finally figured it out. It was a trick, a simple prank." Again, his father paused and quietly coughed. He then raised his voice and answered. "I never sent you an envelope with anything in it, let alone a painting. Why would I?" George said he didn't know. "Well, you like to occasionally pull pranks on people, don't you?" After another pause, his father issued a quick denial. "I may have occasionally but I certainly did not send you an envelope with a painting in it." George then quietly asked his father to confirm his answer. "Honestly, George, I didn't send you any envelope with a painting in it. By the way, what kind of painting did you receive?" George was happy to respond, thinking that maybe his father could give him a hint about the painting." Well, it was weird. It was a painting of a man with his back to the artist facing my door to my apartment. It looked like it could have been me." His father had no opinion.

<hr/>

It was almost a week later. George continued to occasionally ruminate about the receipt of the painting but his concern grew weaker. Understandably, he had spent a fair amount of time after he had received that first envelope contemplating the possible implications, if any of the painting which it carried. That first week, he debated the issue endlessly with himself, going through maybe a half a dozen scenarios it seemed before calling it a mystery and ending consideration of the matter, at least in his own mind. His growing apathy in that first painting continued until George received the second envelope two weeks later. He practically sprinted up the stairs with the envelope, opening the door to his apartment, placing the envelope on the dining room table and then sitting down there to examine it as if he looking through a microscope. The painting appeared to show the same man as in the first painting ----- himself. He was in a similar pose, shown from the rear, his balding head prominent, wearing a black pinstripe suit, and holding a fedora with a grey hat band in his left hand. He was standing halfway down the hallway from the doorway.

He was carrying the second painting. He laid it down beside the first painting on the dining room table and went to the refrigerator where he extracted two Labatt Fifty pints which he intended to use, as he frequently did, to help him deliberate with himself. He started with comparing the two paintings. First of all, there was the matter of location. The first painting showed the man, presumed by George to represent himself, facing the door to his apartment while the second painting showed the back of the same man, having opened and then presumably closed the door, standing in the middle of the hallway of his apartment, looking towards the kitchen, the bedroom room to his right and the bathroom to the left. He was facing in the same direction and was dressed identically in both paintings. As with the first painting, he had no idea what the second painting meant or could mean either. He went through the two bottles of Labatt Fifty as he gazed out the dining room window without any inspiration. He had invested, if not wasted enough time pondering the two envelopes and the two paintings.

THE THIRD PAINTING

——◇——

The third painting arrived in his mailbox less than a week after the second painting had been found. Again, the figure, presumably George again, was painted from the rear. He was seated at the dining room in front of now three paintings arranged in a neat line on the table. There were several differences between the third and the other two paintings. He was sitting, not standing, he was in the dining room, not in the hallway, nor outside the apartment and he was looking out the window, and not into the kitchen. He was in the hallway, looking into the kitchen. George felt that it was some sort of story out of *Weird Tales* or some such publication, an existential fantasy. Although they had no method of ascertaining George Fenwick's reaction to the receipt of the three paintings, Harry and Hector still managed to discuss the progress of his prank at their next meeting at the Glebe House. Harry said that it was virtually impossible unless and until George Fenwick somehow displayed some sort of response to one or all of the paintings that he had received so far. One if not the only way of knowing his reaction to their prank would be to somehow monitor George Fenwick to verify the achievement of the prank. They came to the quick conclusion that there was probably no way of determining whether George had been effected by the prank in some way. They agreed, after their third draft each, to overlook any progress of their prank. They decided to just continue with their plan and hope for a favourable outcome, an assurance that Hector called, in an obviously sarcastic tone, "our best bet."

After they discussed the three paintings that had already been left in George's mailbox, they reviewed the paintings they intended to slip into his mailbox in the next few weeks: the figure of the man standing in the window, the figure of the man standing and looking out the window, and the culmination of the series, a painting of the park through the window. As they reflected on their plans for the rest of the prank, Harry said that he had another painted scene to add to the series of six which they had already arranged. "We can add a painting with a woman in it. I'm pretty sure that George isn't married and I really don't know if he has girlfriend but placing a girl in a painting could make a difference for the results of the prank. It might throw him a slight jolt." Hector slowly nodded, looking sleepy, lethargic, not surprising since he was working on his fifth draft of the evening. He then asked, "Do you think your artist friend can produce another painting in two weeks or so? I figure you'll want to slip another envelope in his mailbox shortly, right?" Harry returned Hector's nod. "Yeah, you're probably right. I'll ask him on Monday. By the way, do you have any idea what the woman should look like?" Hector suggested that it didn't matter. Harry agreed but then said. "On second thought, maybe putting a girl in a painting is really not a good idea. It might confuse the audience, so to speak." Hector replied. "Not to mention us." They both laughed.

They spent the rest of the evening, drinking a couple of more beers and theorizing once again about the possible effect of the three paintings they have left so far in George's mailbox. Harry and Hector looked at each other, leaning toward the middle of the table, both seriously drunk and apparently out of inspiration. Hector knew the least about George Fenwick but seemed to want to talk about him the most. "I don't know the guy but from what you've told me, he's sort of strange. I mean, didn't you tell me that Fenwick not only designed the Parkdale Court building he lives in but insisted that paintings be hung in every apartment in the building, just like his old man. Nobody knows the reason for either of their obsessions. Maybe it's a family thing, you know, something that is inherited, like a genetic thing, a family trait." Harry explained that his father, who lived on the same floor as George Fenwick, told him that both Fenwicks like to practice magic and their propensity to hang paintings on apartment walls. Hector then admitted that he hadn't reached any particular conclusion about George and his unusual characteristics. He then summarized his thoughts on the affect that the progress of the prank has had on George Fenwick. "So who knows what the hell George thinks about our little trick. I know I don't." And he then added. "But on the other hand, he gets to receive three more paintings. Maybe then we'll know something."

THE FOURTH PAINTING

---◆---

It was a Friday evening, a little later than normal, when George arrived in the lobby of Parkdale Court to find his fourth envelope with the painting enclosed. There was one neighbour on his knees fumbling with his mailbox key while an older couple were leaving the building, the man carrying a small suitcase. No one said anything although the man fumbling with his key nodded at the older couple. George managed to open his mailbox without incident and left the lobby while the man with the malfunctioning key was still trying to liberate whatever was waiting for him in his mailbox. George was already on the third floor when the clumsy neighbour finally opened his mailbox only to find it empty. For some reason, George thought of the neighbour when he had a brief problem opening the door to his apartment. He wondered whether the neighbour was also having a problem opening the door to his apartment.

George then stood at the entrance to the dining room, opened the envelope, removed the most recent painting and stared at it like he was inspecting an artistic work on a wall in a museum. Again, the figure in the painting, a man presumed to be George, was pictured from the rear, framed by the window facing the front of the building, when the evening hour made the bustle on Bank Street less conspicuous than it normally was. The figure was facing the window, both arms spread out as if he were leaning out to carefully survey the street, his head down, almost in reverence, apparently watching for something about which he was not certain. George was fantasizing he supposed, thinking about something that may have happened may not have happened or may happen sometime in the future. In any event, George looked at the three paintings sitting on the dining room table and then placed the fourth painting above the other three, forming a small triangle.

Did the addition of the fourth painting on the top of the other three paintings mean anything that George had not thought of previously? Sure, so he had been ruminating about the three paintings he has received so far. He had started to wonder whether the paintings, starting with the first one he received more than a month ago or so, were not practical jokes at all but were somehow messages or more precisely messages about the future. In other words, predictions, prophesies or prognostications, whatever he wanted to call it, they were messages about the future. It was the last painting that meant the most he thought, at least to him, looking out the window, into the future. On the other hand, rather than contemplating the purpose, if not the theme of the messages, George also thought about the perpetrator of the scheme. He thought that there had to be somebody behind the scheme, some malevolent force he feared.

On reflection, as he struggled with sleep several hours after receiving the fourth painting, it was predictable that he would remember a fellow member of the group that used to meet at Fred Magic's Shop. His name was Larry and he was proficient in pulling pranks, which seemed perfectly acceptable to his other student magicians. It was no surprise therefore that he was very popular with the other people in the group, including Fred himself who was particularly entertained by several of his tricks, including the traditional water balloon over the transom prank, fake telephone calls and telegrams, and impersonating women. Over the next few days, that recollection, which may have been partially fictional given his occasionally faulty memory, eventually lead to his conclusion that Larry Something Or Other was behind the prank. It seemed to make sense, even though he had only seen him a couple of times over the past few years, both times on Sparks Street during the lunch hour. That settled, George then went back to congregating his thoughts on the objective of these paintings. They must have some purpose. He just didn't know exactly what that was. Yet, if ever.

THE FIFTH PAINTING

I t wasn't that long before George received the fifth in the series of paintings. It had become his habit, more like a custom, to expect an envelope every month or so, until the fifth envelope was found in his mailbox only two weeks after his most recent one. He immediately realized that there was something special about this most recent missive. The envelope itself was coloured tan as opposed to the usual white, the address and the stamp in their normal positions, suggesting that there was something unusual about it. As was his practice, he hurried up the stairs, clutching the envelope and opening the door, as if he was expecting someone or something. He also made it to the dining room table before he opened the envelope. Inside he found a painting that looked a lot like previous one. Again, it showed a man from the rear facing the window of the apartment's second bedroom, which faced the Glendale Park, which accommodated several children's play structures, an ancient, decrepit baseball diamond, and a slight hill on which people occasionally skied. The man in the painting was leaning over and looking through the window into the park. Unlike the painting's predecessor, where the man was simply gazing out the window without any particular objective in mind, the man in the fifth painting was clearly searching for something in the park, specific but unknown. George was fascinated and a little frightened.

The meaning of the fifth painting remained elusive, a customary situation that prompted George to continually contemplate it, like it was a dream that frequently returned to him involuntarily. He didn't know how to deal with it. More than the other four paintings, the fifth painting seem to be beckoning him to respond in some way, to take some sort of action. Every day, sometimes several times a day, he walked into the apartment's second bedroom to look down at the park from the window. He stood before that window, sometimes for more than five minutes, staring down at the park as if it were another painting. He thought of it as a curious juxtaposing of perceptions, one imagined by an unknown artist, the other clear to anyone looking down from the third floor of the east side of Parkdale Court. Each time he was left that room after gazing out that at the park below, he went immediately to the kitchen where he pulled a bottle of cheap scotch out of a cabinet, a libation that he did not normally enjoy, beer being his normal drink, and gulped down several ounces as quickly as he could. He usually left the kitchen a little inebriated and as mystified as he was before he walked into that second bedroom. As he figured that he would visit the second bedroom frequently, he thought it expedient to purchase several more bottles of cheap scotch.

Within weeks, he was consulting with himself in the second bedroom at least twice a day, a practice that inspired all sorts of visions, not least of which suggested that he was imagining things. He was overwhelmed with his contemplation of the fifth painting, so much so that he began to think that he needed advice. While he didn't have any close friends, either left over from his school days or currently one of his colleagues at JH Roberts or even his parents, in whom he could not confide or he simply could not get the idea of sharing his obsession with someone else, anyone else who could find his way into his bewildered head. One person who he imagined could help him out of the quandary, psychological or otherwise, was a woman named Sylvia, who worked for Fred Ennis, who was an associate in the legal department of JH Roberts. Sylvia, aside from being a secretary also advertised herself as a fortune teller, a profession that annoyed some people but captivated and fascinated others, a group that could count George among her admirers. He did not confer, however, with Sylvia about personal matters while most, if not all of George's colleagues sought her guidance about their lives outside the office. In fact, some of George's colleagues would sardonically suggest that Sylvia needed her own office, particularly after office parties when people would seek her advice. Regardless of the fact that he never sought her counsel, George often thought he was just eccentric enough to consider it.

It was entirely predictable, therefore, that George would want to share with Sylvia the fortune teller his trepidation with the five paintings, especially the most recently received one. Close to seven in the morning, a good half hour before his usual starting time, George had slipped a note under the pad on her desk, imploring her to provide him with guidance on his future, not specifically mentioning his continuing concern with the paintings which was the actual objective of his pursuit of Sylvia's abilities. That morning, a little after ten when most of the support staff were at the company cafeteria for their break, George went to Sylvia's desk to follow up on the note he left her earlier in the day. As usual, the door to Mr. Ennis's office was closed. George was therefore able to talk to Sylvia without worrying about her boss, an imperious superior to say the least, interrupting them, not that he planned to speak to her for very long.

<hr />

It was her idea that they meet for dinner two days later at a restaurant called *The Dark Moon,* a diner in lower town. George never heard of the place. It was dark, dingy and disturbing, characteristics that seemed suited to some sinister purpose. There was space for twenty patrons in four booths with another six on stools in front of a counter. There were various mosaics on the wall. The kitchen was in back, its swinging door the only sound aside from scattered overlapping conversations and soft Oriental music. Sylvia seemed to know the man who greeted them at the entrance, a man wearing a dirty apron and a grey speckled beard. She addressed him as Gus, greeted him with a quick wave, and pointed to a booth in the back. Gus nodded and handed her a menu that looked like it had been laying on the floor of the kitchen. George and Sylvia both sat down. Sylvia ordered a Turkish drink called Raki while George requested a tea. After the waiter, who Sylvia identified as a man named Ahmet, took their drink orders and left, Sylvia said that Turkish meatballs were the specialty of the *The Dark Moon* and recommended that they both order it for dinner. When Ahmet returned with the drinks, they both asked for Turkish meatballs and then got down to the purpose of the dinner.

Not surprisingly, Sylvia asked him why he had approached her. After all, she noted that he hardly, if ever spoke to her about anything and here he was seeking her guidance. She simply asked about the basis for his interest in her. "You don't give me the impression that you're the type that is interested in having his fortune told." Sylvia observed. She then signalled Ahmet for another drink of Raki. George looked stunned, like he was momentarily scrambling for an answer. "I don't know, I just thought that maybe someone like you could help me with a problem I'm having." Sylvia started on her second drink, Ahmet having just delivered it. "What do you mean, someone like me?" Sylvia asked. George answered, "I thought that since you're a fortune teller, you might be able to give me some advice. Not that I want my fortune told, at least I don't think so." Sylvia put her drink down, looked up, sighed and then asked an obvious question. "Which is it?" George looked at Sylvia with a confused look on his face and answered a second time. "I'm not sure, I'm just not sure."

George's doubts about the meaning of the receipt of the five paintings and the possible implications they may have for him, his present and his future. That necessitated him to provide Sylvia with a historical narrative about the receipt of the paintings, describing each painting and the timing of its receipt. Once he had finished his account, both were almost finished their Turkish meatballs, Sylvia's third Raki and George's first Raki, when Sylvia decided that she had heard enough to offer some sort of prognostication, particularly with respect to the last painting, the one which had the man gazing out the window of the second bedroom in his apartment at nothing in particular. "You seem to me to be unusually concerned about your future. Without knowing a lot more about you and your situation, I really couldn't tell you anything more than that."

THROUGH THE WINDOW

 ◆

At first, George Fenwick's leap from apartment 302 of Parkdale Court was almost uneventful, a strange observation. The fact was that George lay in a contorted heap for possibly an hour before his lifeless body was actually noticed in the grass beside Parkdale Court by a neighbourhood woman walking her miniature poodle. He was found across Glendale Park between Powell Avenue and the apartment building from which he had just jumped. The woman, who was so disturbed that she was unable to introduce herself to the police for at least ten minutes, had come across George Fenwick at four in the afternoon. She managed to creep up the stairs from the park to Bank Street before she fainted, motionless until a couple who had just disembarked from a city bus going south managed to rouse her sufficiently for her to point at George Fenwick's lifeless body laying at the base of Parkdale Court. Amazingly enough, her miniature poodle was sitting quietly by her supine form. A cruiser stopped when the couple stepped a few feet into the street to get police attention. Two officers got out of the car, two relatively beefy men.

The couple spoke to the officers. "I think this woman came across something in the park. She was pointing down there before she fainted." explained the man, whose name was Brian Burns. For some reason, he had introduced himself and his companion, his wife Margaret, to the officers before he provided the explanation. The officers themselves looked confused for a moment, nodded wordlessly and headed down the stairs. Margaret was assisting the woman who had been lying on the sidewalk, patted her dog, and helped her to her feet. The woman then spoke. "I think there's a man down there in the park who may be hurt." Brian Burns then responded, "I think the officers know that.", pointing down to the park. By this time, both police officers were kneeling by the body of George Fenwick, gently poking him, one had his ear listening to his chest, both hoping that his leap off Parkdale Court had not had the effect that they both worried it might have had. All three spectators on the sidewalk looked at each other with sudden and sad shock on their faces. They saw one of the police officers on his radio, presumably calling for either an ambulance or the coroner, the latter the most likely.

By the time the coroner arrived, in a black van with two doors in the front of the van and two doors in the rear, a large crowd had assembled. It had taken the black van twenty minutes to arrive. The two beefy police officers were still in attendance, there to greet the two men dressed in white coats disembarking from the van. They pulled a gurney out of the rear of the van, and headed down the stairs to George's body. The large crowd of bystanders were all looking down and shaking their heads, their hands on their hips, waiting for news. Brian wondered how many of the crowd lived in the apartment. Another man was seen exiting the apartment building from a narrow door that looked like it was connected to the basement of the building. One man was overheard saying that he had seen a man in a fedora talking to the police and scribbling in a notebook. Brian wondered how an apparent journalist, either that or a psychologist doing research on suicides, was on the scene of a possible suicide so quickly after a man apparently leapt from an apartment building. He had moved closer to the crowd of bystanders but did not see a man in the fedora holding a notebook. He then wondered where the story came from. He did not see the man, only heard about him. On the other hand, maybe he had misheard the bystander.

Brian had followed and moved closer to Fenwick's body as the two coroner staff members were preparing to lift him onto the gurney, move him up to the street and into the van. They then started to pull the gurney through the crowd, which understandably moved aside to allow it to get up to the stairs where the men in white coats and the two police officers began to lift Fenwick up the stairs and into the black van. The two police officers then went back down the stairs and returned to the crowd which was waiting to disburse but seemed to understand that they had to wait for the police to question them, an obvious conclusion, at least to anyone who read newspapers or read detective stories. It would be required somehow. The woman who originally was witness to George laying in the park between Powell and the apartment was now leaning on the black cast iron fence overlooking the park. She had her miniature poodle on a leash by her feet. The dog was silent. It appeared to be asleep. She watched the crowd envelop the officers who began to record the names of the people who were standing there in the street. A majority of the crowd seemed to want to give evidence. They were actually lining up, like they were in elementary school. On the other hand, at least two of the bystanders left as the police started to take names. They seemed to be walking away in a hurry. Most of the crowd, including Brian and Margaret, who were in the street with the others, spotted them. Maybe they had police records.

The two police officers looked serious, their crew cuts looking more intimidating than normal. Still, they were trying to record the names as quickly as they could. The people in the line also looked serious, hardly speaking to each other, most of them looking at their feet, presumably contemplating the event they thought they had witnessed, which they hadn't. Each person dutifully provided their names, their addresses and their telephone numbers and walked away, their civic duties fulfilled. Every time a person gave his or her information, both officers looked at the back of the line of spectators and continued their gathering of information. After maybe two dozen spectators had reported, a man who many of the crowd did actually see exiting from a door in the apartment building basement seemed to gently seize the officer's right arm and started to whisper in the officer's ear. Once he was finished whatever it was he wished

217

to impart, the man returned to the apartment. He had identified the man laying in the park as George Fewnwick who he said lived in the building.

By the time Brian and Margaret Burns reached the officers to give their names and details, the crowd had thinned out somewhat. Margaret Burns asked one of the officers, who introduced himself in a quietly surly voice as a Constable Dixon, if the police intended to schedule an interview with her and her husband at some point in the future. Wearily, the Constable answered as if he had been asked the question by every person he had spoken to since they had returned from helping his partner and two men in white coats place the deceased into the black van which by then was on its way to the city mortuary. "We'll be getting into touch with any person who could be a witness to what happened here today." With that explanation, Constable Dixon looked like he was tying to be patient. Brian, who was listening to his wife, was trying to coax his wife away from her conversation with Constable Dixon. He interrupted, "Thanks, officer." With that, he ushered Margaret away, They took one last look down at the park and headed home.

<hr />

An article appeared in the *Ottawa Journal* edition of April 5, 1949. It reported the details of his death in a straight forward, journalistic manner. It was the first time that both Harry and Hector were informed of George Fenwick's demise.

OTTAWA ARCHITECT
KILLS HIMSELF

———◆———

G eorge Fenwick, an Ottawa architect known for designing
buildings in the downtown area, killed himself yesterday
by jumping from the open window of the top floor of
Parkdale Court, a twenty one unit apartment building he
designed in 1935. According to building landlord Lawrence
Wallace, Mr. Fenwick, who was unmarried and was living
alone, was a well spoken and courtly gentleman who was
the perfect tenant. "He always paid his rent on time, never
disturbed his neighbours, and maintained one of the most
tastefully decorated apartments in the building." said Mr.
Wallace.

According to several of the tenants who had gathered
in front of the apartment on Bank Street where the body
was found, Mr. Fenwick seemed to be distressed recently,
nervous about something or other. According to the other
tenants, who spoke to this reporter, Mr. Fenwick was not
close to anyone in the building, having few friends, if any
friends in Parkdale Court. Police have indicated, however,
that the circumstances of Mr. Fenwick's death appear
to be obvious and therefore did not warrant any further
investigation. Officially, Mr. Fenwick's death would likely
be ruled a suicide.

According to city records, Mr. Fenwick had either

designed or had a hand in designing over a dozen downtown apartments and was commonly regarded as one of the most prominent architects in the city. Mr. Fenwick was 52 years old and had lived in apartment 302 of Parkdale Court since the building opened in 1936.

There was no doubt that both Harry and Hector were shocked by the news as reported and were a little surprised to learn that authorities were able to come to the conclusion that George Fenwick's jump from the top floor of Parkdale Court would likely be ruled a suicide. While there was some ambiguity in the last sentence of the second paragraph of the *Ottawa Journal* story, Harry and Hector had immediately questioned how the authorities would have come to such a conclusion within less than twenty four hours after George Fenwick had fallen or jumped from the top floor of the Parkdale Court apartment building. Since building landlord Lawrence Wallace was mentioned as a source for the relevant details included in the story, it was clear that the police officers had done some investigating, as preliminary as it was.

There was only one short follow up in the *Ottawa Journal* after the April 5 article about the death of George Fenwick It was published two days later and confirmed the original determination that George Fenwick's death was in fact a suicide. Neither Harry nor Hector nor anyone else the two of them imagined were surprised by what they realized was now the final verdict. Predictably, the article was printed on page two of the April 9 edition. Also predictably, if not ironically, his obituary also appeared in the same edition, although appearing on page thirty five, the second last page of the third section. The text of the final celebration of his life, which was hardly a celebration at all, it was a little different from any other announcement of death. It was, lacking a more adequate description, surprisingly brief.

Fenwick, George Richard *He passed away on April 4, 1949 at the age of 52. Son of Richard and Edna Fenwick and nephew of an uncle who was known to be living in Calgary. George is a graduate of the School of*

Architecture of McGill University in Montreal and worked for almost thirty years for JH Roberts where he was eventually promoted to the position of Vice President where he was responsible for the design of many local buildings, most particularly apartments and houses. A visitation will be held on the afternoon and evening of April 10 at the Whelan Funeral Home on Cooper Street and a funeral will be conducted the next morning at the St. Barnabas Church on James Street

<hr/>

It was the day after the article regarding George Fenwick appeared in the April 5, 1949 edition of the *Ottawa Journal* that Harry and Hector met in the Glebe House to discuss what Harry had referred to as "A tragedy that we may be responsible for.", an insinuation that made Hector very uncomfortable and very guilty. As soon as they sat down at their usual table, the two of them looked at each other with a certain angst on both their faces, expressions that were immediately noticed by Matt, their normal waiter, who asked if there was sometime wrong. Harry and Hector both looked at each other with a certain apprehension but did not reply. They both ordered four draft beers each and returned to looking at each other with desolate looks on their faces. Harry continued with his sombre reflections. "I can't help but think that our paintings obviously led to this. I don't know why but without them, I don't think he would have jumped off that damn building. It's my fault, it's our fault. I think we never realized how sensitive George was ---- we pushed him over the edge." Hector looked at Harry with more than hesitation on his face. He was hoping to coax Harry away from wallowing in his self-pity. "It wasn't your fault, it wasn't our fault." Hector paused for a moment and then continued with his attempt to console his friend.

With Matt arriving with the beer, their conversation about any possible responsibility for George's leap from Parkdale Court subsided into a discussion of the likely reactions of the tenants to his death. Since he designed the building and lived in it since it opened thirteen years ago, and many of the tenants, particularly the ones who lived on the third floor, were long time residents, Harry in particular said that he would be interested in those reactions. The realist of the two, Hector pointed out that it was unlikely that anybody could provide them with any reaction, particularly since the only building residents they knew, Harry's parents, were on holiday. On the other hand, they could consult other sources for reactions, like the police or the newspapers for example. They both said that they wanted to know the reason for his passing. In any event, Hector summarized his advice. "Look, we don't know why George did it but he did it. I don't know how but we should find out why. There must be a reason." They both sat there, looking blankly across the table at each other. Harry then came up with a suggestion. "Why don't we just talk to whoever wrote the article about his death for the *Ottawa Journal* or even his obituary? Maybe they can give us a hint" Hector agreed. He added another helpful conclusion to their discussion. "Well, at least we won't have to submit a sixth painting to George."

⇒·◦·⇐

The two of them attended the visitation at the Whelan Funeral Home on the evening of April 10. They were not surprised at all when they discovered there were only four other mourners in the room when they arrived. It became apparent within five minutes that one of the four was Mr. Whelan's son Malcolm while another introduced himself as someone named Frank who worked as a file clerk at JH Roberts. The other two individuals were obviously a married couple who were sitting by themselves in the last row of the eight that were available. At the front of the visitation room was George Fenwick laying in a mahogany coloured coffin, surrounded by several flower arrangements. Harry and Hector shook hands with Malcolm Whelan and Frank Montague, the clerk from JH Roberts. They also nodded their consolations to the couple in the rear of the room. For several minutes, they knelt before George in his coffin and then got up and sat in the front row of the chairs. They sat in them for maybe twenty minutes before leaving a room that was now empty. Malcolm Whelan was standing by the entrance to the room with a bored look on his face.

He reminded the two of them about tomorrow's funeral at St. Barnabas on James Street. They ended up attending the funeral. There was several dozen congregants at the funeral. They were told by one of the boys participating in the service that most of the attendees were regular church goers and could be counted on to attend most church services, regardless of purpose.

A few days latter, Harry telephoned the *Ottawa Journal* news desk, the number being published on page two of every daily edition, and asked to speak to a reporter who followed city news. The man who answered the telephone introduced himself as Bruce Nolan, assistant to the municipal affairs editor. Harry introduced herself and told Mr. Nolan that he was looking for further information on the suicide of George Fenwick, telling him that his father was an old friend who wanted to know what happened to him, what persuaded him to presumably jump from the top floor of the apartment building in which he was living. Nolan managed to summarize the situation almost immediately. "And you want to talk to the reporter who wrote the story to find out whether there was a background." Harry was pleased, happy that it seemed that he would not have to invest too much time and effort to uncover any interesting facts about George Fenwick. "Sure I want to talk to whoever wrote the story and the obituary. As you suggest, he might have some further background. My father was disturbed by the original newspaper story which reported that George was distressed. The reporter should be able to explain the reasons for George being described as being distressed. I think both my father and I would be interested in any explanation." Nolan then recommended that he contact Mr. Mark Lamarche, the reporter who worked on the city desk and had written the article and obituary on George Fenwick. He gave him his telephone number.

———————————

It took Harry three days to arrange an appointment with the reporter Lamarche to discuss his two pieces on George Fenwick. He and Hector met him at the Prescott tavern in Little Italy around two in the afternoon. Lamarche looked like a reporter, an overweight, bespectacled man who wore a straw hat, smoked unfiltered Players cigarettes and spoke very fast, like he was trying to say something worth saying. Harry explained his objective in contacting him. "So the two of you want to know what was bothering him, if something was bothering him, you know which could have explained his decision to jump out the window of his apartment." Both Harry and Hector agreed. "Well, we would really like to know what the circumstances were before he decided to kill himself." Lamarche nodded, lite his next cigarette, and began to disclose what he had found out about the situation that may have precipitated George's untimely demise. "Well, I spoke to the manager of Parkdale Court. He said that George was a generally quiet individual with some curious habits." Harry asked whether his habits were in any way related to his death. Lamarche nodded slowly and answered tentatively. "Well, not directly but in a way indirectly I guess. It's not a fact but given his strange habits, you could make the argument."

Hector was the one who asked the next question "What argument would that be?" Lamarche offered the two of them a shy smile and went on with an explanation. It sounded like the reporter was providing them with what one could call a psychiatric assessment of George Fenwick's behaviour. "As you may know, at least from my article, George was an architect who designed the apartment building, the Parkdale Court, where he has lived since the place opened. When the place was built, he insisted that paintings be placed in every apartment in the building. Most of the paintings were small sized and always seemed to show similar looking men, men that looked a lot like George when you thought about it. In addition, they were hung inconspicuously, as if he didn't want the occupants to notice any of them, even though many of the inhabitants I spoke to did. No one knows why. In addition, he also had the habit of relocating the pictures every couple of months of so, so they told me. Again, no one knows why either. Apparently, he just sneaked in the apartment when no one is home and replaced the painting. Again, no one knows why. As I said, the guy was a little, what can you say, eccentric." Lamarche then concluded his narrative and awaited comment from either Harry or Hector or both of them.

Their reaction was understandable, if not predictable. Harry made comment. "I know you said that no one, at least no one in the Parkdale Court, knew the reason George hung paintings in the apartments of the building he designed. Did anyone you spoke to ever give you the impression about whether anyone else, like his family, friends or even people at work knew about this strange habit?" Lamarche nodded and then told Harry the facts of life the way he saw them. "I shouldn't have to point it out but I'm a reporter, not a historian. You can do the research yourself, if you two are that interested." The two of them momentarily paused, and Hector answered for them. "No, I don't think we'll be doing anything like that. As interesting as George's predilection with the paintings are, I don't think we're that interested. Maybe there is no particular explanation." Lamarche reacted. "However, I have do another thing that might be of interest to you. In fact, I found it fascinating. It was like something out of a book or a movie." Hector questioned Lamarche. "Well, what are we talking about? Does it have anything to do with the paintings?" Lamarche replied, "Without a doubt."

After waiting for several moments, during which time the three of them finally ordered their beers, Lamarche resumed his explanation. "Well, the police officer who investigated George's death allowed me into his apartment after his body was taken away. He said that he noticed something that he couldn't figure out and thought I would be fascinated with. I was." There was a silence between the three of them. After their beers arrived, Lamarche continued. "Well, there were three paintings on the dining room table, one laying under the front window and another under the window in the back bedroom. It wasn't George in the pictures but they could have been. But that didn't make the paintings unusual. All five pictures were paintings set in his apartment on the third floor, in sort of a sequence that concluded with the man facing out the window above where his body was found, face down in the grass of Glendale Park. All showed the man from the rear." Lamarche then went on to to describe the other paintings. "The first painting showed the man facing the door to his apartment, apartment 302; the second painting showed the man in the corridor inside his apartment; the third painting showed the man sitting at the dining room table; and the fourth had the man facing out the front window of the apartment. And you know the fifth painting."

Almost like having seen an inexplicable magic show, Harry and Hector sat transfixed, looking at each other, like there was an event or a thing in a hallucination that defied any sort of explanation. Lamarche recognized their bewilderment and confusion. "I couldn't figure it out either and I still can't. They may be illusions. I was told by some of the people who live in the Parkdale Court that they had similar experiences with the paintings in their apartments although those did not involve more than one painting at a time. There were sequences but it often took weeks, sometimes even months to provide some sort of sense. Most, if not all of them, the others I mean, would provide predictions of coincidental actions, like moving furniture around the apartment, buying new clothing, stuff like that. One man said one day the painting would show the wall in the dining room one colour and then, a couple of weeks later another, another colour. Another resident claimed, and I'm not sure about his story, that one day, the painting on display by the front door showed the same painting in the kitchen, which the couple ended up moving there themselves. On the other hand, when I questioned some of the other tenants, none of them reported any sort of painting predictions, so to speak." "Painting predictions! Now that's some sort of strange term but that fits, sort of." observed Harry. He couldn't believe it.

Here was a reporter telling her that the paintings in Parkdale Court had somehow foretold the future. It was hard to believe. In fact, it was impossible to believe. So it was natural that both of them questioned Mr. Lamarche's story. "You're kidding, right? You have to admit that it is a pretty strange story." Harry then reflected for a moment and then made another observation. "One thing. I can see why you never mentioned any of this in those reports you wrote for the newspaper. No one would believe it although if you submitted a story about those paintings to a tabloid, some readers might believe it. But I see why nothing like that would appear in the *Ottawa Journal*, unless of course the paper decided to open a tabloid section." Lamarche snickered at that comment. Both Harry and Hector joined him in sneering at the absurdity of that suggestion. The three of them then sat silently, all lost in contemplation.

PONDERING THE PAINTINGS

———◇———

It was three days after their meeting with the journalist Lamarche when they resumed their regular rendezvous at the Glebe House. It was a Friday evening after work, a little after six o'clock when they took up their usual table in the northern corner of the lounge. Their customary waiter Matt arrived almost immediately to accept their drink orders, specifically three draft beers each. He also handed each of them a menu, a document with which both Harry and Hector were quite familiar. The three of them conducted a perfunctory conversation regarding the weather and other minutiae. As soon as Matt left to fetch their beers, Harry introduced the issue that both of them anticipated would be central to their discussion that evening. "Like I said on the phone, I've spent, like you, a lot of time, if not all my time, thinking that the paintings that we sent to George Fenwick may have resulted in his suicide." Hector nodded and agreed with Harry. "Particularly after we spoke to the reporter, Mr. Lamarche. He seems to think that the five paintings that were found in Fenwick's apartment somehow persuaded him to jump out of that bedroom window. I've thought about it a lot. I'm sure you have too." With that observation, Harry held his hand up and suggested that they wait until they had a beer before discussing the circumstances of George's death and whether the paintings bore any responsibility. "After all, we'll probably make more sense to ourselves if we've had a few." Hector agreed. Coincidentally, Matt arrived with the drafts and the two of them ordered fish and chips, a customary selection.

They both drank most of their first drafts in silence. They both had almost rueful looks on their faces. Hector was the first to speak. "I don't know about you but I've begun to think that maybe George had psychological problems, that maybe he had some sort of mental illness. According to that reporter for the *Ottawa Journal* Lamarche, Fenwick was pretty well fixated on paintings, for whatever reason, for years. I mean, Lamarche said that some of the residents of Parkdale Court told him that he insisted, when designing the apartment building, on installing paintings in every one of its twenty one apartments." Harry nodded his agreement and continued George's story. "Yeah, I know. My parents, who have lived in Parkdale Court for years, knew that his father was also obsessed with paintings. The walls of the family house were always decorated with paintings, hanging from every wall in the house, including the lavatories, the basement, and sometimes the front and back doors. My father said that Mr. Fenwick would often alternate paintings between the rooms. He also would trade paintings with local galleries. No wonder his son George ended up being preoccupied with paintings." Hector added further detail to their analysis of George's behaviour. "I heard that magic was a serious hobby of his. I remember that one of my teachers at Hopewell School, a man named Clarke, was a member of the Ottawa Magic Society for a while and took our grade four class to a show that was sponsored by Fred's Magic Shop. George, who we were told was a architect, performed some simple magic tricks for us. For the next few years, we would see posters and signs advertising local magicians, including George Fenwick, performing at various venues, places like the Mayfair Theatre and the Aberdeen Pavilion. But by the time I left school, people were going to movie theatres instead, I think that George was no longer doing magic shows. I don't know if he continued to be interested in magic." Harry had been patiently listening to Hector as he was enjoying his fish and chips. He interrupted his dinner and pointed out to Hector, "He probably abandoned magic but like his old man, he had developed this strange obsession with paintings which he demonstrated by having a painting presumably placed in every apartment in every apartment building he designed. We know that there were paintings in every apartment in Parkdale Court. We can only presume that paintings were hung in every unit in every apartment building he designed. Aside from an inexplicable fascination with paintings, I don't think one can ever assign any specific reason for this strange compulsion, if that's what you can call it."

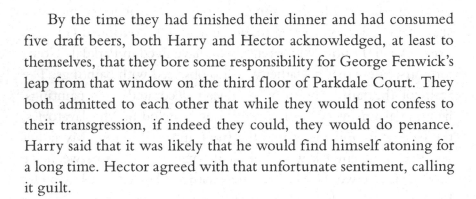

By the time they had finished their dinner and had consumed five draft beers, both Harry and Hector acknowledged, at least to themselves, that they bore some responsibility for George Fenwick's leap from that window on the third floor of Parkdale Court. They both admitted to each other that while they would not confess to their transgression, if indeed they could, they would do penance. Harry said that it was likely that he would find himself atoning for a long time. Hector agreed with that unfortunate sentiment, calling it guilt.

THE DELANEY PLAN FOR THE PHOTOGRAPHS

It was the day after the Delaney's original discussion of the mystery of the photographs they had found in apartment 302 of Parkdale Court, the mailbox of its lobby andP the single photograph in the mailbox of 64 Brighton Street. After a number of drinks, which was unusual behaviour for Patricia but standard conduct for John who was still a regular patron of the Prescott on Preston Street. John and Patricia had agreed that while the pursuit of a private investigator was an uncommon plan for an uncommon problem, it was the only plan of which they could conceive. John had promised Patricia that, as originally suggested, he might seek the guidance of some of the boys on the baseball team. He thought that there were at least three guys on the team who he thought might be qualified to give him advice on hiring a private investigator.

The first opportunity to consult the first of the three guys he planned to approach came during the next Thursday's game, more than a week after he promised Patricia that he would initiate the plan. The first teammate from whom he sought advice was one of the team's better players, a guy named Marc Bertrand. Aside from his playing abilities, Mark was rumoured to have had extensive experience driving a tow truck that John figured would probably have brought him in close touch with ambulance drivers, police officers, paramedics, personal injury lawyers, and of course other tow truck drivers, all of which might have developed an acquaintance with private investigators. In fact, Marc, who played right field with a certain elan, often entertained his baseball playing colleagues with stories about the various automobile accidents in which he had participated or witnessed. By fortunate chance, he got to sit beside Marc on the bench between the first three innings. John casually asked him about the best locations to wait for car breakdowns or accidents and therefore possible business opportunities. Marc answered fairly promptly, identifying that most of the entrances and/or exits to and from the Queensway were prime areas, mainly because they provided enough space within which to park his truck and wait for possible clients. John acknowledged Marc's comments, smiling and nodding, waiting for an opportunity to question him about his towing business. He thought of ingratiating himself to Marc by complimenting him on his job.

"Tough job I'll bet. But you always have company. You know, ambulance drivers, cops, medics, lawyers, and other truck drivers." John looked at Marc who seemed to be staring at the game and not listening to him. He then got up from the bench, Bertrand looked back at John and made a final comment. "Yeah, I run into those guys all the time. Most of the time, guys like me are often the first ones at the scene. It's usually us, then the cops and then the rest." During the next inning, John took the opportunity to seek advice from a bench warmer named Malcolm Nichols, who he thought worked on the telephone switchboard at the police station. Malcolm was profoundly inept as a ballplayer, a characterization about which he seemed to be aware of but was not particularly bothered by it. He was, however, capable of considerable humour, often coming up with absurd commentaries, his specialty the coining of nicknames, about which he was particularly inventive.

At his first opportunity to engage Malcolm in conversation, he asked him if he still worked the switchboard at the city police station. He replied. "Sure, five days a week, listening to people who liked to report their complaints ---- everything from public peeing, I mean urination to shoplifting, I hear it all. It probably funny when you think about it. It's like bad television, if you can follow me, right."

John offered him a grin and then asked him if he could talk to him after the game. Malcolm looked surprised for a moment and then answered in the affirmative. "Sure, okay." John was surprised that he accepted. He seldom hung around with anybody after the games. When the game was over, he told John that he would meet him in the *Newfoundland Pub* on Montreal Road. For some reason, John was surprised when Nichols knew the place. John had the impression that maybe there was something strange about the place. It was after their second pint, both having ordered on Malcolm's recommendation a Black Horse ale, John said that he was interested in hiring a private investigator. Malcolm said that his job occasionally gave him access to private detectives although he seemed more interested in the reason for John's search than the search itself. Their third Black Horse already consumed, John explained that he and his wife Patricia had anonymously received ten photographs and both wanted to get to the bottom of the situation. Malcolm looked at John with a goofy look on his face, as if he was auditioning some sort of joke. Malcolm asked John to repeat his purpose in seeking a private detective, expressing disbelief. "You want to hire a private dick to identify who anonymously left you a bunch of photographs and find out why they were left there." John quietly laughed and commented, "I know it sounds a little crazy but well, I would just like to know." Nichols then replied. "And you think I could give you some suggestions. Right?" John nodded.

Malcolm suddenly placed a hand in the air in the direction of the only waitress in the *Newfoundland Pub*. Her name was Gloria. She came over to their table. John was halfway through his third Black Horse Ale as Malcolm was trying to order his fourth. Waitress Gloria shook her head, pointed to the clock on the wall and announced that on Wednesday nights, the place usually stopped serving by midnight. Nichols then smiled, reached for John's glass and finished his Black Horse Ale. Gloria the waitress, seeing Malcolm's theft of John's partially consumed third beer, smiled and offered the two of them a single beer between them. John smirked, paid for the beer and waved Gloria away. The fate of a last beer settled, John then asked Malcolm,

"So are going to give me a suggestion, a name?" Malcolm took the first gulp of his newly filled glass, leaned back in his chair, which John thought might threaten him into falling on the floor, and finally replied. "I know a few private dicks." said Malcolm, "Most of them are creeps whose assignments are usually pretty dull. It's not like on television. There are no crimes, no criminals, nothing like that. The last time I heard anything from any private dick I knew involved a guy who was hired to follow a husband supposedly on a diet enjoying large lunches instead of going to the gym. Another dick was taking pictures of a neighbour who was allegedly dancing naked in the front window of his house after dark. Another, a private detective named Vince, monitored the evening activities of some poor bastard for at last a month because his wife thought he was gambling. Turns out that the guy was spending most of his evenings in strip clubs." John looked at Malcolm with a bemused look on his face, which then morphed into a clownish smile followed by quiet laughter. Gloria the waitress, the grim faced bartender and the three other patrons who were still enjoying the hospitality of the *Newfoundland Pub* all woke up long enough to take notice of John's slight eruption of laughter.

When John's laughter subsided, he repeated his request for a recommendation."I really need a suggestion from you. I want to get to the bottom of the mystery about the photographs. It's really affecting my wife. She's scared. She thinks our house is haunted. That's why we came to the idea of hiring a private investigator and that's why I came to you." Nichols grinned and finally provided John with a suggestion. "Pimm is probably your guy. He'll take any job, investigate pretty well anything. I mean, as I told you, some of these guys take on some weird jobs and Pimm has taken on some real beauties. For example, Pimm told me a couple of weeks ago that he was looking for a nameless girl a client might have taken to a high school dance more than twenty years ago." John interrupted Malcolm's story with an obvious inquiry. "Nameless?" Malcolm chuckled for a moment and then continued with his commentary. "Well, Pimm told me that this guy said that he had been having repeated dreams of a girl he thought that he might have escorted to a high school dance twenty years ago but couldn't think of her name. He wanted Pimm to find her, the only clue he provided being a bleary photograph of a shy high school couple staring blankly at a camera presumably held by a chaperone. He could remember the name of the school and maybe the year but not the name of the girl. And by the way, I don't know Pimm's first name but I think I can found out."

John just sat there collecting his thoughts and then asked for the results of that investigation. Nichols leaned across the table, swallowed the last of the beer and told him, "Well, after about about a month of researching social activities reported in Ottawa high school yearbooks from late 40s and early 50s, he gave up on the project. He told me that despite the poor nostalgic bastard's disappointment, he paid his fee without complaint. Pimm also told me that he wouldn't be surprised if he continued the search himself." Before they separated, Nichols was kind enough to provide John with Pimm's telephone number to make arrangements for a meeting. John telephoned Pimm and suggested that they meet for a few beers after work on Preston Street, specifically at the Prescott. Pimm had quickly agreed to a meeting the next Wednesday. John also asked Pimm's Christian name. It was James, a.k.a. Jimmy.

⟶•⟨⟨

It was the next Wednesday afternoon a little after four when the two were sitting at one of the round Formica tables in the Prescott. John had immediately recognized Jimmy, from the physical description provided by Malcolm; an overweight, if not outright fat individual who easily could have played a rumpled detective on television. It was obvious to John that Jimmy had been sitting in the Prescott for a while. There were papers spread out before him, a partially consumed quart of Molson Export as well as a still smouldering cigarette in the ash tray before him when John arrived. Jimmy greeted him cheerfully, invited him to sit down at his table and motioned to the waiter, who immediately appeared to take

John's order, not to mention another beer order from Jimmy, with whom the waiter was obviously familiar. John ordered a quart of Labatt Fifty, which was unusual since he would normally ask for a pint, while Jimmy asked for another quart of Molson Export. John wanted to ensure that he did not look like a wimp, especially while attempting to hire a private investigator, an occupation that meant that Pimm was a tough guy who ordered quarts of beer, not pints or drafts. Jimmy offered John a cigarette, an Export Plain, another tough guy brand, while John fired up one of his Player's Lights, a brand that definitely did not suggest that he was a tough guy. Their beers arrived at the table, which prompted Jimmy to immediately initiate a conversation about the investigative assignment for which John was considering him. They both filled their glasses and took single swallows. John then removed the mystery photographs and spread them out on the table, explaining the purpose of the proposed investigation. In addition, John laid a copy of a fragment of a newspaper article as well as a copy of the entire *Ottawa Journal* article from which the fragment came, the date of the paper being April 5, 1949. "So you want someone, someone like me, to find the source of these photographs." John nodded and then asked, "Can you cover a job like that?" He then delayed for a moment and followed with a couple of more relevant questions. After several more swigs of his Molson Export, Jimmy allowed a broad smile to sweep across his face and responded to John's questions with one answer. "Sure, why not? I don't think I have ever investigated mystery photographs but as I think Malcolm told you, I've had a few jobs that involved some pretty unorthodox situations. This one, as weird as it seems, probably would add some appeal to my resume. As you may have gathered, I'm not exactly what you'd call a specialist. In fact, you can call me, you know, a Renaissance man, whatever that is. That's what one of my clients used to call me."

John enthusiastically responded to Jimmy's acceptance of the assignment. He then asked about the the terms of the contract that he and Jimmy would conclude before the latter began his sleuthing. Jimmy seemed to be mildly taken aback. He was usually the one to initiate any discussion of the terms of any arrangement with a client. Jimmy proposed that they could delay any consideration of his fee in particular until such time that he had the opportunity to study the photographs and devise some sort of plan to investigate the origin and purpose of the photographs left in the possession of John and his wife Patricia. After a couple more swigs of beer, Jimmy said that he was prepared to agree to the research project. As for the fee, Pimm explained that while he usually charged clients on a daily basis, this not looking like a normal case, martial cases being a prominent part of his livelihood, in which he monitored someone's activities for a specific period of time. But in John's case, Pimm was being asked to look into something like photographs, something that could be solved quickly or take a fair amount of time ---- it was impossible to estimate.

Besides, most of Jimmy's clients would be unlikely to retain his services unless first having a fair idea of what they it would cost. That meant a flat rate. So it come as no surprise that John asked Jimmy for a figure, to which the latter said that he would prefer if the client, which in this case was John and Patricia, would indicate an amount they were prepared to pay. Both Jimmy and John were probably aware of the possibility that, no matter the extent of anyone's effort, any private detective would have difficulty determining the origin and purpose of the photographs. Although he would have preferred to consult with Patricia, John decided to name a figure of $500. Jimmy shrugged and then said he agreed. John then asked if they required a contract. Pimm said he could agreed to that stipulation as well.

After they both ordered another beer, their attention was diverted when an older patron, a grey haired man wearing a three piece suit and sitting alone, vomited on his pants and the polished concrete floor. The waiter who had been serving him quickly arrived at the vomiting man's table, carrying two white towels and sporting a pair of yellow gloves. The waiter motioned to a colleague who assisted him with the older man in walking toward the closest men's room. As soon as the man disappeared into the washroom and a teenage boy, who Jimmy said was the son of a man who worked as a cook in the kitchen, mopped up the residue of the old man's stomach accident, Jimmy asked John if they could agree on a contract. In fact, Jimmy was bold enough to propose that they come to an agreement as soon as they could. John volunteered to draft a pact for the three of them, Patricia included at John's suggestion, to possibly sign by early next week. The proposed arrangement, complete with the $500 fee, was agreed. .

On Thursday evening, after they had dinner delivered from a pizza joint on Sunnyside, John confirmed to Patricia that Jimmy had agreed with their proposal of a contract calling for an analysis of the photographs that had been left in Parkdale Court and then 64 Brighton Avenue. Patricia was happy with the development and asked if he was sure that Pimm would not complicate any arrangement that John presented to him. In that context, Patricia was somewhat surprised that Jimmy he want John to write the contract, particularly in view of the fact that Pimm had experience with contracts involving investigations while John did not. On the other hand, Jimmy had admitted to John that that he did not usually demand a contract although many of his clients demanded them. When John asked about his obvious disdain toward contracts, Jimmy said that he just did not like lawyers. In any event, after discussing the matter of contracts for maybe fifteen minutes or so, John and Patricia agreed that it would be sensible to propose a contract to Jimmy, particularly in view of their lack of experience in such matters. John told Patricia that he would research the library in the General Records Centre, a building that across the street from where John worked as a clerk. He thought that he could take an early lunch the next day and hopefully have a document that he could copy for their purpose and then submit to James Pimm for his consideration on Monday. Patricia said that the two of them now felt like private eyes just like on television, just like Joe Mannix or Jim Rockford. Surprisingly enough, it took

John less than an hour to locate a sample contract governing private investigators in the official document section. It was the shortest sample contract he could find. He copied it and then spent the rest of the day, the afternoon in particular, working on a contract. Once he had finished his final draft, which was a significantly condensed version of the sample contract he had found, it was almost quitting time. He placed the contract that he had just completed into his briefcase, an accessory that he did not usually use unless he had work to bring home, something he seldom did. The sample was obviously important to him. As soon as he arrived home, he wanted to acquaint Patricia with the contract. He presented the draft to her.

CONTRACT FOR SERVICE

———————◆———————

Agreement for Professional Investigative Services
By James Pimm Investigations
703 Percy Street, Ottawa

John and Patricia Delaney do hereby agree to employ the services of James Pimm Pimm Investigations, Ontario Private Investigator License #191260, a private investigator, for the purpose of investigating the following.

Assignment:

James Pimm, investigator, is assigned to determine the origins and purposes of the two photographs found in the apartment 302 of Parkdale Court, 612 Bank Street, Ottawa, the origins and purposes of the photographs found in the mailbox of apartment 302 of the aforementioned Parkdale Court and the one photograph in the mailbox of 64 Brighton Avenue, Ottawa. In the course of the investigation, James Pimm may use and reply upon information obtained from a variety of sources, including any public records, including newspapers and any other relevant documentation. James Pimm Investigations will endeavour to ensure, in so far as it can, that the sources of information are known for reliability but that the undersigned, John and Patricia Delaney, waive and release James Pimm Investigations from and with respect of any information based on the accuracy or inaccuracy of any information obtained in the course of this investigation.

Payment Terms

This contract establishes an amount of $500 to be paid to the James Pimm Investigations plus reasonable expenses as agreed for the completion of the assignment as agreed by the undersigned, John and Patricia Delaney. The James Pimm Investigations agree to conclude its research within a reasonable time to be stipulated after agreement by the parties to this Contract for Service.

Date: June 15, 1978
Client: John and Patricia Delaney   Investigator: James Pimm Investigations

PIMM'S INVESTIGATION, PART I

B oth the clients, John and Patricia Delaney and the private investigator James Pimm, signed the formal albeit abbreviated contract three days later during a dinner at Giovanni's Restaurant, which was situated almost across Preston Street from the Prescott. As John expected, Jimmy commented on the contract, emphasizing not only its brevity but its simplicity as well. He said that the contract looked like it had been composed by a college student who had consulted a law book for beginners. "Like I told you the other night, I don't like lawyers and I don't like to sign contracts that are hard to understand unless you have a law degree. So I'm more than happy to sign this." Jimmy then smiled, signed both contracts, one for himself and one for John and Patricia. The latter had already signed the contracts. He then said that he had sufficient time to begin his investigation almost immediately, mentioning that he had just completed the study of the adulterous activities of the husband of a lady named Catherine. The three of them then toasted each other. Patricia ignored her diet for the evening and ordered Tiramisu and then a Cappuccino before the evening ended.

The next morning, Jimmy arranged to deliver his report on the Catherine's husband at her place of work, a hair saloon downtown. While he could have easily mailed the report to Catherine, who he assumed would soon be looking for a divorce attorney, Jimmy was a little short of cash, his expectation that his client would pay him his fee, hence the need for hand delivery. Catherine, who was attempting to make a middle age woman look less mature, threw her scissors across the room when Jimmy offered her a quick summary of the report he was there to provide. Despite the flash of Catherine's anger and after an appropriate delay, Jimmy nevertheless asked her for payment of his fee as agreed. His client, whose own customer was looking nervously over her shoulder, obviously wondering whether Catherine would continue with her hair, watched as Catherine headed for the rear of the shop, presumably to get her purse to pay Jimmy's fee. By the time Catherine arrived with her purse, through which she was rummaging, her client had moved to another hairdresser and an assistant had picked up the scissors. Within less than a couple of minutes, Catherine was sitting in the chair that her customer had just deserted to fill in a cheque for Jimmy. She still looked angry. To Jimmy, there was a hint of a possible argument about the fee. She offered him the cheque --- Jimmy practically had to tear it out of her hand. In a loud voice, Jimmy immediately noted that Catherine still owed him $500. Catherine the stylist shrugged, then turned and retreated into the back room. Neither Catherine nor Jimmy said another word to each other.

Next stop was the Bank of Montreal on Laurier and O'Connor where Jimmy deposited a cheque in the amount of $1,000, the better part of the total fee of $1,500 owed by Catherine, into his account. The teller who took the deposit was surprised, basically because the amount in his bank account was usually much lower. Jimmy happily withdrew $200 from the deposit and headed home to 703 Percy Street to start investigating the photographs given to him by John and Patricia Delaney, but not before stopping at the well known *Shanghai Restaurant* on the corner of Bronson and Somerset Streets. After enjoying a luncheon meal of shrimp fried rice and a pint of Tsingtao beer, Pimm returned to his studio apartment at 703 Percy Street, on the first floor of a three floor, six unit house that was likely built late in the previous century. He sat down at a small desk, which faced the front window of the house, less than ten feet from the sidewalk on Percy Street, and stared at the first two photographs that the Delaneys had given him.

As he examined the photographs, he came to the same conclusions that his clients had made, both of them resembled each other. The similarities were evident. Both photographs were black and white, possibly, if not likely to have been taken around World War I, both portrayed a family with a father, a mother, four and five children, one with a dog, one without, and both clearly, if not apparently taken in a local park, and finally, both photographs were taken by photography studios, one in the Montreal, the other in Ottawa. In addition to the photographs, there was the evidence of the *Ottawa Journal* article dated April 5, 1949 reporting on the suicide of former Parkdale Court resident and apartment building architect named George Fenwick. He sat at the desk facing out the window, contemplating the histories of the two old photographs and the newspaper article.

Searching for whoever took the two older photographs seemed to be a more likely method to decipher the mystery than any other means. So Jimmy came to the conclusion that he would have to make inquiries at the two photography studios, that is if they still remained in business. Perhaps those two studios had files that might identify the photographs, when they were taken, where they were taken, who took them, and who was in them. His first move then was to consult the main public library on Laurier Street where he was certain that the telephone books for both Ottawa and Montreal were available. He was pleased with the development of a plan in a little less than a day after signing a contract to the mysterious photographs. Understandably relaxed and looking for entertainment, he immediately telephoned two of his friends, both fellow private detectives, Des Bradley and Ted McPhee, and invited them to the Dominion on Bank Street for beer and maybe a selection of the many delicacies that a dumpy tavern had to offer for dinner. All three of them agreed to met at six that evening, hopefully to observe the wild life, which was generally the description that most people applied to the denizens of the Dominion. As the three of them arrived, the tavern was well populated, only three tables available.

Jimmy appeared first and managed to reserve two chairs for his dinner guests. Jimmy declined to order anything until Bradley and McPhee arrived. When they did, both looked like they had spent the afternoon drinking rather than pursuing private detective work. Jimmy was not particularly surprised with the apparent condition of his colleagues, drinking to excess sometimes a requirement of the job. A slow moving waiter, a man who looked like he might weigh close to three hundred pounds, approached the table and asked for their order. All three of them ordered four drafts each and then passed the menu among themselves. Des could hardly read the menu while Ted had trouble sitting straight in his chair.

Jimmy's favourite aspect of any fraternizing with his fellow private detectives, regardless of where and in what circumstances it occurred, were the stories of their interesting and unusual assignments. They were well into their brews, particularly Ted who had already finished his second draft before they received their food orders, when Des entertained the boys with the story of his most recent hire, a matter of investigating a dog kennel, scrutinizing the treatment of the dogs, their exercising, their feeding, their grooming, their housing, and their general handling. He had been hired by an elderly lady who had engaged the kennel when she had to travel to a family funeral but could not bring her dog, a hound named Lizzie. Jimmy and Ted did agree that the task was unusual, an interpretation that was also accepted by Des. All three of them chuckled somewhat and agreed that it was, after all, a living. As they began to eat their dinners, Ted gave his two dinner companions an accounting of his current undertaking, a temporary security job protecting the stock in a small dollar store, a recent epidemic of shoplifting a concern of the store owner who considered hiring a private investigator more beneficial that installing additional surveillance cameras. According to Ted, however, the job had benefits than went beyond the per diem he was receiving for sitting on a small stool in the stock room of a dumpy little dollar store. When asked, Ted said that the owner of the store, a Mr. Denman, would pay him half the retail price of any merchandise that he caught any customer attempting to steal, the other half Denman would claim as stolen, take a loss on his income and therefore reduce his taxes.

Their dinners finished, Des ordered three more drafts while Ted and Jimmy ordered two more each. Jimmy followed with a short explanation of his assignment on behalf of his clients, the Delaneys. At first, both Des and Ted were surprised but not particularly interested in the details of the job, observing that researching the origin and perhaps the purpose of some photographs hardly had any entertainment value, unless of course there was adultery involved somehow. Jimmy told them that he was planning to talk to the photography studio that had taken the two oldest photographs. He also mentioned an old newspaper fragment that had been left in his apartment after or during a party the Delaneys threw. Des allowed a puzzled look to slowly come over his face and then stumbled into a comment and then into a question. "Man, that seems pretty mysterious. Were you able to find out whether the fragment was attached to an article?" Jimmy then relayed the story of an article reporting on a man named George Fenwick who threw himself off a building on Bank Street, in which John and his wife Patricia eventually lived thirty years later. Jimmy noted, "The article mentioned that Mr. Fenwick lived there since the place opened. Not only that but he was the architect that designed the building." Both Des and Ted expressed more than mild interest. Ted observed. "The guy was the architect of the building. Jesus, and maybe more than ten years after he moves in, he jumps out of a window in his apartment on the third floor. Now, there's a story. Too bad all of this happened thirty years ago. You would be in the middle of a big case if it happened recently. Why did he do it? It sounds a lot more exciting that chasing cheating husbands or shoplifters or lousy dog kennels." And the boys looked at each other and nodded.

Over the remainder of the evening, the three private investigators discussed the origins of their chosen occupation, always an interesting topic, particularly when it was fuelled by more beer. All three of them showed amazing resiliency in avoiding complete drunkenness. Des astounded his two colleagues by ordering four more drafts, a performance of consumption that not only impressed the hell of Ted and Jimmy but also confirmed the veracity of his reputation as a drinker of miraculous proclivities. Fact was even before Jimmy met Des, a local conference of private eyes was the event, the two of them were aware that Des had been fired from the Cornwall police force for excessive drinking, a charge that he did not even bother to dispute. Nevertheless, neither Ted nor Jimmy were aware of any circumstance in which his drinking affected his work. In any event, on that evening and presumably any other evening during which they might share a libation, both Des and Jimmy would and did remain impressed by Bradley's ability to consume alcohol. In fact, it was central to his reputation..

Before the evening ended, only McPhee was able to come up with any advice that might help Pimm with his project, guidance that Pimm did not need since he was already planning to consult with the studios that were responsible for the two photographs that had been left in the Parkdale Court apartment. Pimm wasn't really surprised since McPhee, even though he had consumed fewer beers than Bradley, was intoxicated enough to apparently forget that Pimm had already informed his colleagues of his intention a couple of hours ago. All three of the private detectives left the Dominion around midnight. Fortunately, given their condition, none of them had driven to the place, Des and Ted living within blocks of the Dominion while Jimmy took a cab.

———◦———

It was the next Monday morning that Jimmy discovered unsurprisingly, after consulting a city telephone book in the main office of the Ottawa Library on Laurier Street, that there was no current Ottawa listing for the Blair Photography Studio. He wondered whether the library held on to old city telephone books, a possibility that seemed unlikely but he went ahead and asked one of the older women behind the library counter nonetheless. As Jimmy approached the counter, he noticed that both ladies behind it were recording the return of library books. He first stood before the lady on the left, who was happily humming as she violently stamped each one of the returned books. She looked up from her work and inquired of Jimmy who was standing there with an inquisitive expression on his face. "Good morning, sir. What can I do for you?" Jimmy quietly replied. "Well, I came down here looking for a telephone number for a photograph studio that took a picture a long time ago." The lady behind the counter looked puzzled and asked an obvious question. "When was this picture taken?" Jimmy shrugged and provided the library lady with his estimate regarding the age of the photograph. "To me, the photograph, which was taken by the Blair Studio or so it said on the back of the photo, looked like it was taken sometime around World War I. So I wanted to see if the Blair Studio had anything in their files on the photograph and whoever paid for it."

The library lady looked sympathetic. "Well, we don't keep telephone books for more than five years or so. I can't explain the reason but one of our former head librarians established the policy a couple of decades ago, as trivial as it seems." The lady lightly laughed and brought her hands together made a suggestion. "I'm sorry I can't help but I do have a suggestion. Why don't you visit the research department at the Bell Canada building and ask if they keep old telephone books although I can't tell if Bell Canada actually retains them, or even if they published them back then." The previous expression of dismay on Jimmy's face slowly faded to be replaced a minute later by something that could be interpreted as slight expectation. He managed a smile, thanked the library lady and headed to Bell Canada on Elgin Street.

The Bell Canada building was tall and white coloured constructed less than a decade ago across from the former Ottawa Teachers' College on Elgin Street. The college, which was built in 1875, was closed in 1974 when responsibility for the education of teachers was transferred to the University of Ottawa. The building itself was sold to the federal government in 1978. Jimmy walked into the building from the Metcalfe Street entrance, past a branch of the Bank of Montreal, an exclusive men's store named Fitzgerald's, and a small coffee shop, and checked in with one of the three uniformed men seated behind a long counter underneath a large sign announcing the Bell Canada offices. Pimm stood and waited in front of the man seated on the right. A badge on the left side of his shirt identified the man as Richards. Pimm introduced himself, as a private investigator working for a family interested in their ancestry, and asked if the Bell kept telephone books going back to the turn of the century. Richards looked puzzled and came up with a nervous, inadequate answer. "I really don't know, sir. I can check though." he said as he looked to his two colleagues also behind the counter, hoping for assistance. Receiving none, Richards then picked up the receiver of the telephone that was sitting in the middle of the counter, dialed a number and asked for someone named Mr. Kirkland.

He waited for a moment, evident that Mr. Kirkland had come on the telephone, and then posed his question."Mr. Kirkland, this is Richards down at the front counter. There is a man down here at reception asking if the company has phone books going back a hundred years or so." It was obvious that Mr. Kirkland, whoever he was, was asking for the reason that Jimmy wanted old phone books. "I'm sorry, he didn't say. Maybe I can sent him up to the fourth floor to your office to talk to you. His name is Pimm." Richards nodded, replied in the affirmative, and returned the receiver to its cradle. Richards then returned to Pimm and instructed him on how to get to Mr. Kirkland's office on the fourth floor. Richards said that Mr. Kirkland was the company's archivist. Jimmy could tell that Richards was uncomfortable with the term. Jimmy thanked Richards and, as directed, walked toward the elevators. He stood before the three elevators for several minutes before one of the doors opened, disgorging three talkative young ladies who looked like they were going to the coffee shop. A late arriving well dressed gentleman joined Jimmy in the elevator, greeted him and pressed the button for the twentieth floor. Jimmy pressed the button for the fourth floor and the man sharing the ride asked if he had business with public relations or advertising. Looking back, Jimmy looked at him with a quizzical look on his face. He then nodded.

Exiting the elevator, he stood before a large sign announcing the business of the fourth floor as "Marketing". To the left was a conference room behind a tinted glass wall. The room was occupied, maybe a dozen people watching a woman using a pointer and placing transparencies on an overhead projector at one end of the room. The rest of that side of the fourth floor featured the doors to a number of offices and a men's washroom. Jimmy stood staring at the conference room when a man walked by carrying papers. Jimmy called out to the man who stopped, turned and asked about his search. Jimmy walked closer to the man and asked if the man knew the location of Mr. Kirkland's office.

The man expressed a certain surprise. "You mean, old man Kirkland? " He was now standing maybe a couple of feet from the man. "Yeah, I'm looking for Mr. Kirkland. I understand that he's the curator of the office, the company librarian." The man nodded, shook his head, and smirked a bit. "Right, the company librarian, the old guy ---- he has an office to the right on the other side of the floor. You know, he's a kind of a company legend. He's been with the Bell for more than fifty years. Now, he's sort in charge of the company's history." The man then pointed to the other side of the building, past the elevators and then to the right. The man who had given him directions then continued down the corridor past the conference room. By the time Jimmy reached Mr. Kirkland's office, which was at the end of the corridor, he could hear somebody stacking books. He peaked into the room and saw an elderly man placing books on the shelves of a series of storage racks. He looked further into the room and noted that were ten rows of shelves, each five tiers high. About half of the shelves were filled with what Jimmy assumed were, as anticipated, used telephone books, both personal and business. About a quarter of the shelves held Bell Canada annual reports, as Jimmy was subsequently informed, to before the turn of the century.

As soon as Jimmy stepped into the room, Mr. Kirkland looked up from his job of stacking books from one shelve to another and asked if he could help him. Jimmy asked, "Excuse me, Mr. Kirkland, do you

THE CHANGING MYSTERIES OF PARKDALE COURT

keep telephone books going back sixty, seventy years or so?" Jimmy was now standing in front of Mr. Kirkland's desk, the occupant now sitting and looking up. Kirkland looked at Jimmy with a bemused look on his face and answered. "Sure, we have telephone books going back that far. They are kept over there on the shelves over by the door where you came in. Until the twenties, Bell distributed telephone books every two years. Then, after that, they came out every year." Kirkland then motioned his hand toward the shelves over by the door and invited Jimmy to go through them. He nodded and walked over to the shelves by the corner of the room. He started with the telephone books for the 1920's. "You can take that desk in the corner over by the door if you want and started looking through them. I assume you're looking for a specific name." He nodded in the affirmative and walked over to the shelves as directed.

As he planned, the first telephone book he consulted was city directory for 1920. The publication, which had a 8 X 11 dust jacket over a reference book entitled the "Ottawa City Directory", was advertised on the inside cover as an alphabetical list of all business firms and private citizens to which street and telephone numbers are included. He noted that the population of the city was 150,000 citizens, which did not suggest how many telephone numbers may be listed. In that regard, the directory had 40 pages of telephone numbers. He found the Blair Photography Studio telephone number and address on Dalhousie Street, the address that appeared on the back of the photograph left in the Parkdale Court apartment. Satisfied that he was on the right track with the telephone books, he skipped a decade and pulled the city directory for 1940, where he found the telephone number for the Blair Photography Studio. He noted that the studio had moved to Queen Street but its telephone number was unchanged. By the time he reached the city directory for 1960, which may have been the most recent location for the Blair Studio, he was hopeful that the gallery was still in business. The Blair Studio was still situated on Queen Street in 1960 but was not listed in any way in the 1970 city directory when the city was populated by 475,000 people. That meant of course that the Blair Studio went out of business sometime in the 1960s which seemed curious since the city population had grown by 100,000 possible subjects for photography in the decade. Researching the directories back from 1970, the last listing for the Blair Studio appeared in 1962, which also registered the studio as being situated at 225 Queen Street, clear evidence that the photography studio went out of business sometime in the early 1960s.

Having recorded the details of the last place of business for Blair Studio, Jimmy returned to the front of the archive room to seek the advice of Mr. Kirkland. Mr. Kirkland looked up from his desk with an inquisitive look on his face. He now seemed to be considering a crossword. "Any luck?" he asked as he put down his pencil, sighed and started to fiddle with a cheap cigar that looked like it had been extinguished some time ago. Jimmy answered in a low but hopeful voice. "Well, I was able to find out that the Blair Photography Studio seems to have gone out of business maybe twenty five years ago or so, maybe sometime around 1963 when Bell stopped listing the gallery in the telephone book. The last place they were located was an address on Queen Street, 225 Queen Street to be exact." Kirkland nodded as if he expected the results of Pimm's investigation. Both men were silent for a moment and then Pimm continued, asking Kirkland if he had any suggestions as to how he could locate anyone who might have owned or worked at the studio. "Maybe there are still files that could give me a hint as to the identity of the people in the photograph that I am researching."

Kirkland looked at Jimmy with a momentarily vacant look on this face. It had been less than a minute when Kirkland abruptly arrived at an idea. "You know, I think there's a couple of waiters that have worked for decades at the Centretown Tavern which is still just down Queen Street from where your Blair Photography Studio used to be. And the Centretown has been there for more than thirty years. So maybe you should think about talking to one of those waiters. Maybe they'll be able to tell you something about the studio and the photographs they may have taken." Jimmy was pleased, thanked Kirkland and then asked him if he had either of the waiters' names. Jimmy was inspired by the thought that Kirkland may have spent a lot of time in the Centretown Tavern. The confused look on Kirkland's face turned into bewilderment, a state with which he was probably fairly familiar. After seemingly staring into the rows of shelves and resuming his fiddle with that abandoned cigar, Kirkland suddenly reacted to Jimmy's inquiry. "The only waiter I know over there is a guy named Murray, Murray Davidson. I'd check him out ---- he's still working. The man's over 70 years old and he's still slinging drafts. He used to tell me all the time that he started working there just after the war which, by the way, he also liked to talk about all the time." Jimmy stood in front of Kirkland's desk for a short delay, thanked Kirkland, reached out, shook his hand, and turned to leave the room. Mr. Kirkland wished him good fortune.

⊷⊶

After enjoying lunch at the Elgin Street Diner, a couple of blocks south of the Bell Canada building, Jimmy walked over to the Centretown Tavern on Queen Street. It was around two in the afternoon and the place was practically empty. There were four patrons sitting separately, three towards the back wall and the other by the front window. Jimmy sat in the middle of the room, one table over from the bar, behind which stood an older waiter wearing an apron and wiping down draft glasses. He looked up from his efforts and nodded. Recognizing that the older waiter, who Jimmy had almost immediately supposed was Murray Davidson, so much so that he didn't feel that he had to ask him his name, was not about to come around the bar to take his order, Jimmy got up from his chair and walked over to the bar where he asked for two draft beers. As Murray started to pour the drafts, Jimmy leaned over the bar and asked him if he had been familiar with anyone who worked at the Blair Photograph Studio which he thought closed in the early 1960s. Murray finished pouring the two drafts, looked up, offered what sounded like a grumble, and quietly replied. He sounded annoyed, as if Jimmy's question had been an obvious intrusion.

"Yeah, the guys from Blair used to drop by almost every day of the week for couple of brews and lunch. And sometimes after work and sometimes in the evening, the boss, a friend of mine named Carl Weinstein, also used to come in here. Hell, I must have served Carl and the photographers who worked for him for thirty years before the studio went out business maybe fifteen years ago." said Murray who pushed the two drafts Jimmy had ordered across the bar." And funny thing is that Weinstein still comes in here occasionally, he and a guy who used to take photographs for the studio." Jimmy was now sitting on a stool at the bar, having moved from the table he had originally claimed. Jimmy Pimm continued with his inquiry. "My name is Jimmy Pimm, I'm a private investigator." He had a business card in his hand which he had placed on the bar and slid toward Davidson the waiter. "I have a client who has hired me to identify people in an old photograph that he found in his apartment. The photograph was taken by the Blair Photography Studio, so it was stamped on the back of the picture. I found out from a man who worked over at Bell Canada, a kind of company librarian, that the last time the Blair Studio had a telephone number, it was located on Queen Street." Naturally, Murray the waiter asked Jimmy why he was telling him about some photograph that was taken by the Blair Studio. He explained that "The man over at Bell Canada, an older man named Kirkland, knew you by name and said that a couple of guys who used to work at the studio still come in here regularly. And it seems that he was right. You know this guy Weinstein and maybe he can give me some information on the photograph, maybe he can remember the photograph itself, maybe there are copies of the photograph, some records, some files. I know it is a long time ago but you know sometimes people know things they don't think they know."

Murray poured himself a beer, took a gulp and commented on whether his longtime customer Weinstein could be any assistance to Jimmy. "Hell, I don't know if Weinstein can help you out but you can always try. Look, I have your card here. If he comes in here, I'll give you a call." Jimmy thanked him and then, just before finishing his second draft, asked how often Weinstein actually came into the

Centretown. Murray shrugged his shoulders and gave Pimm a non-committal wave of his hand."To be honest, not very often." he said, "Maybe once a week, maybe more, different days, I can't really say. Look, I'll call you if and when he comes in, Okay?" Jimmy smiled, paid for his two draft beers, and thanked Murray the waiter. He then left the Centretown Tavern. He didn't think he had enough information to report to the Delaneys. Besides, he had to plan his trip to Montreal to investigate the telephone number and possible location of Brown Studio, at one time of Ballantyne Street.

——— ⊳•◦•◁ ———

The main office of Bell Canada in Montreal was located on Beaver Hall Hill, a couple of blocks away from Central Station. Before planning to reserve a seat on the morning train from Ottawa, he thought he would telephone the Montreal office to determine whether they maintained a library in which past telephone books were kept, just like the archive that Mr. Kirkland kept in Ottawa, maybe even find a name and perhaps even arrange an appointment. The next day, he started telephoning at nine o'clock in the morning. After speaking to several individuals, two of whom did not seem to understand his inquiry, he was provided with a name, a Pierre Juneau who was supposedly responsible for the company's files, which could include previous telephone books he presumed. He was able to contact Juneau after speaking to three more Bell Canada employees, including a woman who told Jimmy that Mr. Juneau had retired from the Bell several months ago. The other two employees gave Jimmy the same telephone number although both of them said that Mr. Juneau was an eccentric man who seldom answered the telephone even if he were to receive a call. In fact, one of them said that Juneau often left the receiver off the hook, which wasn't much of a problem the colleague said since Juneau seldom, if ever received a telephone call anyway. Accordingly, both recommended that if Jimmy wanted to talk to Juneau, he should make plans to visit him. Otherwise,

Jimmy was told that, whatever he wanted, he was going to have get it from Mr. Juneau in person and not over the telephone.

So Jimmy was on the next day's train to Montreal. He arrived at Central Station around ten o'clock on a Thursday morning, disembarked and headed to the Bell Canada on Beaver Hall Hill along de la Gauchetiere Street. Unlike the Bell Canada office in Ottawa, the edifice housing the head office of Bell Canada in Montreal was completely constructed in 1928, almost fourty years earlier than the building in Ottawa. At the time, as he was to discover from his initial research, it was the headquarters of the entire Bell Telephone Company in Canada. It was a 22 floor neoclassical building that had dominated that particular area of the city for the next three decades. He disembarked and entered the building from the de la Gauchetiere Street entrance. As he expected and as was standard in most buildings, there were two attendants sitting behind a black marble counter. They were both men. The one on the left was an older balding man with a bushy moustash while the other was a much younger man with long hair and a pair of tinted spectacles. The younger man, who had had a bored look pasted on his face like a bandage, surprisingly stood up and asked if he could assist Jimmy who was happy he had worn his only sports jacket on the trip to Montreal. He had concluded that if he looked presentable, he might get a better reception from people manning the counters. That was why Jimmy thought the office concierge seemed so courteous to him. Jimmy said he was looking for Pierre Juneau.

Jimmy approached the counter, introduced himself and repeated that he was looking for an employee named Juncau. The younger man grew a blank look on his face while the older, balding man started to laugh. He moved his chair over from the left and interrupted any conversation he was about to have with the younger man. "Mr. Pimm, you're looking for Pierre Juneau, the man who is responsible for taking care of the company's files, right?" asked the older man while the younger man maintained his stare. Still, Jimmy could tell that despite his lack of expression, the younger man may be interested with any answer that he might provide. "Yeah, I'm looking for him. I tried to contact him by phone but there was no answer. I was told by a couple of people here that Mr. Juneau never answers the telephone. That's why I came down from Ottawa." To Jimmy, that had seemed like a reasonable explanation. The older man commented. "Look, I'd like to help you but you might have a problem." Jimmy then asked, "What problem?" The older man smirked and explained that Mr. Juneau often wasn't talkative. Jimmy said he was willing to try. "Well, I'm here today, so I'll give talking to him a try."

After that promise, the younger man handed his colleague a page of the company directory. The older man looked at the page, ran his finger down it, found Mr. Juneau's name, and directed him to room 1612. With that, he motioned to the elevators behind him and wished him luck. Jimmy then asked if Mr. Juneau was in his office. The older man said that he didn't know but he wouldn't be surprised if he wasn't. By the time Jimmy was standing by the elevator with three men and two women, he was beginning to doubt whether his trip had been worthwhile. He noted that the five other people in the elevator had taken particular interest in Jimmy pressing the button for the sixteenth floor. One of the women in the elevator, a younger woman asked if he was planning to visit Mr. Juneau, the company archivist as she called him. As he was to discover no more than several minutes later, there were only two doors to what appeared to be the only room on the sixteen floor. One of the entrances was an ordinary door beyond which there was Mr. Juneau seated at a desk, facing a room entirely filled with rows of shelves on which a various files sat. Jimmy presumed that Bell telephone books going back to the turn of the century and probably before were somewhere in those files. The other door, which was on the other side of the sixteenth floor, was the size of the entrance to a garage. That door looked like it was seldom opened. Apparently, the room on that side of the floor held office equipment, including most particularly new telephones.

He was standing in the doorway of Mr. Juneau's side of the sixteenth floor when Mr. Juneau looked up from his desk and sternly asked him what he wanted. He had heard the elevator opening, a noise he seldom heard. "What can I do for you?" he asked, a request that sounded like he did not expect an answer. Jimmy said that he was looking for old telephone books. "I know it sounds strange but I'm researching a photography studio that used to do business here in Montreal and may be able to identify an old photograph that I found." Juneau shook his head slowly and explained the material kept in the archives. "The company keeps old telephone books for Montreal going back before World War I. I think you will find them on the third and fourth rows over from the left on all five selves. They may not be too well organized, so it may be difficult to find anything you are looking for but I think they are all there, at least as far as I know." Jimmy moved into the room and stood by Mr. Juneau's desk. Juneau nodded and commented. "You know, I have to admit that your request is a strange one. Fact is that the only people who ever ask to consult the old telephone books are policemen and they don't come by very often." Wondering, Jimmy then asked why the Bell kept previous telephone books. A casual smile and Mr. Juneau attempted an explanation. "I don't really know. When I started here ---- I used to work in accounting but that was almost thirty years ago --- both sides of the floor were close to completely empty then. But, as time went on, the floor filled up, with financial statements, press releases, reports,statements, and finally, of particular interest to you, previous telephone books."

Jimmy walked to the back of the floor, to the fourth row from the left, and started looking through the telephone books. He started with 1975, his purpose to determine whether the Brown Photography Studio was still be in business at that point. He would then work backward in the chronology of Bell telephone books if it wasn't currently operating and forward if it was, the latter unlikely since the company had not recorded the most recent telephone book. which for Montreal was 1977, the same as in the Ottawa archive room. As he had planned, he started going backward into the history of the telephone books. At first, he was flipping through them casually from 1975 until he came across a telephone number and precise location for the Brown Photography Studio, the last known listing recorded in 1958. It showed the number and an address on Ballantyne

Street in the area of Montreal known as Verdun. He concluded that the Brown Studio had gone out of business shortly after 1958, presumably in 1959. For some reason, Mr. Juneau had been standing behind him as he was looking through the telephone books and was therefore aware of the fact that the 1958 book possessed the most recent listing for the Brown Studio. Pimm was disappointed. That was twenty years ago. He had hoped that the Brown Studio was still in business but doubted it.

Sensing his dismay, Mr. Juneau tapped Jimmy on his shoulder and made a suggestion. "I'm surprised that you haven't thought of this but if I were you, I'd take a cab over to the studio's old address and see if any store in the area remembers anything about the place ---- you know, walk around, talk to some of the other shop owners, find out if you can why they went out of business --- you know, that sort of thing and maybe find out what may have happened to anyone who worked there." Jimmy thought it was a fine idea and thanked Mr. Juneau. Then, before he left the sixteenth floor, asked Mr. Juneau, on the off chance if he might know something about Verdun, maybe even something about the Ballantyne Street. Juneau looked a little blank for a moment and then said that he grew up in Verdun. "Not exactly the neighbourhood around Ballantyne Street but I think I can remember walking by the studio when I was a kid." Jimmy, his private detective cynicism receding for a moment, was immediately interested in the possibility of one of Mr. Juneau's childhood memories helping him find past staff of Brown Studio, a store that evidently went of business years ago. "It was a small store, had a white store front, you know like a facade, with a black awning. There was a restaurant called Abbie's on one side and a confectionery store on the other. And there was also an older duplex right across the street, down the block I think. " Mr. Juneau stopped his report and waited for Pimm to respond.

"Based on what you just told me, on what you remember, I'm going take a cab to Ballantyne Street and see what I can find out. Maybe there are people still working in that restaurant, in the confectionery store, in whatever business may have replaced the studio, even people that maybe still be living in that duplex and other places in the area who can give me a clue as whether there is still anybody around that knows anything about what happened to the Brown Studio." Mr. Juneau went back to his desk, smiled and wished him luck.

Pimm rented a black Ford Focus from the Budget Car Rental just after he had lunch in a sandwich shop in the basement of Place Ville Marie. In addition to the car, Budget gave him a complimentary street map for Montreal. It was no surprise that it took him more than forty minutes to arrive on Ballantyne Street, where he found number 4515, as indicated in the 1958 telephone book, near the cross street of Willibroard. The address now identified a small store named Essence Books. It announced itself with a sign above the clear glass door. To the left of the door was a large picture window, three rows of five books each displayed in the window, each book about some aspect of World War II, suggesting that the store concentrated on selling used history books, an eccentric retail strategy for any book shop, particularly for a working class neighbourhood where used history books were unlikely to be a popular item. Jimmy parked across the street and took notice of the two establishments on either side of Essence Books, a diner called Sutton's, a curious moniker for a restaurant, and a crumbling confectionery store with a banner announcing itself as The Corner Store, two letters of the latter barely hanging on. He decided to enter the bookstore. He thought that it would not be very busy. It wasn't.

The man who Jimmy immediately recognized as the likely owner approached the front door, as if emerging from a back room, through a heavy curtain. He was an elderly man, clearly elderly, too mature it seemed to be working anywhere but maybe helping if not living in a nursing home. He greeted Jimmy with a slow, shaky wave, and then asked casually whether he could be of any assistance. He noticed that the man, who he assumed was the proprietor of the store, was having trouble walking. He could not help but notice that there were narrow rows and rows of what appeared to be well worn history books, similar to the volumes advertised in the store's front window. As Jimmy was standing closer to the door of the shop, the older man stepped into the light. Jimmy saw the man clearly for the first time. He looked like a sheet of paper, his skin almost like parchment. He had a shock of white hair, a long sad face that looked like it had been painted in chalk. He was dressed entirely in black. He looked like he was wearing a priestly vestment, a virtual cassock with a wrinkled sash around his waist. Jimmy noticed that his garment looked like it was stained with nicotine, which was hardly surprising since he had a unfiltered cigarette smouldering in his left hand. All that was missing in his costume was a clerical collar and a shadowy confessional hidden somewhere in the store.

Jimmy Pimm introduced himself as a private detective, clearly announcing his name and occupation. He explained his objective in visiting the address on Ballantyne Street, which was to determine the fate of the departed Brown Studio, that is of course if the owner of Essence Books actually knew.

"Well, Mr. Pimm, my name is Joseph Cass and I have been operating this place for twenty years, even since I bought the store from a man named Albert Valois who had to retire after he got cancer. He had three photographers working for him but none of them wanted to take over the studio. I understand that all three of them eventually managed to secure employment as photographers for one of the large studios downtown. We were friends, Albert and I, so I knew about his plans. At first, when he offered to sell me the place, I wasn't very enthusiastic. I was at least ten years from retirement but the more I thought about it, the more attracted I was to the idea." Pimm wondered but did not ask nor did Joseph Cass what he had done for a living before he took over Essence Books. Regardless of what Jimmy was thinking, Cass continued his explanation. "In any event, when Albert told me that he and his wife Emily were planning to move into an apartment building for seniors, he also told me that they wouldn't be able to take their books with them ---- he and

Emily always had a lot of books, mainly history books but others as well." Jimmy immediately connected the latter declaration with his ownership of the bookstore in which they were now having the current conversation. Joseph continued with his narrative. "You see, I lived alone in a large house --- my parents left it to me ---- and I guess they thought that I had room for their books. But instead, I decided to take over the lease for the space held by the Brown Studio and start a bookstore with his books. So I sold the house and started Essence Books, specializing in used books, mainly history books. That was twenty years ago." Jimmy did not pursue the question of the man's previous occupation.

After listening to Mr. Cass delineate the history of 4515 Ballantyne Street, at least as far as his commitment to the Delaneys was concerned, Pimm decided to confide his entire purpose of his visit to Verdun. He told Cass about how John Delaney was obsessed with two photographs that he found in an apartment he had rented several years ago, had hired him as a private investigator to determine the origin and possibly the purpose of the photographs which, as Jimmy pointed out, portrayed two separate families. Jimmy went on to say that both photographs were apparently taken around World War I. Jimmy also said that the first photograph found depicted one family with a father, a mother, four children, and a small black and white dog while the other showed a father, a mother, and five children but without a dog. "Both photographs were identified as being taken by a photography studio in Ottawa, a place named Blair, and the other in Montreal studio named Brown. The latter brought me here."

Cass reflected on Jimmy's explanation for a moment, staring past him through to the front window where he saw a old woman who looked like she was trying to read one of the books in the window of Essence Books. Jimmy was about to turn toward the window and the woman when Cass pressed on with his questions. "So what have you found out so far? Have you found the other studio, the one in Ottawa?" Jimmy nodded, "The Ottawa studio, which was called the Blair Studio went out of business years ago but I found a bartender who still knows a man who worked in the place. According to the bartender, the guy was and still is a regular at the tavern where he used to drink. So all I have to do is accidentally run into him there and maybe I'll find out about the photo. My new bartender buddy will let me know when he comes in and hopefully I will be able to talk to him."

Cass smiled for the first time, his decaying teeth visible for the first time. Looking at Cass showing his grin disturbed Jimmy, almost frightening him, at least for a moment. "Well, Mr. Pimm, it seems that you may be onto something although, as far as I can see, it doesn't seem worth your client's time and I guess his money." Then Cass smirked, which to Jimmy's relief required Cass to discontinue his grin and therefore any display of his unfortunate teeth. "Well, I hope so. I was also hoping, in fact I am hoping that you can give a clue about a photo taken a long time ago by your friend's studio." With that explanation, Jimmy pulled the black and white photograph by the Brown Studio of a family with five children out of his back pocket and handed it to Cass. With the smirk just about to fade from his face, Cass's eyes widened as he took hold of the photo, lowered his face close to it and began to examine it. He then looked up and allowed a startled smile to spread across his face. He then looked at Jimmy with a smile transforming itself to an expression approaching captivation. Then it was Jimmy who looked surprised. Still holding the photograph, Cass simply said, with a certain wonder in his voice, "I've seen this photograph before." He then handed it back to Jimmy and waved him toward the rear of the store.

Jimmy took a couple of steps forward and then asked a question. "What you mean, you're seen it before? How can that be?" Cass said that it was a story of some peculiarity.

<hr />

Jimmy had followed him into the rear of the store where Cass related to him an account of fortunate consequence. Cass told him that as part of the arrangement he had made with Albert and Emily

Valois when he bought the Brown Studio from them, he took the photographs that were on file in the studio as well as the books they had collected and kept in their home. In the back of the Essence Books, separated from the remainder of the store in a small alcove, were four grey file cabinets, three drawers in each respective cabinet, all ultimately shown to be close to full. Cass, having led him down to the rear of the bookstore, stood in front of the cabinets and presented them as if he were planning to sell them. He then slid the top drawer of first cabinet open and held up a handful of photographs. "I think your photograph is in this cabinet; this drawer has most, if not all of the family pictures. I'm sure, in fact I am certain that a copy of the photograph you showed me a couple of minutes ago is in this drawer. Look, take a look."

Jimmy started flipping through the photographs in the the top drawer, examining both sides of each picture. They appeared to be filed in chronological order, starting with the first photograph, a hazy, profoundly out of focus wedding picture of a couple descending the steps of an old church surrounded by a large contingent of celebrants, well wishers all, grinning haphazardly into the lens of a photographer from the Brown Studio. On the back of the photograph was a stamp announcing Brown Studio as its originator and a handwritten script identifying the newly married couple named Mary and Daniel Dover. There was also a date: June 20, 1919 and the name of the church, Notre-Dame-de-Bon-Secours. As he was contemplating the photograph, as he would consider a lost history book, Cass brought him out a chair with two small armrests asked him to use it as he looked though the photographs.

He sat down in the chair with a batch of photographs. Most of the photographs showed pictures of weddings, many in the month of June but some in other months, in every year from 1920 to 1929, in various churches all over Montreal. There were also other group events, birthday parties, Christmas parties, anniversary parties, even funerals, all with a large variety and numbers of guests, usually formally attired, standing and sitting in rows, posed in usually frozen postures for portraits to be taken by a cameraman working for the

Brown Studio. Copies of them were likely preserved in hundreds of photograph albums, collections of bits of celluloid film squirrelled away, usually forgotten but occasionally reviewed at family gatherings. Amazingly enough, after about a half an hour of examination and analytical curiosity, most of the photographs started to look identical to each other, people dressed in the same clothes, wearing the same expressions, standing and sitting in the same posture, making Jimmy's search more difficult than it had to be.

For an unknown reason, Cass returned to the alcove to help Jimmy with his investigation. He heard Cass firing up another filterless cigarette just as he approached Mr. Pimm, the latter having just finished searching the first drawer of the second cabinet, having already rummaged through three drawers of the first cabinet. Jimmy turned to look at Cass who had a quirky little expression on his face, saying "Getting any closer to finding your photograph?" asked Cass. Jimmy acknowledged Cass with a tired and exasperated nod. "I have the feeling that I'm close, at least I'm hoping I'm close." Cass then laughed, a strange menacing little laugh that momentarily scared him. "I know you're close, Mr. Pimm." Jimmy had the feeling that his host was about to show him where he had seen the photograph before.

He stood beside Jimmy and then reached into the first drawer of the second cabinet, bending over as he did. He could feel his breath on him as he fingered his way through the photographs, looking for a specific one, or at least Jimmy thought he was. Cass looked at Pimm over his right shoulder, another strange smile on his face. "As you have assumed I guess, I knew you were looking for a particular photograph. When you showed me your photograph, I did not immediately but eventually came to recognize it." Jimmy acknowledged Cass, having anticipated that the revelation by Mr. Cass was not really a revelation at all but a guess. With that admission, Cass continued to look though the top drawer of the second cabinet. For his part, Pimm stood silently, watching Cass and waiting for him to find what he was suggesting he was searching for. Several moments later, Cass pulled a photograph out of the top drawer, turned to

Pimm, and announced surprisingly casually that he had found the photograph. He held it up and then motioned to Jimmy who stood beside him and almost let out a quiet gasp when he recognized that the photograph he was holding was the same photograph he had originally shown to Cass.

Cass then showed him the back of the photograph. Aside from the stencilled declaration of the origin of the photograph, there was a written script identifying the individuals in the picture itself. It was exactly the information that Pimm and his clients the Delaneys had been pursuing. He overcame the immediate urge to call his clients to advise them of his discovery. For a second since Cass has pressed the photograph into his hand, Pimm studied the script on its rear surface and read it as if it were written in a foreign language. *The Dennison Family, Old Port Montreal, Summer 1921.* Jimmy wondered whether the photographer had provided the script or had the father or mother Dennison contributed the penmanship. It reminded Jimmy of the penmanship of not only his parents but almost every adult of that generation he had ever come across. He theorized that most students in those days had been instructed to write in a certain manner or face discipline from teachers with acrimonious looks on their faces. Finally, and most importantly, Jimmy pondered the possible reaction that the Delaneys might have to the photograph with the note of identification on the back. On the other hand, they may not have a reaction. Pimm did not know, nor did he have any particular notion about their motive in hiring him, aside from some sort of assumed curiosity. Again, he thought again of telephoning the Delaneys to inform them of his discovery. He didn't. He would change that opinion the next day.

—————⟫·◦·⟪—————

Jimmy finally left Essence Books and its owner Joseph Cass around five o'clock in the afternoon, an hour before the store closed. For the last twenty minutes or so, the two of them discussed Cass's reason for only selling history books. Cass explained that he started the store with a large number of used history books that he had inherited from Albert and Emily Valois. Jimmy then asked whether he had thought the store would stay in business very long. "Do you actually think that there was a large market for used history books?" asked Jimmy. Cass looked like he was reflecting for a moment and then, after a few moments of apparent contemplation, came up with the only answer he could in the circumstances. "Well, to be honest, at the beginning, I didn't really care. In fact, I thought I would just read the books I couldn't sell. But then, Emily came up with the thought that the store could attract students. I told her that that the store wasn't exactly downtown, where the schools were, but she said that maybe the students would start taking a bus out here to save a few bucks."

Jimmy accepted the explanation with a certain incredulity which he managed to hide. Jimmy inquired about the success of Emily's suggested plan. Cass smiled and shook his head. "Not much of a business plan I'll admit but the store gets by. It does attract students looking for used history texts but surprisingly, most of our customers are people around our age. They come in to browse. Sometimes, they may buy one or two. But the fact is the store is more like a library." Then, Jimmy asked Cass another pertinent question, one that had escaped him until that moment. "Where do you get any new books ---- I mean, more books to fill any empty shelves, that is if you have any." After a short silence, Cass answered with further clarification. "I should mention that I take in a lot of copies of the same books. After all, a lot of the history courses require the same books."

And with that, Jimmy had completed his education regarding the fundamentals of operating a used bookstore and library. He left with the original photograph of the Dennison family in the Old Port of Montreal in 1921 in his pocket.

THE PIMM INVESTIGATION, PART II

-------◇-------

He returned the Ford Focus to the Budget Car Rental near Place Ville Marie just as the clerk who had rented him the car earlier in the day was about to close the office. He looked a little annoyed but allowed him to park the car and complete the transaction. He existed the office and found himself on St. Catherine's Street, standing in front of Eaton's, looking if not staring at the displays in its windows and ruminating on his next move, wondering whether he could or even should make the 7:10 PM out of Central Station, the last train to Ottawa on weekdays. It was a little after 6:45 PM and while he could probably make the 7:10 PM if he deployed a slow trot, he decided that he could stay overnight at the Queen Elizabeth Hotel on Dorchester, which was two blocks south through Place Ville Marie and directly connected to Central Station where he could take the train first thing the next morning. He wasn't worried about the cost. He would stay the night and have the Delaneys pay --- he intended to charge them for the train tickets as well as car rental anyway --- even though they had not agreed on what would constitute reasonable expenses. But Pimm didn't think that he would have a problem convincing his clients that the expenses he had incurred were justified. He did have the original photograph which had identified its subjects as the Dennison family. That might satisfy them. In any event, the other detail remaining was to purchase a change of underwear in the first men's store he came across in Place Ville Marie. Fortunately, the stores were still open, it being a Thursday evening.

About thirty minutes after Jimmy had checked in, he had: dinner in Rosely's Cafe in the hotel itself, was told by the concierge that the earliest train from Central Station to Ottawa was 8:00 AM, walked over to the Central Station, bought a ticket for Ottawa, left a wake up call for 6:00 AM at the front desk and headed up to his room on the fifth floor. As soon as he was ensconced in his room, he took out the Dennison family photograph and scrutinized it again, this time under the hotel desk lamp. This time, he inspected each figure in the photograph as carefully as he could, starting with assumed father Dennison. He looked like he was in his fifties, balding with a full moustache and a sad expression on his face, not quite a frown but not anything resembling a smile either. His eyes were downcast, like he was contemplating something that was not evident in the picture in which he found himself, like he wasn't really there. He was wearing a white shirt, its sleeves held in place by adjustable armbands, wide striped braces holding up his trousers. To his left sat his presumed wife, who looked older than her husband. She wasn't bald but possessed a nimbus of white hair parted in the middle. She had a flat face, the countenance and colour of pancake batter, a flat face that looked like a painting that had not turned out quite right. She was wearing a skirt that appeared to be capable of covering a tent that could house a small family. Nevertheless, despite these shortcomings, she looked pleasant. To her left was one of her four sons, the youngest child leaning on her with a sleepy smile on his face. Jimmy then assumed sitting in her lap was her only daughter, who seemed to be looking over her right shoulder at her mother. Her hands were gently folded in her skirt which she may have been attempting to flatten out. Her hair was hanging in her face, an inconvenience that she did not seem to notice.

On the other side of the photograph, to the right of the elder Dennison, were the other three boys, almost sitting in each other's lap. To the far right was the son who appeared to be the eldest of the five children. He had a pensive expression on his face, maybe verging on nervous. He was leaning toward his brother who did not appear to be related to anyone else in the family, at least the individuals portrayed in the photograph. As he examined the brother on which the elder brother reclined, he noted that his nose in particular was completely dissimilar from the noses on the faces of the rest of the family. It was slender, almost graceful in its bearing, it reminded Jimmy of a priest or a teacher. His face was also narrow, unique and thoughtful, as if he belonged in another family.

It was the next morning, on the train returning to Ottawa, when Pimm decided to relate the news of his discovery of the inscribed photograph of the Dennison family to his clients and then make arrangements to turn it over to them as soon as possible. So, as soon as he arrived home at his office/residence at 703 Cooper Street, he called John Delaney at his place of employment in Health and Welfare. He figured he might be at lunch so he delayed his call until after the early afternoon. In the meantime, he watched the news and then listened to the Rolling Stone album he had purchased two weeks ago.

"Mr. Delaney, John, I was down in Montreal yesterday where I found the original photograph of that family taken by the Brown Studio. The studio closed in either 1958 or 1959 and is now a bookstore. Its current owner, a man named Cass, had the original and gave it to me. The identity of the family as well as where and when the picture was taken was written on the back. Apparently, the owners of the Brown Studio, Albert and Emily Valois, left all the original photographs they ever shot with the building, which was on Ballantyne Street in Verdun, when they sold it to Mr. Cass. We found your photograph in the files Mr. Cass keeps. There was a silence on the other end of the line followed by a question that was both unexpected and expected at the same time. "Why did this new owner Cass keep those photographs? Does he think that they are worth something? And on the other hand, why didn't the previous owners just throw the old photographs away?" Jimmy answered almost immediately, having contemplated that question among others for the last day or so. "I don't know. I've thought about it but never came to a conclusion." Before John Delaney had a chance to ask another question, Jimmy tried to explain. "Mr. Cass was a strange individual. On top of the photographs, he also accepted a large collection of history books from the Valois couple and used them to start this bookstore." Before John had an opportunity to comment, Jimmy said that he didn't think that Mr. Cass expected that the bookstore ---- he told him it was called Essence Books ---- to make any money. "I just thought it was just something for him to do in his retirement."

Finally, John arrived at the fundamental question, the purpose Jimmy thought of his telephone call. "So what does it say on the back of the photograph?" Jimmy replied without a trace of melodrama whatever. It said "The Dennison Family. Old Port Montreal, Summer 1921". He heard John taking in a breath and repeating several times the name Dennison. He then asked a fundamental question that Jimmy could understand. "I wonder if any of those Dennisons were related in any way to the man who used to live in the apartment where I found those photographs that you are researching." John then stopped for dramatic effect. "That man was also named Dennison. Talk about a coincidence but let's face it, it may not be." And having come to that conclusion, Delaney then asked about his plan for the other photograph, the one with a father, a mother, four children and a black and white terrier.

That photograph had bewildered Jimmy ever since he saw it. Unlike the Dennison photograph, so named by Jimmy since he discovered the identity of the subject's family in the the picture, the other photograph was unique in that the father, the mother, and the four children all looked remarkably similar, including both the father and the mother, who looked like they could have been brother and sister. Both had broad, pudgy faces and similar wide smiles, grey hair styled in the same way. Their four children, two boys, two girls, all looking to be in the range of three to twelve years old, all with chubby cheeks, wide smiles, similar ears, full heads of dark hair, looked alike as well. While Jimmy could understand the predictability, if not inevitability of the children in the same family looking almost identical, he was puzzled by parents who looked so similar in appearance. On the other hand, the dog did not look like anyone else in the family.

In any event, Jimmy continued with his report by telling John that he was waiting to hear from a waiter named Davidson who sometimes served a man named Weinstein who used to run the Blair Studio in Ottawa. In reply, John asked if Weinstein kept files of the photos his studio took over the years, just like his fellow photographers who worked for Valois in Montreal. Jimmy thought that John was kidding, attempted sarcasm he supposed but he answered seriously. "No, no I don't think so. My plan is to talk to him when I get the chance and to see if I can find out if he recognizes the photo and can tell me if he can identify the people in it." Predictably, John agreed with his plan. Jimmy then informed Delaney that he would deliver the Brown Studio photograph sometime after dinner that evening.

⟶◆◆⟵

It was five days later, during an afternoon repast at the Centretown Tavern, waiter Murray Hamilton greeted him with three drafts and a wink. Jimmy asked if he had a few minutes to chat. Waiter Hamilton checked with the bar, finding no further orders and returned to Pimm's table. He then pointed to an older man who was hunched over a table across the floor on the other side of the tavern. "That's Weinstein. Here's your chance to speak to him." Jimmy got up, swallowed his first draft and walked over to Weinstein's table. He sat down to address him. "Excuse me, Mr. Weinstein, I'm a private investigater. I have a client who is interested in identifying people who may be in this photograph." Pimm had the photograph in his hand and pushed it across the table. "I know the photograph is fairly old, at least judging by people in the picture and the way they're dressed. But my client found it one day and wants to know who those people are." Weinstein looked a little confused, a condition possibly facilitated by his age and his consumption of beer that afternoon. He asked, "Why come to me?", an innocent inquiry. With that, Jimmy

272

turned the photograph over to reveal the stamp Blair Studio in large letters. "Since I've been told that you had worked for the Blair Studio for many years, I thought that maybe you would recognize the people in this photograph? Maybe you were the photographer who took the shot."

Weinstein sat slumped behind his draft beers, Murray having just added two more draft to his collection, three empty glasses were waiting to take away. He was pondering. After a sensible interval, Weinstein confessed to remembering that the family in the memory was possibly named Quinn. Of course, the name didn't mean anything to Pimm but he was more than happy to pass it along to the Delaneys. He started to think. In fact, he was prepared to conclude that his contract with the Delaneys was fulfilled, having realized that he could no further explain the photographs. Jimmy was undoubtedly surprised by Weinstein's recollection. "Are you sure? The picture has to be fifty years old. I mean, it looks like it was taken in the park, maybe right next to that apartment building where it was found." Weinstein nodded, took another swallow, tried to look sober, which was usually difficult for him anytime in the afternoon, and responded. "I remember 'cause we did not usually take photos outdoors much. And this family, I think their name was Quinn, had four kids and a dog, just like in the picture." Weinstein picked up the photograph which had been laying on the table between the two of them and brought it close to his face to inspect it. "Yes, this looks the picture of the Quinn family. I remember them. The father was kind of well known around the area. Or so I understand. Mr. Blair knew him well. I think he was an entertainer. In fact, I understood that he may have been a magician. Mr. Blair told me that Mr. Quinn was a part owner of a magic shop downtown ---- I don't think I remember, maybe I never knew the name of the place." Jimmy started to pay closer attention to his narrative. He now had something to tell his clients. He thought of researching the magic shop. On the other hand, maybe he would leave that mystery to the Delaneys to pursue.

Weinstein continued his story of the photograph. "Anyway, the Quinns said they wanted a portrait taken in the park. I think the father paid Mr. Blair, the man who owned the studio, twice the normal fee. I helped Mr. Blair himself take the photograph. He used lights outside, which was not normal. He kept on telling us that he wanted certain types of shadows in the picture."

So Jimmy was now ready to complete his report to his client. He telephoned John as soon as he thought that he might be home from work. Although he thought he might expect it, he was admittedly surprised that John proposed that the three of them, he, John and Patricia, get together for dinner. John told Jimmy to meet Patricia and himself at Hy's Restaurant on Queen Street. He assured Jimmy that he would make a reservation for seven o'clock that evening. Pimm was impressed. He had never been in Hy's Restaurant, a relatively new five star eatery on the ground floor of the Metropolitan Life building which opened less than a year ago. He thought that maybe the Delaneys probably hadn't dined there either.

He sort of expected it but was surprised nonetheless when he arrived at the entrance to Hy's and was immediately conducted to a table at which the well dressed John and Patricia Delaney were waiting, each with a drink in their hands. Jimmy, regretting that he had not worn a necktie, an oversight that he realized that the host had noticed, was escorted to the Delaney's table. Patricia, to whom Jimmy Pimm had never been introduced, stood up, as did her husband, to greet their guest. Jimmy thought Patricia Delaney was remarkably attractive. He shook her hand but only nodded to John. All three of them then sat down.

"Thanks for meeting with us." said John. "We've been looking forward to your report and we are quite pleased that you were able to complete your investigation so quickly. We were willing to give you more time. After all, it has been only a few weeks." Patricia looked at Pimm and raised her glass toward Jimmy, as did her husband. Jimmy, who was yet to order a drink, simply smiled, not expecting the Delaneys to be so effusive. Instead, he was thinking of ordering something other than beer, which seemed somewhat unseemly given the circumstances. Eventually, he had decided that he would order a scotch, a libation that he used to drink when he was patronizing nightclubs in Hull. He acknowledged their comments. "I just got lucky about the history of those two photographs." With that short admission, he handed the two photographs to the Delaneys. Jimmy's scotch arrived, he took a tentative sip, it had been years since he had taken a taste, and continued with his explanation. "Well, I've already told you about the Dennison photograph." said Pimm as he nodded toward John. "Anyway, the other photograph was identified by a former employee of the Blair Studio named Weinstein. I found him through a waiter at the Centretown Tavern named Murray. He told me that he remembered the photograph you gave me. He thought it was a picture of the Quinn family." Jimmy glanced at John and thought that he had a perplexed look on his face. Pimm waited and then added another detail that had made the stunned look reappear on John's face. "This guy Weistein also said the father of the Quinn family dabbled in magic and used to put on the occasional show."

John and Patricia Delaney looked at each other like they had just been told that the Quinn family in the photograph currently lived next door to them. They knew, courtesy of George Casey, the custodian of Parkdale Court, that a Harry and Florence Quinn lived just down the hall from them on the third floor when they lived there. The two of them just sat across the table from each other happily transfixed. Predictably, Jimmy was the first to speak, asking his two clients if there was something peculiar about the information he had just given them. John looked up at Jimmy and nodded reluctantly, as if he was about to reveal a secret. Patricia also gazed up at Jimmy and then returned to staring down at the table, her right hand spread out on the table, her left hand still holding her drink. "Do either of you know someone named Quinn? I mean, the look on both of your faces suggest that maybe you do." John and Patricia hardly knew what to say. They had strange looks on their faces.

Jimmy again tried to convince the two of them to explain their apparent reluctance to account for their reticence on the subject. He started to feel like he was a detective on a television show. "Look, I'm really interested in knowing what is disturbing you about the information I just gave you." John then revealed the secret he was hiding from Jimmy. "You may find this hard to believe but we had neighbours in our old apartment building named Quinn. Not only that but both of the Quinns, they lived in apartment 307 and we lived in 302, always seemed weird, at least to me. I've seen both of them dress up, you know like they were masquerading for some sort of party. In fact, I've seen Harry Quinn dressed up like Mr. Peanut, with a top hat right down to spats, both in his own apartment and on Bank Street. As for his wife Florence, she liked to dress up as well but I can't remember what imaginary character she was playing but she did like to dance, particularly in the third floor corridor. So you see, being told that a man in an old photograph that I found in our apartment may be related to a man who lived in an apartment down the hall from where we used to live is a little hard to believe. We just don't know what to do now."

As soon as John finished his disclosure, as theatrical, if not difficult as it seemed to be, Jimmy tried to offer the Delaneys some sympathy. "I know it seems strange but at least you may be closer to knowing why that photograph ended up in your apartment. It is likely more than a coincidence, don't you think? It could be lucky I suppose but that seems unlikely. How that photograph got into your apartment, who put it there and why? I don't know and neither do you but at least you know who's in that picture." With his testimony complete, Jimmy then looked at the two Delaneys with as much understanding as he could in the circumstances.

All three of them ordered their second drinks and then their dinners, John and Patricia asking for lobster cobb salads and Pimm, to ensure that he was acting appropriately with his surroundings, ordered seafood pasta. Before their dinners arrived, during which time Pimm and John discussed the Centretown Tavern, both of them exchanging stories about their experiences there. It came as no surprise that Jimmy had more stories to tell, his occupation the obvious reason for the multitude of his anecdotes. While Jimmy was careful not to provide his current client with any confidential information about any of his previous clients, he did have enough amusing and beguiling reminiscences to hold the attention of his dinner companions for most of the evening. The Delaneys were fascinated by Jimmy's stories about those patrons of the tavern who were also bookies, their reputations so well known that the waiters usually keep their tables empty when they weren't there, provided they had the space. Stories involving certain gamblers, some of whom would arrive in the tavern with desperation written all over their faces, were particularly interesting, if not fascinating.

So it was over desert, they all had tiramisu and coffee, Jimmy asked his clients about their own efforts to investigate the photographs left in their mailbox in the Parkdale Court and the one outside their place on Brighton Avenue. Jimmy said that, unlike the two old family photographs, there weren't any people in the other photographs that anyone could identify no matter how hard they looked. Patricia interrupted Jimmy's explanation by making a fairly obvious observation. "All the other pictures were taken near our old apartment building on Bank Street, the Parkdale Court. They were basically shots of the street, from one direction and then the other. There were also pictures of a car like ours, a picture of a nearby garage. And the photographs were all current, all taken recently." John nodded and added another comment. Pimm acknowledged that his contract with the Delaneys obligated him to ascertain the photographer as opposed to the photograph. "I don't think I can find out who took those photos or why but it is likely that it was someone who lived nearby. I cannot tell you why. You will have to ask whoever took them." The comment elicited quiet laughter from the three of them.

<hr />

By the time they arrived home from their evening with Pimm, during which they had finalized the disposition of their contract with Jimmy Pimm, paying him the $500 as well as certain expenses Pimm had incurred in his search for the origins of the photographs John had found in the apartment. John suggested that their new move was pretty well obvious. Both of the families identified in the photographs that could quite possibly be related to the people who currently resided or had recently resided in the Parkdale Court apartment building. Any search, if indeed either John or Patricia wanted to continue to search for the ancestry of the two photographs would involve interviewing anyone who possibly knew or remembered either the Dennison or Quinn families those decades ago. Patricia pointed out that both names were associated with families who had lived in Parkdale Court, including Hector Dennison whose death allowed John Delaney to become the next lodger in Apartment 302. As for the Quinn family, who may still live in Apartment 307, it was possible that the two of them, Harry and Florence Quinn, could be related to the Quinns who a certain Mr. Weinstein, who used to be employed by the now defunct Brown Photography Studio of Ottawa, had recalled and assisted in their studio photographs.On the other hand, both Delaneys decided they should approach Casey custodian of Parkdale Court regarding the background of Hector Dennison, is so far as he was aware of it. Patricia eventually suggested that someone must have claimed the body of Hector after he dropped dead in Apartment 302. The two of them discussed an appropriate method of discovering who claimed the body, finally agreeing to simply ask Mr. Casey. John asked Patricia what kind of excuse would they use to approach Mr. Casey about the body. After all, it had been more than three years since Hector Dennison had died and more than six months since the Delaneys moved out of Parkdale Court to Brighton Avenue. Later during dinner. several evenings after they had had their most recent and presumably last meeting with Pimm, Patricia proposed they simply tell Mr. Casey the truth. They wanted someone to possibly identify the Dennisons in an old photograph that John had found in Apartment 302. They were wondering whether Dennison, the occupant before John Delaney moved in, was a child in the photograph. Patricia volunteered to call on Casey the next Sunday afternoon.

———◆◦◈———

So Patricia arrived at Parkdale Court just after lunch on Sunday. John and Tyler dropped her off on Bank Street just across from the apartment. Patricia said that she would walk home after speaking to Mr. Casey. She entered the lobby and pressed the button for Apartment 102 for Casey, identified as custodian. She had to press the button twice before a voice sounding like its owner had just arisen from a nap. In the background, Patricia could hear an elderly woman hollering at who she assumed was her husband. "Mr. Casey, my name is Patricia Delaney. My husband John and our son Tyler lived in Apartment 302 for a few years until about a year ago. Maybe you remember us?" Casey answered with a short, raspy cough and then a question. "Who are you? Do you live here?" Patricia was momentarily stunned but recovered quickly enough to respond, "No Mr. Casey, my husband and I and our young son used to live here --- we had an apartment on the third floor. About a year ago, we moved to a house further south in the Glebe." Despite this scant explanation, Mr. Casey then buzzed her into the building. "Turn left at the bottom of the stairs." was Casey's instruction. She already knew that.

He was waiting with the door to his apartment open, peering out into the hall with a suspicious look on his face. Although Patricia recognized him, she was still a little frightened but approached him with her hand out. Mr. Casey shook her hand and then retreated into the apartment, inviting her in. Mr. Casey motioned her to sit in an armchair across from Mrs. Casey, who was sitting on the sofa with a knitted blanket in her lap. Patricia also recognized Mrs. Casey even though she seldom saw her, coming home from church with her husband every Sunday was the only occasion. Patricia sat down. She and Mrs. Casey exchange smiles. Patricia noticed that Mrs. Casey had lost most of her front teeth. The look seemed to suit her. Mr. Casey sat down on the sofa next to his wife and waited for Patricia to get down to the purpose of her visit. "Mr. Casey, we would like to see if anyone who knew Hector Dennison would know if he was in this photograph as a child." She handed to Mr. Casey the old photograph of the Dennison family taken by the Brown Studio in Montreal. Casey, though still puzzled, certainly seemed to be listening now. "So we thought that maybe you knew someone who was connected to Hector, like someone who may have claimed Hector's body when he died. We just want to know whether Hector Dennison was in that photograph. We are curious." At first, with the puzzled look on his face remaining, he seemed to be waiting for Patricia to continue her explanation. Mr. Casey asked Patricia why she and her husband were curious about Hector. "I don't know, just interested I guess." She wasn't going to tell Mr. Casey about the plan, if indeed Hector was in the photograph, to talk to some of his former neighbours about him. Maybe they knew something about his history, something about him personally. She also didn't tell Mr. Casey that she and her husband thought that maybe the photograph was left in the apartment on purpose and that they were interested in discovering what that purpose was.

After exchanging trivia about recent developments in the building, Patricia reminded Casey of her request for the name of the person who may have claimed Dennison's body after he died. Casey had been staring blankly at his wife who had looked like she had been lapsed into slumber on the sofa. Patricia had to raise her voice. "Do you remember any name, Mr. Casey?" He was stirred from his temporary snooze and suddenly answered, "Fenwick, his name was Ernest Fenwick, who said his uncle used to live in the building years ago. It was before my time. The police said that he just showed up at the morgue a day or so after poor old Mr. Dennison had his stroke. He said that Fenwick's name and contact information had been found in Dennison's wallet and that the police had informed him of Dennison's death." Patricia then asked Mr. Casey if there was a funeral held for Mr. Dennison. Mr. Casey answered after a brief delay. "No. I don't think there was anyone else who wanted to have a funeral for Hector. According to a city constable who I knew pretty well, Fenwick didn't want a funeral, a memorial, anything to commemorate Dennison. And there was no one else who wanted to arrange anything." Patricia asked what Mr. Fenwick did for Dennison's death. Mr. Casey again returned to an empty expression. He then told Patricia. "Nothing, Fenwick didn't do anything for Dennison." Patricia continued to pursue Mr. Casey about Fenwick's handling of Dennison's passing. "Do you know where he's buried?" she asked. Mr. Casey looked at Patricia blankly. "No, I don't, I don't think anyone but Mr. Fenwick would."

Patricia was now convinced that Ernest Fenwick could confirm whether Hector Dennison was related to the Dennison family portrayed in the photograph that the Brown Studio had taken maybe fifty years ago. She then asked Mr. Casey if he knew where Fenwick could be found. He said that he had no idea, not even knowing whether he lived. He suggested that the police might know since they had contacted Fenwick in the first place. Thanking him for his advice, Patricia got up from the sofa, left the apartment and then the building. She then started to walk home, south on Bank Street. On her way home, she contemplated their next move. While she was not as taken, or as obsessed with the photographs that had been found in Apartment 302 as her husband, she realized that considering all their efforts, if not their financial investment, particularly the hiring of Jimmy Pimm, it would be pretty well pointless to abandon the project since another step in the process had been reached. So by the time she had crossed the Bank Street Bridge, she had formulated a simple plan. They would consult the police to get Fenwick's contact information.

It was the next Saturday when Patricia, John and Tyler drove over to 1411 Morrisette Avenue off Merivale Road. It was the address found in Mr. Dennison's wallet. There had been a telephone number but it had been disconnected. They were pleased when they found that the 1411 Morrisette was the address of a fairly large apartment, the only such building on a block of suburban houses. Both of them had noticed that the building looked like it had been constructed more recently than the houses on the rest of the street. They also noticed that there were two "For Rent" signs out in front of the building, advertising several two and one bedroom units. The three of them entered the apartment and scanned the directory of more than a hundred residents until they located the rental office. It was on the first of four floors, near the stairs. Patricia said she wondered why the building did not have any elevators. "Perhaps that's a way for the owners to keep the rents down somehow. Lower construction costs you know." They walked toward the rental office and knocked on the door. There was a notice that announced the occupant of the room as the building supervisor. It sounded like there were two people in the room talking. Both of whom might have been smoking. There was a radio playing quietly in the background. After more than a minute or so, an older man named Ed Brooks got up from behind his desk, opened the door and introduced himself. "What can I do for you? By the way, this is my assistant, Paul Dewys. We were just going over recent applicants for leases. Are you looking for a lease? We have half a dozen openings." Brooks then made a gesture and his assistant Dewys got up and left the room. Again, Brooks gestured, this time to direct the Delaneys to take the two seats in front of his desk.

John answered. "No, we're not looking for an apartment. We're wondering if you have any information on someone who we think used to live here several years ago." Mr. Brooks asked for the man's name. "His name was Ernest Fenwick and he lived here back in 1977 and likely before then as well. But, after 1977, he disappeared, at least from the telephone book. We are hopeful that he is still alive somewhere and somebody can tell me where that may be." Brooks looked a trifle annoyed with the request although he seemed to loosen up somewhat when Patricia took up the appeal. "We don't want to bother you, Mr. Brooks, but maybe you can look through the building's files to see if you have any information on him." Brooks sighed a bit, pushed out from his desk, stood up and then opened up the cabinet files behind him. He pulled out the first drawer and started flipping through the resident cards in it. He managed to find the card for Fenwick, Ernest about the three quarters the way through that first drawer. He pulled it out of the drawer, held it up and read the few facts recorded on the card.

> **Fenwick, Ernest**: Signed a one year lease on June 1, 1973 for single occupancy of an one bedroom suite at a monthly rent of $185.00. Renewed for further one year leases on June 1, 1974, June 1, 1975, and June 1, 1976 at monthly rents of $195.00, $210,00, and $225.00 respectively.

"Well it appears that Fenwick was here for four years and then moved in the spring of 1977." concluded Mr. Brooks. Predictably, John then asked if he knew where Mr. Fenwick moved. Brooks smiled and nodded. "Yeah, I understand he got a room in the Lake Retirement Home out there across from the Queensway Carleton Hospital in Bells Corners." John, though relieved by the information, asked if Brooks had been in touch with Ernest Fenwick since he moved. "No, I haven't. Fact is that I don't know if he's still there." Patricia then followed up by asking if Fenwick had any friends in the building who could still in touch with him or may know where he is or what happened to him. Brooks looked at the two of them and raised his arms up. "I don't think him had any friends in the building. He was usually on his own, almost all the time. I do recall though every now and then someone would visit him. Not often but enough times for me to remember them. " Patricia continued. " Do you remember the last time you saw anyone with him? " Brooks shrugged and answered. "The last time I saw him was when he came into the office to tell me that he was moving to the Lake Retirement Home. And that was three years ago?" The Delaneys thanked Brooks, got up and left the building supervisor's office. By the time they reached their car, they decided that they would visit the Lake Retirement Home and contact resident Ernest Fenwick, that is if he was still there.

———————————◆-◇-◆———————————

The next day, their enthusiasm to resolve whatever mystery they had created still existing, they presented themselves at the front counter of the Lake Retirement Home. It being Sunday, there was a queue of visitors, relatives John and Patricia presumed, awaiting to announce themselves. There were maybe a half dozen people waiting in line in front of them. The woman at the counter greeted each visitor, acquired the appropriate name and room number, and waved them to the elevators, which were behind the front counter, the office and to the left of the nurses station. One of the visitors, a middle aged woman wearing a maroon beret, was told that the resident she was looking to visit, a supposed relative, had passed away over a year ago, a statement that the woman was obviously disputing. The discussion with the middle age woman who disagreed with the fact of the death of her relative went on for at least five minutes before she left. Patricia then told the counter woman that she and her husband were there to visit Ernest Fenwick. The counter lady giggled a bit and pointed to the audience gathered in the corner of the lobby. "Which one is Mr. Fenwick?" asked Patricia, an obvious question given that he was one of maybe fifty people sitting in a circle of sofas and chairs. The counter lady giggled again and replied. "He's the man standing in front of the audience with the microphone. Every week or so, he entertains the residents with either a magic show or some kind of nightclub act where he tells jokes, that is if he can remember any of them or if you call them jokes."

The Delaneys walked toward the corner of the lobby and stood behind the crowd. The man standing in front of the audience was easily in his late seventies, maybe even in his eighties. He was almost entirely bald, might have been six feet tall at one time but was now stooped over, was carrying a paunch and was dressed in shabby suit that might have fit him properly more than decades ago. He was standing in front of an audience of maybe three dozen people spectating. Fenwick was fumbling through a bit about people he sometimes recognized but never saw before but couldn't remember his middle name. He followed that with an observation involving an erection and dentures although it was clear that Mr. Fenwick didn't know what the joke may have meant even though he had just told it. In any event, the quip prompted an avalanche of titters, particularly from the women in the crowd, including Patricia. Fenwick then sat down on the chair that he usually kept by his side during his shows and pulled a deck of cards out of his suit jacket pocket. He then tried to perform a couple of simple card tricks but lost control of the cards, a misfortune that frequently occurred commented the counter lady who was now standing near the Delaneys. Later, on their way out of the Lake Retirement Home, Lilly Martin, the counter lady, told them that his inability to properly perform magic tricks was a surprising development since he grew up in a family of magicians. Mrs. Martin said, somewhat uncharitably, that people said that Mr. Fenwick suffered from theatrical Alzheimer's and were more entertained by his blunders than anything else he did behind the microphone.

After Fenwick's magic/comedy show, the Delaneys introduced themselves to Ernest Fenwick as delicately as they could. "Mr. Fenwick, I'm John Delaney and this is my wife Patricia. We're sorry to come and visit you like this. We hope we're not troubling you or anything but we wanted to show you this old photograph. We found it in an apartment we rented a few years ago in Parkdale Court on Bank Street." He held it in front of Fenwick who looked at the both of them with a puzzled look on his face, as if he had neither heard a word John had said nor had seen the photograph. "You see, the man who lived in the place before us had a heart attack and was found died in the apartment. His name was Hector Dennison. We were told by the custodian of the building that you claimed Dennison's body after he died." Fenwick still stood there, tranquilized it seemed, not saying a word. Again, Patricia thought that she would try to explain their presence. "Anyway Mr. Fenwick, I thought you might know why that photograph was left in the apartment.."

The three of them stood looking at each other, considering their next comment. Then, Fenwick broke the silence, "I have to go to the nurses' station. I have to get my ears syringed. They're always plugged up." John and Patricia looked at each other, bewildered as to a possible response. After no more than a minute or so, John replied with a promise and a question. "We can wait for you. Where exactly is the nurses' station?" Momentarily, Fenwick looked confused and then pointed down the corridor toward the elevators. The nurses' station was about halfway down the corridor to the exit. The Delaneys looked at each other again, still perplexed. John then told Ernest that while he had his ears syringed, they would wait for him in the lobby. Fenwick seemed satisfied with John's reassurance and headed down to the nurses' station. But he returned to the lobby maybe five minutes later, telling the Delaneys that one of the nurses, he couldn't remember which one, informed him that he didn't need any syringing, reminding him that he didn't need to have his ears done every day. John then suggested, with a certain weariness in his voice, that the three of them retire to the lobby, pointing casually to a corner sofa. Patricia helpfully noted that there was still coffee and tea left over from Fenwick's show. For his part, Fenwick mentioned that he did not want to miss dinner, which was due in more than two hours. John and Patricia looked at each other with befuddled expressions on their faces. Both of them then shrugged and walked over to a sofa.

Patricia took a cup of tea while the other two declined. In a strange aside, Ernest mentioned that he was certain that the kitchen of the Lake Retirement Home spiked the tea with whisky which explained how he was able he said to draw an audience anytime he put on a show in the lobby. Again, John and Patricia exchanged inquisitive looks. They were seated comfortably on the sofa. Patricia whispered to John that Ernest gave off an unidentifiable aroma, an odd comment thought John but he ignored it. He then asked Ernest, unusual smell and all, if he had any explanation for the photograph he had shown him only a few minutes ago. John held up the photograph he had previously shown and waited. At first, Ernest appeared to have never seen the picture, staring at John like he trying to remember but couldn't. He then brought one hand up to his eyes, contemplating. John tried to urge him to reply, slowly waving the photograph in his face. Ernest looked at it as if he had been hypnotized, his head turning to follow the picture. Ernest finally stopped, starred at the photograph, and came up with a realization, a sudden recognition. He then spoke, as if struck by a surprising inspiration. "I think that I can remember. The police called me one day a few years ago and told me that they had found my telephone number in the wallet of this man named Hector Dennison who had a stroke and had dropped dead in this apartment."

John and Patricia were waiting for Ernest to explain how he knew Mr. Dennison and why his name and number was in the descendant's wallet. They both figured that was the original purpose of their pursuit of Mr. Fenwick in the first place. They waited a few moments and then they asked him directly. "Ernest, how did you know Mr. Dennison or how did he know you?" Ernest replied a bit tentatively, as if he wasn't really sure of any answer that he might provide. He was, however, telling a story that started to make a certain amount of sense. "Well, Mr. Dennison was a good friend of my uncle who also lived in the building where Dennison and you two lived." John then asked why that photograph was left in the apartment, which was the original purpose of their investigation. "I really don't know but it is an old photograph of the Dennison family." John and Patricia both nodded. Ernest then made a startling statement. "I'll wager you didn't know that Hector Dennison was in the photograph." He just put out his hand and took the picture from John who was still holding it. He then pointed to a young boy on the right side of the front row of the photograph. "Did the thought occur to either of both?" asked Ernest. Both of them shook their heads and then just sat there, a little stunned by the confirmation. To Patricia, after sitting there for maybe two minutes or so, it made a certain amount of sense if the Dennison family photograph had simply been forgotten in the clutter and junk that Mr. Casey had asked the Saint Vincent de Paul people to remove to prepare the apartment for the next occupant. Either that, or the photograph had been purposefully hidden in the apartment for some reason and not been retrieved until John had stumbled across it.

In any event, Patricia was the first to come to her senses. She thought that Ernest Fenwick could probably be of further use in their continuing search. She whispered the suggestion to John who agreed and then asked Ernest, who looked like he was about to fall asleep, how his uncle and Hector Dennison become friends."Well, let me see. I think I remember that my father's brother, my uncle George, was an architect who not only designed the Parkdale Court apartment building but lived there as well, was a member of the same club as Hector Dennison. It was a club that practised magic tricks. It was run by a guy named Fred something or other. Eventually, they became friends and remained friends for years. I don't think I can remember anything else. Then my uncle jumped out the window of the apartment building that he designed and that was that."

Two days later, after getting approval from Gladys Tennant who happened to be the Director General of the Lake Retirement Home, John and Patricia made arrangements to visit Ernest Fenwick after dinner. They arrived at 7 PM, knocked on the door to his room, and waited for Ernest to answer. He didn't. They called out to Ernest until he replied with a simple grunt, or what could have sounded like a grunt. John took that for permission to enter his room, room number 252. Fenwick was sitting in an easy chair, monitoring the weather channel with the sound off. Patricia spoke to him first, standing in front of him, not disturbing Ernest at all. "Sorry to bother you, Mr. Fenwick, but we did have a meeting scheduled. As we mentioned to you when we spoke to you on Sunday, we are interested in knowing anything you can tell us about what may have happened between your uncle and Hector Dennison. John and I are just curious, that's all." Ernest looked up at Patricia, looked back at the television, and then returned his gaze at Patricia. John was still standing in the background, waiting for Patricia to make progress in her negotiation with Ernest. The object of her pursuit started to looking around from his chair, from one side of the room to the another, like he was thinking about what Patricia had just explained. John added. "As Patricia said, you can help us if you can tell us about the relationship between your uncle and Mr. Dennison. We think there will be probably something intriguing about whatever it is that you will tell me." Room 252 grew silent, waiting it seemed for somebody to say something informative about the history of George Fenwick, Hector Dennison and maybe Parkdale Court.

After an appropriate interval, Ernest held a shaky arm up and pointed to the desk on which the television set sat. "Look in the first drawer. There's a newspaper article in there that might kind of explain some of mystery or intrigue or whatever it is that makes the connection between my uncle George and Hector Dennison of interest to you two." John pulled the drawer open. He then he came across a faded front page article out of the *Ottawa Journal* dated April 5, 1949. John could barely see it but did read the article, aloud. Patricia moved closer to John and listened. So did Ernest. He had leaned back in his easy chair. John was reading the newspaper like he was reciting a prayer. No wonder Ernest's eyes were closed.

OTTAWA ARCHITECT
KILLS HIMSELF

———————◇———————

George Fenwick, an Ottawa architect known for designing buildings in the downtown area, killed himself yesterday by jumping from the open window of the top floor of Parkdale Court, a twenty one unit apartment building he designed in 1935. According to building landlord Lawrence Wallace, Mr. Fenwick, who was unmarried and was living alone, was a well spoken and courtly gentleman who was the perfect tenant. "He always paid his rent on time, never disturbed his neighbours, and maintained one of the most tastefully decorated apartments in the building." said Mr. Wallace.

According to several of the tenants who had gathered in front of the apartment on Bank Street where the body was found, Mr. Fenwick seemed to be distressed recently, nervous about something or another. According to the other tenants, who spoke to this reporter, Mr. Fenwick was not close to anyone in the building, having few friends, if any friends in Parkdale Court. Police have indicated, however, that the circumstances of Mr. Fenwick's death appear to be obvious and therefore did not warrant any further investigation. Officially, Mr. Fenwick's death would likely be ruled a suicide.

According to city records, Mr. Fenwick had either designed or had a hand in designing over a dozen downtown apartments and was commonly regarded as one of the most prominent architects in the city. Mr. Fenwick was 52 years old and had lived in apartment 302 of Parkdale Court since the building opened in 1936.

John looked at Patricia with more than mild surprise on his face. He expected Patricia to be equally incredulous. They had both previously seen a fragment of the article which they first saw on the floor of their apartment the morning after a party they had hosted shortly after they had both moved in. John had later found the full article after consulting the microfilm archives in the main Ottawa library. They both looked at Ernest who leaned forward in his chair in response to the faintly flabbergasted looks on his guests who quickly told him that they were quite familiar with the article regarding the demise of George Fenwick, Ernest's uncle, and friend of Hector Dennison. For the first time during their conversation, as peculiar as they had seemed, Ernest Fenwick laughed, not a simple snicker but an actual guffaw, an intonation that seemed entirely unusual for an old man with ear problems. John and Patricia both wondered whether a Lake Retirement Home attendant would be alerted that there was something amiss in Room 252, a quiet cackle the likely cue. But no attendant came.

Ernest's laughter, such as it was, subsided as he began to acknowledge their reaction. To both John and Patricia, Ernest seemed to be suddenly more astute in talking to the two of them, more discerning than he had been a few moments ago. "I can understand your apparent consternation," Ernest pointed out, the use of the term "consternation" somewhat peculiar, "the article may well have been left there although not by my uncle. Fact is that my uncle was already dead by the time that particular article was published. I know it might seem somewhat bizarre but someone other than my our uncle undoubtedly left that fragment." Before either John or Patricia could register a reaction, Ernest continued his commentary, "Before you say anything, I can assure that I am familiar with the article that you just read aloud because I saw it in a family photograph album a long time ago. I know that there was a background story to my uncle's likely suicide but I never heard all of it. Fact was that I was too young and while my family, my mother, my father, my brothers, my sisters, my aunts, my uncles, and some of my cousins might have had their own versions of what actually happened that day, I wasn't one of them." John and Patricia were looked at each other, confounded, not quite knowing how to continue their interview of Ernest Fenwick. It was obvious that there was more to the story than had been disseminated in the newspaper.

So John asked Ernest. "So there is more to George Fenwick's death than was a simple leap from the third floor of the apartment building thirty years ago?" Ernest moved back and forth in his chair, exclaiming with a certain amount of enthusiasm that anyone who knew his uncle back in April 1949 claimed to know something about the incident or tragedy or whatever it is you want to call it. "But I can't really tell what that something could be." he admitted. Patricia then followed up on her husband's inquiry, to which neither of them expected a sensible answer, "So there are a fair number of theories about the whole thing?" Ernest slowly shook his head and replied. "Not really. I mean, the main theories are that George jumped out of that window on his own ---- a suicide; or was pushed out of that window ---- a murder; or fell out of that window ---- an accident. In the end, the suicide story became the conclusion of the police and most people I guess." Ernest looked up and added another comment. "I also remember that there had been a theory that a local *Journal* reporter who unsuccessfully tried to write about in the newspaper. I forget what the theory was but some people at the time were fascinated by it, mainly because it was strange......at least I think it was strange." It was obvious that both John and Patricia had grown interested in the story but Ernest was about to disappoint them. "But I can't remember the damn story at all. I wish I could but I can't."

Ernest then learned forward to renew his interest in the weather channel and grew silent. John and Patricia then concluded that it was time to leave the Lake Retirement Home.

⟫◈⟪

It had to be more than a week since they had visited Ernest Fenwick. Patricia's mother, who lived in Toronto, had arrived for a visit and was staying with her sister Margaret who insisted on hosting dinners for the relatives who lived in Ottawa practically every evening for almost a week. John showed an extraordinary amount of patience at such suppers, having to listen to the same family stories from different relatives for five consecutive nights. Patricia was so pleased with John's tolerance that she complimented her husband every evening on the way home, a habit that eventually became tiresome. As a consequence, John and Patricia had no occasion to consider their next move in their search for the answer to the mystery of the two abandoned photographs, that is if it there was a mystery left to be solved. In that context, John would lay in bed at night believing that Patricia and even himself were becoming increasingly indifferent or even dismissive to the whole project. So he decided that he would have to convince Patricia or re-convince Patricia and maybe himself that the pursuit of the purpose of the two photographs that he found in Apartment 302 was worth recalling. He managed to convince her, however, by pointing out that it would be a shame to waste all the time and money they had already invested in the investigating the source of the photographs.

———⋙✦⋘———

They finally concluded that they should approach the Quinns in Apartment 307 although John had yet to devise an explanation for his visit beyond simply showing Harry and Florence the photograph that had been identified as an old picture of the Quinn family. It would therefore seem natural that he would consult with the Quinns who lived five doors down from the apartment in which the photograph was found. John started to realize that despite his entreaties, Patricia's interest in the photograph project was waning. He had to raise the prospect of continuing with the search for the answer to the mystery of the photographs several times before she finally agreed with his most recent suggestion. He could tell, however, that her agreement, or whatever it was, was intended only to appease him, if nothing else. Eventually, they decided that they would drop by the Quinns the next Sunday afternoon.

———⋙✦⋘———

"Didn't you say they're a little off? I mean, you've told me of a bunch of incidents where the Quinns have acted and dressed a bit strange. I mean, doesn't Mr. Quinn like to impersonate Mr. Peanut? Didn't you often see Mrs. Quinn dancing in the third floor hallway? We can't therefore expect either of them to tell us the truth, that is if that would do us much good anyway." commented Patricia, her fading interest in the pursuit of the purpose of the photograph left in Apartment 302 now almost entirely evident. It was understandable then that John spent some time in considering their approach to dealing with the Quinns. In any event, John telephoned the Quinns and, after speaking to Harry Quinn for five minutes, arranged for a visit the next Sunday afternoon.

So, the next Sunday, having dropped Tyler at the grandparents for the afternoon, the two of them, John and his reluctant wife, drove over to Parkdale Court to call on Harry and Florence Quinn. They were nervous about approaching the Quinns. John, having been exposed to them often enough not to be fooled by anything they might say, was wary. He could hope, however, that the Quinns would identify the people in the family photograph he intended to show them. Patricia was basically along for the ride. They found a parking spot halfway down Patterson Avenue across Bank Street from the Parkdale Court, adjacent to the Economy Car Agency. They walked across Bank Street to the lobby of Parkdale Court, where John pressed the button to the Quinn's place. There was the normal delay, during which time a middle age couple both John and Patricia may have recognized were leaving the building. John pressed the button again, after which point Harry Quinn answered the buzzer in an almost secretive voice. He was almost whispering. "Is this John Delaney? Do you have your lovely wife Patricia with you?" John answered in the affirmative and wondered for a moment whether Mr. Quinn had ever met Patricia.

A VISIT WITH THE QUINNS

John provided Harry Quinn with a crisp expression of consent, took his finger off the buzzer, opened the lobby door, and he and Patricia began to climb up the marble stairs to the third floor. Inside the apartment building, there was a strange silence, faint echoes of a radio show heard in the distance. The afternoon sunshine was streaming through the windows at west ends of the three floors, the light almost poetic in its effect. To John and Patricia, the sights and sounds felt strangely familiar. By the time they arrived on the third floor, they felt like they were still living in Apartment 302. They looked down the hall and saw the door to Apartment 307 partially open and heard a faint tone of maybe a Broadway musical. They walked down the corridor to the Quinn residence, stood before the slightly open door, noting that the name "Quinn" was emblazoned on the door, and lightly rapped. The sound of the music that seemed to be coming out of their apartment grew louder. Patricia thought she could also hear, every now and then, alternating bursts of what sounded like hand claps. They then stopped.

"Do you hear those noises?" she asked, as they both stood waiting for the Quinns to come to the door. "They sound like hand claps or maybe those wooden clickers that teachers used to have." John heard the noises too. "Yeah, I hear them." Then, the noises suddenly stopped and Harry Quinn opened the door. He was dressed formally, a dark maroon tuxedo. Behind him was his wife Florence, attired in a pink chiffon evening gown. Florence was holding a walnut coloured clicker In her right hand. The Quinns were both smiling. John and

Patricia looked at each other quizzically, as if they were pondering whether to actually enter the apartment. Harry recognized their hesitation. "Don't worry about Florence. She just likes to occasionally entertain herself with that thing." explained Harry. John and Patricia were still looking at each other, seemingly questioning their decision to visit the Quinns. John leaned in and whispered to Patricia. "It's like an asylum or something." Again, Harry seemed to understand his former neighbours' discomfort. "Oh don't worry about Gertrude. She does stuff like this all the time. I think one of you already knows that." He nodded in John's direction and continued his narrative. "I know you're seen Florence act a little unconventionally, you know like dancing in the hall." That admission seem to startle Patricia but not John, who had already developed the suspicion that Florence, if not Harry as well, were somehow involved in entertaining people, possibly for money. John happily nodded at Harry and Florence and particularly at Patricia who seemed to have maintained that mildly surprised look on her face. Unlike her husband, she had never seen Florence dancing in the apartment hall or anywhere else but she could imagine it.

Florence changed the subject, the Delaneys thought accidentally, by inviting John and Patricia into the apartment's dining room to serve them, as they announced, tea, tea cakes and sandwiches. On their way into the dining room, John and Patricia took note of the fact that the layout of the Quinn apartment was identical to the geography of Apartment 302, the Delaney residence until they moved to Brighton Avenue almost a year ago. Patricia did point out, however, that the picture window in the living room faced part of the park and beyond that Lyon Street South. Patricia thought that she preferred the view out of their apartment which was Bank Street and the Economy Car Agency. All four of them sat down at this vintage deep brown dining room table. Around it, there was four chairs decorated with petty point needlework. Florence had picked up and was then holding a silver tea pot from which she was shakily attempting to pour tea. Harry stood up, helped Gertrude for a moment, completed pouring the tea and then invited the three others to sit down. "My grandmother gave us the tea service a lot time ago but we don't use it very often. We don't have visitors very often." said Harry who then gestured toward the tea, tea cakes and sandwiches. "Please have a sandwich and a cake. Gertrude worked all morning on them."

They were sitting at the table sampling the sandwiches, watercress and egg salad, and the tea cakes, almond and lemon, while sipping tea, when John slipped the Blair Studio photograph to Harry Quinn. Gertrude got up to look over her husband's shoulder as he casually scrutinized the photograph as if he were looking at a picture that he found in somebody's family album. After lingering over the photograph for what could have been three minutes or so, Harry looked at Florence and said simply "I've seen this before." and then started to push it back across the table. John and Patricia looked across the table at Harry. "Where did you see it before?" they both asked, befuddled and enlightened at the same time.

Both Harry and Florence started to laugh and then Harry paused long enough to explain the basis for their mirth. "Fact is that I've seen the picture many times. Fact is that I have a copy." he continued with a more astounding revelation. "Fact also is that I am in the picture." Both John and Patricia stared across the table and at each other. They then questioned Harry's declaration with an stunned incredulity. "You're in the picture? You're actually in the picture?" John asked. Both he and Patricia leaned over as Harry slid the photograph across the surface of the table and tapped his finger on a boy sitting on the left side of the photograph. "That's me when I was eight years old. The photograph was taken in a park near we used to live, in old Ottawa South." John then asked how another copy of the photograph ended up in Apartment 302. John punctuated the question by reaching into his shirt pocket and showing Harry and Florence the other photograph that had been left in their apartment, the same one found in the cabinet in the archive of Essence Books in Verdun. Harry and Florence looked at the photograph and then nodded to each other. "That's the Dennison family back maybe fourty years or so." said Harry. John and Patricia were stunned, the latter bringing her hand over her mouth. John thought for a moment that there was maybe some sort of strange incestuous ambience in Parkdale Court. Harry and Florence portrayed no particular expression. They acted as if there was nothing unusual about Harry's statement. But the Delaneys thought otherwise. How did he know that it was the Dennison family? That was the question that bedevilled them. They sat across from the Quinns waiting for illumination.

Harry smiled and then, as expected, explained his assertion. "You know that the Dennison family lived here in Ottawa. But they had relatives ----- a widowed mother, two brothers and a sister who all lived in Montreal. During one visit, Gordon, one of the brothers, arranged for each one of the Dennison families, the three sons and the daughter, to have their photographs taken. So on one of their visits to see the mother, they had their family portrait taken in a park near where she lived in Montreal." John then interrupted the flow of Harry's story." And you saw the photograph when Hector Dennison moved in this building, right?" Harry smiled and then shook his head. "No, I saw the photograph before he moved into the apartment after George Fenwick, who as you know designed this building, took his own life by jumping out of that window on the third floor. I knew Hector before he moved in here." Harry paused for a moment and added. "And by the way, a family named Bailey lives there now." Mr. Quinn smiled again.

—————◦◦◦◦—————

John and Patricia spent the rest of their visit in the Quinn apartment listening to the story of Hector Dennison and the photograph. According to Harry, with Florence adding the occasional detail, Harry met Hector when they became members of the Ottawa Magic Society, which met regularly at Fred's Magic Shop on Sparks Street. They were novice magicians, both attempting to learn rudimentary magic tricks, like sleight of hand or using forced decks, and enjoying the appreciation of other students of the Ottawa Magic Society. They became fast friends, a relationship which endured for over fourty years, almost twenty five of which was spent in the same apartment building, on the same floor, five apartments away from each other. Over the years, if not the decades, both Hector Dennison and Harry Quinn, as well as a number of other members of the Ottawa Magic Society, not only had developed a facility for magic but also for the pursuit of pranks. While most of them were concerned with phony letters, bogus telephone calls, food containing dirt, soap, and other unfortunate ingredients, and other actions that could only be described as trickery or, as Florence would prefer to call it ---- tomfoolery.

After Hector Dennison moved in, several years after construction of the apartment building was completed, Hector's father Thomas told him that every apartment in the Parkdale Court was blessed with a small painting that was a permanent feature of each unit. Both he and Harry thought it curious that an apartment was equipped with a painting. The Dennison apartment was decorated with a portrayal of a family in which a father, a mother, two girls, and a boy were illustrated in a Victorian Era style. He told Harry that he had wondered whether the residents were favoured with different paintings in different styles, like abstract or cubist. Not that it mattered, commented Harry. John and Patricia didn't think it mattered either.

A MYSTERY FINALLY FADES

———◇———

Almost as soon as they left the Quinns' apartment, they initially looked at each other with blank expressions on their faces. After a few moments, they had both fell into guilty giggles. They had expected an answer or answers to the serious mystery of why a Quinn family photograph had been left in Apartment 302 for the Delaneys to find many years later. The whole thing sounded like the plot of a television soap opera. They both agreed that despite the generally compelling and extensive reminiscences of the years the Quinn spent living on the third floor of the Parkdale Court, their accounts of relevant events did not help explain the reason for the discovery of the photograph of the Quinn family that the Delaneys had made in Apartment 302 more than fourty years after the photograph was taken. Even at the beginning of their quest, they had realized that there was a scant possibility of the Quinns, who supposedly were familiar with Hector Dennison, the previous tenant of Apartment 302, actually knowing the reason for the photographs being left in the apartment. That photograph, along with the fragment of that *Ottawa Journal* article reporting on the suicide of a man named George Fenwick, had been beguiling the Delaneys ever since they had found them.

For reasons they could never determine, even to each other, they nevertheless felt they had to explore the background of these two artifacts. They felt compelled. They couldn't explain it but it prevailed regardless. But despite their best efforts so to speak, the most recent of which was a visit to the Quinns' apartment, they were still mystified by the events, particularly the discovery of photographs and a newspaper fragment, that unfolded in Apartment 302 of Parkdale Court, the apartment in which they had resided for more than a year. They had to admit to each other that they had grown weary, if not entirely exhausted of discussing their efforts to clarify, if that was possible, the reasons, if there were any, for photographs that were abandoned in their apartment in Parkdale Court as was a fragment of the *Ottawa Journal*.

Patricia continually asked what was left. She said that it was getting absurd. So, as they were enjoying diner that evening after their visit with the Quinns, she asked the question for the thousandth time. "Is there anything else either of us can do to discover what we are or have been dealing with?" John looked at his wife as if he was just about to fall asleep and answered as simply as he could. "I really don't know. I've thought about it a lot and I have to admit I'm stumped. More than that, I'm sick of the whole thing." Patricia threw her head back and slapped the table with both hands. "There must be something we can do, John, there must be something." John was surprised with the force of her insistence on continuing their pursuit of the photographs. He pointed out that they had even hired a private investigator and she countered by saying that while Mr. Pimm was able to identify the families in the two photographs, he couldn't tell them why the photographs were left in their apartment and why George Fenwick threw himself out of that window. Patricia then implored John to consider another way of discovering the answers to those two questions.

Patricia continued to pursue her ambition after dinner and Tyler went to bed. "Are there any other people who can maybe give us some further answers, I mean aside from the ones that Mr. Primm or the Quinns or Ernest Fenwick already gave?" she asked. John was hesitant. He answered reluctantly. "Maybe there aren't any more answers. If there are, maybe we will never know them." Patricia offered the final answer. "I think we can just call it a mystery."

Printed in the United States
by Baker & Taylor Publisher Services

Printed in the United States
by Baker & Taylor Publisher Services